THE DISAPPEARING SEASON

Cienna Collins

AJC Publishing
PO Box 8050
Oakleigh East Vic 3166 Australia
aj@ajcollins.com.au
ajcpublishing.com.au

ISBN
978-1-7637190-0-2 Print
978-0-9954140-8-2 Ebook
978-0-9954140-9-9 Audiobook

Interior design: AJC Publishing
Cover design: GetCovers
Image licensing: Depositphotos
Photography: Robyn Slavin

Typeset in EB Garamond 12
Printed and bound by IngramSpark
First edition 2024

Also by Cienna Collins

How You Left Me (Part 1)
How You Found Me (Part 2)
The Disappearing Season

What if all the world's mirrors were broken
and you could only see yourself
reflected through your loved one's eyes?

Author's Note

When I first began writing this book, the question I was burning to answer was "Why did she stay?". Perhaps I was looking for clarity in my own life decisions. It wasn't until I read Jess Hill's book *See What You Made Me Do* (Black Inc., 2019) – an examination of the intricacies of domestic abuse – that I realised my question didn't need answering. As Jess so insightfully suggests, the question we should all be asking is "Why does *he* do it?".

Content warning: References to domestic violence, alcoholism, health conditions and some anti-religious sentiments. Respectful portrayal of LGBTI+ characters.

Grammar note: This book uses Australian spelling and grammar conventions.

Disclaimer: While the setting of this story was inspired by a small town in Far North Queensland, the location, characters, places, businesses and public services are the product of my imagination. Any resemblance to actual entities or persons living or dead is entirely coincidental.

For every person who has been there.
There is hope.

Cairns Wed 29 Dec 2010

Way, way below there's an endless density of green canopies. An ocean too, full of creatures that maim, kill. Especially this time of year – the wet. I hope for a glimpse of those tourist-tempting, deadly white shores, but the plane's oval window has its limits. And it's getting dark now anyway, wispy grey clouds enveloping. I sit back, listen to the cranks and whines of hydraulics, this beast banking, descending. A thump, shudder, squeal of rubber on tarmac, the pull of reverse engine thrust.

Breathe, Georgia.

Tourists, too impatient, fill the aisles. A mess of hands, elbows, bag-clutching. I count my breaths ... inwards slow ... outwards slower. Tell myself there's no urgency. That I should take this moment to refocus, to tamp the small panic festering low in my gut.

A pause in the procession. I rise, pull my carry-on from the overhead cabin, then follow-the-leader toward the exit. Something pink and fluffy falls to the ground ahead of me. A small child is reaching over her mother's shoulder, her face crumpled as if she's about to begin wailing. I know how she feels. I bend and scoop up the toy, hand it to the kid, the woman none the wiser.

"Thank you." A nod from the flight crew member. A white, white smile.

Outside at last, and my lungs aren't prepared for the heat, for the soaking of thick, damp air. Ugh. Queasy. It's funny how your brain can tell your body what to expect, but the physical doesn't get it. Not until it experiences it for itself.

Flashes of red and yellow flicker off the tarmac, its surface shiny with early evening drizzle, puddles, mist rising like precipitative ghosts. I've never walked across a tarmac – through a passenger tunnel sure – but not this. This feels primitive. Elemental.

Is this place distant enough? Hazy enough to disappear in?

The terminal corridors are painfully ablaze with vibrant tropical touristy promotions: Kuranda Railway, Skyrail, a crocodile sanctuary. I retreat to the toilets and throw up – the wine I drank probably not helping the adrenaline. "I hear it's your birthday," the flight attendant had said, handing me a mini bottle of sparking white. I should have asked for vodka instead. But that's got to stop.

I sit, head in hands, absorbing what I've just done, where I am.

Andreas has probably called Katie by now, asking why I left my mobile at home and checking if I made it to her place for dinner, and if we really are seeing a movie. "Which one? Where?"

I told him, twice. But he'll have re-checked the cinema and time. Later, he'll call her house – the landline, to make sure I'm actually there – on the pretence of saying goodnight. I can picture Katie, hand on hip. "Give it a break, Andreas. It's her birthday, and you can never be bothered doing anything for her. No, I'm not going to fetch her, she's in the shower. She'll call you tomorrow."

Tomorrow, if I'd returned home, he would have asked to see a receipt for popcorn, a choc-top, anything from the cinema. Proof. My heart pumps hard at these thoughts, telling me to keep moving. Hand on my chest, I breathe, deeply, slowly. Release. Repeat. Splash my face with cold water. Check my reflection in the water-dropped mirror. My brown eyes almost black with lack of sleep and stress. A tangle of mouse-brown hair. Maybe I should have left it blond, just cut it short.

At the bus counter, I ask for a transfer to the closest budget accommodation. Cheaper the better. The attendant tells me there's a hostel in the town centre, ten minutes away. I picture rooms full of bunks, young things sitting cross-legged on sagging couches, sun-bleached hair falling over smooth open faces yet to be shadowed by life's darkness. And thirty-something me, carrying that heavy shade within.

It's only one night.

"Sure." I pull out the envelope I found in my pocket after Katie dropped me at the airport. Two thousand dollars in Visa gift cards to add to the few thousand in cash I'd scrimped on the sly. "No cyber trails" her note said. "I have more if you need". God, I love my baby sister.

Out in the humidity again, while I wait at the cement bus bays, I pull out Katie's old phone – a 2006 Nokia, almost five years old now. The "burner" we called it, injecting some humour into the direness of our rebellion.

I text Katie: *Hey Kit. Made it.*

She'll be wanting reassurance that no one asked for my ID when I checked in, screwing up the ticket booked in her name. I wait to see if she responds. Nothing. Probably busy on her late shift. Ambulances wait for no one.

A small crowd has grown around me. I hang back. By the time the minibus arrives and people clamber in, the only seat remaining is behind the driver. "No suitcase?" he asks. I and sit, carry bag poking into my stomach. He shuts the automatic door, reverses the bus.

Close your eyes. Relax now. But the circular air vent in the ceiling is doing its best to drill ice into my forehead. I push the outlet aside.

It's not been a long flight, just over three hours, but what came before it, the utter panic, the ache of holding things together, the not daring to breathe, has taken its toll. I'm guessing backpacker hostel rooms don't come with minibars.

2

Andreas

Katie hadn't liked him from the get-go. Red flag. Should have listened. Hindsight.

But I wanted someone. Needed someone. I'd never been popular like Katie, and a six-year drought had desiccated my confidence. I was overripe for the taking. As a young woman, I'd always been discerning – prudish, according to Katie. She was the butterfly; I was the butterball.

And no nice girl was going to meet a nice boy in some club, in the dark, in the loud music. In an eco-system of predators. Bad move. But there we were in the midst of beer, vodka and noise. No longer girls, but women.

I let go.

Then woke up in his bed, wondering who the heck he was – not his name, his job, his address but who. And for that matter, who the heck was I? Lying next to him, morning edging around bedroom blinds, him on his back, solid and muscular, sandy hair a mess of careless waves, I was kind of proud. "You're a slut, Georgia," I whispered, smirking to myself.

He woke and grabbed my butt. "I like a woman with curves." Insisted on breakfast – croissants at a beach cafe a few bright, squinty steps toward the end of his street.

He wanted my number. I wasn't sure. He wouldn't let me go until I said okay. Then he rang me, while I was standing there.

His arrogance annoyed me, but I was flattered too. He was interested. Really interested.

Too interested.

3

Morning brings another minibus and a stocky, grey-haired driver who's way too cheery for this time of day.

"Heading north?" he says.

I nod and give him the name of my accommodation, booked online last night in the hostel's communal lounge. The bus is empty; this must be his first pickup for the day. I move toward the back, but Mr Happy doesn't take the hint, looks in his rear vision mirror and calls out.

"First time up here?"

"Uh huh," I call back, my voice cracking with tiredness from a night trying to sleep through my roommates' earnest philosophical oversharing or questions about where to hook up or buy Mary Jane or mangoes. "Travellers", they called themselves. Not tourists. Though their snores and narrow-bed-fraught booty calls seemed no different to students back in my uni days.

"Where you from, darlin'?"

"Mel ... Sydney." I need to get better at this.

"Ah, thought you looked like a southerner."

He's psychic – nothing to do with my ankle boots, jeans and a turtleneck shirt already clingy with sweat. I make a mental note to fix that. Camouflage – the first tool in my armoury.

We head out of the city centre, past the beachy esplanade clustered with resort towers, suburban fringes fighting back mangroves trying to reclaim swampy lowlands, creeks curling like wrought iron flourishes. I've heard there are crocodiles in those waterways, "crocs". And pythons. Not just urban myth.

We pull into the airport again, collect half a dozen passengers. I eye each one as they enter, telling myself I'm being paranoid, that it wouldn't be possible for Andreas to know my location ... yet. They're oblivious to me sitting down the back, too caught up in their own wide-eyed holiday mood.

Before long, the drive becomes long and winding. To our left, tall cut-in cliffs, their red muddy faces reinforced with drilled steel and mesh. To our right, rocky beaches peek through stretches of rainforest shrubbery. And the palm trees ... another time, my heart might have been lighter at the sight of the sturdy tropical icons, their firework-splayed heads bent in supplication to the sun and sea winds. I would have looked through their fringed tops in search of young green coconuts, my mouth watering at the thought of drinking fresh juice, not the pale liquid that comes in plastic boxes.

An hour later, we've reached the outskirts of town. The bus stops periodically, picking up or depositing passengers at lush resorts. I'm dropped in front of mine – not the pristine, large-pooled, beachfront resort it purported to be. More the two-storey, cement-paved motel with a kiddie pool. It's a half-hour walk into town, so the website said. Pushbikes available.

"Booking for Sally Smith?" I had no headspace for creativity last night and now own a Gmail address for this non-existent woman.

The desk clerk gives me a cursory glance with hooded eyes, red with weariness ... or perhaps Mary Jane. "ID, credit card." He pulls at the collar of his Hawaiian-themed shirt, then winces as if he's woken up with a wry neck. I get the feeling he'd rather be snoozing on a plastic lounger in the middle of the kiddie pool, preferably with a beer in hand.

I pull out a wad of cash. "How about I just pay for two weeks in advance? There's an extra fifty there."

He doesn't respond to my meaningful look, just lazily reaches for the money and hands over a key – the type you insert and turn, not a swipe-card. "Fifteen. Ground floor. Hundred and fifty for lost keys."

Something tells me that fee would go straight into his pocket, not on a replacement lock.

The room, described as a one-bedroom apartment, is more of a bedsit. Compact, confined, but comfortable looking. Its kitchenette has a hotplate, kettle and bar fridge with a freezer just big enough to hold a bottle of vodka at an angle. I hope. I flip on the aircon, sag onto the edge of the bed with its obligatory floral cover, take my boots off and rub a foot.

I guess I should think about buying some food, suitable clothes. But I flop onto my back instead, stare at the unremarkable ceiling. Welcome to my home for the next however long it takes to decide what to do with myself.

⸺◈⸺

When was the last time I rode a bicycle? Can't be that hard to pick it up again, save being unfit. A wire basket clings to the rusty handlebars. Handy to bring back a few things from the supermarket, get the rest delivered later. I set off, up the highway, staying close to the gravel shoulder, conscious of how nervous I always feel when driving past cyclists, giving them a wide berth, hoping they won't suddenly veer closer.

It only takes a minute to work up a steamy sweat in the glare of the unforgiving sun. Note to self: buy sunglasses and a hat. So many things I didn't pack in my overnight bag. Just in case he checked.

The motel's website was right – it'd be a half-hour walk, twelve minutes by wobbly bike. Traffic is light on the main strip, and I slowly glide, checking out the stores – clothing boutiques, eateries, surf shops, chemist. A discount department store. Great. First stop for some lightweight cheap clothing.

I prop my bike against a wall outside the shop. It seems a friendly enough holiday town, no one waiting around to steal a rust bucket on wheels.

The cool inside is tangible, blissfully cold, tingly on my skin. I browse the aisles with a shopping basket, choose several t-shirts, a soft cotton blouse – loose because my buttons always pop – and a couple of pairs of shorts. I pause at a row of office skirts. No. I'll worry about clothes for a job interview once I'm more settled. If I end up with a cleaning job or similar – something simple, stressless – I won't need formal clothing. I throw in undies, sandals, sunnies and a hat, then stop in the swimwear section. Shall I? Why not? It's a beachside town. It'd be stupid not to. Boyleg shorts, halter tankini and a matching loose shirt to wear over it will do fine.

At the counter, the shop attendant gives me side-eye when I ask if I can use the changerooms to get out of my jeans. I'm beginning to doubt the myth of Queenslanders having a disposition as sunny as their weather.

Shorts, sandals and blouse donned, I tuck the rest of my goodies into the bike basket. My Melbourne clothes go straight into a nearby street bin. I only have a moment of non-recycling guilt, but it's soon overridden by paranoia – Andreas checking op shops might be a stretch, but why take the chance?

The supermarket is next. In the bread aisle, my stomach grumbles, but it'll have to wait until I'm back at the room. Cafe brekkies are off the menu for now. Before I head back, I stroll my bike past the rest of the shops to see what else the town has to offer. An ice cream shop gives me pause, and I stop to gaze at the myriad flavours. My stomach grumbles again. I guess an ice cream would be a cheap brekkie. Protein, dairy, fruit.

A cone of Mango Delight in one hand, I continue until I reach a wide-fronted pub with tables and chairs spilling onto the pavement. A singleted bloke nods to me as he sips a beer. He seems happy enough, but my stomach contracts at the thought of alcohol this time of the morning – a relief that my body knows some limits. A dog lies next to the man's thonged feet. Shaved into the brindle fur on its back are the words "I bite". The dog looks up at me, wags its tail. Is this Queensland humour?

"Go on," the man says, holding up his beer as if it's a universal symbol of trust. I balance my bike against my hip, bend and scratch the dog's offered chin.

"Is it okay, if I ..." I gesture with my ice cream.

"Sure. Bertie'll love you forever."

I offer Bertie the last of my cone. I swear he grins. The ice cream is gone in a second. I'm surprised by my own flicker of joy, the first in what seems like an age.

Brekkie beers and non-bitey Bertie dogs. I think I'm going to like it here.

I head back along the opposite side of the street, call into the bottle shop to buy the cheapest vodka – lemon flavoured – then stop at a beauty shop offering a special on pedicures. I weigh up the cost of something so frivolous. Screw it. I deserve one crazy little splurge before I knuckle down to reality. I lug my shopping inside, apologising to the beautician for taking up so much space.

4

Andreas

We met on weekends – we had jobs. He worked in finance; I worked in childcare. I drove to his place. Always. He didn't have a car – no need since he lived so close to the city. On a daytrip down the coast, he asked if he could drive.

Why not?

It became routine.

A part of me wavered at the concession of giving up a portion of my power, my independence.

Another part of me – an old-fashioned heart, witness to my dad caring for Mum in her latter, leaving-us days – embraced it. I wanted a loyal man like that.

5

It's a lucky glance down a side street that causes me to see the sign: "Job Centre". I pause ... Maybe I should ride back to my room, get changed first. No, too much of an effort in this heat, and I'll be just as sweaty by the time I get back. It's not like I'll be interviewing. Just seeing what's available, checking the lay of the land in these parts.

I head up the ramp and pull the glass door open. The agency has one of those buzzy alarms on the door. Why it needs one, I don't know; the office is practically a hole in the wall, with just enough room for a desk and one visitor chair. I suspect the space may have had a previous life as a coffee stand. I hesitate in the doorway. A woman wearing bright-red, slim-line glasses is squeezed behind the tiny desk. She ignores me, continues typing for a few moments, her eyes dark, crow-like in their concentration on her computer screen. When she looks up, she examines me with a sharp swoop, from my loose, messy hair down to my newly acquired sandals.

She doesn't smile. "Looking for a job?"

I admire, but have never been comfortable with, people who do that – get straight to the point without any niceties, don't bother to send out snail antennae to test the energy around another person. Her voice is jarringly loud for this minimal space.

"Yes. Just wanted to chat about what's available this time of year."

"Sure, sure. Take a seat."

I glance outside to my bike, propped against a light pole, my shopping still in the basket. There's really no room for my things in here.

"You okay?" the woman asks.

I remind myself this isn't the city; no one's going to steal my cheap clothes. At least my vodka is buried beneath the frugal groceries.

"Yes, thanks." I close the door and sit opposite her.

"So what sort of work are you after?"

"Anything really."

She leans back in her chair, crosses her arms. "Not helpful."

I swallow. "Well ... something easy, I guess. Room cleaning?"

"You think that's easy?"

I flush. "I didn't mean—"

"You don't look like a mould scrubber to me. Used-condoms, snotty tissues, soggy towels? I don't see it. What was your last job?"

"Um ... I worked at a childcare centre for the last five years, on the—"

"You're kidding me!"

I frown. "No."

"Were you fired?"

"No."

"Why did you leave?"

"I, uh, just moved states. I needed a change of scenery."

She narrows her eyes, pauses. "Looking for short-term or long?"

I pause, unnerved by her rapid fire. "Either, I think."

"You think so or know so?"

"Um ... I'll take whatever you've got."

"Six-week contract. Immediate start. Nannying."

"Ah ... sure. Sounds good."

"Incredible. I can't believe this. I have the perfect job." She shakes her head, as if she *really* can't believe it.

I'm equally intrigued, yet concerned.

"Don't move." She picks up the phone and dials.

I glance at the nameplate on her desk: "Evelyn". It's blue with white embossing. Plain. Functional.

"Hi, Margie. Me again. Is Daniel there?" Evelyn arches her neck, looks at the ceiling, closes her eyes. "Yes, yes ... I know. Well, pickings have been slim. Tell him I'm sending someone over ... I know, I know. This is the one, I promise." She pauses, covers the phone, leans forward and whispers. "You have a Working with Children Check, don't you? No issues with the police?"

"Yes. Working with Children. But does it apply interstate?"

"Good point. We'll get you a national Police Check instead."

What?

She returns to the phone. "Great. Thanks, Margie ... right now?" She glances at me again. "Sure, sure. Give me an hour."

I madly wave, shaking my head. She holds up a solid palm, blocking me.

Crap.

She hangs up.

"Are you kidding?" I say. "Look at me. I can't go to a job interview dressed like this. And I don't even have a résumé with me."

Evelyn closes her eyes, rests her head in her hands for a moment, sighs deeply. When she looks up again, she's composed. "Finished?"

Rebuked, I nod and quieten, impressed by her unflappable presence, as if she deals with flighty, panic-stricken clients every day yet still manages to place them in the perfect job.

"Daniel, Mr Moretti, is a busy man. If you don't go today, he's handing things over to a Cairns company."

"But I need time to prepare."

"Prepare what?"

"I ..."

The woman softens. "Look, it's just a small family job, not a five-star resort manager. You look fine. This is FNQ. Nobody dresses up. Just go. He'll think you're wonderful. Trust me."

I look out the window to let my mind breathe. She's argued everything away. "If you're sure ..."

"Eh. If you don't like it, you'll be out in six weeks anyway." She leans in. "But I'll tell you a secret. I know this guy, how he thinks, and I know you'll be perfect." She winks, then sits back again, softness gone. "Put it this way. Would you rather earn nineteen dollars an hour cleaning toilets or forty-five driving a ten-year-old little miss to school?"

I blink. *That much?* "No brainer, I guess."

"Okay. Welcome aboard. Now, résumé. Can you download one? Do you have one in Dropbox or something?"

"Uh, no. I haven't needed one for—"

She sighs again, then reaches into her desk draw to pull out a bottle of tablets. Prescription by the look of it. She pops a couple, swigs from a water bottle, then shrugs. "Headache." She returns to her computer, types a few lines, then looks up again. "Talk to me."

"Sorry?"

"I'm making you a résumé."

"You're making one up for me? You can't do that."

She peers over her red frames. "Watch me. I'll just need some ID – for the Police Check. You have that with you?"

I hesitate. "I do, but ..."

She looks at me now, sharp. "Anything I should be worried about?"

"No ... it's just ... there's someone ... I'd rather he not know where I am. He has ... contacts."

She screws up her mouth, considers me, then nods. "Look, no one's going to see the application but me. It's just in case. Mr Moretti's wife, *ex*-wife, is ... difficult. She'll probably want the Police Check, so I'll get you to ..."

She must see the panic on my face, the blood draining.

"Tell you what. We'll put your address as my office, okay? I promise I won't run the check unless it's absolutely necessary. And I'll let you know if I have to do it. And ... tell you what. You give me his name and number – in case he somehow manages to contact me. Then I can warn you. Okay?"

Something about her confidence, her been-there-done-that attitude seems to make it okay. "Sure." I hand over my driver licence.

"Happy birthday for yesterday. And you'll need to change to a Queensland licence after three months."

Great. All the details I never considered.

Forty or so minutes later, I stand to leave, a copy of Evelyn's a-little-too creative résumé in hand. She runs a critical eye over me, then retrieves something from her desk drawer. It's only now, as she rolls her seat backward, that I realise she's in a wheelchair. She spins the chair and rolls around to my side of the desk. Now that I can see the whole of her, she's wiry like a whippet.

"Stare a little harder," she says.

"What? Oh, god. Sorry." She's right; it's rude. I don't try to justify it.

She ignores my awkwardness. "Here." She flips open a compact. "Bend. I can't reach you from down here."

I lean in, and she dabs the applicator on the foundation base and reaches toward my neck. I shy away. "What are you doing?"

She sighs, impatient. "You want that showing?" She points, and I instinctively raise my hand to the bruising I'd forgotten about. I flush, mortified. "No. I guess not."

As she presses, I watch her face. She signals nothing, just dabs. "It's a little pale for your olive skin, but it'll do." When she's finished, she pulls my hair forward over my shoulders, then places the compact in my hand. "Touch ups," she says, then looks at my hair. "You'll need to keep up that colour job too, you know."

I flush again, laugh awkwardly as I pull on a few mousey strands. "Thanks. It's taking some getting used to. Thank you."

"No problem." She narrows her eyes a fraction, lowers her voice. "Been there."

"Oh."

She sniffs, straightens her shoulders and rolls back around her desk. "All good?"

I nod, my throat tight with gratitude, head giddy with how fast things are moving. "Thank you, Evelyn. I mean it."

"You'll be fine."

—◆—

A few minutes in, my legs give out like a seal trying to blubber its way up a rocky beach, and my hands slip on the handlebar as if it's greased. What the heck made me think I could ride a bike up this hill? I hop off and hobble beside it, humidity sapping my resolution, my lack of thigh-gap rubbing, stinging, and one side of my shorts riding up. Push. Push. I must be almost there.

A sharp pain jars me to a halt. Something so small – a pea under the princess's mattress – a tiny rock in my sandal – stops the world of my mind turning. I hadn't noticed the bitumen become gravel now that the incline has levelled out.

The air is deeply stagnant. No sea breeze today. Leaves hang like green drips, wet and heavy. Damn it. As if I'm not soggy enough with sweat, a shower breaks. I take refuge under a Moreton Bay fig, whose generous glossy leaves seem to cup the rain, saving it to drop a baptism of splashes on my head. *Thanks.* Behind me, a rustle. I snap my head around, trying to see through the dense foliage, but the rainforest is too jungle-like. Anything, *anyone*, could be hiding in there. *Pull yourself together.* I check the time on my phone. Heck. Keep going.

The rain eases, and I pace my steps to the interminable timekeeping of the bike's gears. Click. Click. Click.

Apparently, this is the area where the other half lives – on the highest point of the peninsula. I'm guessing from the multi-level designer residences jutting over the clifftops – sleek cement and glass sentries, their chins lifted in sovereignty over the township below – the property I'm looking for will be just as ostentatious. Stands to reason; it's not the average person who can afford a full-time nanny. Here, carved into the rainforest, are gardens of lemony frangipani, verdant lawns, infinity pools, views to die for. Retreats for the privileged. Andreas would be at home. He'd love it. Bask in it. But not me. These are not my people.

Andreas. And here come the incessant what-ifs, the what-am-I-doing jitters, the will-he-find-me woes. I touch my neck, wondering if the foundation has smudged away in the heat, exposing the truth branded by his hands. And now a pervasive shadow sinks over me, dragging on my resolve, telling me I won't fit in here, I won't belong. People will know. He'll find me.

Screw him. I'm here now. I need a job. I'm no quitter.

A few more metres of plodding, and I'm drained again. I pull at my sticky shirt, wanting to just sit in the road, let the heat melt me. But through a gap in the dense foliage, I glimpse the beach, its arc languorous and palm-lined, its stretch dotted with clusters of holiday resorts and apartments. Sigh.

How much further? I swallow, throat claggy. Why didn't I think to bring water? I glance at my shopping bags. Vodka? *Don't be stupid.* Where on earth is this place? Onwards.

As I round a bend, there it is – a curved stone wall embedded with a bronze plaque: "Moretti".

What if the kid's precocious and hateful? What if the father is a jerk? What if ... Look how vibrant the hedge is, all prettily red-tipped, yellow and green. Lush. People here must have full-time gardeners – not a dead leaf or stray branch. I crunch myself and the bike up the driveway. Gravel for drainage, I suppose.

A massive redwood door, reminiscent of a cathedral entrance, looms. Pray for me. I could use a miracle. I prop my bicycle against a giant pot plant, straighten my blouse and pull at my shorts again. Khaki for god's sake. With my dyed mousey hair, this guy is going to think I'm an Irwin family wannabe. Too old to be Bindi, too young to be Terri.

I brush the soles of my sandals on the doormat, notice my hot-pink nail polish. Should have chosen something earthier, more sensible. This colour isn't me. That'll teach me for trying somebody else on for size.

I grab my résumé folder from the bicycle's basket, a little scrunched from being jammed in with my shopping, and head up the porch. Here goes. Nothing to lose except more self-esteem. The doorbell echoes, giving the impression of a cavernous space beyond.

6

Andreas

Our first argument. They say three months is the turning point – the make-or-break time.

"You're being insecure," he says.

"I am not. If you say you're going to call someone, you should call."

"I was tired."

"You could have texted me. I waited home all day Sunday."

"I didn't ask you to."

"You didn't answer your phone. I could have gone out with friends."

"You should have. Stop playing the victim. Nothing happened."

God that hurt. But maybe he was right. Maybe I needed to toughen up. Not be so needy.

7

The man's face is gaunt, could do with a shave. He's younger than I expected, late thirties perhaps, but the whole tanned Mediterranean thing he has going on with his loose linen shirt works for him.

"Ms Wright."

"Yes. Mr Moretti?" I juggle my folder and stretch out a hand. "Georgia Wright. The agency sent me." Idiot. He already knows my name, knows why I'm here.

He ignores my greeting and glances at my shorts and sandals.

I snatch my hand back, hug my folder to my chest. "Sorry for my ... they didn't give me a chance—"

"You're late."

His tone isn't accusatory, it's more ... bored. I guess Evelyn was right – I'm that one-too-many interviewee.

"I'm new to the area and ... I had a bit of trouble getting my bike up the hill. It's a lot steeper than it looks. Then it started raining ..." I push a hand through my stringy hair and grimace. "I guess I should have been better prepared – they say it rains at the drop of a hat here. You're probably used to it, but it took me by surprise, and now I'm such a mess."

He's glowering, so I fall silent, pursing my lips into an apologetic smile. Bad habit, running off at the mouth. He steps back, motioning me inside.

"Ahhh, that's nice." Instant cool tingles my skin, and I wipe my sweaty forehead with the back of my hand, then wipe that on my shorts. "What a relief." I take in the ceiling fans, the abstract paintings in the hallway and the ornate, Balinese-style hall table. "Nice house ... big."

He brushes past me. "Hmmm. Through here."

I get a closer look at the paintings as we pass by. No idea who the artists are, but the works are bright and beachy with sea blues and greens.

We pass through the lounge, the dining area. This is no family home. The décor is ultra-modern, everything perched perfectly in its place. Even the cushions on the settees are expertly positioned to exhibit their colour and texture. Does anyone actually sit on those couches? Polished wooden surfaces, expanses of white walls and white-tiled floors. It's beautiful, for a museum.

I bet the man's wife – oops, ex-wife – looks as if she's straight off a magazine cover. And the kid. Probably in an ivory tower somewhere. I bite my lip. *Judgemental, Georgia. Do you want this job or not?* That's the trouble though. I don't know.

We head out to a wide patio overlooking the ocean. The faultless blue of the sky drops into the darker hues of the sea's horizon, where island peaks rise, their outlines softened, breast-like, in the haze of humidity. Out on the bay, yachts glint as they ferry passengers to and from the Great Barrier Reef.

"Lovely view," I offer, for want of something less trite to say.

"Ms Wright, can I offer you—"

"Georgia. Just Georgia." I wait for the reciprocal invitation. It doesn't come.

"Can I offer you a cold drink?" He leads me over to a wicker outdoor setting, where an acrylic tray holds what looks like a jug of iced tea with lemon slices. At least he doesn't have a maid to do his pouring for him.

I puff my gratefulness. "Sure." Pity the drink isn't something harder to calm my nerves. I'd hoover it up in a second.

While Mr Moretti pours the tea, I shift from one hot, swollen foot to another, looking longingly at the chairs.

"Here you go." He hands me a glass.

Did his eyes just pause on my chest? I glance down. My blouse is stuck to my bra, the dampness showing an outline of my breasts. A flush burns my face as I juggle the tea and my folder, trying to pull the fabric loose. When I look back up, Mr Moretti has already turned away to pour his own drink.

"Take a seat."

Finally, the magic words.

I place my folder on the table and sink onto the cushioned chair. Bliss. It's deep though, designed for lounging back, relaxing. I struggle forward to perch on the edge. "You have a lovely place here." Did I say that already?

He sits, one leg crossed over the other, and sips his drink. Doesn't answer, just stares.

Awkward. I take a big gulp of tea, accidentally sucking up an ice cube. Do I spit it back into my glass? Too gauche.

"Your résumé says you don't have experience with children older than five. Reilly is ten. What makes you think you'd be suitable?"

I almost swallow the ice cube whole, but manage to cough it into my hand, then shove it back in my mouth. The man isn't pulling punches. And how does he know what my résumé says? I put the glass down and hold up a hand while I crunch the ice. It takes forever, but eventually I swallow, then grimace and press my forehead.

"Ugh. Sorry. Brain freeze." I shake it off. He must think I'm an idiot. "Well, yes, I've worked mainly with younger children. I'm a qualified kindergarten teacher. But I practically brought up my younger sister. Our mum died when we were kids, and I took over her role. Dad, who's passed too now, was a shift worker, so he kept odd hours, and we had to fend for ourselves. Katie and I turned out okay. We both worked to put ourselves through university, and ..." I catch myself, unsure if his look is bemusement or annoyance, but he's doing that thing where people hold your gaze for too long, making it personal, awkward. My temper flares. I'm chuffing hot and dehydrated from the struggle up the hill, and the pressure of the interview, and just being here is such a fluster.

He sighs, lowers his head, as if he's given up on me already. He looks ... weary, dark circles. He's not sick, is he? Oh god, what if he's terminal, and that's why he needs a nanny to ...

"Mr Moretti?"

He doesn't look up.

"Mr Moretti, are you alright? You're not ill, are you?"

He jolts his head up as if he's woken from a micro sleep.

"Should I get someone for you?"

"No. Go on."

"Okay, well ... I know I'm probably not the perfect candidate, but children are children – listen to them, treat them with respect, and they'll learn and thrive. I've got a solid work ethic. I don't steal, I don't do drugs, and I only drink socially." *Liar.* "I've held down long-term positions in childcare. Did I mention I'm planning on living here permanently? I am." Another lie. I don't have a clue yet. "I adore kids and would love to have my own one day. That's about the long and short of it." I pick up my résumé folder and thrust it at him.

He blinks. "I've seen it. The agent faxed it through."

I hold firm, challenging his gaze. And soon it's too late to back down. Oh geez, am I being a jerk, or am I showing him I'm not a featherweight? I decide the latter. Go hard or go home.

Finally, he leans forward, accepts the folder and opens it – a courtesy, no doubt – his face is set, passive. He takes forever, exaggerating his attention on each page. Is this some sort of intimidation tactic now? How long does it take to read a three-page résumé? Maybe he's tired – he looks it – so he's having to read things twice, that thing where information doesn't make it from your eyes to your brain.

"No police check?"

He's read *too* closely. Now he's going to ask for one. What parent offering a childcare position wouldn't? I have an impulse to snatch back my paperwork. I could lie low for a few months, even if that means cleaning toilets and eating into my savings. "No. But I do have a Working with Children Check." I hold my breath. Maybe he'll let it slide.

"Well, it appears you do have a stable work history. This job here"—he points to an entry—"your last one. Why did you leave?"

I press my nails into my palms. How much should I divulge? My personal life isn't his business, but I have to say *something*.

He narrows his eyes. "Was there was a problem?"

"No." For a nanosecond I consider lying again. Nope. If there one thing I'm terrible at, that's it. Katie used to say my ears turned red and swelled. I sit up straighter, hands neat on my lap. "I loved my job, I loved the children, but I was in a relationship that didn't work out. Things became difficult, so I decided on a fresh start."

"Oh." He closes the folder.

"Such is life." I smile, shrug, hoping he'll leave it there. "But that's why I moved up here … among the rich and famous." I grin now, hoping I sound flippant, funny, not stupid. "I mean, I love the touristy aspect of this village. Everyone here is on holiday. They're determined to have a good time, you know?"

"And you think taking care of a child would be a 'good time' then?" There's a sarcastic edge to his voice. I've dug myself a hole.

"No, I just meant … the atmosphere here is—"

"Do you have a boyfriend now?"

"Excuse me?"

"Do you want me to repeat the question?"

"No. I heard you." I fold my arms. "I just think it's inappropriate to ask."

He clears his throat, a nerve twitching in his cheek. "I don't allow strangers onto my property. The position requires the nanny to live in. You know that?"

I nod. I didn't, but—

"If you have men friends …"

"Ohhh, I get you. No, I won't be bringing any friends here. Male *or* female. I've only just arrived. I don't actually know anyone." I brave another sip of my iced tea to buy some recovery time. When I look up, he's studying me. Is he expecting more? I hold his gaze, but I can't help shifting, tucking my feet under my chair. He follows my actions, maybe involuntarily, like a cat distracted by movement.

"Was there something else you needed to know?" I ask.

"No. You fit the bill. I want someone young enough for my daughter to 'hang' with, as she calls it, but mature enough to keep her out of trouble. You're thirty-four, yes?"

Again, inappropriate. I nod. "Not exactly *young*, but ..."

He snaps the folder shut. "I like your spirit. You're going to need that."

I baulk. What does he mean? Is the girl a problem child? "I'd like to know more about your daughter. Does she—"

"I need someone down to earth. Not a socialite. Someone who can take responsibility, get on with the job without constant supervision. School pick-ups, extra-curricular activities, help with her homework, keep her busy on weekends, or when I'm away on business. That sort of thing. Do you think you can handle that?"

Doesn't he want to add "keep her out of my hair"?

"Yes. I think so." But details. Does the child have any issues? Physical? Emotional? And what about ? Where do I sleep? Am I expected to be on duty 24/7?

He stands. "Can you start today? The last nanny left in a hurry. I assume the agent discussed wages with you?"

I fumble to my feet. Is he serious? Just like that? Thursday before New Year's seems such an odd day to start a new job. Surely, he needs time to think things over? "Um, sure. I was thinking I'd start next week but ..."

He frowns, sighs, looks out over the sea as if I've just dumped the world on his shoulders. Does he suffer from depression? He looks miserable, and now I feel guilty. I scrunch my nose. Would it be so bad to start today? I don't have a good reason not to. Sheesh, I'm such a sucker.

"Today works."

"That would be best. I'm heading overseas Monday, so if you can get settled in over the weekend that would be more convenient."

"Great."

"Good. My housekeeper will get the final say; you'll be working closely with her. She'll fill you in on everything else. I'll get my VA to attend to the employment forms."

He's already leading me back into the house but stops suddenly. I almost walk into his back. This close, I have to crane my neck to look up at him – taller than I thought, and lean – but something about him seems to take up more space ... not space ... more energy, or perhaps it's me who feels smaller. Is it his eyes? The odd depth to the dark brown, like damp wood, not cold fossilised wood, but sturdy, worn of ages ...

"Thank you," he says, stepping back a little. "I'm trusting my gut instincts here. I hope I'm not *wrong* about you ... Ms *Wright*."

Woah. The iceman made a joke. Is that a smirk? "Thank *you*, Mr Moretti."

"It's Daniel. Right, well, I need to get back to my office." He moves through the lounge, heading back toward the hallway, and calls out, "Margie?"

A fifty-something, red-headed woman appears, tea-towel in hand. She's curvaceous like me, and I thank god the first woman I meet in this house isn't a supermodel.

8

Andreas

Another argument. On the day we moved in together. It was about where to keep shoes. He called me stupid. Said I didn't know anything.

I sat on the floor of our bedroom and cried. Couldn't believe I was moving in with someone so awful. Was it too late to change my mind? We'd signed a lease. I'd let my last place go.

But he was just stressed, he said. Hugs would make it all better. Moving in with someone was scary. Things would settle down.

That night we had sex for the first time in our new bed. He called me "baby", came quickly, not bothering to satisfy me. In truth, I was just glad to be held, to know he still loved me and everything would be okay. Anything was better than the loneliness of my years passed.

We could work on it. Never mind the infantilising.

9

Margie regards me for a moment, smiling as she sizes me up. The woman is a ginger puff, no, a gingernut – her expression sweet and inviting, but the sharpness in her eyes hints at a core of spicy grit. She wipes her hands on the tea-towel, and ignoring my outstretched hand, grabs me into a hug. I'm not quick enough, so she pins my arms to my sides. Okaaay.

"Welcome aboard the good ship Moretti." Margie smells like icing sugar and holds me a little too long. Is she physically assessing me? Maybe she's one of those airy-fairy types, trying to feel my vibrations, my aura.

Mr Moretti cuts in. "I'll leave you two to get acquainted. See you at dinner."

Margie lets go, steps back. She nods to him. "She'll do."

"You'll fill her in––"

Margie flaps a hand, and he strides off.

"So!" Margie says. She's loud when she speaks, really loud, and I wonder if she's a bit deaf. She reminds me of a grandmother – not mine; I never met either of my own – but what I imagine a grandmother should look like – tell-tale silver streaks, soft wrinkles framing warm eyes, a floral apron. But there's nothing cliché about the bright orange lipstick that clashes with her hair, though she owns the look. "I'm glad of some female company who's beyond her teens. How old are you? Early thirties?"

I nod, confounded. I've never met someone so gregarious, so in-your-face confident. The employment agent was forthright, but this is next level.

"Don't mind me. You'll get used to my fifty questions a day." Margie's laugh is loud and husky, like a rock singer who's spent a lifetime yelling over a too-loud band. I bet she has stories to tell. "Come on. I'll show you the ropes. So, you're from Melbourne?"

"Is it that obvious?"

She winks. "Evelyn mentioned it, love."

Love. Funny how when some people use the diminutive, it can irritate like a press on a tender bruise, but Margie makes it sound like a compliment. As if she thinks I *am* a "love", worthy of affection. She pats my shoulder. "Not to worry. You'll fit in soon enough. This town has a way of wearing your edges off."

I imagine myself an odd-shaped rock with someone chipping away at my angles until I fit perfectly into a predetermined space in the stone wall of this community. I'm not sure I want that. I need to remain vigilant, sharp. I let go once before, let Andreas erode my foundations, cement me to his own bedrock, all while I smiled too easily, the girl needing to please.

Never again.

As I suspected, the house is larger than life, the stark absence of homely, personal belongings, even photos, more evident as we pass by other living areas. The brightly lit kitchen, with its multitude of appliances, is pristine.

"This is my baby," Margie says. "My pride and joy. Everything has its place. Grew up an army brat. Can't shake it off. You know?"

I don't know. My own family always muddled through in a mess. Dad coming and going at all hours for his train engineer shifts, leaving sandwich crumbs and spilled coffee from his thermos all over the kitchen bench. And Katie's socks, undies and hair elastics a regular feature on our bathroom floor. But this house here ... it's something else.

"Don't stress about making a mess," Margie says. "Help yourself to anything you like, anytime. Just let me know if you use the last of something. There's a shopping list stuck on the fridge. Just whack it on there so I'll know."

"Sure."

She moves to the bench, picks up an electric kettle and fills it at the sink. "Never-ending iced tea in this house," she says. "Disgusting stuff if you ask me, but they like it. Brekky is served on the patio if it's not raining, else in the dining room. Lunch, you can fend for yourself, there's always heaps of left-overs in the fridge and plenty of cafes in town. Dinner's at seven. Reilly's allergic to shellfish – and bee stings – but mostly things with calories, so make sure she eats. She tends to think a carrot stick constitutes a meal." Margie sets the kettle down and switches it on.

I wish I had a note pad to jot everything down.

She turns, hands on hips. "Any food preferences yourself? Allergies?"

"No, I eat pretty much anything."

"That's what I like to hear. A woman should have a healthy appetite." She pats her rounded stomach. "Maybe not quite as healthy as mine." She laughs, then leads me off down another hallway. Outside a fully furnished bedroom, she points. "Yours. There's an en suite through there. Have a look around if you like. I've got a spare set of house keys for you, and the car keys live on hangers above the hallway table.

Make sure you put them back whenever you're finished with them."

"Okay. But I ... I'm floored that you're going to trust me with so much. Just like that."

Margie chuckles. "It's a small community, love. Not much you'd get away with. You have a licence, don't you?"

"Sure."

"Good. Daniel doesn't drive, so you'll need to get Reilly to and from school. There'll be general appointments, running her to her mother's, to friends, outings and whatnot. Errands for Daniel, and chauffeuring when he needs it."

"He doesn't have a licence?"

"No. I'll explain later. It's a brain thing, medical. A glitch of sorts. And take no notice of his lack of social filter – it's not personal. He'll grow on you."

"Oh nooo." I press my fingers to my lips.

"What's wrong?"

"I told him I had brain freeze with my iced tea."

She laughs. "You duffer. Is that all? Well, he shouldn't be serving that foul stuff to guests anyway. I only make it because he likes it."

I wander into the bedroom, press on the queen-sized bed, then head over to the French doors, which give direct pool access from my own patio. I spin back to Margie. "This house feels like a resort."

She nods. "Pretty cushy. But you'll find you'll earn your keep. Families are families no matter where you are."

I come back to the bed and bounce on a corner. "Is that why the last nanny left? Mr Moretti says she didn't stay long."

"Call him Daniel, love. 'Mr Moretti' was his father, god rest the old bastard's soul." Margie pulls a face, and I laugh. "Don't miss him at all. Glad Daniel doesn't take after him –

sure he's abrupt at times, you don't want to get on his wrong side, but he's a softy compared to his dad."

"Tell me about Reilly. This has all happened so fast, Mr Moretti ... Daniel ... hasn't told me a thing about her."

"Reilly," Margie says, leaning against the door frame and folding her arms. "Well ..." Margie scratches her nose. "She might come across as uppity, prissy, like her mum, but there's deep waters, like her father. Just watch what you say around her. She has big ears, and I can't guarantee anything we say or do doesn't go straight back to the cow. And by 'cow' I mean Cynthia." Margie smirks.

I laugh again, unsure if it's nerves or because Margie is gold. She already feels like a confidant.

She straightens. "Reilly will be at school camp all next week, so that'll give you a chance to settle in, get to know the ropes. I expect you'll want to organise transport for your stuff? I can make a call if you like. There's room in the garage if you need storage space. Where are you living now?"

"A little one-bedroom place, on William Street. I don't have many things."

"Left in a hurry, did we?" She gives me a knowing smile.

I blink. It's way too soon to be spilling those beans, though I suspect Margie would be someone who could keep a secret, when it counted. I chew the inside of my lip. "Just one of those spur-of-the-moment decisions."

The lights above us flicker.

Margie clucks. "Kettle's boiled."

I frown. "How—"

She points to the downlights. "Had the halogens replaced with LEDs recently. Now, any switch we turn on or off on this circuit makes them flicker." She throws her hands up. "Well, help yourself to a tour of the house and gardens. There's a gym next to the garage if you're into that sort of thing. I'll be in the kitchen when you're ready. Just stay clear of Daniel's office and his bedroom – they're the two rooms closest to the front door. He travels often. Doesn't like to wake Reilly when he leaves early. Reilly's room is next to yours."

"Thanks."

"I'm glad you made it. I think you're in the right place. Evelyn is rarely wrong."

"Sorry?"

She's gone, but her words hang, enigmatic, an unfinished invitation.

While I puzzle, I take Margie's advice and stroll out through the French doors. The air here is softer, breezier. I can't get enough of the ocean, the sweet lemony scent of frangipani. I take my sandals off and sink into the thick buffalo lawn. Cushy is right.

So this is my life now. Kid sitter. I just hope Daniel doesn't follow through on the police check. I'm betting he won't. He looks too harassed, too tired.

I stroll over to the pool and dip my hand in. Baby-bath warm. So tempting. But there'll be plenty of time for that. I can make better use of the rest of the morning by clearing out my motel room and doing a bit more shopping – some decent clothing, shoes, personal stuff. A hairdryer. Don't forget a hairdryer. Maybe a small present for the kid – I'm not beyond a bribe.

Speaking of, since her room is next to mine ... I wonder what ten-year-olds like to do these days.

⋯◆⋯

A breach of trust probably isn't the best way to start a relationship with the kid, but sneaking about her bedroom is something to keep my mind demons at bay. Katie still hasn't responded. She's okay. Of course she is. There have got to be countless reasons – I mean, a paramedic dealing with someone's heart attack takes precedence over my insecurities. She'll be fine. She's smart. She'll get back to me when she can. And stressing doesn't serve her or me. Yet self-help positivity talk won't stop Andreas strangling or gut punching her. God, I hope she's alright.

So let me focus on Reilly. How do I get an upper hand on winning the girl over? Apart from the pink bedspread, a silver-handled hairbrush on the dresser and a framed photograph, the room has very few personal items. The bookcase holds school texts, not the squidgy toys, pop magazines or novels I'd expect to see in a young girl's room. Where's *A Wrinkle in Time*? Where's *Little Women, Anne of Green Gables, Diary of a Wimpy Kid, The Princess Diaries*? Perhaps they're all at her mother's place in Palm Cove? Margie says Reilly visits her every other weekend. That's not enough time to enjoy personal treasures. Perhaps they're all neatly hidden here, behind the cupboard doors? Should I? No. That's going too far.

But wait, along a window ledge there's a collection of snow globes, each containing a replica of an iconic landmark: the Eiffel Tower, Big Ben, The Statue of Liberty, Niagara Falls. Has the child been to all these places, or does she wish to go one day? I shake the Eiffel Tower globe, watch the silvery flakes flutter then settle. Who thought these up? Something so simple, so sweet.

Over at the dresser, I examine the photo. Is this Reilly's mother? The attractive blonde is standing near a waterfall, her bikini-clad body lithe, nothing maternal about it. Beside her is a much younger man, arm clasped around her waist. Not the grip of a son. How does her kid feel about that? How does Daniel feel about it? Does he even know this photo is here? There aren't any others around the house. At least, not that I've seen. I'm sensing I've walked into a minefield.

I sigh, deep and good. I could use a drink.

10

Andreas

I signed up for weekly art classes.

He hated being left at home at a loose end.

"Can't a friend give you a lift so you can leave the car for me?"

Somehow, the car keys became his.

11

Oh wow. The cars. A bright-red convertible Audi – too incongruous for pulling up to my budget, paint-flaking motel, as if I were a VIP from the more exclusive, child-free, boutique resorts closer to town, slumming it for the day. Next to the Audi is a bright-yellow four-seater Mini Moke. More my style, but isn't it a collector's car? You wouldn't know from the immaculate paint work. I wheel my pushbike over to it and lift, trying to keep the wheels straight and praying I don't scratch anything as I squeeze it between the back and front seats.

It's relatively easy to back out the driveway, and off I zoom, wind in my hair, grin where all grins belong.

The motel clerk, the same beer-belly dude who checked me in, is tight-lipped as he calls up my booking on his screen. He leans on one hip and, without making eye contact, announces he can't refund me.

"Why not?"

"You paid cash. Didn't put down a credit card."

"So?"

He doesn't say anything, just stares.

"Fine." I'm busting to tell him the room at my new place is three times the size of the dumpy one here and comes with a chef and a real pool. But I get the feeling it'd be lost on him.

And I don't like this precarious feeling of where I've landed. Someone might kick my feet out from under me at any second. Take all the privilege away. Not that it would matter. Andreas was the coveter of pretty things, expensive things. Things that were always out of my grasp when I was growing up. Out of my hemisphere. Things held by glossy people in magazines, who implied you were unworthy without this watch, this perfume, this perfect body. Was I subconsciously jealous? I don't think so. What my father, Katie and I had was something better – the closeness of blood, someone having your back, no matter what stupid things you did. Even if Dad was never a hugger, he showed his affection in other ways – a wink, a nose twitch, a genuine laugh at our nonsense. We didn't need much, but what we did need, he provided. That's not something you can trade on the stock exchange.

So why am I feeling so ... uptight? Katie would tell me to just enjoy the ride. "Geegee, don't get so tied up in your head." As a kid, a fleeting delight – a ridiculously enormous cloud of fairy floss – would have Katie googly-eyed, even though she knew a stomach-sickening sugar overload awaited her afterward. It was the moment of joy that mattered.

I head over to the motel room, shove my few belongings into my carry bag, then kneel beside the bed. In the far back corner of the bedside drawer, tucked behind the bible, is a small red velvet pouch. I retrieve it, open the drawstring and pick out the red, yellow and blue *misanga* Katie sent me from South America – back in the days when she was still backpacking, living in the moment, finding herself.

How contrary is life, inverting our roles like this? I stroke the embroidered threads. I've never worn it – too afraid Andreas would rip it from my wrist. "What the hell is that rubbish?" Its symbolism of my being loved by someone else would have been an affront to him. Especially when that someone was Katie, who'd made it clear from the start how she felt about him.

"I don't trust him, Geegee. His energy is dark."

"You just don't know him. Give him a chance."

She'd looked sad, knowing she was dampening my newfound joy, though she refused to back down. She was too honest for that. She would have felt my hurt but held my pain anyway. Somewhere along her journey, she'd learned that fairy floss can be toxic. How had I not seen it myself? I was the elder. I'd always been the down-to-earth one.

I sit now and enjoy the moment of tying the bracelet on, bittersweet, knowing my beautiful, cheeky, wobbly-in-life-and-love kid sister is now a grown-ass woman. Thank god for her. I'm so proud.

Once I'm done, I tip the pouch up, and out tumbles something else – a steely, sparkly piece of fairy floss – a handcuff made for one finger, which never brought the joy I dreamed it would. I was stupid not to leave it, but everything had been such a crazy, hectic rush. Now I'll have to find a way of safely returning it without leaving a trail. He'll want it, the ring is a family heirloom, even if he can't have the trophy he thought it would buy.

As if on cue, my phone beeps.

Katie: *He knows.*

Me: *Surprised it took him this long. You okay?*

The text indicator keeps repeating the response dots. I wait and wait, my mind working overtime, imagining her body pressed against her front door, hands pressed over her ears, terrified that Andreas might actually be able to follow through on his bellowing threats to bust her door down. I should have insisted she come with me, but she has her job, her friends, her life. And Andreas would have found the ticket trail … somehow.

Still no answer.

Should I call her? What if he's there, in the room with her, and hears it's me? God, I'd kill for a vodka.

Please be safe, Kit.

Margie's kitchen smells of fruit and cinnamon. "Apple pie. Family favourite," she says, sifting flour from a packet. "Making one for dinner and a couple for the freezer. Pour us a cold drink, would you, love?"

"Delish. Who doesn't like apple pie?" I open the fridge. Two bottles of white wine sit on the bottom shelf, neither of them opened. I bite my lip, glance at Margie. I guess meeting your new charge with alcohol on your breath wouldn't be a good look. My nerves are going to have to cope on their own.

"Never trust people who don't eat dessert," Margie says. "Lemonade for me. There's a jug on the left. Oh, and try some fudge."

Maybe the sugar will help settle me. I take a small piece of a latte-coloured sweet from a plate and pop it in my mouth. "Mmm, that's divine. Caramel?"

"And vanilla."

"Does Reilly's mum eat dessert?" I could bite my tongue, but the gossip will help take up some mental bandwidth I'm currently devoting to worrying about Katie. I carry the lemonade to a bench, then glance around the cupboards.

"Glasses are in that one there," Margie says, nodding to her left. "So you saw the photo? No, that woman wouldn't let a spare calorie past her trout-pout. Way too skinny for my liking. Setting a bad example for Reilly. Young girls have enough pressure these days without a mother who thinks eating the odd pineapple doughnut is selling your soul to the devil. Ha!" She adds half a cup of flour to a bowl of oats, desiccated coconut and brown sugar, sending up puffs of white as she kneads in small knobs of butter. "Moderation in everything. Until you reach my age. Then anything goes."

Her laugh is so raucous, it *almost* makes me smile. As I pour the lemonade, my hand shakes, clinking the jug against the glass. Margie glances but says nothing.

"What about Daniel?" I ask.

"Daniel's a bit of a health nut, but he appreciates my cooking. His problem isn't food, it's mood. Ever since Cynthia ran out on him"—she turns and gives me a pointed glance—"with one of his business managers, a close friend no less, he's been like a black cloud over a barbeque. Never know when he's going to drop a downpour and sizzle out the sausages. Can't blame him though, can you? I'd want to kill them both."

"Is that why there aren't any photos around the house?"

Margie nods as she kneads. "Ten years of family memories, and she was in every one of them. Narcissistic much?"

I store away the information. Poor guy. Having your wife walk out on you and your child is one thing, but rubbing it in your face with someone you trust? I push Margie's lemonade along the bench, then pour one for myself. "I noticed the guy in the photo seems a fair bit younger." I'm prying, but I can't help it. If I'm going to live here, I need to know the ins and outs of this family. Besides, Margie seems to love a good gossip.

"No, no. That's Stuart, her latest boyfriend." She walks over to the stove, stirs a pot of syrupy mixture, then turns off the burner. "She left the other guy a couple of months after they'd set up home. Don't know why and don't care.

Any man willing to get involved with that woman is asking for trouble."

I sip my drink, wondering if Andreas's mother is saying the same thing about me, even though she's never met me.

"I know what you're thinking: Why did Daniel marry Cynthia in the first place? Can't answer that one. He listens to me about most things but didn't this time. He was obsessed. She tried to give me my marching orders when she first moved in, but I told the cow I was employed by Daniel, so I get fired by Daniel. And look which one of us is still here!"

She picks up her glass to cheers, as if celebrating. I can't help but laugh with her; the woman's candour is as delicious as her cooking. Oh, to be so comfortable, so at home with yourself and your surroundings. I wonder if I'll ever have that again.

I watch her work, mesmerised by her hand movements, she's chopping almonds now with a quick rolling movement of the knife.

"Margie. About what you said earlier. Is Evelyn your … sister?"

Snick, snick. She doesn't even pause her chopping. "Nope. We've been together near on twenty years now."

"Oh, nice. Longevity seems rare these days. But has she had an injury or …"

"MS."

"I'm so sorry."

She looks up. "Why? It's not your fault."

"I … don't know. It just … seems the right thing to say, I guess."

She laughs then goes back to her almonds. "I'm just yanking your chain, love. So what about you? Would have taken courage to leave."

I take in a sharp breath and touch my neck, but she doesn't look at me now, and I'm grateful for the space. I don't bother trying to deflect – it's obvious Margie and Evelyn have exchanged notes – though I do purse my lips, which desperately want to share how worried I am about Katie. *Not yet.* "I guess so."

She nods, continues her cooking.

As I sip my lemonade, I pull my phone from my pocket. Still no message. "So ..." I say, too brightly, "has Daniel always been so quick to decide when hiring nannies?"

Margie pauses, shakes her head. "No. No, he hasn't. But the last one left us in the lurch. She was supposed to cover my upcoming leave, but let's just say she had other ideas of what the job entailed. Fringe benefits, if you get my drift."

I'm not sure I do. Did she break the boyfriend rule? Steal? Not pull her weight?

"Now we're heading into the off season, so not a lot of choice of hires – about the only downside of living in a holiday town. And Evelyn and I really need this break. She's having more bad days than good lately."

"I'm so sorry." There it is again, my useless "sorry".

"Thanks, love." She eyes the kitchen clock. "Would you look at that? Better get a move on. Reilly will be getting out in fifteen. Can't keep the princess waiting." She scrapes the almonds into a bowl, then rinses her hands. "I'll fill you in more in the car."

12

Andreas

He didn't like my friends. Not that he had many himself.

"I don't want them in my house. Especially your sister. She doesn't like me."

"My house? Do you hear what you're saying?"

"I live here, don't I? A man should be king of his castle." He laughed as he said it. A joke. I should get over it.

Then came my birthday. Katie was determined to visit. "Screw him, Geegee. You're my sister."

He shut himself in the bedroom until she was gone. Didn't talk to me for a week, except to say he hoped Katie had kept the receipt for the dress she'd bought me as a present. "Makes you look fat."

And nobody would want me if I was fat.

13

"Orientation Day," Margie says. "Preparation for high school next year. Never had those in my day. Personally, I reckon it's just babysitting so parents have time to prepare for New Year's Eve tomorrow."

We're waiting in the Audi with the top down, outside Reilly's school – as one does. I study each kid as they come piling through the school's gate, voices high, noisily excited like birds in a nesting tree.

"It's one of those alternative set-ups," Margie says. "Cynthia chose it. Convinced Daniel they have better teachers. They don't. Just higher fees. But Reilly had settled in, so we didn't want to move her."

Margie's "we" intrigues me. Has she that much sway? I glance toward the gate again, wondering if I can pick the girl from the crowd. Moody and serious like her father? Long-limbed and lean? Or is she all blond self-composure like her mother? Please tell me she doesn't have a Disney princess backpack and perfect hair.

As if to taunt me, a wisp of my own mousey hair flies across my face. The colour still surprises me. *Light Mocha*, the box said. Peanut, more like. Katie said it was boring, that I should have dyed my hair dramatically black. "That's the whole point," I countered. "Boring is invisible."

My mind turns back to what Margie has just told me about Daniel, how he has brain misfires that prevent him from driving. "Nothing serious," she said. "It's like an electrical fault."

"Like epilepsy?"

"Sort of. They're called absence seizures. Often, you'd never know he's having one. It's like he goes off into his own little world for a while, disconnects. It's no big deal. Doesn't happen often. But he gets fatigued afterward."

"Is there—"

"Nope. Nothing you need to do. He only needs rest. Always worked with kiddies, have you? Never wanted to do something else?"

I've been readying answers for moments like this, but the sudden change in topic throws me. I also get the feeling Margie has an inbuilt bullshit detector. "I've always fancied baking, cake decorating, that sort of thing. Maybe I'll do a course one day."

"There she is!" Margie points to a petite blonde with pigtails in ribbons. Princess it is then, though it would be hard for any young girl not to look princessy in a uniform of powder-blue with a white Peter Pan collar. The kid waves to another child, then turns, searching the line of cars. Spotting the Audi, she breaks into a run. Margie gets out and opens the rear door. The kid halts when she reaches us, stands glaring at me.

"Why is she sitting in the front?"

"Reilly, this is Georgia. Your new nanny."

I smile, reach out my hand. "Hi, Reilly."

She climbs in, takes off her backpack – not Disney, kittens. "Another one?" She sighs in that heavy, dramatic way kids do.

Margie leans in to buckle Reilly's seatbelt.

"I can do it myself!"

Margie pulls back but stands and watches to make sure Reilly's secure. With that scowl, the kid must take after her father. Great. Prissy *and* moody.

"How long is this one going to stay?" Reilly asks, crossing her arms.

I beam, an expert at giving smiles I don't feel. "As long as I'm needed."

Reilly pouts. "I don't need you at all."

Wow. My first thought is that being a cow must run in the family. But I have to remind myself that I don't know her or what she's been through at home.

Margie is impassive as she returns to the driver's seat. "Watch your manners, young lady. I'm sure you and Georgia will get along just fine. Especially as Georgia is going to take you for ice cream now." Margie winks at me. "Isn't that right?"

I have a momentary impulse to tell Margie I've already had an ice cream today, but I get the ruse. "Sure. What's your favourite flavour, Reilly?"

"I don't like ice cream."

"*What*? That's unheard of! What little girl doesn't like ice cream?"

Reilly tightens her crossed arms, looks daggers, then slowly and deliberately, as if I'm hard of hearing ... or stupid, says, "I'm *not* a little girl. I'm almost eleven."

Geez, pre-schoolers were so much easier. Okay, strike one. I have to lift my game. "Well, that's a shame because I found a shop that has thirty flavours." She must know it; the town is too small for anyone to miss the window decal – a huge tongue licking a cone.

Reilly looks uncertain, lowers her eyes. Her arms are so tightly squeezed, they're losing colour. "Thirty-one. They now have liquorice."

I exaggerate wide eyes at her. "Thirty-one! I stand corrected."

"You're sitting."

"Sorry?"

"You're not standing corrected. You're sitting."

She's a little drier than I gave her credit for.

She uncrosses her arms, flops them by her side. "I suppose I could have a diet lemonade."

I flick a look at Margie that asks if Reilly's allowed to drink the stuff.

She shrugs. *Bigger mountains to climb.*

Margie drops us on the street outside the ice cream shop, then leaves to do a quick grocery run and pop in to see Evelyn. A deep gutter runs between the road and the footpath, wide, like all the gutters on the main strip. Catering for the heavy rainfall, I expect. While I contemplate jumping over it, Reilly turns and walks away.

"Where are you going?"

She ignores me, reaches a cement walkover, crosses, then heads back toward me.

I opt to jump. Piece of cake.

The kid's face is solemn when she reaches me. "It's not ladylike to jump over dirty gutters."

"It's"—I glance back—"not that dirty." It's *not*. I've seen worse. Cheap holiday destinations where sewerage flows along rubbish-littered curb-side trenches. What's a few leaves and ... big seeds? *Are* those seeds? They look like chewed mango pips.

And why am I defending myself against this precious little cow? My inner child wants to flick the back of her head.

At the counter, Reilly stares at the massive display – thirty circular pictures of ice cream flavours. She points. "See?" A piece of paper has been tacked to the side of the display board: "31. Liquorice".

"Okay. Would you like that flavour?"

The shop assistant finishes serving a customer, then turns his attention to us.

Reilly drops her gaze. "A diet lemonade, please. With a straw."

At least she has manners for other people, if not with me. I consider mentioning the ecological impact of plastic straws, but a lecture isn't going to win me any points.

"And you?" the assistant asks.

I wonder if he remembers me from this morning. If he does, he's not showing it. I choose three flavours, including the double chocolate fudge. Reilly watches him scoop generous serves into a cup, piling layers until it's an Everest of ice cream. I hope my tactic pays off; there's no way I can eat all that. I wink at the kid, but she gives me side-eye.

Look how neat she is – Pigtails, clothing, shoes, all immaculate. Even her voice is clipped. Where does she get that from? Her mother?

The assistant places our orders on the counter. While I pay, Reilly takes her lemonade to a curb-side table, leaving me to juggle my ridiculously large cup of ice cream. I lay out two napkins and two spoons. "I got an extra one, just in case."

She shrugs and looks over my shoulder as she sips her drink.

I take a large spoonful of ice cream. "Ohhh yes. It's really good. You should taste the coconut. It's sooo coconutty."

Reilly frowns as she continues to stare off into the distance.

I try again. "And the chocolate one. Oh. My. God."

She looks at me then, pulls a look of distain before my wrist catches her attention. "What's that?"

I tuck my plastic spoon into the ice cream cup and twist the bracelet around so she can see the intricate embroidery. "A gift from my sister. It's called a misanga, a friendship bracelet. I can teach you how to make one if you like?"

She shakes her head, glances over my shoulder again. "I don't have a sister."

Her tone is flat, but there's an edge of sadness in her eyes that makes me think of Katie. How life might have been growing up without her – unbearable, after losing our mother. Sure, we had petty disagreements as kids, resentments as teens, jealous barbs as adults. But none of that has lingered in my memory. Katie is now Diana to me, goddess of hunting, the moon.

"Don't you have a best friend? You could always—"

"That man keeps looking at us."

A flood of crawling nerves hits my chest. Fight or flight. "What man?"

I turn, follow her gaze, but can't see his face – he's holding up a magazine with a motorcycle on the cover. The familiar compact bulk of him makes me shudder. I can't run, leave Reilly here on her own. Instead, I pin myself to my chair, try to drive my nails into the plastic. Wait. Focus on my breath, cool as it slides up my nostrils, warming my lips as I slowly, deliberately, breathe out through my mouth.

The magazine lowers a touch. The top of his head shows. Oh god. Sandy hair. Will it curl over his forehead? Will his eyes be muddy, too close set, full of loathing? His bottom lip too generous, too pillowed, for the vileness he'll spit: "Leave me? You ungrateful slut."

Will I see the tapering scar over his left cheek, the one he swore he got boxing? "You should have seen the other guy." *Liar*. His brother told me – he'd been drunk, hit his face on the pissed-stained step of a pub, back in their uni days.

Reilly touches my hand. I startle, turn back to her.

"Do you know him?" She looks scared, pale. My fear is rubbing off on her.

"I—"

A chair scrapes. I spin back to him. He's standing, magazine folded under his arm. Sweet relief. Not Andreas. He glances at us. Frowns. He must think we're odd, staring at him like that. Acutely embarrassed, I face Reilly again.

"You look ill," she says.

"I'm fine," I say brightly, picking up my spoon. "Look at this. It's to die for." I gulp more chocolate ice cream, make a slurping noise. Anything to distract her. And myself.

"That's disgusting." Her eyes fasten on the smudge I've left across the top of my lip.

"You've got—"

"What?"

"You've got chocolate on your face."

"Where?"

She points, and I touch my forehead. "Here?"

"No. There!"

I touch my cheek. "Here?"

"On your lip!"

I cross my eyes and pull a face, trying to look at my lip before running my tongue around my mouth. "I was going to save that bit for later."

Despite herself, Reilly laughs. "My mummy would never do that."

"What else would your mum never do?"

I can't help it – I take a quick glance over my shoulder. He's gone. Good.

Reilly pauses. I've freaked her again. The kid is perceptive. I'm going to have to watch myself with her. "What wouldn't she do?"

"She wouldn't hold her spoon like that."

I check my grip, wrapped over the top of the plastic cutlery, instead of underneath. I dig the spoon into the ice cream again, gouge a gigantic mound and pretend to stretch my mouth around it.

Reilly glances about, checking for witnesses. "Don't do that! You'll get it all over yourself."

I hold the spoon aloft. "Is that why you don't eat ice cream? Because you might get it on your clothes?"

Reilly's focuses on the creamy treat. I'm sure she's salivating.

"Does your mum disapprove of this?" I dip my finger into the ice cream and smudge it on the front of my blouse.

Reilly gasps. "What are you doing?"

I shove the spoon at my mouth, squishing a trail of dribbles out the sides and down my chin. "And this?" I mouth through the mess.

Mortified, Reilly giggles. "You look ridiculous!"

I give her a chocolatey grin. "I do. And see? Nothing bad happened." I push the spare spoon closer to her. She shies back as if it'll bite her.

"Go on. I'm not going to tell anyone."

Her hand inches toward the spoon.

"It'll be our secret," I whisper.

She grasps it, tastes a smidge of the coconut, closes her eyes with a tiny sneaky smile. Heaven is in her mouth.

Smack!

Her eyes fling open, and she looks down at the splodge of bright green I've flung at her pristine t-shirt.

"Pistachio," I say, matter-of-factly. "You're not eating it quick enough. It's melting."

She doesn't move. Have I gone too far? No turning back now. I load my spoon again, ready to flick another creamy projectile. "You better get in there, or it's coming your way."

Reilly jerks forward and heaps up her own spoon, ready to launch. We're at a stalemate, each keeping our eyes on the other's missiles, locked and loaded. I tilt my head, inch the spoon toward my mouth. She follows suit. We swallow, then freeze, waiting for the other to move. Suddenly it's on, both of us digging into the cup, shovelling spoonful after spoonful until we're scraping the bottom.

As we sit back and laugh, I pass her a napkin. "You've got drips all down your chin."

Something shifts in her eyes, and just like that, tears well. She grabs the napkin and hides her face.

"Oh, honey. It's okay, it's okay. Nothing that won't come out in the wash."

Reilly shakes her head. "I'm going to be fat."

I suck in my breath. What on earth has the kid's mother put into her head? She's a healthy size. Petite. Not overweight in the slightest. Not that it should matter. "Sweetie, one serving of ice cream isn't going to hurt you."

"Mum says we should eat to stay neat."

What the hell? Is this woman some relic from the fifties? I bite my tongue, remind myself I don't know the woman ... yet. "Well, you know what? If you ate a whole tub of ice cream on your own, sure, she'd probably be right. But sharing a few scoops with a buddy is perfectly fine. And I'm always happy to share. Now let's get you home, washed up and changed. You'll feel a lot better. Shall we walk back? It's not that far is it?"

"No! I don't want anyone to see me like this. And you've still got a dirty face too."

I wipe my mouth, deflated. How can a mother do this to her child? The kid should be outdoors, digging up mud crabs, climbing trees, making daisy chains. She's way too young to be thinking like this.

I fish around in my bag for my mobile to call Margie. While I dig, I ask Reilly, "What does your father say about this?"

"Daddy doesn't care. He says he's had enough of women."

With an ex-wife like that, I'm not surprised. "I'm sure he does care, sweetie."

Reilly shrugs. "No, he really doesn't. And my name is Reilly, not sweetie."

I've been told.

Margie gives me a querulous look as she pulls up to collect us. "Looks like you two had fun." I give her an I'll-tell-you-later look, then offer Reilly the front seat, but it seems dairy products render the kid a glowering, speechless, backseat lump.

As soon as Margie pulls the car into the driveway, Reilly is out and running for the front door. I guess I won't be seeing her until dinner time – unless she thinks the calories she's consumed means she has to forfeit her meal? I doubt Margie will let that go down. Or is force-feeding my job now?

The house is quiet. Mr Moretti … Daniel … must still be in his office. Dinner won't be for another couple of hours, and there isn't much for me to do, since I'm already unpacked.

Margie tells me to relax, so I head out to the patio with a magazine she's left on my bed. The intensity of the day must be catching up with me; my eyes droop as I lie back on a lounger.

"Why aren't you changed?"

Amazing. I've only known the kid for less than a couple of hours, and I recognise that tone. She stands with hands on hips, wearing a pink bathing suit, a towel slung over her shoulder and sunscreen plastered all over her heart-shaped face.

"Excuse me?" I lift my sunglasses.

"Why aren't you changed? Come on! We have to go before it gets too late and they pull the booms in."

I sit up, puzzled. "Sorry? Where are we going?"

"The beach! Swimming! Hurry up and get changed."

She's kidding right? "You can't swim this time of year. The stingers ..."

Reilly rolls her eyes. "You're such a tourist."

"Sorry?"

"The nets! *Come on*, get changed. We don't have much time."

14

Andreas

"No, I don't feel like cake and coffee. We have coffee at home. You can make sandwiches. You should stop spending so much."

"It's just a coffee."

"Every dollar adds up. You know what? We should put our money together. In a joint account."

He worked in finance. It made sense, especially once we'd managed to save a decent amount and he transferred it to a term deposit.

Where was the harm in an investment for our future?

15

We head off down the short road, then work our way down the sandy cement steps that lead to the beach, me still unsure if this is a good idea. The scene looks as inviting as any other coconut-tree-lined, towel-strewn, tropical beach, but I don't know if I dare dip a toe in. Far North Queensland marine life is murderous: saltwater crocodiles, sharks, stingrays, and the jewel in the crown of things that can potentially kill, stingers – deadly Irukandji or box jellyfish. God knows what else. Reilly has no such reservations, assuring me again we're safe swimming within the nets. "Besides, there's lifeguards on duty." She springs across the two hundred metres or so of packed damp sand, sending little crabs skittering to their burrows. "Come on! You're so slow."

"Wait!" I call, stopping to read a bright-yellow noticeboard stuck into the sand on a pole. Today's risk is medium. Is that good or bad? Attached to the noticeboard, a short piece of plastic piping holds a bottle of white vinegar – apparently the best first-aid action for stings – that and a trip to the hospital while you writhe in agony.

Reilly isn't having any of it. "Look." She points. "See the booms?" I follow her line of vision to where three long white flotation tubes cordon off a fifty-metre square section of water between the swim flags. "The stingers are out at sea.

And even if they do get brought in with a wind change, it's okay as long as there's been no rough weather to wash them over the sides. We're cool."

"Not the Irukandji," I insist. I know that much. They're small enough to swim through the holes in the net.

Reilly sighs. "The lifeguards do regular sweeps; they'd know if they were about." She dumps her towel, flings off her thongs and runs into the throng of swimmers. I stand watching from the water's edge. Are these people crazy, or am I just a big chicken? Everyone seems to be having a good time in the languorous waves. I dip my foot and sigh at the baby-bath temperature, such a contrast to Melbourne's water temperatures. Even in the heat of summer, they feel Antarctic to me, making me gasp at the cold, but this is heaven. I wade in a little deeper. If my skin could sigh, it would.

I scan the water to see where Reilly has disappeared to. She's heading toward the rear of the boom. "Reilly! Come back." Maybe she can't hear over the trills and laughter of the other kids. I yell, louder.

She turns to look back as she paddles on the spot. "No! Come and get me."

I wade further, until the water reaches my waist. "Reilly!" She ignores me, paddles away. I take a breath, dive under a wave. The deeper water is a breath of coolness, still heaven. When I resurface, Reilly has reached the boom and is swimming along beside it. I tread water, waiting for her to bore of her game.

Eventually she swims back to me. "See? Nothing happened. Just like your ice cream."

"Touché. You've had your fun. Now, please stay away from it. There might be jellyfish caught in the net."

"You can't tell me what to do."

"It's my job to look after you, and you're worrying me."

Reilly considers me for a moment. "Adults are such bores. If you don't like it, you don't have to stay in." She turns and heads straight for the boom, leaping up and resting her arms over the top of it.

"Reilly! I'm not joking. Get off there."

"Make me!"

Several other youngsters leap onto the boom further along. Great. "Look what you've done. The sign said to stay off them."

"I'm sick of rules."

I'm about to yell out to her again when an announcement comes over a loudspeaker:

"Please do not lean or climb on the booms. For your own safety, stay off the booms."

Looking chagrined, Reilly eases off, her eyes shooting hateful darts at me, as if it's all my fault. But the kids further along ignore the warning, laughing and splashing each other.

"EVERYONE OFF THE BOOM."

"Okay, Reilly. We're done. Let's—" A high-pitched scream spins me toward the other kids. A small boy of perhaps six or seven is holding his arm up.

"It hurts, it hurts!" he cries.

The other children let go of the boom and tread water around him, looking unsure of what to do. An older teen boy tries to grab the boy around the waist, but the youngster flails and smashes him in the face.

I turn back to Reilly. "Swim to shore." She doesn't move, looks confused. I don't want to frighten her, but I need to know she's safe. "Do it. Now!"

She splashes off as I swim toward the children who are trying to calm the boy, but he's screaming and keeps slipping under the water. I grasp him and fling him onto his back so

I can wrap an arm over him and drag him behind me. *Am I doing this right?*

"It's okay, it's okay. I've got you."

He lashes out and screams, sobbing as I push toward shore. "I know it hurts. I'm going to help you."

He struggles harder, and I tighten my grip, striking harder, sucking air and spitting salty water between the roll of waves. A lifeguard pelts across the sand, followed by another. They charge into the shallows between startled adults wading out to meet us. A woman yells – his mother? As my feet touch shallower ground, the lifeguards close in. "Watch his arm," I say, as they take the boy from me, carrying him out of the water. It's only now I see the tentacle still clinging to his wrist.

I bend forward, resting my hands on my knees, puffing from exertion as the lifeguards lay the boy on the sand. He's fallen quiet, still. "Is he going to be okay?" I ask. A crowd gathers while the loudspeaker crackles to life – everybody out, they're pulling the boom in. Now they're pumping the child's chest and giving him mouth-to-mouth. I'm nauseous, wanting to collapse to the sand, but Reilly is standing a couple of metres away, face pale, obviously terrified. I go to her, put my arm around her shoulders. "Come on. Let's leave them to do their job."

Someone touches my arm as we squeeze through the crowd. "Good job."

I nod, sapped, unable to respond.

As Reilly and I trudge back toward the hillside steps, the wail of a siren grows louder.

Have I screwed up my job before it's even started?

———◆———

Ritual is what I need now: soapy hair, a hot cleansing, to feel my own skin – the only familiarity I have. Can I just stay in this small space forever? The world has gone crazy outside; I've fallen down Alice's rabbit hole. Did a kid nearly die in my arms just now?

Breathe.

Eventually, I have to forfeit the comfort of the hot water. I wrap myself in a towel and sit to untangle my wet mousey hair, wondering how long the colour will last. God, I don't even have … I snatch open a couple of drawers under the sink. Thank god. Margie thinks of everything.

The hairdryer's motor doesn't drown out the devil questioning what I'm doing here, why Katie hasn't responded, or the call of the vodka bottle I've hidden in the washing basket next to the bath. Just a sip, to calm, to help me survive the awkward dinner to come.

I gulp.

Again.

Again.

Screw it, I'm going to call Katie.

Her message service stonewalls me.

———◆———

I'm the first one in the dining room. Did I get the time right? The table is laid for three. Guess Margie won't be joining us. Does she normally? She's lit a couple of citrus-scented candles. They highlight the maple inlay through the centre of the walnut table, setting the wood's golden swirls on fire.

Are the candles a regular thing, or a special touch to welcome me? I wander around the room, reluctant to sit lest I usurp someone's usual seat.

A painting on the feature wall takes my attention. Its colours are florid with no particular pattern – my day captured in acrylics – stark against the white of the wall. But it catches the hot pink of the bougainvillea in Margie's table centrepiece.

Where is everyone? I check my phone. No messages. I saunter over to the French doors – ubiquitous in this house. Outside, the sun has slipped behind the hills, stilling the bay into an early bruised twilight. The intermittent red flash of a plane's navigation light pulses in the darkening sky. A glint of white sail – tourists returning from a dinner cruise perhaps.

How long until I feel at ease here? Until I become inured to this privilege?

I wander back over to the table, and it's only now I notice the A5 yellow envelope on one of the seats, my name scrawled on the front. I guess that answers one question. The envelope contains a letter of employment offer, a tax form, other bits and pieces. No mention of a Police Check. I close my eyes and sigh. One less stress.

Reilly enters the room, head bowed, and I shove the documents back into the packet, tuck it under my arm. The kid looks pink-faced from a shower, hair straggly and damp. Would it be too much to offer her one of my new frangipani clips to pin her hair back? Would she take that as a peace offering ... or a smother?

She doesn't greet me, just takes a seat at the head of the table, the spot I assumed would be Daniel's. Interesting. She doesn't seem upset, traumatised. But kids can be good at hiding that stuff.

Daniel appears, even more dishevelled than this morning – hair ruffled, eyes red rimmed. Has he had one of his "misfires"?

He clears his throat as he sits. "Evening, Georgia. Pumpkin." His voice seems deeper. Tiredness, perhaps.

"Evening." I can't bring myself to call him Daniel yet. A muscle in my cheek twitches, and I smile to cover it up. *Say something. Something not banal.* Then I remember the envelope under my arm. "Thanks for this."

He nods. "I'll forward them to my VA once you've completed them."

Margie enters carrying a tray – plates of teriyaki salmon fillets and salad.

Daniel glances across to Reilly. "Been for a swim, Pumpkin?"

Reilly nods keeping her eyes on the plate Margie is placing in front of her.

"You must be starving then." Daniel attacks his meal, taking a large mouthful and chewing thoughtfully before turning to me. "The water should be warming up this time of year."

"Yes, it was like a baby's bath. Lovely."

He focuses back on his meal. I stick a fork through a cherry tomato, pop it in my mouth, then steal another look at him. Lean body, strong hands, dark hair falling over his forehead, but there's a shadow in his eyes, a strain in his features. He's watching Reilly out of the corner of his eye.

"Not hungry, Pumpkin?"

Reilly shakes her head as she pushes a piece of lettuce around her plate. "I had some ice cream."

Daniel lowers his cutlery to study her. "You did? When?"

Reilly sighs. "In town. Georgia took me. She eats messy."

I flush. "It was just a little treat."

"Huh. That's a first," Daniel says. "She never eats sweets." He focuses on me now, doing that thing where he holds my gaze for too long, trying to see past my skin. "Takes after her mother."

The word "mother" hangs, nuanced, a coughed-up fish bone.

I stay silent, wait, unsure if he suspects or expects Margie has dished the dirt.

He releases me, goes back to his meal. "You'll get to meet Cynthia on Saturday when you drive Reilly over. Usually has her from Friday night to Monday morning, but, you know, tomorrow's New Year's Eve, and I don't trust Cynthia will be"—he glances at Reilly—"in a fit state. But she's going overseas for a month and wants to see Reilly before she leaves."

"Okay."

"And I need you to drive me to the airport on Monday."

Reilly looks up. "You're going away again?"

"I have to, Pumpkin."

"But you just got back!"

"What have I said about complaining about the unavoidable?"

Reilly's lip trembles. "Yes, Daddy."

"You'll be away at school camp anyway. You won't miss me at all."

There's no anger, no trace of admonishment in his voice, yet his words obviously hold sway. Reilly returns to her lettuce while I attempt to break the tension.

"We had a bit of drama at the beach this afternoon."

Reilly's face pales, and she glares at me. I've said the wrong thing.

Daniel halts midway through pouring iced tea. "You were swimming in the sea?"

Reilly sighs. "In the nets, Daddy. There were lots of people."

"We have a perfectly good pool."

I swallow. Is this a black mark already? "I'm sorry ... I admit I was worried about letting her go in, but ... there were lifeguards on duty, and as she said, plenty of other people in the water. It's just that some of the kids were hanging over the boom, and—"

Reilly clangs her fork.

"Sheer stupidity," Daniel says, thumping the iced tea jug down. "If I ever hear of you being silly, Pumpkin"—he turns his gaze on me—"there'll be no more swimming at the beach. Off season or not."

I glance at Reilly, avoiding his intensity. "I'm sure Reilly will listen to reason."

A flicker of shrewdness in her eyes.

Daniel sighs, wipes his mouth with his napkin. "Who's up for a day's sailing tomorrow? Thought we'd go to the outer reef. Nice way to bring in New Year's. Then we can go see the fireworks in the park later."

And just like that, the tension vanishes. Is this how Daniel manages his daughter? With promises of privilege? Does he bring expensive gifts back from his travels to buy his daughter's heart?

Reilly shrugs.

"I thought you'd be happy to go snorkelling, Pumpkin?"

She manages a smile.

He glances at me.

"Love to." What else am I going to say?

Eventually, I excuse myself, citing the need for an early night. Back in my room, I have a closer read of the paperwork. I'm to be employed through Evelyn's agency. I toss the documents aside, lie back on the bed and check my messages again.

Relief.

Katie: *Yes hun. Sorry! Thought I'd pressed send on prev txt. All good. Had to turn my phone off. Shithead has been calling and texting me all day. I've blocked him now. You okay? Can I call?*

Me: *God yes please.*

16

Andreas

"We should have lunch here. It's Italian. They do good lasagne."

"How do you know?" I asked. "I thought you said—"

He opened the door and ushered me in. Once wasn't going to hurt. He was hungry.

Short-skirted and long-legged, the waiter smiled at him. A lot. As if she knew him.

"Ugh," he said. "Tell her my coffee is cold."

"Tell her yourself."

"Don't be difficult. I'm going to the toilet. Just do it."

That night, I lay in bed wondering at his faithfulness. I consoled myself with the thought that things could be worse. At least he didn't get drunk. At least he didn't hit me.

At least I wasn't alone.

17

Sunlight filtering through white plantation shutters. Empty pillow beside me. The lightness, the fan-freaking-tastic ridiculous privilege of my new reality.

This is not a dream.

I stretch, long, languorous, not worrying about waking *him*, about slipping out of bed before he can grab, pull, pin, force his hand over my mouth because he likes the rapey feel of it. Did I encourage that? Did I like it myself as first? Submission. Easier not to fight. Quicker.

I rise, reach for the ceiling, touch my toes, lean left, right. This is my body now. Shall I start the day with the luxury of a bath? Maybe I won't even shave my legs.

As I lie back and soak in the momentary, exquisite pleasure of *me* time, my mind has other ideas. Reilly and Daniel. Such an intriguing pair. I'm keen to see them interact more. Reilly's obviously pushing her boundaries, as any tween would, should. It's healthy. I've had worse from toddlers. But Daniel feels like an enigma. Still, a whole day out of the house together might relax them both, give me a glimpse under their skins. And if it takes a champagne cruise to suss them out, well, there are worse things in life.

Loose white shirt over my bathers, khaki shorts, sandshoes. I'm all set. Tote in hand, I head out into the bright-blue day. I'm hiding in plain sight with my Jackie O. sunglasses and oversized floppy hat, tourist clichés, but who cares? I like the look; it's fun. I've forgotten what that's like – a simple pleasure. Not sure I'll be brave enough to get back in the water. I wasn't even brave enough not to shave.

Daniel is already sitting in the passenger seat of the Moke. For a moment, I'm thrown. I'm driving? Of course, I am. His seizures. He looks more relaxed than yesterday. Maybe it's the t-shirt and shorts, his arm stretched over the back of the seats, which he withdraws now.

"Morning," he says, touching the peaked cap keeping the sun off his face.

"Happy almost New Year's. Great day for it."

Reilly comes charging out of the house, trailed by Margie. The kid jumps in, not a whisper of complaint about being in the back seat. Margie places a picnic basket on the seat next to her. "Few sandwiches and snacks, in case you get hungry."

Reilly rolls her eyes. "There's food on the cruise, Margie."

"Yes, pet, but not *my* food."

It's only a fifteen-minute drive to the harbour, but I hadn't anticipated the awkwardness of sitting next to Daniel in a compact vehicle. The gear shift is right up against his knee, and it's difficult to manoeuvre it without bumping him.

"Sorry."

"Don't worry about it."

But I do. It's not a coy game; it's plain uncomfortable.

"Everything okay?"

"Uh huh."

"Settled in?"

"Uh huh."

"This from the woman who claims to have running-off-at-the-mouth disease."

Something tightens inside me, and I have to remind myself not everything is an aspersion. "Just a bit nervous about driving a collectable car. This must be antique by now, no?"

"Are you a car fancier?"

I take a corner a little too fast. "Sorry. No, just ... my dad used to buy and repair jeeps."

"Well ... technically, it's not a jeep. And to be classified as an antique, it would need to be at least forty-five years old, but you could call it a modern classic, since it's a Leyland 1981. Last year of manufacture."

"Cool." Great. Thanks for confirming my fear. Now I have two things to be nervous about.

"But don't worry about it. It's had its fair share of repairs over the years. It's just a get-about."

Huh. His knee is still too close.

⋯⊰◦⊱⋯

At the marina, my sandshoes hit the ground before anyone unbuckles their seatbelts, and I busy myself with retrieving Margie's lunch basket. We stroll along the pier with its rows of shiny vessels gently bumping against their moorings, soft metal chinks of rigging, the faint sour scent of seaweed. I try to guess which one is Daniel's, but we don't stop until we reach the end of the pier where I suck in my breath.

"Holy shit! That's not a yacht; it's a ship."

Reilly is quick with her admonishment. "Language!"

Daniel laughs.

"Sorry," I say. "I just assumed we'd be going on a private yacht."

Daniel shrugs. "We are. Not bad, is she?" There's a note of pride in his voice.

I'm still confused – there must be thirty or so passengers seated on the rear deck.

"Paying clients," Daniel says, offering his hand to steady me as I step across the gangway. "No point wasting a trip. Only taking three people on this baby is a waste of resources and unnecessary pollution for the reef."

His line sounds like practised tourist patter, but if this had been Andreas's, he'd be boasting about having the whole damn thing to himself.

"Plenty of room at the fore," he adds.

"The ...?"

"Front." Reilly thumbs toward to the pointy end. "It's more fun up there anyway. Come on. I'll show you." She leads me by the hand, confident in her steps and direction.

Once we're settled on one of the padded bench seats circling the front deck, Daniel asks, "Do you get seasick?"

"I don't know. To be honest, I've never been on a yacht."

"It can get a little choppy once we get out of the bay. We've got plenty of sick bags"— he points to a nearby pile of foiled-lined paper bags—"but you might want to take something now, before we leave. Pretty sure we've got some Kwells downstairs."

"Hmmm. I think I'll be fine. If I can tolerate the Big Dipper at Luna Park, I'm sure I can handle a few bumps on the ocean."

He looks doubtful. "You sure? It's pretty miserable if you do get sick. Once it hits you, there's no stopping it. I'll get some anyway. I need you to watch Reilly, and you can't do that if you're unwell."

A familiar lump forms in my throat, and I have to remind myself he's just being sensible. This isn't about control; his first concern is his daughter. "Alright. Thanks."

He turns to Reilly. "What about you, Pumpkin? Will you be okay?"

Reilly is lying on her stomach, kicking her legs back and forth. "I'm always okay, Daddy."

"Okay, honey. Just stay close to Georgia, alright? I don't want you annoying the guests. And when we get there, let them have first go at the snorkel equipment. There'll be plenty of time for you afterward."

What the? He's letting her swim outside of a net? I try to keep my voice light, non-accusatory, but I'm truly puzzled. "I thought you didn't want us swimming in the sea?"

He pauses, looks confused.

"Yesterday. At dinner."

"I think what I actually said was I didn't want Reilly being silly on the booms. We supply stinger suits for all our guests, plus keep a close eye on the stinger forecast. We don't take risks."

Reilly flops onto her back, folds her arms across her chest and mutters, "It's our boat. I don't see why I have to wait until last. Mummy wouldn't make me."

Daniel's face tightens, but he says nothing, grabbing Margie's basket and heading off, leaving me with his sulky child. Distraction is what we need. I think about the present I've stashed in my tote but decide to save it for a more dire moment.

"Reilly, there's no problem with stingers out at the reef?"

"Not always. Sometimes."

So comforting.

"Daddy has plenty of stinger suits on board."

"Stinger suits?"

She huffs and gives me a don't-you-know-anything look. "They're like wetsuits, but not as thick." She stares up at the sky, twirling her hair.

We have the whole front deck to ourselves. Why not relax? I sit and tilt my head back to let the sun graze my face, but a sudden breeze stirs over the marina, and I have to snatch my hat before it blows over the side.

Reilly springs up. "Good catch! You'd be better off with a cap though. They've got some downstairs. I'll grab you one."

I'm about to tell her no, to stay with me, but my phone beeps, and in that moment of distraction, she's off, leaving me mid-refusal as she dodges an elderly couple who've come to inspect the area. I contemplate following the child, uncomfortable that my charge isn't close by. Still, the yacht is a confined space. Even though it's big, seriously big, how far can she go?

I smile at the couple, who shuffle toward the bench opposite, then dig out my phone to check the message. A banking notice. Someone has tried to reset the password on my credit card account. Good luck with that, Andreas. I bet he's blocked me from our joint account too – as if I'd be stupid enough to keep using it. Or maybe he's left it open to trap me. Whatever, I'll have to set up a new account. Somehow. If I have enough identification documents.

I lean back and lift my chin again. The air shimmers with moisture, the early heat not biting yet. Water slaps against the hull. A voice on the loudspeaker announces we're departing in a few minutes and for everyone to take a seat. The elderly couple have settled in for the journey. It seems safari jackets and long socks with sandals are still popular for older gentlemen. They hold hands like long-time lovers. I smile again, fascinated by their unusually pale hair and skin but not wanting to stare.

"The water's clear from what I'm told. Should be good viewing on the reef," I say.

They nod, "Yes, sounds good."

"Where are you from?"

"Helsinki," the woman answers, her accent thick.

"Ah, Finland. I expect you're enjoying the warmth here then. Have you been out long?"

"Two weeks. It's our sixtieth anniversary present from our kids," the man says, patting his wife's leg.

Married young, still giving each other comfort in old age. "Congratulations," I say through a sad wish for something I'll never have.

A deep vibration rumbles beneath our feet, and I glance toward the rear. No sign of Reilly. Should I look for her? I don't want to smother the child; she obviously knows her way around. I'll give her a couple more minutes.

Soon the vibration grows stronger, and the yacht inches away from the pier. Okay, that's it. Time's up. I stand, intending to trace Reilly's steps, but Daniel appears from the other side of the yacht.

He looks about. "Where's Reilly?"

"Downstairs." I point in the direction she disappeared. "I'm just going to fetch her."

"No, she's not. I just came from there."

"Well, she must have wandered down the back."

"You're supposed to be keeping an eye on her."

"I am—"

"So where is she?"

I stiffen, tell myself to shut up, apologise, admit I've failed already, but his tone ... "You can't put a ten-year-old on a leash. It's a boat. Where is she going to go?"

Daniel flushes crimson. "Have you never heard of someone falling overboard?"

"I—"

"She's your responsibility!"

His tone stings, and my own face heats up. "She's not silly," I stammer.

"Slipping overboard is silly?" he hisses.

My chest tightens, instinct clamming me up. *Don't argue. It'll only escalate.*

He seems to notice my discomfort, takes a breath, lowers his voice. "Even so, she's not supposed to be annoying the other passengers. You sit there. I'll find her. We don't need two of you going missing."

"She's not missing!" I shoot back.

The thunderous look he gives me makes me sit like an obedient dog. This must be what Margie meant about getting on his wrong side. It rankles. So much for not allowing myself to be pushed around anymore. I guess I need to pick my battles. And this isn't about me; it's about his daughter's safety. He's entitled to be angry. I would be.

"Here." He hands me a packet of tablets. "Take two now."

Before I can answer, he stalks off.

I clench my shaking hands and glance, hot faced, at the Finnish couple, who are politely looking out to sea.

⸻ ◆ ⸻

"What are you thinking?" Reilly asks, close by my side now that Daniel has read her the riot act. She's not to move from this deck unless she's with me.

"Not much. I'm just enjoying the fresh air and the sail." *I wish.* The weather, the view and the sea are perfect. I *should* be enjoying them, but I'm still niggling at how to win back Daniel's trust. If I'm not able to handle such a simple task, how does he think I'm going to handle something more serious?

"No, you're not. Your forehead's all creased. Daddy does that when he's thinking."

Reminder to self: the kid is sharp in the observation department. I choose my words carefully. "I guess I'm hoping things will go well between you and me."

"Why wouldn't they?"

"Well ... you don't know me, and your father is about to go away on a business trip."

Reilly shrugs. "I'm used to being on my own."

"Don't you have any friends?"

"Yeah, Sammi Siva's my bestie. But she's with her dad right now in Ko-ala Lumpur."

I smile inwardly but don't correct her pronunciation. Not this early in our relationship. "Is Sammi from there?"

"No. Just her dad. She's visiting."

I nod as I think of Katie. Sisters make the best friends – once all the "me" of being a teenager has fallen away. Once you understand the preciousness of someone who knows how crap you are at karaoke but still comes along and manages to only cringe when she thinks you're not looking. Once you've got yourself stuck in a bad place and they have your back, time and time again, until you're ready to save your own butt.

"Hey." Reilly taps my forehead.

I jerk a little, surprised by her touch.

"You were doing it again."

I smile. "You got me. So what about your father? Does he have many friends?"

"No, Daddy is all work, work, work."

"But he's out here today. This isn't work."

"Wanna bet? He'll have some big client on board. You watch."

We fall silent for a while, Reilly bumping a foot against the bottom of the bench. I relent on my "dire" ruling, reach into my tote and pull out the brown paper parcel I've stowed.

Reilly looks at it, curious. "What's that?"

"Wouldn't you like to know?"

She gives me side-eye, and I laugh. "Actually, it's for you. A sort of reverse welcome gift. I picked it up in town yesterday."

Her face brightens. "For me?"

I hand it to her, and she rips at the paper, revealing a book: *The Knife of Never Letting Go*. It might be a touch old for her, but I think she can handle it. I'm determined for her to have some fun with her reading, to use her imagination, to know a child can survive adversity.

Her enthusiasm fades. "I don't like books. They're boring. I have to read enough for school."

I cringe in mock-horror. "How dare you! Patrick Ness is *not* boring."

She looks doubtful but runs her hand over the bright-red cover. "What's it about?"

"Well, I guess you'd call it science-fiction. It's about a young boy living on another planet and—"

"B-o-r-ing."

"And he can read people's minds and talk to his dog, and there's a girl who flies starships."

Here's the side-eye again. She's an expert at it. "Really?"

"Give it a try. If you don't like it, you can hand it back."

Reluctant, she lies back on the bench and opens it. After a moment, she giggles. "Poo, Todd!"

The line made me chuckle too when I first read it. Such a great hook. I mean, what else would a talking dog say to its owner? It's a delight watching her turn the pages, her amusement, her uncertainty, then worry as she takes in the story. She's a couple of chapters in by the time Daniel reappears. He sits next to me and absently rests his arm along the railing behind me. Is this part of his lack of a social filter – being unconscious of personal space? I inch away on the pretence of straightening my shorts and resettling myself.

"What have you got there, Pumpkin?" he asks.

"It's a *not* boring book," Reilly says without looking up.

I can't help smiling. "A present."

He nods. "Nice." He sounds genuine, not snide at all. "How's it going?" He takes his cap off and rubs sweat from his forehead. Maybe it's the sunshine lightening the deep brown of his eyes to a hue of gold, or the wind catching his hair, but he looks healthier today.

I sit up straighter, still wary I might be in for a second round of berating. "Fine."

"Good. I was hoping you two would hit it off. Evelyn seemed convinced. When she and Margie join forces"—he holds both hands up in surrender—"it's beyond reckoning."

I chuckle. "You think?"

"My trip Monday ... I might be gone a while. A week at least."

I'm not sure if it's his close proximity or the heat and humidity causing this nervous tightness in me. I shift a little further still. "Okay. We'll be fine. Won't we, Reilly?"

Reilly keeps her eyes on her book but answers. "Sure. I'll take Georgia on a tour. Maybe we'll go hot air ballooning."

Something tells me this is a regular button push. Daniel laughs for the first time today, the skin around his eyes wrinkling as he smiles at his daughter. It's a deep and genuine reaction that makes me wonder why Reilly thinks he doesn't care about her. He's clearly besotted. "That's not happening. You'll be too busy on your school camp. And behave yourself while you're away. You hear?"

"You're so boring, Daddy."

He shrugs while Reilly turns and flops onto her belly, leaning on her elbows to read.

"Anyone like a drink?" He turns to me. "There's chilled champagne on offer for all the guests."

So tempting. "Just a soft drink or mineral water, thanks. I need my wits to keep an eye on this one."

Daniel looks sheepish. "Yeah, sorry about that. I was probably a bit over the top. Bit tense. Investors on board. Deal's almost done now, though."

Reilly pipes in. "See? Told you."

Daniel pretends to glower. "She can be a handful, but she's a good kid."

Reilly looks up. "Hello! I'm right here."

Daniel leans over to ruffle her hair, then pushes her face down into her book.

She laughs, and so do I. "You have a nice smile, Daniel. You should use it more."

I'm mortified as soon as I've said it – the amount of times the comment has infuriated me. A favourite line of Andreas's: "Babe, smile. You're not one of those women who's pretty when she's angry."

Daniel doesn't seem fazed. He leans back, rests his hands behind his head and looks at the sky. "My mother says I have a killer grin."

I can't help it; I stare at his mouth, and I'm surprised by the laugh lines there. Given his gruffness yesterday and this morning, I expected downturned lines that unhappy people wear. "Is she local?"

Daniel shakes his head. "No. Mum's in Tasmania now. Had enough of the heat. Reilly only has me ... and her mother." He runs a hand over his mouth and chin, as if he's trying to block talking about Cynthia. "Margie filled you in?" he murmurs.

I nod. No point lying. I respond in kind, voice low. "I didn't want to pry ..."

"No, that's okay," he whispers, then glances at Reilly. "Forewarned is forearmed."

Reilly looks absorbed in her book, but I change tack anyway. "So ... I haven't quite got a handle of what business you run."

"Own," he says. "Property development. Took over when my father died a few years back."

"I'm sorry. I know how it feels to lose parents."

"Don't be. He was an arsehole."

I'm shocked, but Reilly isn't. "Daddy, language."

He chuckles. "Sorry, Pumpkin. Guess I owe you another snow globe."

"Your version of a swear jar?" I ask.

Suddenly, I'm lurching forward. Daniel grabs the railing with one hand and my arm with his other, pulling me back onto my seat. "Rogue wave. You okay?"

"Sure." I shuffle away to recover, rubbing my arm where he's pressed too tightly.

"Sorry, if I—"

A noise from Reilly diverts our attention. The child is looking pale, miserable.

"Reilly? Are you okay?" I get up and squat beside her. "Sweetheart? Are you sick?" She nods, and I turn to Daniel. "I think you better get a sick bag."

He grabs one from a nearby stash, then squats beside me to rub Reilly's back. "Pumpkin, it's better if you sit up. Keep your eyes on the horizon and take deep breaths. It'll balance you."

She groans at the movement, and as I lean in to help, she vomits all down my shirt.

"I'm sorry," she sobs.

"It's okay. It's okay, sweetheart," I manage over the hot stench.

She retches again, and I grab the bag from Daniel, hold it open as she vomits, sags then moans. "But I've never been sick before."

Daniel gets up and somehow materialises a bunch of napkins, passes them to me. "Happens to the best of us," he quips. "You'll be okay."

I wipe Reilly's face, her tears, then attempt to clean my blouse. "Maybe it's the reading while the boat is moving. I'm sorry, sweetheart, I should have thought of that." Great, another stuff up. I help her sit up properly. "Deep breaths and look out at the horizon, like your dad said." I turn to Daniel. "I didn't realise how rough it had got."

"Just a choppy patch. Could have been a bit of backwash from another vessel." He bends to brush Reilly's damp hair from her forehead. "You'll be fine, Pumpkin. Hang in there. We're almost at the reef. I'll get a steward to bring you a wet towel."

Andreas

A night out at the theatre. On the way there, he pulled the car into a petrol station and pointed to the windscreen.

"Clean it off."

"What?"

"Are you stupid? The bird shit. It wasn't there before you did the groceries this morning."

"I'm in an evening dress. I'm not going to—"

He got out of the car, came around to my side and hauled me out. "Do it or we're not going anywhere." He meant it.

My first bruise. The anger in his eyes terrified me.

19

We dock at a jetty that stretches to a coral cay, picture perfect – sparkly, sandy-white and palm fringed. Reilly and I disembark, leaving Daniel with his clients and passengers, all summoned downstairs for a safety briefing and allocation of snorkelling gear and stinger suits. Below the jetty's weathered decking, the water is shallow, sun-dappled and clear, though there's not much to see except rippled sand, pebbles, bits of broken cauliflower-like coral and a few small silvery fish that dart and sway together. I guess the serious coral is further from shore.

Once we reach the sand, it's gritty and shelly under our feet, not the sift-through-your-fingers smooth I expected. We set off further down the beach to find some shade. Reilly drags her feet, a towel slung over her shoulder. She yelps when she steps on a lump of rock hidden in seaweed, limps for a moment.

"You're having all the bad luck today. Shall I take a look at it?"

She shakes her head, soldiers on.

I head toward a clump of palms, but Reilly says no. "See? They've got coconuts hanging. You don't want one of those falling and hitting your noggin." She leads me to another less fruity clump and we lay out our towels. Within minutes, she's dozing on her back, snoring softly like a snuffly cat.

I get up, remove my khaki shorts and head down to the water's edge to rinse the vomit from my shirt, startling a school of tiny fish in the shallows. I stand in the sun for a few moments, letting its rays soak in, vitamise and revitalise. It doesn't feel as harsh as Melbourne's. Maybe it's the humidity. I stroll back up to splay my shirt out on a shrub behind us.

Reilly is still out of it. I study her flushed cheeks, her tight features that should be relaxed in this haven. Even at rest, she lacks the innocent sweetness of a sleeping child. What trauma has her parents' separation caused her? Or maybe it's Daniel's condition that stresses her. An electrical glitch in the brain, a misfire, sounds devastating to me, dangerous. How must it feel to Reilly?

The kid wakes to take a few sips from the bottle of lemonade I thought to grab from the yacht, then settles back again.

It's now I can exhale, release the tightness I've been carrying in my chest. I roll my neck back and forth, breathe deep, turn my attention to the swell of the waves and the ever-changing colour of the reef, darkening then lightening as patches of stray clouds pass over the sun. Lulled by warmth, I lean back on my elbows and close my eyes, almost falling asleep myself.

"Lunch anyone?"

Daniel is laden with a couple of bulky carry bags and Margie's picnic basket. I scrabble to my feet, flip my towel out lengthways to make room for him, then sit crossed legged at one end. He puffs as he deposits the carry bags on the sand, eases himself onto the towel and sets the basket between us. It's always puzzled me how some people sit so heavily, just let their bodies dump down without regard. Andreas was a dumper, bouncing the whole couch when he sat. Or the bed, the earthquake of his movements waking me every time. Not Daniel. He seems aware of his own mass, the space he takes up.

He's undone the buttons on his shirt, which now hangs loose, exposing his toned midriff. I turn away, wondering at my aversion – whether it's just him, or my own state of being.

He opens the basket and pulls out a pack of sandwiches. "Chicken and salad," he offers.

Reilly sits up and grimaces. "Dad!"

Daniel chuckles and pulls out a box of dry crackers. "Here you go. Didn't think you'd be up for much."

Reilly accepts the box, rips it open and nibbles at the salty biscuits.

"Make sure you take some Kwells for the return trip, hey?" He looks at me. "Around three o'clock, so they've got a good hour to kick in."

"I'll make sure."

Reilly puts the crackers aside and lies back to resume her napping, an arm slung across her eyes. Daniel and I eat our sandwiches, then sit quietly, watching the guests snorkelling further down toward the yacht. After a while, he reaches into the carry bag and pulls out some flippers and stinger suits.

"Thought we might have a dip. Water's fantastic. You girls should jump in, have a paddle at least."

Reilly moans. "I'm too tired, Daddy."

"It'll make you feel better, Pumpkin. I promise."

"Maybe later. I just want to stay here."

"You?" He fixes me with a hopeful look.

Cooling off does sound tempting. "Don't the stingers get your hands and feet, though? Your face?"

"They can, but we've done a sweep, and the water is clear at the moment. It's usually a strong wind or tide that brings them in."

"Then why is everyone wearing suits?"

"Policy." He shrugs. "Makes our guests feel better about the whole experience and lowers our insurance. I mean, there's always other larger jellyfish around – not deadly, just a bit painful if you get in their way. You don't have to wear one if you prefer. I'm not going to bother today."

Now it's just awkward, a challenge. "We've just eaten. Shouldn't we wait an hour?"

"Old wives tale. We'll just be fossicking around, not swimming laps."

"Right, well ..." I reach over to my shirt on the shrub, squeeze the bottom edge. "I don't want to get this wet again. It's only just dried after I washed the vomit out. I don't think it'll have time to dry again before we leave."

"Why do you need your shirt?"

"I'll get burned."

He lowers his sunglasses and peers at me. "I'm sensing some resistance here."

"Not at all. I just forgot my sunscreen."

Heck, yes, there's resistance. Swimsuits and bosses? Not my idea of comfortable.

"Problem solved," he says, reaching into Margie's basket and pulling out sunscreen.

Damn it.

"Turn around. I'll do your back."

I hesitate. Doesn't he know how inappropriate he's being? Is this what Margie meant about lacking a social filter?

He holds up his hands. "Oh geez. I'm sorry. Am I making you uncomfortable? I forget myself sometimes."

"No. It's okay."

"No pressure. It'd be a shame to miss out though."

His smile might be beguiling to some. Not me. *Just say no. Or wear the damned suit.*

"No, it's fine." I turn my back to him, telling myself I'm overreacting; my boyleg shorts and tankini are so modest a nun would be comfortable in them. It's only my shoulders and upper back he needs access to. I hold my breath, bracing for the uncontrollable flinch at his touch.

Think about the cool water, the coral, the fish.

He's quick, business-like in his application. When he's done, he passes me the sunscreen. "Here you go."

I apply it to my arms, chest, face, neck and legs.

'Ready?' he asks.

I nod. He turns to Reilly. "Last chance, Pumpkin."

"*Daaad!* I'm sleeping."

He hands me a pair of flippers and goggles with a snorkel, and we head down to the water's edge. Daniel heads straight in, but I pause in the gorgeously warm shallows, hopping on one foot in an attempt to put on my flippers. Daniel has waded deeper. He turns back. "Ah, you might want to wait until you're a bit further out. They're hard to walk in, especially in the shallows."

"Oh, okay." I tuck the flippers back under my arm and stride in deeper. "Damn it!" I've toed a lump of coral. I didn't think there would be any this close to the shoreline.

"Careful where you're walking, or you'll get a nasty cut."

"Now you tell me!" I say, hopping on one foot, trying to rub the other.

The water temperature drops at waist deep, and I suck in my breath, acclimatising. Daniel stops to put his flippers on. I try to follow suit but keep losing my balance. "Here." He holds out an arm for me to lean on. Flippers finally secured, we stand face to face.

"Okay?" he asks.

"I think I've got it." I wobble.

He grabs my arm. "You sure?"

I nod, and he reaches up to my forehead, pulls my goggles down, helps me fit them snugly over my eyes and nose. They press hard above my upper lip, giving me duck face.

"Guess I'll fit right in with all the fishes."

"Huh?"

"Trout pout."

"Oh, yeah. All good then?" he says, tightening the straps more.

Mouth full of snorkel now, I give him a thumbs up.

He fits his own goggles. "Blow into the snorkel to clear it before you breathe," he says. "Like this." He gives a quick couple of blows, and I follow suit. "Great. Now keep within eyesight of each other, and just tap me or yell out if you get into any trouble."

"What trouble?" And how does he expect me to yell with my mouth full of rubber and plastic?

"You'll be right." He splashes off.

I take a quick look toward to shore, to check Reilly is still sleeping, then anticipating the cold shock of dipping my head, I hesitate, take a breath and plunge into a fantasy world where ribbons of purple seaweed dance on the desert-like ridges of the ocean floor. Glittering schools of disc-shaped silver and yellow fish dart ahead of me, as if teasing me to follow, and a huge spotty pout-lipped fish – a grouper, I think – stares at me with protruding eyes that roll back and forth in their sockets. I've forgotten to breathe and have to still myself to blow into the snorkel before sucking in more air, a little panicked that water might rush in and fill the tube. It's all good. I relax into the rhythm.

The further out we swim, the deeper the water, and the coral forest thickens, colours more vibrant, as if a child has taken to them with a packet of crayons, randomly colouring in – missing some but glorifying others. To my right, snuggled between two boulder-like corals, a giant grey clam sits, its massive corrugated mouth sealed with a bright-blue mottled lipstick.

Occasionally, I glance around to ensure I can still see Daniel's legs kicking nearby, but otherwise I'm lost in my own wonderland of spiky, crumbly, rocky, vibrant creations. I drift from coral to coral, peeking into crevices, reaching out to curious fish that seem to tease by keeping just a finger's breadth way. Time dissolves as I float, watching, breathing, until a dark shape drifts below.

As much as I try to override the adrenaline-fuelled panic of my primitive brain, try to reason away the probability of danger, there's no denying what the shape is – long, grey, unmistakable fins.

Fuck. *Fuck*.

Body. Rigid. Sinking.

Whip the snorkel from my mouth. Release of air. Craze of foamy bubbles. Madly pushing up. Breaking surface. Chaotic fountain.

"Shark! Shark!"

I spot Daniel's snorkel. I've drifted too far from him. He can't hear me with his head underwater. I spin toward shore.

Stop. Don't attract its attention.

"Oh god. Oh god. OH GOD!"

Stay calm. It might swim away. Pleeease swim away.

I don't want to look. But have to. I grip the snorkel mouthpiece in my teeth, dip my head back under. It's gone. Where? I gently weave my arms through the water, slowly spinning my body for a better view.

A brush against my leg. I scream, jerk my knees up, my brain charging into overdrive. Visions of that girl at the start of the Jaws movie, in the dark, alone, screaming. I scream again.

A splash behind me. Daniel surfaces, laughing. "Hey, calm down. It's just me."

"No! Down there," I say, treading water. "Look underneath us. There's a shark!"

Daniel grins. Is he enjoying my distress? Doesn't he get it? We need to get out of here.

"Shhh, you're okay," he admonishes. "I saw it. It's harmless. They're very sensitive. And rare up in these parts. We're lucky to see one."

"What?" He's crazy. I shove my snorkel back in my mouth and make to swim toward shore, but he grabs my arm and tugs me back.

"Let me go!" I splutter.

"Wait a minute." He pulls my snorkel away, pushes my facemask up.

"What are you doing? Let me go! I want to go back."

He grabs my other arm, holds me steady. I'm now relying on him to keep me afloat. "Calm down. You're going to start sucking water, and then you'll be in all sorts of trouble. You need to stop panicking."

"Let me go."

He does ... and I sink. He reaches for me again, and I grip his shoulders, livid that he's *still* laughing.

"It's a Grey Nurse. Wouldn't hurt a fly."

"I don't care if it's somebody's bloody fish and chips tonight. I don't want to be near it." My heart still sprints at the thought that, any second, the monster might rise up and savage us. I move a little closer to him, try to look under the water, reluctantly grateful for something solid to hold on to, and there are more legs than just mine for the shark to choose from.

He cracks up again. "Well, that's not going to happen; they're a protected species. It's not going to hurt you, I promise. They're docile. They don't eat humans. Breathe."

I do as he says, taking deep breaths. "Are you sure? How do you know?"

"Look, we can swim down there, and I'll show you how to identify it. You can tell by the shape of its snout and the rounded dorsal fins."

"No!"

"Alright then, just relax. You're perfectly safe."

I still feel inclined to pull my legs up, let it bite him instead, but I calm, lean my head back in the water. "Oh god, I thought I was dead."

He chuckles.

I look him in the eye. "I'm serious. I was terrified." It's now I realise how close we are. How little protection my bathing suit provides against his skin. I clench my panic down, use his mirth as an excuse to push him away, then tread water. "Stop laughing at me."

"I've stopped," he says, still grinning.

"Then wipe that smirk off your face and stop making fun of me."

He falters. "I wasn't laughing *at* you."

"Yes, you were."

"No, it was just the situation. Come on, you have to admit it was funny. Wasn't it?"

He reaches a hand to my face, but I flinch and he jerks his hand back, eyes wide. "Did ... did you think I was going to hit you? I was ..." He shakes his head. "You've got seaweed tangled—"

"I think it's time to go in. Reilly's been on her own long enough."

I twist away and swim toward shore, not caring if he's following.

———◆———

The seasick tablet has made Reilly sleepy. She's flaked out on the yacht's bench cushions, her head resting in my lap, ringlets gently kicking up in the wind like small blond flames. I don't know how this happened, how she's attached to me so quickly – if she has. The thought makes me squirm. What if I can't stay? What if Andreas finds me, and I need to leave in a hurry? I shiver; the wind seems cooler on my heat-soaked skin.

Daniel stands. "I'll get some hot tea, shall I?"

"That would be so good."

It's a relief when he leaves. Since we re-boarded he's been constantly glancing at me, while I've kept doing my best to not make eye contact. Why? He hasn't done anything. It was just one of those moments. And he was right; I panicked. I'm overthinking it. Let it go. It's only my feelings that were hurt.

He returns from the galley with two mugs, plus a cotton blanket slung over his arm. "Thought you looked a little cold," he says. He puts the mugs down, then drapes the blanket over my shoulders and down over Reilly's sleeping form. The child stirs and turns onto her side, her face squashed into my stomach, thumb resting against her lips as if she wants to suck it but knows she's too old. My heart.

Daniel hands me a mug and sits, leaving some space between us.

"Thanks."

"Least I can do."

I sip the sweetened tea, comforted by its warmth.

"Another half-hour until port," he says.

I nod.

"Listen," he whispers. "I didn't mean anything back there. I hope you don't think ..." He thumbs the rim of his mug, glances at Reilly. "I hope you don't think I was inappropriate. Grabbing you like that. I would never ..." He shakes his head. "I just wouldn't."

"Don't worry about it. It was nothing." I watch his face, unsure whether to continue. His concern seems genuine, his gaze soft. I can't imagine him forcing, abusing anyone. Then again, I'd thought the same about Andreas in the beginning. Have I lost the ability to judge character? Maybe. But there's something about Daniel, something in his expression, his voice, that makes me want to trust him. "It's not you. Just bad memories. That relationship I mentioned."

He looks at his feet, as if to give me space to talk. "I'm sorry for whatever happened to you."

Simple words. I'm grateful he's not pulling out platitudes but can't help reaching up to tug my shirt collar over the bruise on my neck, wondering if Evelyn's re-applied make-up has washed off in the water.

"Relationships are overrated," he says. There's an ache in his voice that reminds me I'm not the only one who's suffered at someone else's hands. "You don't owe me any explanations," he adds.

"I know. I appreciate it. I just hope you don't think you've hired a weirdo to look after your daughter."

He glances at me then, his smile crooked. "No one's perfect here. A little bit of weird is a good thing."

20

Andreas

"Who's that guy?"
"What guy?"
"The one you were waving to."
"No one. A work colleague. We catch the same train home."
"Catch a different train."
"But that'll make me late home."
"I said, catch another train."
A black eye, sprained wrist.

21

Margie has prepared a chicken and mango salad, sweet and tangy with a hint of curry. Daniel and I wolf down crusty homemade bread with it, while Reilly sections off most of her meal to one side, then pushes a piece of spinach leaf around like a green boat in a lake of saffron-coloured salad dressing. Her elbow rests on the table, head propped on her hand, squishing her cheek. I feel for her. I'm weary myself from the sea and sun, but she looks pale under her sun-flushed cheeks.

I keep my tone gentle. "I promise it'll make you feel better."

"I'm not hungry."

"Just a little?"

"I'm *not* hungry."

"Shall I get Margie to make you some toast?"

Reilly slams her fork on the table. "You're not my mum! Don't tell me what to do!" She gets up and runs from the room.

What the? I'm all mouth ajar, the sharp clatter of her cutlery still resonating in my skull. I scrape my chair back to follow her, but Daniel stops me. "Leave her."

I drop back into my seat, my instinct to obey orders – given under the breath or yelled – kicking in. Conditioning for self-preservation. "She's upset with me. I should go talk to her."

"It's not you. It's her mother's access visit tomorrow. I think Reilly might need some more therapy. She's been getting worse lately."

I look at the remnants of my meal, guilty at having such a huge appetite when Reilly's struggling with hers. Is her mother really that awful? From what I've seen of Reilly so far, she doesn't seem to be a button pusher or hateful – sure she's testing the waters with me, but that's understandable. Margie's words "a cow of a mother" come to me, and it pains me to think of Reilly's spirit squashed, her young energy muted to suit an inflexible adult. I steel myself with a sip of wine – a concession, mealtimes only. "Does she have to go? I'm happy to look after her."

"No choice," Daniel says. "Cynthia has rights."

I'm stupidly angry on Reilly's behalf. The child is obviously traumatised. I glance at Daniel, wondering if I really want to risk his ire. I know so little about this family. I should shut up. "Can I ask why Reilly doesn't like going there?"

Daniel stops chewing, puts down his cutlery. A tendon in his neck flexes as he swallows. I've pressed too far. Andreas always said my big mouth was the source of all our problems – if only I would shut the hell up and let him make the decisions, let him figure things out without whining in his ear.

"I'm sorry," I say. "I'm prying."

Daniel picks up the wine bottle, offers me a refill.

"I probably shouldn't." But I shrug acceptance. "Just a half, thanks."

He pours for us both. The moment seems to take forever, as if the wine is defying gravity, hay-coloured liquid taking its time to slide out of the bottle.

"Reilly's okay," he says. "She just gets lonely."

"Huh."

"What that's supposed to mean?"

I blink. "Nothing."

He looks at me then, hard and long. Too long.

I take a swig of my wine for distraction ... or comfort. "I'm not judging you," I say. "I just want to understand her. See if I can ease things. For all of you. That's why I'm here, isn't it?"

He runs a finger up and down the silver of his knife handle, carefully lining it up so it sits flush with his plate. His hands are sculpted, veined with blue-green tributaries. So different to Andreas's meaty, possessive paws, digging into my flesh. I shiver.

He clears his throat. "I get all ..." He purses his lips before continuing. "That woman's name seems to bring out the worst in me."

"Sure." I don't know what else to say. Can this get any more awkward? I guess this is the "families are families" bit Margie talked about.

He looks me in the eye for a moment, as if assessing, then sighs. "I guess you need to know the status quo if you're going to stay."

"It'll be helpful."

"Yeah, well, it's the alimony," he says. "I'm convinced it's the only reason she's holding onto Reilly, when she makes it clear she's an imposition. She won't let her have friends over, doesn't spend time with her or take her anywhere. It's homework, TV or swimming. Alone. Reilly hates it. She's a child. She needs stimulation, company. But as long as

Cynthia's not mistreating her, she has to go. It's part of our custody agreement. If I break it, Cynthia will take me back to court. I don't want to put Reilly through that again."

I bite my lip. Wait.

"But I'm worried about the kid she has living there. Him being around Reilly."

"She has another child?"

"Ha! No. Her boyfriend."

"Oh, yeah. I saw Reilly's photo."

"Reilly has a photo of him?"

"Umm ... no, I meant Cynthia and ... him. On her dresser." Heck. I think I've just dropped Reilly in it. Surely, she's allowed one picture of her mother? Even if she seems not to like the woman.

Daniel pushes his chair back, stands.

I panic. "You're not going to take it are you?"

A tight frown pinches his face. "What?"

"The picture."

"No. Why would I do that?" He picks up his plate, leans over for Reilly's, then reaches his hand for mine. I pass it and watch him scrape the remains onto one plate. His movements are slow, deliberate. A meditation.

How long is it since Daniel's been in his daughter's bedroom? Doesn't he kiss her goodnight? Read her a story? When do kids get too old for that? It makes me wonder what Daniel's own mother was like. She seems to have taught him self-sufficiency, decency. I think I'd like her.

Daniel pauses his scraping, as if he's picked up on my thoughts. His expression softens. "Look, I feel as though we haven't quite cleared the air about this afternoon."

Again? I stiffen, shake my head. "No. We're good. It's fine."

"I want you to know I'm not like that. Don't think for a minute I'd try to take advantage of you."

He has no idea how much that sounds like a line.

"Or mock you."

"I didn't." *I'm such a liar.*

"And I hope you don't think that's why we let the last nanny go."

"No, of course not. I hadn't really thought about it." *Liar, liar.*

"She"—he struggles, scratches his chin—"thought her role included ... 'extracurricular activities'."

Stop. Please stop. Margie's words fall into place: "fringe benefits".

"I mean you're a very attractive woman, but I'm not—"

I laugh, taut. "Okaaay, you better quit while you're ahead."

He shoves the dishes aside, puts his hands on his hips, shakes his head, then looks up. "Sorry. I can't see the line sometimes."

I smile. "You and me both. We'd make a good pair."

Margie enters with her apple pie and a tub of ice cream. She fusses about, clearing space. There's a decent chunk missing from the pie already. Has she helped herself first? Daniel seems oblivious.

"I took Reilly some pie," she says. "Poor pet's devouring it."

I chastise myself. Why did I think it was any of my business? It's only food. And Margie made it after all. "That's a relief." I'm curious now. Maybe Reilly only eats in private? She doesn't look anorexic. "Does she want to walk to the park for the fireworks?"

"No. She's almost asleep with her spoon in her mouth. I wouldn't push it."

Margie carves out a chunk of pie and slips it into a bowl. Steam curls up from the soft, juicy apples as she dollops ice cream on top. It smells like heaven. I didn't think I could eat any more, but my gaze follows the bowl as she hands it to Daniel, who takes it and stands. "I've got more work to do, so I'll say goodnight." He touches Margie's shoulder. "Thank you. Delicious as always."

•

Margie gathers the used dishes and cutlery, her movements efficient – muscle memory from a thousand previous clearings. She whisks them off to the kitchen while I dig into the pie. God, it's good. Sweet, succulent, the pastry melt-in-your-mouth. She returns with an extra wine glass and a small fruit platter. "Come on," she says, heading toward the French doors. "Bring that wine. You can't drink it all yourself."

I baulk, eyes wide, mouth still full of pie. Did she think I was going to?

She pauses at the doors and motions with a tilt of her head. I grab my glass and the half-full wine bottle as I swallow and follow. "Are you allowed to do this?"

She wanders over to the edge of the pool, puts the fruit platter on the paving stones, removes her shoes and sits, feet dangling in the water. "Do what? Drink wine? It's the only place I can. Not allowed to at home."

"I meant … well … you're the housekeeper."

And there's that deep, throaty laugh. "I've worked for this family for over nineteen years. Trust me, if Daniel had a problem with me, I'd know by now. This is FNQ, not Sydney." She slaps the pavers next to her. "Come on, have a seat."

I place the wine bottle between us, then sit to remove my sandals. The pool lights sparkle in ripples as I slip my feet into the water. It's blissfully tepid.

"So ... why don't you eat dinner with the family?" I ask.

Margie pokes at the fruit plate and chooses a chunky piece of watermelon. "I have my own life. I'd rather eat with Evelyn. Once you're settled in, I'll be able to leave earlier. That's the plan anyway."

"Makes sense." I yawn.

"Big day?" Margie says, catching a stray piece of watermelon that breaks off as she bites.

"I guess."

"Penny for your thoughts?"

I give her a wry look. "Do people still say that?"

"Excuse me?"

Oh, heck. Is there anybody in this house I won't offend before the day is out?

Margie ribs me. "God's sake, woman. Loosen up. I'm pulling your leg. One day you'll learn to give as good as you get."

I slump. "I'm just weary. It's been a crazy couple of days."

Margie pours herself some wine. "Told you it wouldn't be a picnic. And it's likely to get worse before it gets better. Daniel's filing for divorce as soon as he gets back from his trip."

"Really? I assumed they were already ..."

"Nope. Need to be separated a year. And since she chose last New Year's Eve to run off on him, let's just say there won't be much celebrating in this house."

"That explains a lot."

"Bit moody today?"

"Mmm."

We lean back on our hands and look up. A bright crescent moon sits between wispy clouds. I close my eyes, enjoying the feel of the water on my feet, the alcohol soothing my blood, until an eerie screech carries up from the beach.

"What the heck is that?"

Margie chuckles. "Curlew. Local bird. Pretty things."

The call comes again. I don't think I've ever heard such a mournful sound, full of pain and longing, a soul whose one and only love has moved to another plane of existence, leaving the other to endlessly wander the earth alone.

"Sounds like a baby being murdered, doesn't it?" Margie says.

I laugh, poetic mood shattered.

"A dollar for your thoughts?"

I smirk. "Inflation?"

"Revelation. You can't keep it hidden forever."

I run my hand over a chipped pool tile, an imperfection in paradise. "Tell me more about Daniel. About Cynthia."

Margie sighs. "Third time unlucky. Poor boy."

"Third?"

"First one got sick of waiting for a ring. Good thing too. Didn't like her any more than I did Cynthia. The second one was sweet but couldn't handle Daniel's ... quirks or his working hours or travel. Too insecure."

"Quirks?"

"His brain condition. His lack of social filter. I told you, didn't I? My own brain's getting a bit slow these days. Often find myself repeating things."

Margie seems sharp enough to me.

"Daniel's not great at reading cues," she says. "He's smart, don't get me wrong, but he sometimes comes a bit unstuck. He can't always decipher expressions. Can't read between the lines. He needs to be told straight what's what."

I dig her in the ribs. "Isn't that most men?"

She laughs "And ..." She bites the side of her thumb, as if contemplating. "This might be a bit too much information, but I've long suspected things might be a bit unusual in the bedroom department."

"Oh. Yes. Definitely too much information."

We settle into a quiet contemplation, watching the stars, swishing our feet in the velvety warm water, me wondering what "unusual" means, then mentally chastising myself, and Margie, for what's none of our business. I slap at a mosquito.

Margie drains her glass, pulls her feet from the water and stands. "Come." She holds out a hand. "Walk with me."

"Where are we going?"

"The beach. Less of the little bloodthirsty tyrants down there in the sea breeze."

I accept her help getting up, then follow, both of us barefoot, down the steps to the beach. They seem steeper tonight, and I cling to the guard rail, the wine and warmth making my steps loose.

The sand is soft now, still holding the day's heat, not yet wet from the tide. Something rustles in the undergrowth beneath the coconut palms, and from under moonlit flat-leafed vegetation, a small tubby body with a long snout snuffles out, then disappears back into the shrubbery.

"Bandicoot," Margie says, then points further down the beach. "And there's your curlew."

A tall bird trots a solitary route along the water's edge, its lanky legs slicing back and forth like two pick-up-sticks, avoiding the dance of frothy fringes reaching to dampen the sand again. I breathe deeply, salty mist in my lungs – it doesn't matter whether it's night or day here, the humidity is like a faithful dog, always ready to cover you in damp kisses.

Margie reaches into her pocket and pulls out a pack of cigarettes, offers me one.

"No, thanks. Don't smoke."

"Neither do I. Tell anyone and you die. Especially Evelyn."

God, I like this say-what-you-mean woman – a softer version of her lover. Her river runs strong and sure, no shifty undercurrents to work the ground out from under your feet. Maybe she's developed that trait as essential for living with Daniel.

"Who are you running from?" she asks.

I flinch. "What makes you think—"

She scowls, gently mocking.

I bite my lip, look out to the ocean, moonlight highlighting the froth on the breakers. Am I about to screw things up? Once she knows I'm a coward for not disclosing the truth, that I might be putting this family at risk ...

"Don't think too hard."

Ah, to hell with it. If she sacks me, she sacks me. "Andreas. His name's Andreas." My chest tightens, telling me to stop. To not untie the knot holding the blackness in place. "He ..."—I blow out a breath—"just *won't* give up."

Margie makes a sympathetic noise but keeps silent as we walk on.

I shake my head. "I know people don't understand. I didn't. Couldn't. Why did I stay? Why did I let someone abuse me like that? Nobody understands. Not until it happens to you." I choke now, trying to swallow, press my fingers to my lips.

Margie puts a hand on my back. "It's okay, love. You're okay."

"They say 'you don't have kids, what's stopping you walking out?'" I halt now, unable to catch my breath. I suck, deep and long, let it out in a slow steady stream. "I tried. I did. I left. It made things worse and ..." Suddenly I'm on my hands and knees in the sand, retching, as if the stinking truth has tied itself to the bile in my stomach. It doesn't stop until I've evacuated my dinner.

Margie bends, rubs my back. "Let it out, love. Let it out."

I sit back on my haunches, wipe my mouth. "One of his mates found out where I was." I jerk forward, retch again, but there's nothing left inside except my confession.

Margie grunts. "Arseholes come in all shapes and sizes."

I steel my guts, look up into her eyes, waiting to see the disappointment. "I went back." I shake my head in disgust. "I went back to him. Undid everything."

"You were brave to leave in the first place."

"I'm not brave. I'm a coward. I'm just running."

"You're doing what you need to survive." She squeezes my hand, pulls me to my feet, leads me along the beach again. "Come on. Keep breathing."

The motion sobers me, draws me back. "Margie. If I stay ... if you want me to stay ... if you don't think I'm too much of a risk to the family – and it's okay if you do, I'll understand – but if I stay, is there any chance I can be paid cash or a cash card? For a while at least? I don't have a new bank account yet. I'll get one ... once things have settled down."

"Say no more."

Eventually, we reach a wide inlet flushing water from the rainforest. The evening tide is rising, and the inlet – a mini sand-banked Grand Canyon webbed with mangrove roots – looks thigh deep. To our right is a large yellow sign: "Danger Crocodiles". Margie puts her arm through mine and turns me around. "One monster at a time, hey?"

A sudden, deep *boom* draws our attention to the sky – a firework exploding in a giant bloom of red and gold sparks.

22

Andreas

Too scared to face him, I left a note. It was over.

Day three, he turned up at my work – a kindergarten – screaming to kill me. I cowered in the corner of a toilet cubicle, listening to his onslaught. He slammed his shoulder against the door, smashing the door lock, grabbed my wrist and pulled me to my feet.

The storm dissipated with his voice softening. But his grip held solid.

"Babe, what are you doing hiding in there?"

"I ... I'm working." I thought my arm was going to break.

"Let's go home. You know I love you, right? You belong at home."

I went, head lowered, shameful, past the terrified kids and horrified teachers. The police turned up. Talked of charges.

"A misunderstanding. Right, babe?"

Back home, he was glued to my side. Told me how much he loved me, that I was his and his alone. We didn't need anyone else.

From then on, I didn't need to work. He would look after both of us.

23

The day's torrid heat is yet to kick in and lift the overnight rain from the shrubs, drops large and glassy on russet and emerald leaves. From the front porch, I squat to watch a skink, its movements sudden, little lungs pulsing the silvery skin behind each of its front legs. It tilts its head, peers down a crack between the tiles, darts forward, snaps up a juicy bug, retreats.

I breathe deep as I straighten, lift my arms and stretch up, lean left, right, then head over to the car waiting in the drive, top and windows down so Reilly and I can enjoy what passes as morning freshness during the coastal drive ahead of us.

"Nooo ... I don't want to go, Margie. I want to stay with Georgia."

Fun times ahead.

I head back inside. Margie is leading Reilly down the hallway, the child's suitcase in hand. Reilly's face is flushed, teary. She's truly unhappy, not just being difficult.

"Come on, pet. It's only two days, then you'll be at school camp. You love school camps."

"Two days is forever!"

Daniel opens his office door, grim-faced, as if he's already steeled himself for this moment. "Car. Now," he says. "Enough of the waterworks."

Reilly sucks up a sob, lets go of Margie's hand and walks out to the car, head lowered. Poor kid. She must really dislike her mother. Daniel takes the suitcase from Margie and follows Reilly outside. I look to Margie for any words of encouragement, but she shakes her head. "Every time."

"Will she be okay?"

"She'll get over it. Nothing we can do."

Outside, Daniel squats in front of his daughter and takes one of her arms in each of his hands. "Look at me," he says.

Reilly refuses.

He shakes her gently. "Reilly."

She looks up, and her forlorn expression is heartbreaking. A sad puppy couldn't do better.

"You know the rules. I don't have any choice here, else I'd let you stay. But if anyone"—Daniel pauses, shakes his head a little—"hurts you, anyone makes you feel scared, you call straight away. Okay?"

She nods and Daniel stands to open the passenger door. Reilly climbs in and sinks into the seat as low as she can. Arms crossed, she stares at her feet while her father secures her case in the back.

"Seat belt," he says.

She obeys.

"Okaaay," I say brightly, sliding into the driver's seat and popping my mobile in the dash cradle. I've already programmed Cynthia's address in the car's GPS maps app, but fiddle about, hoping my business will give these two a moment to finish their farewell.

Daniel stretches his arms out. "Hug?"

Reilly tightens her arms.

"Okay, but it's your last chance. I'm leaving on Monday. You'll have to wait a week."

She flings her arms up and Daniel leans in. "Be good."

When he straightens, he has an odd expression, as if he's deep in thought, gaze unfocused.

"All set?" I ask, expecting him to close Reilly's door. He doesn't answer. Just stares into the distance. I glance at Margie, catch her eye, and she hurries forward, closes Reilly's door, then braces Daniel with one hand on his arm, her other around his back. Is he having an episode? Should I help?

"Okay, Reilly," she says. "You've got everything you need for camp in your suitcase."

She turns to me. "So you can drive her straight to the pickup point on Monday. Now, off you go," she says pointedly.

I get the hint and reverse the car. Reilly doesn't seem to have noticed the change in her father. She's sulking again, head down. I wait until we're well away from the house before I speak.

"Hey."

She ignores me.

"Hey!" I say louder. She glances up, and I pull a face, stick my tongue out. She doesn't react. Damn. It always worked for my toddlers and pre-schoolers. What makes older kids laugh? I try again. "Hey!" This time when she looks at me, I push my nose up into a piggy snout.

She huffs. "You look silly."

Tough audience.

We have a forty-minute drive ahead of us, scenic, though I'm guessing Reilly's not interested in the rugged coastline, having seen it too often. I have an idea. "I spy with my little eye, something beginning with R."

"Reilly."

"Nope."

"Road."

"Yep." I'm sure she's rolling her eyes, but I keep mine on the ... road.

"Too easy," she says. "Go again."

"Oh what? No. It's your turn."

She huffs. "I spy with my little eye, something beginning with W."

"Water?"

"No."

"Waves?"

"No."

"Ummm ... windscreen?"

"Nuh uh." She shakes her head.

"Wind?"

"You can't see wind!"

"True. Okay, I give up. Tell me."

"Witch."

"What? Where's a witch?"

"At Mummy's house."

I exaggerate a shocked look. "Your mum has a witch?"

"My mum *is* a witch."

"Reilly!"

"I hate her."

What do I say to that? Are ten-year-olds capable of understanding the severity of such language? How deep a word like that can cut? I know she's emotional right now but ... "What don't you like about her?"

"She's boring. I'm not allowed to do anything or talk to my friends or text them. She only eats yucky vegan food. And I hate her boyfriend. He pretends he's all cool, but he's just stupid, prancing around without a shirt on. And she lets him tell me off, and he's not even my dad."

Okaaay. Tween stuff. "That doesn't sound like much fun."

"And then, when he's told me off, he wants to hug me, and he's all like 'we're still friends aren't we?'"

Ugh. Do I put the shirtless thing and the hugging together? How do I phrase this? "Reilly, does he ... does he make you uncomfortable?"

"What?"

"Does he make you uncomfortable? Does he ..." I glance over, to see if she understands.

She's wide-eyed and mouth open, grimacing. "Ewww, no. Not like that!"

How does she even know what I mean? Before I can ask, she says, "They taught us about that stuff in school. Nooo, ewww." She laughs now. "I reckon he's just trying to stay on Mum's good side, and he figures if I'm happy, she's happy. But she doesn't care. I don't know why she even wants me there."

"She's your mother, Reilly. Of course, she wants you there."

"Yeah, that's why she tells me to go outside or go to my room and play. Like I'm a kid."

I fight to hide a smile. Maybe Cynthia is an anti-tech mother, wanting her child to read, or get sun and fresh air instead of being glued to a screen. Not a bad thing.

Reilly stares out to sea.

"Doesn't sound like much fun," I offer. She ignores me. "Hey, did you bring that book I gave you?" She doesn't answer. I glance at her again. "Reilly?"

She shakes her head. "I finished it."

"Wow. Stay up all night, did you?"

She shrugs. "It was okay."

I smile inwardly. I may just be about to turn her day around, but I wait a few minutes to enjoy the anticipation before finally saying, "Did you know there's a sequel?"

"Yes. It says it in the back of the book."

I feel her gaze on me. Is she going to ask? Nope. She's either used to not having expectations, or she's too shy to ask. I fight to control a grin. "It's in the glove box."

Her tone lifts in excitement. "Really?"

I nod as sagely as a grinning quokka, and she reaches forward. While she's busy tearing off the brown paper wrapping from *The Ask and The Answer*, my phone pings from the dashboard cradle. A quick glance, and fear stabs as I take in the one-word text: *Bitch*.

"That's not nice," Reilly says. "Who's Andreas?"

I swallow hard, wishing I hadn't programmed his name into the phone. Just seeing it makes me shiver. I keep my eyes on the road, dying to pick the phone up and hide it. How do I explain this without sounding panicked? "He's ... a friend. It's just a joke between us. Nothing bad. We do it all the time." *Please god, don't let him send anything else.*

Reilly sinks back and opens her book. "Grownups are weird."

I can't answer her. I'm sure the anger, the confusion, the terror coursing through me is going to snap the steering wheel.

⸻ ◆ ⸻

The nearer the house I drive, the more my shoulders ache. I blow out a sigh, trying to relieve tension. Reilly looks up from her book – how she's been reading on the winding roads without throwing up, like on the yacht, I don't know.

"Mum won't actually bite you, at least, not physically."

God, her mother is the least of my concerns right now, but I manage a thankful look. "That's a relief. I was wondering if I should have worn a flak jacket."

"Ha! You're funny." Reilly points to an ordinary suburban house with cement steps leading up a lawned incline. "This one."

That's it? I expected something more extravagant, given Daniel's wealth. Maybe he had her sign a prenup. Now that Reilly's drawn me back into the moment, I wonder if I should walk her to the front door, meet Cynthia up close. She'll be wanting to know who this stranger looking after her daughter is. I would. Has Daniel mentioned me?

"You can park in the driveway."

I don't. I pull up to the curb. The driveway is too steep-looking, and I'm still getting used to the car — reversing has never been my strong suit, and I don't want to embarrass myself in front of this mythical Medusa by grinding the gears, accidentally rolling back or knocking over her letterbox. Not when I'm already jittery.

What sort of reception am I going to get? Not a good one, I expect. But right now, I've got bigger things to worry about. Like how Andreas has got hold of my mobile number.

"You can stay here," Reilly says, unbuckling herself.

"Oh, I think I should at least say hello."

She fixes me with a hard stare. "You don't want to meet Mum."

"Okay. But she might want to meet me, since I'm your new nanny." Geez, I need another word for that. It sounds archaic, as if I should be wearing crinoline and pushing Reilly around in a baby carriage with wide-spoke wheels.

"No, she won't. She doesn't like seeing anyone prettier than her."

I flush with a stupid surge of surprise and pleasure. "But your mother looks beautiful in her photo."

"Mummy is plastic."

"What do you mean?"

"It's what Margie calls her. Plastic fantastic. She says Mummy's surgeon has had his hands on her body more than Daddy ever did."

My jaw drops. "She did not say that."

"She did. She just didn't know I was listening."

"Reilly!"

We both giggle as she pulls her suitcase from the rear seat. I'm bad, colluding with her like this. I get out of the car but stay where I am, confused as to whether I should obey a ten-year-old or my instincts.

I watch the front door as Reilly climbs the steps. No one opens it to welcome her.

Driving back down the coast road with the ocean stretched out beyond the rocky beaches, I should be enjoying the warmth on my face, the sea breeze trailing through my hair, but I've put the convertible top up, closed the windows. I should have a smile of satisfaction – I've got the whole weekend to myself. I should be relaxed, but ... Andreas. I thought I'd made the right decision coming up here. Nobody knows me. Nobody knows where I've gone. And I've landed on my feet. Reilly is a sweet girl. Daniel is ... Daniel! I'd forgotten about him. I wonder if he's okay. Perhaps sleeping off his "misfire". He'll be out of sorts for a few days now, going by what Margie has said. Maybe he'll cancel his Monday flight—

Bang!

I scream. The steering wheel judders. The car swerves to the wrong side of the road. I yank the wheel back, but the rear end traverses toward the rocky edge.

I hang on for my life, teeth clenched as the car slides. There's another vehicle coming around a bend, head-on to me. Its tyres screech. My car keeps sliding. Finally, there's a crunch as the Audi's rear end takes out part of a barrier, then halts. Is that it? Has the world stopped going crazy?

Heart hammering, brain trying to remind me to breathe, I steal a look over the doorsill. I've never been good at calculating distances, but that's a heck of a drop – not the kind that makes cars explode into flames in movies, but enough to crush my skull on boulders if the car had rolled. The rear right-hand wheel is hanging mid-air over the drop, where the barrier has given way. I blurt a laugh, short and hysterical. Holy crap, that was close.

A knock on the passenger window jars me. A man in a peaked cap is bent over, staring in at me. I have a flash of horror – maybe he's the gunman who did this! No, fool, he's the driver of the car I'm blocking – his passenger, a woman in a floral dress, is standing with her car door open, looking worriedly at us. Their hazard lights are flashing, and there's another car slowing up behind them. There's no safety lane here, hardly a shoulder, just the barrier. Soon we'll have a traffic jam.

He signals for me to lower the window. I fumble for the button. Once the glass is down a third, he asks, "Spot of bother?"

I laugh shakily. "Could say that." I swallow, mouth and throat dry. "Do you think it's safe to drive forward? I'm a bit worried about that rear wheel."

"Let me take a look." As he rounds the back of the vehicle, I lower my own window.

He slaps the boot a couple of times and yells, "You're okay. Just take it easy. It's an all-wheel drive. Should be fine. Go ahead." In the rear mirror, I watch him hunch, then strain upward, supporting the rear. I gently release the handbrake – surprised I'd actually had the brain space to apply it once the car had stopped – and ease on the accelerator. The car rolls forward, but there's a ka-thump from the rear.

"Hold up!" the guy yells. "You got a flat."

That explains the bang. Geez, the places my mind went. Andreas. A gun. I've become paranoid.

"Can't change it here," he says. "Too dangerous and the traffic's banking up. There's a lookout stop, a few hundred metres further up. You want some help with it?"

"That'd be great. Thanks. It's not my car – the boss's."

"Sure. You go ahead." He looks back to his car, where there's now another five cars banked up. "I'll have to find somewhere down the road to turn around. You go ahead, though. Slowly, slowly does it. You don't want to damage the rim."

"Thanks."

We wait for a car to pass on the other side of the road, then he waves me forward. "Turn your hazards on," he yells after me, and I snatch looks at the dashboard while keeping an eye out ahead. "Gotcha." I flip the button. The periodic ka-thumping of the flaccid tyre makes me cringe.

24

Andreas

Katie called me every day. Begging me to leave.

I couldn't. I had no fight left in me.

"If you stay, he's going to end up killing you."

"He'll kill me if I leave."

"Geegee, he won't find you. We'll go to a women's refuge. They're safe. No one will know. We'll get an intervention order."

Her persistence wore me down.

25

"Are you sure you're okay?" Margie fusses, running her hands over my head, shoulders, arms, then gives me a firm hug.

"I'm fine. A bit shaken is all. I'm just glad Reilly wasn't with me. I expect Daniel will be angry. Is there somewhere specific he takes the car for repairs? I'll pay for it of course ... once I save some cash. God, first time out on my own and I screw up."

"Don't you worry about the car. That's what insurance is for. Cars are replaceable. You're not. And nothing will be open until Tuesday – New Year's. Come on." She leads me to the kitchen and sits me on a stool. "I'll get you a cold drink. Or would you prefer some camomile tea? Calm the nerves?"

"Something stiffer would be better." It's slipped out before I can stop it.

Margie chuckles and nods to a clock on the wall, its seahorse hands on ten past eleven. "Maybe we'll wait till after lunch, hey?"

Did I sound desperate? I laugh. "Joking. Iced tea would be perfect."

"Ugh. Don't know how you drink that stuff."

123

I gulp the drink she offers, then look down at my clothes, grubby from helping with the tyre, sweaty from adrenaline and humidity. "Think I'll have a shower."

Back in my room, I message Katie. I know she can't drop everything and answer when I call – she'll be busy saving other people's lives besides mine. But I can't help staring at the screen, waiting. Nothing. It must be nearly lunchtime in Melbourne though. She'll take a break and call me soon.

I stand under the warm water, close my eyes, and suddenly I'm in the sliding car again, heading toward the rocky ledge. I bolt my eyes open, shake my head. *Don't do that.* Once was plenty enough. Once was too often. But now the what-ifs come: What if the barrier hadn't held? What if the other car had hit me? What would make a tyre blow out like that? A fault or weakness? Maybe the heat affects tyres more up here, so they wear out quicker?

I drop the soap, my hand shaking as I bend to retrieve it. Probably delayed shock. "You're okay," I tell myself. Nothing awful happened except ... Andreas's message.

How the hell did he get my new number? Did he use his "mates" to triangulate the location? Is that even a real thing? I've been so careful elsewhere: the bus, my room booking, everything I'd bought in town, all cash. Only Katie and this household has my number.

Out of the shower, I check my messages again. Nope. No Katie.

I sit on the bed, stare at the phone. Evelyn? Could she have accidentally triggered something? On her computer? Hard to believe – she'd said she'd protect me, but in this digital world, are we ever safe? Maybe it was Daniel's virtual assistant? But she couldn't have filed a Police Check or Working with Children Check without my sign-off. However it happened, Andreas knows where I am. I should leave. But he'll just follow. How do I get him off my back? What would do that? Him giving me a last beating? A *final* beating?

I nearly jump out of my skin as the phone vibrates and pings in my hand. Andreas again, as if he knows I'm sitting here, freaking out.

I want it back.

Wants what back? Me? He wants *me* back? Well, hell can freeze over, buddy. There's no way you're ever going to see me again, and ... *ohhh, the ring* ... his great grandmother's engagement diamond, a family heirloom. Of course he wants it back. Will that satisfy him? He's welcome to it. Let him pawn it and gamble that away too. I just need to figure out how to get it back anonymously, securely.

Back in the kitchen, Margie is preparing lunch. "You like crab salad?"

"Love it."

"Good. I'll leave it in the fridge. I'm heading out shortly. I have weekends off when Reilly's at Cynthia's. Will you be okay?"

"Of course."

"If Daniel hasn't appeared in a couple of hours, can you take his into his room with some tea? He needs to stay hydrated."

"Oh god! I haven't even thought to ask how he is."

"He's fine. Just resting."

I ask how often he has these seizures.

"Not so often. Maybe every three to four months. We call them "episodes". Have done ever since Reilly was a toddler; we thought "seizure" sounded too scary when she was little. Now she's older ... well, it's stuck."

"But he's okay?"

"Sure, sure. He'll probably be right by Monday ... *if* he rests. But he rarely stops."

"So ... is it epilepsy? I'm still unclear."

"No. That would have been easier in some respects – he could be taking anti-seizure meds." She explains that it's some sort of electrical fault, that he's had it since he was a kid, and in all these years, doctors haven't been able to pin it down to any particular diagnosis. "They hoped he might grow out of it."

"And he hasn't. How frustrating ... and frightening, I expect."

"We deal with it. He's not hurt himself or anyone, it's just the fatigue that comes with it is debilitating. I wish his company directors could understand that."

"Will you tell him about the car, or should I?"

"Ahead of you. I told him while you were in the shower. You don't need that stress in your first week."

"Was he—"

"Totally fine. More concerned about you."

"Thank you so much. Is there a tyre shop in town? I can at least see to that on Tuesday."

Margie gives me the name of the mechanic they use. I mention I'll also call in to see Evelyn to say thank you for the interview, the job.

"You can try. She only works part-time – when she's feeling up to it – and usually has water therapy on Tuesdays, but you never know, you might catch her. Okay, well, I'll be off in a minute. My number is on the bench if you need anything."

"Sure. Will Daniel need anything else?"

"No, love. He just needs to sleep it off. He'll come out when he's ready."

"Okay, thanks. Would—" My mobile rings in my back pocket. Thank god. "Excuse me. It's my sister." I hurry out to the pool patio.

"Geegee, what's happening. Are you okay?"

Her voice melts me. I wish she were here. "Andreas found me."

"What? How?"

"I don't know. He texted me."

"What did it say?"

"Bitch."

There's a pause while she processes this, but I'm impatient, finally letting my brain do what it's been wanting to do since I got the text: panic. "What do I do now? I've barely been here a minute, and now I have to run again? What if I stay and he turns up?"

Katie's laugh stops my litany. What the hell? Has she gone mad?

"Kit! It's not funny."

"I'm not laughing at you. I'm laughing at him. The phone's in my name."

"So?"

"Think about it."

"Ohhh." Tetris pieces of logic fall into place, and I bend over, dizzy with relief. "You've blocked him on your phone, so he's probably gone searching and found this other number in the phone I left behind. He thinks he's got you again. What a dick. Although, I think I'm the dick for panicking and not figuring it out."

"You are so *not* a dick. But make sure you block him. Don't respond, whatever you do, in case he tracks the text location. I can't explain being both here and there. We both know he has ..."

"Mates in high places," we say together, imitating Andreas's obnoxious tone, because we've heard it a million times.

"How's the new job?" she asks. "They treating you well?"

"It's good. Different." I think about telling her I crashed the Audi, but why make her worry for me more? "This is the life. We went sailing yesterday."

"Nice."

<hr>

Daniel is a no show at lunch time, so I eat alone. With only my dishes to wash, I do them by hand, wipe the benches, then retrieve his lunch from the fridge. His door's closed, so I balance the tray in one hand and softly knock. His reply is distant, muffled. I can't understand what he's saying, so I open the door a fraction. The room is dim, curtains closed over the French doors, aircon humming on low. There's a small table just inside the door, so I slip the dinner tray onto it.

"Daniel, I brought you something to eat. I'll just leave it here by the door. Okay?"

"Thank you." He sighs, bedcovers rustling.

I try to keep my gaze averted, not wanting to intrude. But what if he's really unwell? I glance over. He's lying face down on top of tangled sheets, his t-shirt twisted.

"Are you okay? Do you need anything else?"

He mumbles something, but all I can make out is "sleep".

I spend the rest of the afternoon reading, web-surfing and watching YouTube videos of things to do in this part of the country. It's mostly touristy stuff. Expensive if you don't have a decent regular income. Guess the locals have their own networks and fun things to do. Just after six, my phone beeps. Andreas. I turn the sound off, but the screen keeps lighting up in intervals over the next half-hour.

Tell her to come home.

We can work it out.

I love her.

Answer me.

Bitch.

Wait till I get you both.

I turn it over, lay it face down, wondering if this is going to be an evening ritual – if he's going to use his drive time to and from work to harass us as entertainment while he's sitting in traffic. He doesn't know it's actually bringing me a level of comfort: he's there, not here doing it in person.

<hr>

By evening, Daniel still hasn't appeared, so I repeat the process of taking him something to eat. Again, the sleepy reply. At least he's eaten what was on his lunch tray.

I retreat to my bedroom with a serve of pie to watch Foxtel. I was surprised when Margie gave me the spare remote, along with the household wi-fi – not the fact she was giving them to me, but that they have pay television at all. Daniel doesn't seem the type, and I assumed Reilly is on a tight leash with her lack of fun books to read. "I like to sneak in a show or two when I'm doing the ironing," Margie said with a wink.

Her apple pie is just as melt-in-your-mouth as last night. I'm on the verge of going back to the kitchen for seconds when a noise outside my window catches my attention. I freeze, grab the remote and pause the movie. Again, the noise comes – a scraping sound, as if someone's dragging the pool furniture. I slip the dinner tray off my lap, reach for my beside lamp and flick it off, throwing the room into darkness. I listen again, poised on the edge of my bed. A voice, male, low, murmurs panic into my heart.

Painfully slow, I ease off the bed and pad over to the plantation-shuttered windows. I daren't look out, but I have to. I slide a finger into the louvre closest to my eye level and push it down a fraction. The whole shutter moves, and I jerk to the side, flatten my back against the wall, holding my breath, straining to hear. Silence. I release my breath, ease forward, peer through the shutter. A glimpse of shadow moving. Could it be? No. He couldn't possibly know where I am. Should I get Daniel? What would he be able to do in his state, anyway? The scraping noise comes again, then a yell, a splash.

"Ah crap, I fell in."

Giggles.

"Shhh, you idiot."

I reach for the patio light switch, flick it on, fling the French doors open. Outside, a teenage boy has a girl by the arm, midway through pulling her from the pool. She has her knee up on the side, hair bedraggled about her face and shoulders, her t-shirt and shorts soggy and clinging.

They both freeze.

"Hey! What are you doing?" I call, all bravado.

"Run!" the boy yells, yanking the girl to her feet and taking off toward the steep path to the beach.

Two pool chairs sit in the bottom of the pool, as if waiting for a mermaid's picnic.

26

Andreas

Some of the women were screaming. I was too, on the inside. The pain from digging my nails into my scalp wasn't bringing any relief or distraction. I startled as another impact shuddered the door against my arm, my thigh. Still, I pressed against it, as if me being hunched there on the floor could hold back the fury behind it.

Adhira crouched beside me, whispered as she tried to put an arm around my shoulders. "You're okay, Georgia. It's going to be okay." Social worker speak for "things are fucked up right now, but hang in there".

It wasn't going to be okay.

THUMP.

The shudder vibrated through me. If I stayed there, absorbed it, he couldn't hurt the other women.

THUMP. "Give me my wife, you bitches!"

Adhira tried again. "Come on, Georgia. Let's move away from the door."

"I can't."

THUMP. THUMP. "I'll break this fucking door down. Then I'll break all your friends too. How's that?"

27

Sunday morning, Daniel appears in the kitchen. Dressed in a fresh t-shirt and shorts, hair wet from a shower, he looks as surprised to see me as I am him. Perhaps he was expecting Margie.

"Morning," I say. "Coffee? Just brewed."

He stands there looking a bit dazed, scratches his head, then takes a deep breath and blows it out, as if he needed the inhale to force himself into action. "No thanks." He heads over to the pantry and retrieves a box of cereal.

"Feeling better?" I ask.

"Hmmm." He's methodical in his movements, first focusing on the milk cascading into his cereal bowl, then the iced tea into his glass. He picks up both and makes to head off.

"Oh." He turns back. "I'll be in my office today."

He waits for a moment, staring at me. Am I supposed to give him permission?

"Okay." I give him an awkward salute, a stupid smile.

"Right." He turns and leaves.

Lunchtime, I knock on his office door, offering to make him something, but he declines. "I'll get something myself a bit later."

Two-ish, as I'm sitting out on the patio, I glimpse him walk through the lounge, then return a few minutes later with a sandwich on a plate. He disappears down the hallway. This job is far easier than I anticipated.

Mid-afternoon, I take him some iced tea and biscuits. He thanks me, but blocks any attempt at conversation.

Busy, busy man.

Evening, I approach again. "Would you like some dinner? I've made some chicken salad with crusty rolls."

"Sure. I'll be out in a minute."

We eat at the family dining table – too hot outside. He looks drained and has a headache but seems in better spirits. I ask if he still plans to travel tomorrow.

"Yes."

I don't push.

"So ... Margie told you about the car accident?"

"Yes, she did." His head is down, voice flat, so I can't tell if he's annoyed.

"I found a screw in the tyre wall. I'm taking it to get fixed on Tuesday. I hope that's okay?"

"Of course."

"Margie told me the name of the repairer you prefer."

He nods. "Thank you. Not much that woman doesn't know." Still flat.

"I get that impression. I'm so sorry, by the way. I feel bad being my first—"

He looks up now, smiles sympathetically. "Not your fault. Could have happened to anyone. It must have shaken you up. I'm just glad you and Reilly are okay. That's all that matters. Are you still okay to drive? I can get a taxi."

"No ... no, I'm fine. Just a bit wary, which isn't a bad thing on those winding roads."

"Good."

"Good."

We eat in silence for a while.

"Oh, there were some kids out the back last night," I say. "A couple of teens mucking about around the pool. Do you know them? Are they neighbours?"

His forehead wrinkles. "Damn it. They come up from the beach. I've been thinking about putting up a fence, some security cameras, but"—he shrugs—"they never seem to do any harm. More an annoyance than anything. How did you go dropping Reilly off? Did you encounter the Kraken?"

I nearly spit out my mouthful and have to grab a napkin to clean a dribble off my chin. "Um, no. She didn't come to the door, so I didn't ..."

He huffs, takes a gulp of iced tea. "As I thought. Hungover from New Year's."

"How's Reilly's behaviour after she's been at her mother's for the weekend? I hope she won't be as upset as when she was leaving."

"A bit testy, but she settles down pretty quickly once she's back at school."

"Good to know."

The silence falls again, and I blank on conversation.

"So ..."

I jerk my head up as the brusqueness in his tone.

"I'll give you a call when I get back if you don't mind picking me up."

The *if* doesn't sound optional. "Sure. Of course." I bite my lip, wondering if I should ask why he's actually going away, and where he's going. Too nosey? Screw it; I ask anyway.

He looks surprised. "Thailand."

"Nice. I've been to Bangkok once. We landed in the middle of a spectacular storm, lots of lightning. By morning, the streets were flooded, and shopkeepers were sweeping water from their stores. What are you going for?" I hope he doesn't launch into some high-finance money-moving corporate-deal talk.

"I've got an injured project manager."

"Oh, sorry. Is it bad?"

"To be honest, I don't know." He goes on to explain that Somchai is a workaholic, refuses to take time off.

I consider the irony.

"It's hard to get a clear picture. I've only been able to speak to his second-in-charge. He says Somchai is fine, but I feel they're being cagey. I'd rather see what's going on for myself, make sure OH&S is in place and that Somchai and his family are being looked after."

"That's very generous of you."

"It's not all altruistic. Sometimes the communication between local government and the project managers is ... tenuous. If I lose someone who's able to communicate ... negotiate effectively, the project might draw to a halt. And that affects everyone."

He takes a breath, as if he's not used to talking so much and the effort has taken it out of him. Still worn out, I suspect. Or maybe he's not used to having someone to download to.

I encourage him to continue. "And what exactly is 'the project'?"

He glances at me. "I didn't tell you?"

I shake my head.

"A new resort. Because Thailand doesn't have enough, right? But this is a new concept. Totally eco-friendly using only renewable resources. Self-sustaining with water and rubbish recycling. I've got four others completed. One in Vanuatu, a couple in Sri Lanka and another in Vietnam. There's plenty of investors interested in other countries too. My father started the first project, and it's grown from there."

"I'm sure he would've been proud of you."

His cheek twitches. "What about your father? Tell me more about him. Was he hard to please?"

Our meal is finished now, so there's not much to distract us from having to look at each other as we talk. Awkward. I pick up my paper napkin and fold it, crease upon crease until it's too thick and small to fold any further. "Not really. He was a hard-working man. He didn't expect much of either of us really, just wanted us to be happy."

"And your sister?"

The napkin springs open as I set it on my plate. "Katie's a paramedic. Loves her job. Fast and furious. I guess she likes the adrenaline. I don't think she'll ever marry, have kids."

"What about you? What do you want? I'm guessing you want children, since you chose to work with them. Or did that put you off?" He smirks.

I've been asked this so often, I have a stock-standard answer. *Maybe.* But now I take the time to think about it. Do I? Never with Andreas. That was for sure. Though he desperately wanted some to carry on his flawed genes – imagine more boys with his bullish attitude, or more girls to be cowed. "Why do people automatically assume every woman wants kids?"

Daniel runs his tongue over his top teeth as he considers. "I guess ... no, you're right. Some women shouldn't be mothers."

For some reason, this rankles me. "Really? And who gets to choose that? Who qualifies as a potentially worthy mother?"

He holds his hands up. "I'm just speaking from my own perspective, my own relationship. Didn't mean to generalise. Anyway, why are you so angry?"

"I'm not angry!"

"Yes, you are. Look at your hands."

They're balled into fists on the table. I unfurl them, lay them flat, force a smile. "What time do you need to leave tomorrow?"

Daniel sits reading documents in his lap, their edges flapping in the breeze. How does that not make him nauseous – reading in a moving car? Like father, like daughter.

The further south we head on the coastal road, the broodier the pre-dawn clouds become, air heavier, thicker than on the drive with Reilly. There's no top on the Moke, and now I wonder aloud if we're about to get soaked.

Daniel looks up, squints at the sky. I half expect him to suck a finger and hold it up to the breeze. "It'll blow over."

My nose itches with drying sweat as wind rushes over the windscreen. Thank god for sunglasses and ponytails. I yawn, covering my mouth, then grip the steering wheel again with both hands, attention glued to the road, the speed, the sound of the tyres. At least Monday peak hour here consists of only the occasional passing car. Not like the crazy crush back home. *Home*. Must stop thinking that. I don't have a home now.

At the airport, Daniel retrieves his suitcase from the rear seat while I fiddle with the side mirror, adjusting the angle, wiping away moisture with my fingertips, which just smears the glass.

He stands on the cement walkway, pats his pocket. "Should be back Monday morning. Early. I'll let you know what time."

"Sure."

He makes to move off but hesitates. "Sorry."

"For what?"

He shrugs. "For whatever I said yesterday that upset you."

It's the second time he's apologised, and I'm not used to sober, genuine apologies from a man – only post-drunken grovelling and pawing. My throat tightens, eyes prickle. I force a smile, wave him off and move out.

⸻◈⸻

It's just before seven by the time I pull up outside Cynthia's house. I consider tooting the horn in the hope Reilly will come out; I'm not sure I'm ready to meet Cynthia now. Call me a chicken. Within seconds, Reilly is pounding down the pathway, pink suitcase bouncing along behind her. She throws the case in the back and jumps into the front seat.

"Go! Go!" she yells.

"Seatbelt."

"Oh, bloody hell."

"Language!"

Reilly laughs, clicks on her belt, and I press the accelerator too hard, not used to the feel of the Moke. The tyres squeal. I bet her mother heard that. I bet she's already got a list of things to complain to Daniel about. I wonder if Reilly told her about the ice cream episode.

"Where's the Audi?" she asks.

"Long story."

"Huh."

"How was your weekend?"

"B-o-r-ing."

"I just dropped your dad at the airport. He said to tell you he'll miss you."

"Big deal."

Not the response I was expecting. The way Reilly carried on Saturday morning, I thought she'd be pining for him.

"What would you like to do when you get back from school camp? Maybe I can plan something for us."

"Hot air ballooning."

"Umm. Didn't your dad nix that?"

Reilly flops back in her seat, and out comes the jutted chin, bottom lip and folded arms. I shake my head. At least she has personality. She suddenly perks up. "What about jungle surfing up at Cape Tribulation?"

"What's that?"

"You know, zip lining through the rainforest."

What? Where the heck did the pristine little princess disappear to? "It sounds dangerous."

"Oh geez! Life is dangerous."

I nod sagely. "That it is, but I've had way too much excitement in my life this week."

"Really? What happened?"

I glance at her, all big-eyed and keen for some drama. I guess telling her about my accident won't hurt. I can't see it scaring her. This kid is going to give her father hell when she reaches her teens. I foresee an adrenaline junkie.

Reilly's super impressed with my story. "I can't wait till I can drive."

"You young things have no sense of mortality."

She laughs, though I doubt she's grasped my meaning. It's true though. Kids don't seem to understand that death is permanent. They just see unending years ahead of them. Boring years, according to Reilly. Everything is *now*. Risk everything *now*. And this jolts me, because isn't that what I've done? Risked my future, left everything behind, just to have a life at all?

Where will I be in ten years? Still a nanny? Hiding from the world? I haven't thought it through. Everything's been on fast-forward. But if I were still here then, Reilly would be grown up, and I'd be forced to make some long-term plans that didn't include a ready-made family. That's if Andreas leaves me alone.

And on cue, my phone beeps. I snatch it off the holder and stick it between my thighs. "Are you looking forward to school camp?"

"Yes! Sammi is back. Yay!"

Soon we're pulling up outside her school where a large bus is loading up kids and their suitcases and backpacks. I make to walk Reilly up to the bus, but she grabs her suitcase handle from me.

"I can do it. I don't need a babysitter. See ya."

She takes off up the path, while I stand, uncertain whether to follow. Instead, I wait by the car so I can honestly say I saw her board the bus safely. She's on. Just in time, as a woman with a scowl and hi-vis vest comes stomping toward me – presumably the parking attendant Margie calls the parking proctologist. I'm outta there.

Once I'm around the corner, I pull over and reach for my mobile.

This morning's messages:
Tell her I'm coming for her.
Nowhere she can hide.
She better run, bitch.

28

Andreas

Adhira was more insistent now as she kneeled in front of me, grasped my wrists. "Georgia. Listen to me. He can't get through. I've called the police. Let's move."

I let her guide me to my feet, a good girl, doing as I was told. We walked the passageway, women with terrified faces peering from doorways along the hall, some with children clinging to their legs. "Close the blinds or curtains if you can," she told them. "Then stay away from the windows."

The kitchen was at the rear of the house. Adhira sat me at the long table stained with coffee cup rings and sticky jam spilled at breakfast, not quite an hour ago.

"Georgia," she said. "Do you know how he found you?"

"I bet she called him." Eadie was standing at the open backdoor of the enclosed verandah, just outside the kitchen, a smoke in her hand. The woman hadn't brushed her hair in her lifetime. Why did she hate me so much? She'd only known me less than two weeks.

Adhira blanched. "Eadie! I asked you to lock that door."

"I'm having a ciggy."

"*Close the damned door and lock it. What if he gets around the back?*"

"*Let him try,*" *she said, all bravado. But she did it anyway. I recognised that flicker in her eyes. She pretended indifference, but fear was hard to hide.*

29

Convenient. The mechanic is only two streets behind the main strip. A small operation with one of those lift-up doors with glass panels. The service bay is surprisingly clean – no dark greasy stains on the concrete floor, no haphazard piles of used parts left on benches. It doesn't even have that heavy smell of years of ground-in oily dirt.

I can't say the same for the stains on the overalled legs sticking out from under a silver Honda Civic. Is that ... a child? The figure seems too small to be an adult.

"Hello?"

"Yeah?" the voice under the car says. It *is* a child.

"Margie called earlier. Regarding the tyre repair?"

The body rolls out on a trolley. Not a child. A woman. A small woman, sinewy, fit. She sits up without supporting herself, then gets to her feet, the top of her overalls hanging in a fold from her waist, white tank top smudged with grease.

"Moretti's Audi, yeah?"

I nod, mesmerised by the tattoo encircling her neck and spilling onto her chest like a chandelier of black spidery jewellery. Stunning.

"You Reilly's new nanny?" she says, pulling a cloth from her pocket and rubbing it over the back of her neck, then her forehead. Her black fringe is impossibly straight and shiny, like the rest of her hair, all pulled back in a glossy ponytail. How does she do this magical feat in such humid weather? Maybe she's a witch.

She offers her sweaty hand. "I'm Nayla, Samara's mum."

I take her hand, puzzled, trying to place her. "I'm sorry …"

"Samara Parker? Reilly's best friend? Maybe she hasn't mentioned her yet?"

"Samara … oh, *Sammi*. Of course. I get you. Sure. Sammi Siva." I smile, awkward for insisting on her child's diminutive.

"Well, yeah. I prefer her to use my last name, since she lives with me, but she has a thing about sticking with her dad's at the moment." Nayla shrugs her hands onto her hips. "Who am I to stifle her choices? We gotta let them live and learn, hey?" Something catches her eye – several packages piled up just outside the bay. "Tch." She heads over and bends to tuck a package under each arm.

"You have a cat?" I ask. Dumb question; she's carrying kitty litter.

"Nope," she says, dumping the packets and going back to retrieve the remaining two. "Easiest way to clean up oil spills. Your car out front?"

"Yes."

She wipes her hands on her overalls, then strides out of the bay and onto the street, spots the Audi and heads over to it. I follow. She whistles as she inspects the dents and scratches. "Man, you did this first week on the job?"

I didn't think it was possible for my face to get any hotter in this heat. "How do you know it's my first week?"

She gives me side-eye. "You don't get to scratch your nose around here, let alone bingle Moretti's Audi, without a commentary on it."

Great.

"Don't worry. It's not that bad. But my panel guy's booked up till next week. And it's gonna take me a couple of hours to get to your rubber today; I gotta sort out that baby first." She thumbs back toward the bay. "Steering rod's stuffed."

"That doesn't sound good."

"Ah newbies up here not taking care with potholes after rains. Not your problem though. What are you up to now? Hanging around town for a bit?"

"Um, yes, I suppose so."

"Head over to Carey's Café around twelve. I'll drop the car over to you."

"Oh, thanks. You're sure it's no trouble?"

"Nah. Always wanted to get behind the wheel of this mother. And I gotta call in there anyway."

⸺◆⸺

Margie's right. Evelyn's office is closed, so I wander through the shops, pick up a brochure for a Pilates studio – a woman can dream her job might last – then buy a few casual summer essentials: shorts, t-shirts, a pair of runners on sale at half price. When I'm done, I head over to the café and treat myself to air conditioning and an iced coffee, frugality be damned.

The coffee arrives topped with a mountainous pile of whipped cream. I suspect there's a good lump of ice cream floating beneath the surface too. I'm halfway through the drink, licking cream off the long spoon, when Nayla walks in.

"Carey," she calls to the guy behind the counter, waving.

"Usual is almost ready," he says.

"You're a legend."

She comes over to my table, dangling my keys in her hand. "Good news. Tyre's fixed. And more good news: my body guy's had a cancellation. He can start on your car this afternoon. Can you do without it for a couple of days? Should have it done by Friday morning."

"Yes. That would be terrific. Thanks."

She glances at my drink. "That looks nice and cool."

The urge to invite her to join me is instinctual, but I resist. Can't get cosy with the locals. Not yet. "It's delish. Thanks for the tyre. How much do we owe?"

"Don't worry about. I'll add it to the account for the body work."

"Perfect. Thanks."

"Nayla," Carey calls. "Ready to go. Need some more cakes too."

"Goodo. I'm baking a batch tonight."

I blink. "You're a baker too?"

Nayla laughs. "Nah. Just a hobby." She points to the glass display case at the counter, where three cupcakes sit, each exquisitely decorated with lavender icing swirls, sparkles and tiny purple flowers. "Sammi wanted purple unicorn cupcakes for her last birthday. Next thing I know"—she holds up her hands and shrugs—"everybody wants them."

She turns to grab the sandwich packet and bottle of juice Carey is holding, then waves me off as she leaves. "See you Friday. I'll text you when it's ready."

30

Andreas

*Adhira moved to pull the hallway swing door shut too –
an attempt to muffle the yelling. But it carried. And each
bang brought more squeals and whimpers from the women.
I couldn't stand it. This wasn't their doing. It was mine. I
shouldn't have run.*

*Adhira looked me in the eye. She knew us women, knew
what fear made us do.*

"Don't go back, Georgia. It won't stop."

*I knew that. But I also knew he'd only get worse now
if I didn't. He was a hyena, baying for prey, endlessly
persistent. He had to have it.*

*"This isn't your fault," she said. "You didn't bring him
here."*

*"I reckon she did. You can tell the type. Always running
back. Then expecting you guys to protect them."*

"Eadie! Shut up. You're not helping."

*Eadie was right though. I'd do anything to make him
stop.*

*"Georgia, listen to me. I know you're scared. But this is
momentary. We can get through it together. The police will be*

here any minute. If you go back, it'll be a lifetime ... if you last that long."

I nodded, gave her what she wanted. Affirmation. And she was right. Of course she was. But what if he did get in? I wouldn't be the only one he hurt. And he might return ... after. Payback was his favourite flavour.

31

Friday afternoon, Reilly is waiting by the school gates, chatting to a girl who could be her opposite twin – same height, same petite build but a shaggy, scuffed energy – one t-shirt sleeve up, one down, tasselled threads hanging from the hem of her overalls. I park the Audi under the sharp eye of the parking proctologist – working on summer holidays won't be doing her mood any good.

Reilly comes running over, dragging her friend, who's carrying a half-eaten cupcake. "Georgia! This is Sammi Siva, my bestie. She's been away visiting her dad in Ko-ala Lumpur."

Sammi wipes a hand down the bib of her overalls, then rests the other – the one carrying the cupcake – on the doorsill. Ugh. I've just come from the repair shop, and I'd hoped to have the Audi all shiny and perfect to show Daniel when I pick him up on Monday. Sammi reaches over to shake my hand. "Hiya. How's it going?" Her freckled nose seems permanently wrinkled, as if she's about to sneeze. She has her mother's thick dark hair, just not as tamed, but presumably her father's olive skin. A gorgeous child with wide brown eyes and dimples to die for.

I shake her hand. "Reilly's told me a lot about you."

"Has she?" She looks at Reilly with narrowed eyes and a cheeky smirk.

"Well, she says you're fearless at karate and an endless supplier of cupcakes."

Sammi grins. "Yup. That's me. Would you like some?"

I look at the half-demolished cake on offer and shake my head. "Thanks. You enjoy it."

"Georgia, can Sammi come over for a swim?"

Is this my domain? "Aren't you going to be spending the weekend at her house?"

"Yes, but that's *tomorrow*."

There's so much urgency in her voice, I weaken. "Alright, I suppose so. If her mum says it's okay."

"Mum's already said it's okay," Sammi says, turning to wave to Nayla who's sitting in a coupe parked on the other side of the street, too far for me to yell out. And if I stay here much longer the proctologist is going to get huffy.

"She said I could stay for dinner. That's okay, isn't it?"

"Sure," I say, more confident than I should be. But I'm guessing Margie is used to these last-minute impositions. "Do you have a swimsuit with you?"

"Nah, I always borrow Riles's. It'll be grand."

Grand. I smile at Sammi's turn of phrase. Her father's perhaps?

The girls jump in the back, and I pull out. As we pass Nayla's car, I slow and wave.

She yells across to me. "How's she driving?"

"Perfect."

"Great. I'll pick Samara up around eight after class if that's okay?"

"Sure. See you a bit later," I yell back, wondering how on earth a single mother has time to run a business, make cupcakes *and* attend classes. I wonder what she's studying – marketing, business management, entrepreneurship?

The girls chatter non-stop all the way home. A week at camp together, and they still have more to say. I remember when Katie and I were that age. It seemed there was never enough time to tell each other every thought that flew into our imaginations, that nested, grew and blossomed into daydreams.

Margie makes mac 'n' cheese for the girls' dinner and offers me some. "Thanks. Why not?" It's the side of salad that draws an "ewww green stuff" from Sammi, but the huge banana splits with mile-high whipped cream and chocolate sprinkles get a "that's ridonkulous!" Reilly makes an effort at least, eating a third of her pasta and a quarter of her dessert before both girls scamper off to play in the lounge. I manage to scoff all of mine and would have eaten the rest of Reilly's if I'd been left alone with her plate. Thank god Margie clears the table before that happens. Maybe it's the cutting back on alcohol that's making me want to self-medicate with food.

Just after eight, Nayla arrives to collect Sammi. She's wearing a white martial arts uniform. "You're taking karate classes?" I ask.

She looks down, pinches a long dark hair off the front of her shirt. "Not taking, teaching."

Holy cow. She one of *those* women.

"Listen"—she reaches into her pocket—"if you're going to be staying in town a while, you should come along to my class." She hands me a business card: Martial Arts Maven. It has a graphic of a Lara Croft-esque woman mid-flight, ponytail flying. "Beginners welcome," she says.

I take the card and smile, a little insulted – unjustifiably – that she assumes I'm a beginner.

"My studio's on Warner Street, above the Backpackers. Come. It's loads of fun. First three classes are free."

"That's generous, but—"

Nayla shakes her head. "Don't worry about feeling embarrassed. Most of the group are there just to keep fit or get out of the house."

"I don't think—"

"Mummy!" Sammi and Reilly come pounding down the hall. Reilly has her small wheely suitcase behind her. "Is it okay if I stay at Sammi's tonight too?" She looks from Nayla to me, then back, her face so full of expectation I can't bear to say no.

"If it's okay with Nayla."

"Of course."

When they've all bundled off in the car, Margie invites me for a wine by the pool again.

"Just mineral water for me. I'm going dry for a little while," I tell her, though some desperate part of me calls me a fool.

She nods. "I might join you. Doesn't hurt to have a clear out now and then."

We sit, comfortable in each other's company. It's a still night. I slap at a mosquito about to settle on my knee, think about getting up to retrieve some repellent, but I'm too comfortable, too languorous.

"You must be looking forward to your holiday," I say. "Only a week to go."

Margie looks into her drink, swishes the ice cubes. "Hmmm. Yeah."

"You don't sound it."

"No, I am. It's just ... exhausting. Thinking about it."

"I know that feeling. I used to travel a bit. Was always tense, pent up just getting out of the house. Had I organised everything? Packed everything? Forgotten anything? Once I got to the airport, I was fine. No turning back. It's the leaving that's hard … back when I was allowed to. Damn. Sorry. I didn't mean to go there. We're talking about you."

"You still are. That's how I know you so well. I've been there."

"I'm sorry, Margie. I had no idea."

"It's okay. It's important not to forget. Not to fall back." The surety of her words doesn't match the waver in her voice.

We're quiet for a while, watching misty clouds drag themselves across the stars like stretched fairy floss. A satellite flares, traces a path west to east – or is it east to west? I get my directions muddled sometimes. No, that's right, they never travel east to west, something about Earth's rotation. Where did I learn that?

"Evelyn and I met in a support group. Both from broken marriages."

It's almost a gut punch. No wonder she nailed me on first sight. Why didn't I pick that up about her? Have I been too self-absorbed? "I can see how a shared experience might be a strong draw card."

"Too strong." She presses her lips together, corking any further revelations.

I wait. Just in case. I know how important space is … time to process, to decide what's safe to share.

She yawns. "Yes, well. Think I'll head off." She puts her glass down, braces to stand.

"Wait, Margie. Tell me about Evelyn. What's it like caring for someone with MS?"

She pauses, her body seeming to grow heavy, shoulders falling. She sighs, paddles her feet for a bit. "It's frustrating. Exhausting, Exhilarating. Rewarding. It's what you make it – how you take it, how you decide to respond ... most of the time."

"How long has it been? Since you found out?"

Her jaw works as she thinks. "Over four years ago. It came on suddenly. One day, she couldn't lift her coffee cup. We thought she was having a stroke."

"How did they diagnose it?"

She laughs her deep, husky laugh, but there's bitterness there. "Painfully. Took forever. Blood work, MRI, neurological tests, lumbar punctures."

"That would have been tough."

"You're not kidding." She picks up her glass, holds it up to check it's empty. I suspect she's wishing she'd had a wine instead.

"And now?"

"Now? It is what it is. The hardest part is the not knowing. It's unpredictable. Some days you'd never know she had it ... others, it's unbearable. One day she'll be so angry with herself – as if it's her own fault – another, she'll be so full of grace, serene, enduring. Those days I wish I could take on her pain for her." Her voice cracks, close to tears. "I love that woman so much. But pain ... well, it changes you."

I squeeze Margie's arm. She throws her head back, laughs with stoicism. "That's enough dwelling. I'd better get home to said woman." She rises now.

"Margie, take the weekend off."

"No, no. Don't be silly. I'm fine."

"Of course you are. But that's what I'm here for isn't it? Reilly's spending the weekend at Sammi's, Daniel's not back until Monday. It'll be quiet here."

She straightens, brightens a touch. "The fridge is stocked, washing done, house cleaned ... oh, there's a technician coming tomorrow around ten to fix the security shutter in Reilly's bedroom – it keeps jamming, but you've got my number if—"

"I can handle it. Go, relax, look after yourself for a change."

She smiles now, almost. "I might just do that. Thank you."

She wanders off, leaving me with the hazy stars, the silent vampirical flap of a foraging fruit bat and thoughts of cold wine. A few minutes, and the thrum of her car engine carries, fades.

Eyes closed, I let time laze by as the water soothes my feet. And here's the constant whisper in my ear: *I could be doing something. I should be doing something.* I push it away. Andreas is not here. Those days of panicking at his arrival are gone. No more racing around the house, making sure everything is perfect, everything is how he wants it – his meal not overcooking, enough ice blocks in the freezer, the television remote and Scotch next to his armchair. No one checking my every action, my every movement, every word.

I stretch my neck this way ... that way. It's okay. I'm alright doing nothing.

32

Andreas

"Let's have some tea while we wait," Adhira said. Why was everyone's standard response to trauma a cup of tea? I guessed she needed some distraction too.

As she got up to put the kettle on, the three of us startled at the smashing of glass. Adhira pulled her mobile from her pocket. She'd be dialling triple zero again, asking where the police were. She moved out of the kitchen, to the back verandah, perhaps to shield me from the panic in her voice. Eadie was still there, sucking on her smoke, one foot on a stacked milk crate, examining her toes.

I got up, pushed through the hallway door. It swung shut behind me. I was halfway down the hall before Adhira called. "Georgia, stop!"

Glass lay shattered on the carpet. He'd put his fist through the side pane. Now he was growling at his inability to reach the lock. He swore as he cut his arm on the broken pane.

"Georgia! You get out here now!"

"Don't do it." Adhira was closing in behind me.

I reached for the lock, turned it.

"Georgia! No!"

He was mid-swing as I opened the door. "Stop it, Andreas." If I hadn't ducked, I would have worn his fist. "Just stop," I said, softer.

I walked past him, down the garden path. Adhira didn't try to stop me. I was over the threshold. She'd witnessed this too many times. She'd said the statistics were high. That some women left up to eight times before they left for good. I had six lives left.

Andreas followed me to the front gate, pointed to his car. When we reached it, he opened the door for me, all gentlemanly. At first, he was apologetic, wiping spittle from the corners of his mouth. "Don't know what came over me," he said, continually glancing in the rear and side mirrors as he drove. "You know I never meant to hurt you, babe."

"I know."

He promised it wouldn't happen again.

He'd drink less.

He'd keep his anger controlled.

He'd get some counselling.

<h1 style="text-align:center">33</h1>

It's almost eleven, and the shutter technician hasn't shown up. I'm dying or a swim, but I settle for a foot dangle in the pool again. My default position lately. I lean back on my hands, eyes closed, shaded by a sail cloth. Could almost fall asleep, so dreamy, so quiet.

"Mind if I swim?"

"Holy heck!" I spring to attention, hand pressed over my heart. "Daniel, you scared the bejeezus out of me."

"Sorry. Thought you would have heard me." I move to extricate my feet, but he says, "Stay. I'm just here for a quick dip."

"I thought you weren't back until tomorrow?"

"Managed to get an earlier flight, so I got a transfer car back. Didn't want to bother you."

"It's no trouble. That's what you pay me for."

"Not twenty-four-seven. Where is everyone?"

"Reilly's at Sammi's and Margie's taking the weekend off."

"Nice." He pulls a towel from his shoulder, slings it onto a sunbed and kicks off his thongs. He's already in his boardshorts and doesn't waste time diving in. I shy back as his splash sprinkles over me, then watch, entranced by his long-armed smooth strokes, strong kicks and rhythmic pace.

He reaches the other end, does a flip turn and heads back. He does this five more times, then pulls himself up to sit next to me, pinching water from his nose and pushing his hair back to drip behind.

"So, it's Reilly's birthday next month," he says.

No niceties, no small talk, straight to the point. I guess I'll get used to it eventually. "It is?"

"Why would I say it if it weren't?"

"I ..."

"I'm kidding."

I nod. Awkward. A little irritated. How am I supposed to know when he's joking?

"I'm a bit hopeless at presents, so I always ask her what she'd like. And this year she wants you."

My expression must look stupid, but I can't help pulling a quizzical look.

"She'd like me to make you permanent."

"But ... I've only been here, what ... a week? And I've hardly seen her. And I thought the position was only for six weeks?"

He leans down to catch a leaf floating on the water, flicks it away onto the grass. "She's clicked with you."

"That's nice. I like her too. But ... you hardly know me. And what about Margie?"

"I have a good feeling about you. So does Margie. I'm sure she could use more time with Evelyn."

"We were just talking about her."

He lowers his head. "I can't imagine living like that, the increasing disability. Knowing it's only going to get worse."

I do a double take. Does he not consider his own condition a disability? Not being able to drive, having "episodes" that wipe out entire weekends?

"I wish I could do more for her," he says. "Three weeks doesn't seem long enough. I should have booked it for longer. Margie hasn't had a break since I can remember."

"You're paying for their holiday?"

"Sure, sure ... and Evelyn's ongoing treatments. It's the least I can do. Margie is family to me." He pushes himself off the side and back into the pool, then turns to rest his arms on the pavers. "Anyway. Think about my offer. Take whatever time you need, but keep in mind Reilly will kill me if you don't stay."

I smile, awkward, glance away from his earnest gaze. "Thanks. I will. Think about it." I squint at him. "Can I have a couple of weeks? I'm still finding my feet."

He shrugs. "Sure. As long as the answer's yes." He grins. And how it changes his face: cheeky, boyish. "Right then," he says, "couple more laps then I'm off to grab some sleep. Don't worry about my dinner. I'll help myself if I wake up."

"Okay. I'm thinking of popping into town later this afternoon. Check out Nayla's self-defence classes."

"I hear she's scary." He holds his hands up as if defending himself.

"You should come along. Might be fun. Step outside your comfort zone a bit. Get away from your work."

"I have my share of fun."

"Sure," I say, shrugging. "I guess cruising with clients is pretty exciting for some people."

"Pfft." He turns and swims off, reaches the other end and doubles back.

As he nears me again, I pull my legs from the water and stand. "Is it ... okay if I make myself a sandwich?"

He tilts his head. "You don't have to ask."

"No, I mean. Should you be swimming on your own? I can stay until you're done."

"Oh, right. No, I'm all good." He taps his head. "I feel when it's coming on. But thanks for asking."

I nod, turn and head back toward the house.

"Hey," he calls. "What are you doing tomorrow?"

"Ah ... nothing planned as yet. Margie says there's a Sunday market?"

"Afraid of heights?"

"Errr, no ... why?"

"Let's go hot hair ballooning."

"Seriously?"

"Not a fan?"

"I don't know. I've never been."

"Too chicken?"

"No."

"Too out of your comfort zone?"

"Alright, smart-arse."

"You'll love it. See you at 4:30 am."

"*What?*"

He spins around and pushes himself off the side again.

As I'm considering whether I want to be up at such a rude hour, the phone rings, so I hurry inside. It's the shutter tech. He can't come today. The parts haven't arrived. He'll need to reschedule.

I head to the kitchen. There's an open wine bottle in the fridge door, sitting innocently winking at me. Just a little? A spritzer maybe? I'm not on duty. I glance at the kitchen clock. Just past twelve. I pick the bottle up, start unscrewing the cap ... *Stop, you have to stop. You don't need it.*

Sandwich. Mineral water. Foxtel. Distraction.

I eat my lunch at the kitchen bench, then head back to my room, prop myself on my pillow and stare at the ceiling, trying to think. "Permanent". Unexpected. Do I want this? Why wouldn't I? Would it be dangerous to stay in one spot too long? Andreas hasn't found me yet. Maybe there's hope. It only took him less than a week last time. *Last time* ... I slip into the reverie so easily, almost as if I'm there again, crouched behind the door, heart crazy, pulse thrashing, fear gripping me in its fetid jaws, gnawing at my sanity.

Shake it off.

Before I can think more, I head to the bathroom to retrieve my half bottle of vodka and drag it to my lips, swig. I add a good slosh to my glass of mineral water too, then stash the bottle back. Pillows welcome me. Relief. Eyes closed. Deep breaths –four in, hold, six out, hold – slowly, slowly.

Settle.

Calm.

Relax.

It's over.

One last huge breath, and I reach for my phone, surprised by my shaking hand. I text Katie:

Chat?

Working. Tomorrow?

K. Miss you.

⋯⬦⋯

Upstairs, at the rear of a shop, a sign on the wall tells me I'm in the right place: "Martial Arts Maven. Self-defence Salon". I peek through the window in the door. The space is smaller than I expected, wooden floors and high windows along the back wall. I'm not sure what I was expecting. A gym? Equipment everywhere?

Nayla is in her uniform with her back to me. A group of women in shorts and singlets stand around her, listening intently. They look engrossed, as if they're living for her every word. Nayla beckons one of them forward and demonstrates a palm thrust to her face. The woman throws an arm up, fending her off to one side.

The door suddenly gives with my leaning against it. Nayla turns at the creak.

Oops. Sprung.

"Georgia! So glad you came. Didn't think you would."

I give her a small wave, and she turns back to her group.

Unsure if I should join them or take a seat on one of the teak benches near the entrance, I opt to sit, and as I do, kick something under the bench with my heel – shoes, a line of them. The women are all barefoot. Okay. I slip off my sandals and place them alongside the other footwear.

The group breaks into two lines facing each other, and Nayla calls to me. "Come."

Damn it. I wanted to sit and watch for a while. I pad over to her and she places me at the end of one line. I stand, arms dangling by my sides, hands itching to do something with themselves. Anything.

"Everyone, this is Georgia. Georgia, everyone."

Thanks. I wouldn't have remembered everyone's name anyway. I nod, smile, and they return the same, except for one overly enthusiastic woman who looks like she'd be more at home in a wrestling ring. She waves and calls in a surprisingly squeaky voice, "Welcome, newbie." I wonder if she likes to crush new blood.

Nayla continues the class with some warm-up exercises. Ugh. I'm so unfit. A few minutes in, and I'm sweaty and puffing. Now she pairs us up and takes us through some drills. And everything she says makes sense: moves to block attacks, to protect our vulnerable areas, to temporarily disable your attacker – throat, shins, little fingers, groin.

We do the moves over and over again. And again. And again.

I start to enjoy myself. The discipline of the movements, the slight corrections she gives me, the concentration it takes to repeat each move precisely. Balance, breathing, awareness.

Then I start to daydream, wondering why in movie fight scenes men never ever go for the groin first? I mean things would be over in seconds. Is it some sort of honour, besides the fact it would cut the movie time in half?

Nayla shows us how to jab our fingers into our opponent's throat. I squirm. Wanting to hurt someone and actually doing it is vastly different. I guess I'm not taking this seriously enough. And I should be. What if Andreas turns up? What if he tries to drag me by the hair back to Melbourne?

Whack. I cop an open palm to the side of my mouth.

"Arrrgh!"

"Oh, god. I'm so sorry," my opponent says.

I can't speak, I'm too stunned, and my lip feels as if it's already swelling. A wave of fury rises in me, and I shove her, so hard she almost falls backward.

"Georgia!" Nayla grabs my arm. "Breathe."

"I am!" I snort in and out, tears threatening.

"Breathe," she repeats, gentler, leading me aside.

I do. Deeper, holding it in, then easing it out.

My opponent approaches, a young woman who couldn't be more than twenty. She touches my shoulder. "I'm so sorry, I thought you—"

Nayla squeezes her shoulder. "It's okay, Terry. She'll be alright."

"Not your fault," I manage, though I can't look at her; I'm too busy holding the pain in my face.

"Class over," she yells, and the women all quietly step back from each other, bow, then head toward the exit to collect their shoes and belongings.

Shame fills me. Hot, hot shame. I close my eyes, wishing I could fold myself into something tiny and disappear.

"Sit," Nayla says, pointing to the floor. Her tone is calm but solid as a weight pressing down on me. I obey, and she sits cross-legged opposite me.

She looks over her shoulder as the last woman leaves, then turns back to me. "Bad day?" she asks

Day? A bad freakin' *day*?

"It's normal," she says.

I can't look at her.

"Georgia. It's normal. Sudden pain, unexpected like that, makes us want to hit back."

"I could have hurt her."

"But you didn't."

"Because you stopped me."

"Georgia …" She sighs. "I broke a guy's nose once."

I look up now. Nayla tilts her head to one side, smiles crookedly. "He deserved it. I'm not proud of it, but he did."

"Why?"

"He was trying to make me dance with him." She pulls a silly face.

She wants me to laugh, but I can't. I stare at the floor, the scuff marks on the wood. "Why is it, when you're down, life seems to want to stamp its foot onto you and grind you into the ground like a cigarette butt?"

She huffs. "Life isn't always so mysterious. Sometimes, it's obvious. Maybe it's telling you to let go. Release. Have a damned good cry."

"Well, it got its freakin' way today." My words are accompanied by a single, stubborn sob. I suck in air, straighten my shoulders, look to the ceiling for strength as I breathe deep. "I, uh … I don't think I can deal with the violence of this, what it brings out in me. No offence."

"It's not about violence. Or anger. It's about controlling it. It's about response, not reaction. Most of all, it's about defending yourself long enough to get away from danger."

This makes me pause. Am I avoiding responsibility for my own safety?

Nayla seems to pick up on my thoughts. "Nobody should *need* to defend themselves. But being prepared is a good thing, right? We have first aid kits, repair toolkits, fire extinguishers – think of self-defence as a toolkit for your body and mind."

"Sounds logical when you put it like that."

"Okay," she says, slapping her hands on her knees, "I'll stop preaching now. You gotta come to Jesus in your own time. You thirsty? I could kill for one of Carey's iced coffees."

I lift my gaze.

She adds, "And one of my cupcakes?"

"Now there's a class I'd like to take."

On Nayla's request, Carey brings me a napkin with a couple of ice blocks for my mouth, then doesn't disappoint with his frothy mountain-topped drinks, sprinkled with powdered chocolate. Nayla dives almost nose-first into her whipped cream, slurping up the cold, sweet coffee. She pulls back when a lump of ice cream becomes stuck to the bottom of her straw, lifts it up and sucks it off.

Before she can start probing my psyche further, I deflect. "Tell me about Sammi's dad. Are you both of Malaysian heritage?"

"Well, my father's a white Aussie, mother Malaysian. The ex's parents are still there, so he moved back after we split. He's ... not a *bad* person. We just don't see eye to eye on things. Mainly religion. Like, my religion is respect; his is a god who doesn't believe in equality or equity ... well, maybe he does, but, you know, interpretation when suits. Abuse comes in many forms. Like subservience. Can you imagine me deferring to a husband?"

I laugh. "No. No, I can't. So ... how does this all affect Sammi?"

"It's tough. She's infatuated with him, you know, absence makes for fondness. And she's a free spirit – have you seen the way she likes to dress? I'm just relieved she's not doing the whole *binti* thing. I mean, I respect differences in cultures, but that's too Handmaid's Tale for me."

She picks up on my blank look.

"It's traditional in Malaysia – well, maybe not *so* popular these days, but he's recently converted, so heavy on – to take your father's first name as part of yours. *Bin* means "son of" and *binti* means "daughter of". So the children are named 'son of' or 'daughter of' their father's first name – no last names. Hence, 'Sammi Siva'. Have you read Margaret Atwood's books? Remember Offred?"

"Oh, right. Okay. I didn't know that."

I sip iced coffee between icing my mouth, keeping my eyes on her. She's playing with the cream now, dipping her straw in and out, punching holes in the slippery cloud, as if she's trying to sink it along with a bad memory.

"I refuse to talk bad about him to Sammi. We were happy once, here, until he found religion and its particular brand of misogyny. I think his parents got in his ear about bringing a child up 'properly' – a girl child, of course. You know how it is; boys will be boys. But he's always been good to her, provided for her, just not ... he no longer does affection, you know? Not now, anyway. I just worry that, as she gets older and her blinkers fall away, he'll become ..."—she swallows, looks up, an ache in her eyes—"I'm terrified one day I'll send her for a stay, and he won't send her back."

I grab her hand, squeeze it, unsure of what to say.

Her smile is sad. "One day at a time, hey?"

I return her smile, then I motion to her tattoo. "How did he respond to that?"

"Ha!" She grins. "None of his beeswax. It was my break-up present to myself. Anyway, nice segue. This is supposed to be about you."

"No, it's okay. We don't have to—"

"Yeah, we do. Give and take. That's how it works. Let's say, six cupcakes for a half-hour of bean spilling?"

"Make that a cake decorating lesson, and you're on."

"Ha. One lesson and you'll know all my secrets. Actually ..." she narrows an eye. "What are you doing now?"

"Now? Um ... not much. Going home to sulk over my lip."

"I've got a better idea. Come on. My place. Let's go." She pushes her chair back and stands.

"Now?"

"You got anything better to do?"

"Nope."

"Just excuse the house. It's a work in progress. I bought a fix-er-upper. Still waiting on cyclone screens and a few other things."

Three hours and three different cakes decorated later, my beans are well and truly spilled.

Before we leave, I ask, "Could you apologise to ..."

"Terry? Sure. Don't sweat it. Happens to the best of us."

<hr>

It's twilight when I return. Daniel is awake and pulls the front door open before I can unlock it. "Woah, what happened to you?"

"You should see the other guy."

His eyes widen. "Did someone hurt you?"

I laugh. I can now. "Slight mishap."

"Looks painful."

"Nothing a decent pizza won't fix. Do they deliver here?"

He nods. "Leave it to me."

He likes his pizzas spicy, hates pineapple. I tell him he's a heathen. It's good to see him laugh.

34

Andreas

The police car wail reaches us before we see the lights. Andreas pulls over, rests his elbow on the window frame to hide his face, sinks in his seat a little. The vehicle races past. He waits a little longer then pulls out.

His hand is jittery on my thigh as he drives. It's not a sexual thing; it's urgent, as if he's afraid I'm going to jump out at the traffic lights. I look at his fingers digging into my numb flesh. Two weeks of bitten nails, raw around the edges.

When we reach the apartment block, there's a police car out front. No surprise. Andreas's anger seethes back to life. "Don't say a word," he hisses.

I nod.

We get out of the car, stand on the nature strip as the police officers approach. One asks if I'm okay, glancing me over.

No visible bruises. No evidence of assault.

"Ma'am?" He has one hand on his hip, or is it on his weapon?

I look him straight in the face. Do they see my fear, the way I saw Eadie's?

"I'm fine."

"You sure?"

"I said I'm fine."

He asks if I'm here against my will. A fair question since I have a Temporary Protection Order against Andreas. Yet, here I am, returning. My choice. But he'll still have to face charges for the damage, the violence at the refuge. I can't stop that. And I don't want to ... those women were terrified. They've faced enough in their lives.

He swaggers, smirking as he offers his wrists for the cuffs.

"Keep dinner warm for me, baby."

Stop. Stop! Freakin' alarm. Who invented sunrises anyway? I fling back my sheet and sit up, a touch of nausea as well as nervous excitement flitting through my gut. Never been a morning person. Never been in a hot air balloon.

My wardrobe looms before me. What do you wear on these occasions? Jeans, I guess. Imagine falling out of the basket and your skirt flying up around your head.

Daniel's waiting by the open front door, keep-cups in his hands. "Morning."

"Is it?" I grumble, still working my hair into a ponytail.

"Your lip looks better. Nice bruise though."

"Does it?" I press the spot. Still a bit tender but the swelling seems gone.

"This might help." He hands me a coffee.

"Oh, you beautiful person." I take a sip before reaching for the car keys above the hall table.

"You don't need those," he says, nodding toward the doorway.

A smart-looking shiny sedan sits in the driveway. "Ooh, special."

"Not really. We both had a fair bit last night."

He's right. Wine, wine, port. Accounts for the seediness. So much for my "meals only" rule. "I don't guarantee I won't fall asleep on the drive."

"Be my guest. You have an hour and a half."

"And don't blame me if I snore."

"Scoot," he says, chuckling as he motions me out the door.

***

We step through the grassy paddock, wary of the odd cowpat. Ahead of us, several couples and small groups stand watching flames shooting sideways as men hold open the bottoms of two balloons, the bright silky fabric starting to billow with the heat. Slowly, slowly, both the balloons take shape, lifting, swelling, lifting, until two giant vibrant teardrops hang above us, straining against their tethers.

"Oh god, oh god," I whisper. Do I really want to do this? It looks amazing, but ...

The pilots motion for us to come forward, instructing us to climb into the sectioned baskets, ensuring each group is evenly distributed. Daniel and I share our own corner.

The burners blast upward, deafening, heat washing over us. I bite my lip, squeeze my eyes tight, cling to the side, wait to be jerked into the sky.

"Georgia, open your eyes."

"No." I shake my head. "Tell me when we're up."

"We're up," he says. "We're up. It's okay."

I ease open one eye, then the other, let my breath go. Just like that, we're aloft, gently rising as the ground crew release the ropes and the pilot pulls the ropes aboard.

The burners continue to sporadically set the balloons aglow. Soon we're drifting high above the patchwork of paddocks. Daniel points to the horizon where the sun is peeping, gilding the gem-green landscape, making everything seem fragile and new. The air about us holds its breath, utterly still. Bird song carries from the trees way below. How? We're so far away. The lowing of a cow. Caw of a crow. All heralding the birthing of a new day. I wouldn't have missed this for the world.

"Okay?" Daniel asks.

"Mmm." I nod. It seems wrong to break this angelic quiet.

"There's no wind," I whisper.

"Well, there is. We're just moving with it."

We drift and drift and drift, the view constantly fascinating as the day brightens: mirror-like lakes catch the sun and glint in our eyes, soft Kermit-green hills and valleys dimple the earth's verdant face. Quaint farmhouse properties sit in slumber, their land cordoned by rows of wind-break trees; dark patches of earth, trampled by cattle gathering in a follow-the-leader formation to bellow for their breakfast – grain to supplement their grass feeding, Daniel informs me – creeks winding like glittering mercurial snakes. And not far from us, the other balloon glows from the gas burner and the sun. I snap a few shots. "Here," Daniel offers. "Let me take some of you." I fleetingly think about some selfies of both of us, but it doesn't seem appropriate. He doesn't offer.

We rest our arms on the top of the basket and gaze. How do you take in, absorb, store for future, this rare beauty? This defiance of human limitations and the embrace of nature?

"Daniel?"

"Mmm?"

"Can I ask you something? Personal?"

He doesn't turn, keeps staring out. So hard to read.

"Does it ever annoy you? Your disability? Make you wish you could do things you can't?"

He flashes me a querulous look. "What disability?"

I baulk. Was that insensitive? Maybe he doesn't look at his brain malfunction in that way.

He elbows me. "Kidding. I *am* doing things. You don't have to feel sorry for me."

"I'm not. I just ... I wonder if you miss things like ... driving?" I should stop. Now. Before I make an idiot of myself. But I've started this.

The corner of his mouth twitches. "How tall are you? Five two? Three? Do you ever wish you were taller?"

I laugh. "Only when I can't reach things in supermarkets."

"Does that stop you from getting what you need?"

"No. I guess not."

"You work around it, right?"

"Yes. Or ask for help."

"No shame in that."

"No."

"Georgia. *Look around*. Look where we are."

Sigh. Life lesson on gratefulness installed.

The pilot regales us with a story of the first manned balloon flight in 1783. "France," he says. "A condemned prisoner, due to be executed the next morning, was offered his freedom if he survived the flight. The balloon took off and landed successfully, but farmers in the field where it landed were so terrified they attacked the balloon with pitchforks. Then when the prisoner crawled out, still alive, they attacked him. He was saved in the nick of time by the King of France who was following along."

Daniels leans in and whispers. "Fun story, but a fairy tale. The king suggested it be prisoners, but the first pilots were actually two other blokes – a French chemistry and physics teacher called de Rozier, and the Marquis d'Arlandes."

"How do you know that?"

He winks. "Google is your friend."

"Heh. I wonder what the farmers down there think of us spying on them from up here."

He sighs. "My great-grandfather owned property out here."

"He did?"

"Yep. But my grandfather sold it to move into property development. Lost his love of this land after being interned in a prison camp in South Australia. Said farming was for the delusional. Servants for the ungrateful."

"A prison camp? Here in Australia?"

"Yes. Thanks to the National Security Act."

I shake my head, cursing my high school history teacher whose idea of teaching was two hours of dictation from a textbook every Monday morning. I mostly slept through his droning voice.

"When Mussolini joined the war, Italians living here in Australia were assumed to be in support of his fascist government. Many were rounded up and interned. My father, only nine at the time, was left behind to run the farm with his mother. Not all women and children were so lucky."

"It must have been a tough life."

"He survived. Didn't make him a better person for it."

A matter-of-fact statement, but there's a curl of bitterness like the sharp edge of an iron filing. It resonates with my own experience of men who harm, whether intentionally or obliviously.

We both stare at the other balloon ahead of us, the flame shots bursting the quiet.

"I guess trauma takes its toll," I murmur, thinking of my own father. How, for a while after Mum died, he'd come into our room in the early hours after a shift and shake me and Katie to make sure we were still alive, still breathing.

Not dead, like his wife. How he called Katie his fairy angel and me his chubby cherub, then pinched my thigh until I squealed. Because he laughed, I laughed, hiding the small shock of pain. It hurts me now to think of this. To weave any meanness into my memory of Dad. He always came home to us. Never took his temper out on us. He *loved* us.

"Sure," Daniel says. "But when do we stop using trauma as an excuse for someone being an asshole?"

I have to think about this, such a grey question. "I guess I've always preferred to give someone the benefit of the doubt. How much self-awareness do they have? Do they know what they're doing is wrong and still keep doing it?"

Daniel points to his head. "Sometimes, once is enough."

It takes me a moment to process what he's saying, then as his meaning becomes clear, I shrink inside. I don't want it to be true.

"He didn't like the way I spoke to him. One punch. I landed hard. Hit my head. Nearly a month in hospital. He told them I'd tripped and fallen. He never hit me again, but never apologised, never acknowledged that he'd screwed my life. I was seven."

I shudder. "Apologies only mean something if they're genuine."

Daniel shrugs, a pretence at nonchalance, though his strangling grip on the basket gives him away. "It is what it is. Okay, my turn to ask you something."

I stiffen. If he asks about Andreas ...

"I'm not going to press you on the permanent thing, but"—he squints, looks down at his fingers, releases a hand, stretches it—"speaking of my condition, I have an opportunity to take part in a medical trial."

"That sounds promising."

He nods.

"But it's risky?"

"It's not that. It's based in Sydney. I'd need to relocate there for the three months. For daily observation, scans etc. I can run my business from there—"

"But you don't want to leave Reilly."

"Exactly. She's been through enough trauma, and there's no way Cynthia would take her for that long – not that I'd do that to Reilly. And it's too much to ask of Margie with her responsibilities to Evelyn."

"I see what you mean. Difficult."

"I'd need you to move to Sydney with us. Look after Reilly and home school her for that time."

"Oh."

"It's too much, isn't it? Too big an ask. You hardly know us."

"It's not that, it's …"

"Forget it. I shouldn't have asked."

Suddenly, the pilot is yelling instructions for landing. "Hold tight," he says. "Brace yourself. Every landing is different. It might be bumpy. Bend your knees to absorb the impact."

Impact? I'm tempted to crouch in the bottom of the basket, visions of being thrown over the side panicking me. Instead, I cling on for dear life. "Oh god, oh god, oh god."

"Do you want some moral support?" Daniel asks.

I nod. "This looks like suicide." I hold back a scream as we rush toward the ground. I expect him to put an arm around me, but instead, he stands close and interlinks his arm with mine. Side by side, we grip the basket.

"I guess if I'm going to die," I whimper, "it won't be alone."

He makes a bok bok chicken sound, and I laugh. Bastard.

My mobile vibrates in my jacket pocket between us. I could cry. From fear and awkwardness, and from bitterness that it's probably Andreas, unaware he's timing his harassment perfectly.

"Is that your phone or are you pleased to see me?" Daniel says.

My guffaw is lost in the blast of the burner. The basket seems to pause, then glides horizontally, lower, lower.

There's an almighty bump and shudder, and we bounce into the air again. Another thud, and we're being dragged sideways. The passengers scream and laugh, yelling their surprise. As we slow, Daniel lets go of me. "Okay now?" We're almost stopped. One more unexpected bump that jars my back. Hard. "Argh!"

The basket rights itself.

"You okay?" Daniel asks.

I nod, then shake my head. "I think I've done some damage."

The side of the basket reaches above my waist. How am I going to clamber out without hurting my back further? Daniel climbs out first, then holds out his arms for me. I grab the top of the basket, heave myself up, then groan as I sit astride and Daniel helps ease me to the ground.

"Okay?"

"Yeah. It's not as bad as I thought. Probably pulled a muscle."

He helps me hobble off to the side and sit in the grass while the pilot and ground crew give the passengers instructions to help pack up the deflating balloon. Daniel pitches in as they all grab a side, and drag the fabric forward and over itself, folding it into a giant package to be shunted onto the back of a flatbed.

While I'm waiting, I pull out my phone. Not Andreas. Katie, checking if we can still chat today. Good. Andreas hasn't ruined my day. I send her a photo – one I took with my big smiling face in the foreground with the other balloon mid-flight in the background.

After brekky by the sea in Palm Cove, we head back to town. Daniel's question seems forgotten in all the activities. He suggests a visit to the local market. "It's not big, mainly arts and crafts, but you have to try the fruit pooh."

"The *what*?"

"Frozen fruit, like a soft serve. You'll love it."

He's right, the mango and pineapple are amazing – tangy, freezy sweetness melting over my tongue. Then we come across a stall with a man using a drill attachment to shred fresh coconuts in their shells. Mmm, such creamy goodness.

⚬

Hi, sis. Okay to chat now?

Katie calls me straight back. "Ooh! I'm surprised you have time for me now that you're living the high life."

"Don't be daft. It was just a bit of fun. Anyone can hot air balloon."

She's rostered off, she says, enjoying some down time at home, browsing travel brochures. She's thinking of booking an overseas trip. Volunteer work.

"You don't mind, do you?" she says. "It's not till March. I figure by then things will have settled down with Andreas—"

"Go! You can't put your life on hold for me. I'd hate that."

"Thanks, Geegee." Her voice holds a quiet guilt.

"Go. I mean it. It's time we both put the arsehole behind us."

"Cool. By the way, I have a new ambo partner. Jackson."

"What happened to Samantha?"

"Burn out. Taking six months off."

"Poor woman. Not surprising though. Is this new guy good to work with?"

"Who cares? He's cute."

"Kit ... don't go there. You know what happened last time."

She shrugs, laughs. "Easy come, easy go. Tell me what's been happening in your world. Is your boss hot?"

"What?"

"Is he a hottie?"

"So not interested. The thought of another man ... just ... no." I distract Katie with mention that I haven't had any more texts from Andreas.

"That's good news, but you still need to block his number."

Maybe she's right. But how can I when I know he's still out there, festering? I want to know if he manages to get close. Be prepared. I can't block him; I *need* to know.

"Maybe he's done," I say.

"'Maybe' isn't in his vocabulary."

"Hey, guess what? I attempted a self-defence class yesterday."

"Really? That's a great idea. I wanna see you smash the arsehole in the nose."

"*Defence*, you maniac. Anyway, the only one who got smashed was me. I had a fat lip. Check this out." I take a selfie and send her a picture of my bruised lip.

"Ouchy. Who's teaching these rubbish classes?"

"A local woman. Not her fault. I wasn't paying attention. She's nice. She's also a mechanic – I met her after the car accident."

"Wait! What car accident?"

Oops. I fill her in, my laugh edgy when I relay the part about thinking there'd been a gunshot.

"Geez, must have been scary. Glad you're okay."

"Yeah, I'm good. But this Nayla, the mechanic and instructor, makes and decorates cakes too. One of those multi-talented people we love to hate."

"Interesting combo. Fatten them up with sweetness, then take them out with their mouth full."

I laugh.

"Keep up the classes," she says. "It'll be good for you. Build some confidence. You've always been afraid of conflict."

"That's not how it works. It's meant to help *avoid* conflict. Anyway, I have some better news."

"Yeah?"

"Daniel's offered to make me permanent."

"That's fantastic, G! Awesome."

"It's so quick though. And do I want to become grounded while Andreas is still on the hunt? What if he finds me up here?"

"I'm telling you he won't. We've been careful. We'll keep being careful. You're off the radar. He'll shrivel up and eventually go away."

"But—"

"No buts. Take the job."

The thought is appealing. I don't mention the three months Daniel wants me to spend in Sydney with just him and Reilly. I need more time to think that through. "So where are you thinking of going on your next wondrous journey?"

I can hear the smile in her voice as she tells me about her Kathmandu trek – the traveller's heart is never still. I imagine us as children again, lying on our sun-and-moon-and-stars bedspreads, our cherry blossom pyjamas falling back on our legs raised into the air, trying to touch an unreachable ceiling, talking about all the places we'll go when we're grown up.

Then my guts gurgle. I may have overdone the fresh coconut.

36

Andreas

He'd known I'd be back. The fridge was stocked. I made roast chicken and veg. The preparation gave me something to do, something to think about besides consequences. But when I heard him on the stairs, his belligerent footsteps on the landing, my hand shook as I pressed the stovetop burner button, clicking the flame under the saucepan of peas to life – he liked them freshly cooked, still firm.

He went straight to the shower, came out dressed in a fresh t-shirt, jeans, bare feet, even though it was winter and our floorboards were raw with cold. I shivered. Had I forgotten to turn the heater on?

"Smells good," he said, pulling out a chair.

I didn't speak as I served the meal, afraid I'd trigger something we'd both regret. Instead, I waited for him to say what he had to say. And I would agree to it. Whatever it was.

He made appreciative noises as he ate. Not slurping, burping noises – even an animal had its limits. I had to work my throat muscles to force a swallow.

When we finished, and I moved to clear the table, he grabbed my arm.

"Sit."

My voice barely made it past my lips. "Okay."

"I want to show you something."

He held out his phone and showed me a text: Wait till she sees this. She's gonna crack it.

He scrolled down to a second text – the address of the women's refuge.

It's not so much the address that drains the blood from my head; it's the sender's name. A cop. A fucking cop mate.

"Friends in high places, babe. Nowhere I won't find you."

37

I lean against the open loungeroom doorframe, staring out at the dark sea. The house has quietened, settled for the night. Dishes done, Margie home packing for her trip on Sunday, Reilly sleeping over at Sammi's. The girls are making the most of the last of their summer holidays together – another week and they'll be starting high school. I'm so excited for them.

The weeks have flown, and now I'm looking forward to stretching my wings in Margie's absence, making her proud that I can cope on my own, though I'm sure the house's energy won't be the same without her or her apple pie. Daniel and Reilly are going to have to settle for my limited repertoire of chocolate or orange cake, with attempts at icing styling courtesy of Nayla's lesson.

A breeze ruffles my hair, soft, cool. While I wait for the kettle, a digestive tea on my mind – liquorice and peppermint – I watch a vessel in the distance, probably a container ship, faint twinkles from its lights barely carrying across the inky black. There are no sunsets on this side of town; the hills hide the sun before its evening rays can carry to the water. Still, the sunrises over the ocean – if I'm up early enough – are inspiration enough to make me want to do something wonderful with my day. And the moon, peeping over the watery horizon, shivers an unclimbable silver stairway across the water. Stunning compensation.

"Look, you can say no if you want to, but ..."

I startle at Daniel's voice. He's propped against the hallway wall, half in shadow, a handtowel slung across one shoulder of his sweaty t-shirt. How long has he been standing there?

"Geez, you frightened me."

He straightens. "Sorry, I just came from the gym and ... didn't want to disturb you. You looked so—"

The downlights above us flicker, and we both look up.

"Kettle," I say.

"Been meaning to get that fixed."

He stays looking at the downlights, transfixed, and it makes me wonder if flickering lights can set off one of his episodes. The stretch of silence becomes uncomfortable.

"I'm making tea," I say. "Would you like a cup?"

"Sure." He follows me into the kitchen.

"Say no to what?" I ask.

"Sorry?"

"You said 'you can say no if you want to'."

"Oh, yes." He tilts his head, sheepish. "I need to ask you a favour. I've got a client arriving in town next week. I promised to take him to dinner on Saturday. He's just told me his wife is coming with him." He leans against the kitchen counter, crosses his arms and frowns, as if conflicted on whether to continue.

"And you want me to come along to make up the four?"

His frown dissolves. "Would you? It'll probably bore you silly, all business talk, but I'd owe you one. I'm happy to put extra in your pay. Overtime, you know."

I laugh. "It's okay. You don't have to do that. It'll be nice to go out and have some adult company. I'm beginning to talk like a ten-year-old." I open the pantry and run my eye over the collection of tea bags. "I'm sure Margie had some liquorice here somewhere." I poke a few boxes, push some out of the way. "Ah, here it is." I turn to him. "What's your poison?"

"Just plain for me. So, here's the other awkward bit. I don't suppose you speak Italian?"

"No. Why would I?"

"Just a hopeful guess. The wife doesn't speak much English."

I carry the tea bags to the kitchen sink and set out a couple of cups. "That's going to be a challenge."

"And one more thing. The restaurant's a bit classy. I don't suppose you ... have anything ..." He drums his fingers on his chin.

"Hmmm?"

"Dressy?"

I pause, mid-pour. "You're making this outing more and more attractive by the minute. You know that?"

"Let me buy you something nice. Pick yourself out whatever you like. Dress, shoes ... Did Margie give you the household credit card?"

I stare at him, hard, images of Andreas criticising me before we went out because my skirt wasn't tight enough, heels not high enough, my hair not straight enough.

"Georgia? Oh geez, I've offended you, haven't I?"

I bite down embarrassment, go back to pouring the hot water. "No. I just haven't had any need to—"

"Was I inappropriate?"

I swallow, put the kettle down. *Was he?* I thought this would be easier now – making my own choices and creating my own boundaries, but it's confusing. I sigh, turn to him.

His face is flushed too. "I guess not. Intention has to count for something. It just feels a bit 'Pretty Woman'."

"Sorry?"

"It's a ... never mind."

He opens a drawer, then pauses as if he's forgotten what he was looking for. "Ohhh ... No! You thought I meant ... God, no. I'm not expecting anything in return. Cynthia used to buy something new for these occasions. All the time. Thought nothing of it." He passes me a teaspoon.

"You should probably stop while you're behind."

He looks puzzled for a second, then goes back to drumming on his chin. "Sorry. I'm all foot in mouth around women. I shouldn't have asked." He turns to leave.

I laugh. "Woah there. Let's not toss the baby just yet. I've said I'd go. Just ... let me sort out my own clothing. Okay?"

He sighs, shoves his hands in his tracksuit pockets. "Thanks. I get myself into some tight corners sometimes. No wonder Cynthia was always in a bad mood."

"You're not so bad."

He smiles. Raps the bench with his knuckles. "Have you thought any more about my offer to stay on? Reilly's birthday's not far off, and if you don't stay, then I'll have to find an almighty present to curb her disappointment."

"Um ... I do like the idea."

He brightens. "Great! That's so great. Okay, well. I might give the tea a pass and jump in the shower before I do any more damage."

"Oh, wait. Does Margie know about this? About me staying on?"

He shakes his head. "No. I wanted to check with you first."

And he's gone, leaving me with two steaming teas and the quiet house.

38

Andreas

I tried to behave, but nothing I did pleased him.
My meals were crap.
I dressed like crap.
Everything I said was crap.
I ruined everything.
My fault, always.
If I wanted a husband, I needed to lift my game.
He was drinking more of late.
So was I.

39

What the heck? I follow the sound of Margie's humming and find her in Daniel's bedroom. She's removing the bed covers; Saturday is linen day.

"Margie? I thought you were taking today off. Don't you have packing to do for tomorrow?"

"We don't leave until late. I'd rather get things ship-shape here first."

"Still, wouldn't you like to take your time? I *was* planning on doing this, you know? I hadn't forgotten."

She sniffs. "I know."

"Okaaay, so why—"

She throws me a couple of pillowcases. I catch them against my chest. They're super soft, fine cotton, just like in my room.

"I'm giving Evelyn some space. She's a bit uptight about travelling."

"Really? I thought she'd be excited."

"She is ... but, you know ... Evelyn is Evelyn. Not as tough as she likes to think."

I move to the chair where Margie has stacked the pillows, grab one and stuff it inside a case. It's weird being in my boss's bedroom, changing his bedding. I try to be nonchalant as I glance around, seeing the room in daylight this time. There's nothing remarkable about the space: it has the same French doors as the rest of the house; the drapes are demure – a non-descript oatmeal; the floor tiled, cool. A couple of pictures hang on the walls – softer pieces than in the rest of the house.

Margie is sucking in and chewing the right side of her bottom lip. I know that signal; something isn't right.

"She's not doing so well?"

No answer.

I keep silent; I've also learned to let her drip-feed her troubles.

"MS is a one-way trip," she says. "She has good days and bad, but we're grateful for each sunrise. No point moaning about it. We're all heading in the same direction."

"I admire your attitude and courage, Margie."

She sniffs again, and I wonder if she has the beginnings of a cold.

"How long have you been together?"

"What is this? An inquisition?"

I laugh, a little intimidated. "Just asking."

"Well ..." She shakes out a fitted sheet, and I move to the other side of the bed to help tuck and smooth it. "Would be getting on fourteen, maybe fifteen years now.

"That's quite an achievement."

"I guess it is."

I struggle for something more to say. "How do you get these sheets so white?"

"Napisan. Use it in all my white loads."

"Uh huh." I go back to the chair, grab the next pillow. "She must be looking forward to catching up with her brother after so long."

Margie looks up at me then, her face softening. She knows how much I miss Katie.

I probe a little more. "So … does flying affect Evelyn's MS?"

"It can. But she'll have meds and steroids with her just in case. Flying at night will help. Avoids fatigue if she can sleep."

"Have you met her brother?"

Margie stops unfolding the top sheet, lets it fall in a white, meringue-like pile. Her nostrils flare, pulling breath. Her chest heaves – a puffer fish in defence mode. "We're not seeing her brother."

I waver back on my feet, wait, reluctant to break the tension as she composes herself. But the silence becomes too much, and her face is reddening. "Sorry? Did I misunder—"

"We're going to India. To see some rubbish practitioner who's offering her a rubbish cure for forty-thousand fucking dollars." She blows out her breath, a sharp pressure release that deflates her onto the edge of the bed. "He's not even Indian, or Hindu or from one of those temples that cure cancer; he's just some American idiot she found on YouTube. And I'm disgusted with myself for going along with it."

I'm shocked, both because I've never heard Margie swear and because, well, *this*.

She takes another big breath, eases it out. "There. I've said it."

What do I say now? I walk around the bed, ease onto the mattress next to her, place my hand on her shoulder. Her blouse is damp with sweat. "Margie … I'm so sorry."

"You and me both. But I said I'd go with her, and go I will."

"Good on you for being so supportive. It's a tough decision. Really tough."

"It's not what I feel like doing. I feel like slapping her." She chuckles, sniffs.

"Let me know if you need me to hold her down. I suspect you'd have your hands full there."

We both laugh then, and Margie pulls a tissue from her pocket, wipes her nose.

"Well," I say, "I have some news that I'm hoping will cheer you up."

She looks at me, expectant.

"It's about my job here."

She turns to me. "Have you found another one already? I meant to tell you you're welcome to stay on until Evelyn can find you something else, but I've been so distracted."

"No. Daniel's offered me a permanent position. I was hoping he would have checked with you first." I hold my breath, watch her carefully.

She doesn't respond, just stares.

"He thinks you might like to spend more time with Evelyn."

Margie stands. "Does he?" She takes the top sheet and whips it open over the bed. Again, I move to the other side, take an edge, help lay it out. Her face is impossible to read.

"I thought maybe we could job share. But if you're not okay with that—"

She shakes her head, forces a smile, lips tight. "It's fine, love. I'm just a little surprised."

"Me too. I thought he would have discussed it with you first." *Damn.* I've chosen completely the wrong time. "I ... uh ... I don't want to interfere with your job, Margie. If it doesn't suit you, I'm happy to just cover your holiday then leave. Really. I'd hate to upset things for you."

She stops her tugging and smoothing, looks at me. Worry has dulled her eyes. I should have been more sensitive, waited until she got back. She's got enough stress on her right now. This was supposed to be good news, but I'm just adding to her burden. "Margie, if you need full-time money, I don't want to take that away from you. This is your family. I'll leave. Just please be honest with me. Tell me how you really feel."

I wish I could read her mind, but we're kindred spirits – used to hiding.

She sniffs, swipes at her nose with her tissue again, then pockets the ragged remnant. "Love, to be honest, it's been a relief having you around. These bones aren't getting any younger. I'm exhausted most of the time, and a couple of extra days off a week sounds good. Really good. It's just hard letting go when I've been holding the reins so tight for so long."

"I understand. I'm happy to fit around whatever schedule suits you."

"We'll work it out when I get back. Don't stress."

"Thank you."

She nods "It's a good plan. Evelyn isn't going to get any better in India." There's a catch in her voice that breaks my heart. "I'm not looking forward to the moment she realises it's all been for nothing."

"Margie. Can I give you a hug? In case I don't see you before you leave?"

She pulls me in and squeezes. "Now off with you before you make me blubber."

"I'm going to miss you."

"Oh, for Pete's sake. It's only three weeks."

As I'm rounding the bed again, a pillow catches me in the back of the head. "Just so you know, I'm still the Queen Bee around here."

I laugh-snort. "Oh, I nearly forgot. Daniel's asked me to pick up a couple of things in town. He said there's a credit card?"

Margie tries to hide it, but there's a tightening in her jaw again. "Sure, love. In my purse. In the kitchen. It's got the company name on it. I should have thought to give that to you."

I slink out of the room and down the hall, unable to shake the sense of being a usurper. Guilt is a dark companion.

40

Andreas

"You never remember anything."
"You ruined things again."
"How can you be so stupid?"
"What do you do all day?"
"Where's all the money going?"
"You should get another job."

41

Dirty water sloshes in the laundry sink, grey dregs spinning round the basin, rivulets of stubborn sediment in the bottom. Sand, an ever-present irritant of living by the sea – on the floor, on feet, on clothing, no matter how much I shake or wash it away.

As I hang the mop up, my arm muscles complain. I bet the house is laughing at me, and I haven't even finished yet. The beds. I promised Margie I wouldn't forget, but I just ... oh, screw it; an extra night sleeping on last week's sheets won't hurt anyone. Margie will never know.

I wonder how she's doing over in India, if she's coping with Evelyn's treatment, holding back her scepticism, being the good partner. And I wonder how on earth she manages here, caring for Reilly, Daniel, Evelyn and running the household on her own. Where on earth does she get the strength or find time for herself? This week's school holidays have killed me, what with keeping Reilly entertained, visiting Sammi, shopping, driving to Cairns for movies, picnics, swimming, hiking.

I rush through a shower, then dress. Cynthia's back from overseas and wants Reilly for the weekend.

"Quick, quick." Into the car she goes.

She's surprisingly well behaved on the drive. I suspect it's so she won't lose the privilege of a day off school on Tuesday – her birthday.

Outside Cynthia's house, I wait while Reilly heads up the path. If her mother wants to meet me, now's her opportunity. She doesn't appear. Fine by me.

Back in town, I hunt the boutiques, Daniel's credit card in hand. Why is it that when you don't have money, everything jumps out at you? Buy me! Buy me! Today, nothing. This pressure is so damned frustrating and typical of me – I've had a week to sort this out, but procrastination is a sneaky and smooth mistress. *Come on. Just choose something.* At this rate, I'll probably leave empty handed and end up wearing my standard shorts and blouse.

After the seventh shop, I'm done, can't take any more, so I head toward the post office, which is where I should have gone first. And wouldn't you know it? There, in the next window, is exactly what I didn't know I was looking for: a burnt-orange shift dress, its shimmery fabric falling softly from shoestring straps, grazing the curves of a mannequin in all the right places. Okay. Head inside. Last try. But the price tag. Ouch! Pure silk. No wonder.

I head to the changing room anyway.

"How are you going in there? Can Monique help?"

"Fine thanks," I say, wondering if the woman is referring to herself in third person or offering someone else's assistance.

A solid hand, bejewelled with costume rings on every finger, grabs the changing room curtain and swishes it aside. "Let's have a look. Oooh!"

Monique, I assume. She has a voice of lush velvet, the kind you hear on late-night radio.

"It looks gorgeous on you. Trust me, Monique knows."

"Thanks. It feels great. Love the material, so soft. Is the length okay? Not too short?"

"You know, I've seen three other women try on the same dress." She closes her eyes for a moment and shakes her heard. "Honey, they looked like five-day-old milk scum. But on you ... perfection. Where did you get that gorgeous skin from? I bet you tan real easy, don't you?"

I blush, sneak another look. "My grandmother was from the Seychelles."

"Ah! Seychellois! We could be sisters, you and I."

"We could?"

"Mamma Monique from Moa, they call me. Torres Strait for those playing along at home. But there's nothing straight about Monique. So what's happening, my love? What's this dress for? Getting lucky?"

"Nooo. Just dinner. Tonight."

She sniggers. "Holy smokes. You like cutting things fine. What shoe size are you?"

"Six."

"Tiny! I'm an eleven myself. So hard to get sexy shoes. Wait there."

"I need flats!" I call after her. God, how much are those going to cost?

I check the time again. Twenty minutes. The post office might have to wait until Monday. I twist to examine the dress from every angle. Gorgeous. I want it. Really, really want it. The mirror grins back at me. *Georgia, you're such a child.*

"Here we are." Monique holds up a pair of low-heeled, strappy lilac sandals and a matching handbag. The leather is sooo soft. Help me. They're divine. "You, my good woman, are a fairy godmother."

"Monique's alter ago." She smiles, sly. "Tell me, you gorgeous creature, where are you going for this 'just dinner' tonight?"

"Cascades. Have you heard of it?"

She almost mewls. "To-die-for food. Make sure you order the chocolate dessert. It's designed for sharing." Her look is full of insinuation, her giggle plush. "Makes it more romantic."

"Ha ha! None of that. It's with my boss. Anyway, I don't share my chocolate with anyone." I swirl the dress again, twist my feet this way and that, then turn to face her. "But I can't afford *everything*." I return the handbag.

"Honey"—she presses the bag back at me, puts her hands on my shoulders and spins me back to the mirror—"look. Just look. Gorgeous. Meant to be. And didn't you see our sale sign? Thirty per cent off everything."

I bite my lip. "I guess I could always pay him back anything he thinks is too much."

She puckers her mouth, raises a well-drawn eyebrow. "He's paying? Honey, go for it. Women always end up paying in the end. Enjoy it now."

"You know what? Hang it. Sold!"

"Right choice." Now she pauses, picks up a few wisps of my hair, looks disdainful. "No. This won't do. Who did this colour for you?"

I swallow, shrug, look guilty.

She tuts. "You got a couple of hours?"

I check my watch. "I guess so, but I need to get to the post office first before it closes."

"No, honey, you need to get to Arnie's. Get changed."

When I reach the register, she has her phone tucked between her shoulder and ear as she wraps my purchases in tissue paper. "I know, I know. I'll owe you one." I pass her the credit card. "I'm sending her right over now. Thank you, Arnie. You're a darling." She hangs up, then hands me a large paper carry bag and a business card. "Two streets down on the left. Move your tush. He's squeezed you in."

"You're wonderful."

"Monique knows." She winks. "I popped a little something extra for you in the bag."

I leave the shop in a state of guilty pleasure, assuaging my inner miser with purchaser's logic that I've saved thirty per cent on everything. But I only have ten minutes left to reach the post office, so I hoof it across the road, dive inside, grab a small, padded postage envelope off the shelf and hurry to the counter.

"Hi, I need to send something by registered post to Melbourne. Insured, person to person."

"Yes, mam. Pop it up here."

I dig the velvet pouch out of my handbag, place it on top of the envelope on the scales.

"Here on holiday?" he asks.

"No, I've just moved here."

He peers over his glasses. "Welcome! I'm Walter." He shoots out a thick hand covered in sun spots.

"Georgia."

"Family?"

"No, no. Just me. And I'm really sorry, but I'm in a bit of a hurry."

"Well, it's a bit Hotel California here – lots of people come for a short spell and end up falling in love with our little town. This land grows invisible roots in your soul, sturdy as the bloody mangroves. Came out thirty years ago, myself. Wife and kids. Kids went off to uni, but Wilma and I are still here."

I wonder if they handed down their w's to their kids. "I get how that could happen."

"Mind you, living here's a lot different from holidaying." He taps a few keys.

"Yes."

"But if you can handle cyclone season"—Walter pokes my parcel, ensuring it's sitting in the middle of the scales—"tourist season and the humidity, you'll find we're all one big family of sorts. People from all over the world, but we're close-knit. You know? We look after each other."

I nod. Maybe close-knit is exactly what I need, instead of isolation. Closed ranks, protection, but I wish he would hurry up. "Can you please—"

"Person to person, insurance ..." He tells me how much it will cost, then hands me a form with a red and orange label on it. "Okay, Georgia. You'll have to fill this in."

I hesitate. "Um ... will the postmark say where the parcel is posted from?"

He screws up his forehead as if he's never thought about this. "Well ... yes it will. And you need to provide your own name and address if you want a receipt."

Damn. "Okay. Look, I might take this with me and bring it back later."

"But we're closing."

Suddenly, I need to get out. To rethink this. "That's alright. Not in a hurry."

Outside, on the pavement, I take a moment to calm myself. A little bit of pressure with anything to do with Andreas, and I fall apart. Will I ever get past this?

Gentle rain is fuzzing the street, so I stay under cover as I hurry down to Arnie's.

Wow. I can't help it, glancing in every shop window, trying to catch my reflection – my hair, so shiny, long, caramel and blond-streaked. Who is this woman? I stride a little taller, stronger. I'm becoming me again.

Tap. Tap.

"Come in!" Evelyn mouths from behind her office window.

What the? I didn't think she and Margie were due back for another week. She beckons again, and I enter the office. "Welcome back! Did you cut your trip short? Is everything okay?"

She flicks a look at my hair. Doesn't comment. "All good. So I hear you're being made permanent?"

Okay, cut to the chase. Her tone is neutral, eyes on her computer screen. Is she pleased or annoyed? I can't tell. But I recall our first meeting – the way she chatted while focused on her computer. Maybe she has social anxiety.

"It was a bit of a surprise," I say. "But a good one. For me."

"And me. That's a nice little bonus coming my way."

"Sorry?"

"Finder's fee. For your permanency. Well done, you." She looks up and smiles now, but it doesn't reach her eyes. "Pity about Margie though."

"What do you mean?"

"Well, she's getting on a bit, isn't she? Won't be long before she'll have to retire."

"That's not ... I thought—"

"Anyway. Not your problem."

"But I'm not usurping Margie. Daniel assured me. She's family."

"So they say."

I'm not sure what else to say, so I ask how she is. "You're looking really good. I guess the treatment helped."

The sudden hardness in her eyes, the small, sharp intake of breath, signals my stupidity and big mouth. "What treatment?" She pins me with her gaze, and I can't think quickly enough to cover my gaff. There's no point lying now, so I purse my lips and shrug. "Sorry. I guess that should have been private. But ... you're looking fantastic. I hope it was worth—"

She holds up a hand, face slipping back to neutral.

Damn. Margie is going to hate me for this. Stupid, stupid, stupid.

"Here"—she leans to open a drawer—"I've got a little present for you." She passes me a small parcel with a red ribbon. "I was going to give it to Margie to pass on, but since you're here."

I take the present. The shiny white cardboard sticks to my sweaty hand. I focus on it, play with the ribbon so I don't have to show my guilty eyes. "Thank you for this. It's very sweet of you."

"It's nothing. I do it for all my permanent placements. Just some preserved spiced figs. I hope you like nutmeg?"

I'm forced to look at her now. It would be rude not to. "Sure. Sounds yummy." I thank her again, then stand there, unsure of what else to say. "Umm. Okay, well. I need to get to the book café before it closes. I want to see if they have Patrick Ness's third book in stock yet. I've ordered it for Reilly's birthday. She devoured the first two."

"No wonder that girl loves you."

"What a lovely thing to say. I'm kinda getting attached to her too."

42

Andreas

I went back to work, and for a while things settled. Then got worse.

"Where are you?"

"At work."

"Why aren't you answering my texts?"

"I'm working."

"Don't get smart."

I took sick leave until the black eye was coverable with make-up.

A gun appeared in the house. He showed it to me after I'd burned dinner because he couldn't wait for a shoulder massage.

43

The orange shift is still perfect, makes my skin glow, the shoestring straps showing off my tanned shoulders. I spin to check my back in the mirror, *again*. Is it too revealing? It's dinner, not a date. Don't want to send the wrong signal, not after what he said about the last nanny. A wrap will solve that – a fine cream length, swished over my shoulders – Monique's "extra little something". Better. Maybe I should let my hair down too. An up style might say I've put in too much effort. Probably. Down it comes, a shake of my caramel waves, then … up again in a clip – it's too hot.

My stomach grumbles, reminding me I skipped lunch, too busy shopping. I eye Evelyn's package of figs on my dresser. Maybe I should put something in my stomach in case we have pre-dinner drinks. Don't want the alcohol going straight to my head. A tug on the silky red ribbon, and it falls away, revealing a lavender-coloured logo: Cynthia's Creations. Cynthia? Daniel's Cynthia? Is this what she does for living? A line of gift products? Odd that I've never thought to ask what she does.

I forfeit the nicety of unwrapping the tissue paper inside, just rip. The figs look delicious, golden brown, all neatly stacked in two rows. My stomach rumbles again at the waft of heady spice. I pull out a fig, it's stickier than I expect, coating my fingers. The bite is spongey, chewy, Mmm. But they're too rich as an appetiser, so I suck my fingers clean, tuck the rest away and brush my teeth.

***

"You look nice," Daniel says, as I enter the lounge room.

I blush. Dammit. "Thanks. Don't look so bad yourself."

I'm on the verge of apologising for taking too long, when he smiles – slight, unsure. Vulnerability?

"Do you mind walking?" he asks. "It's a clear night, and I could do with a bit of a leg stretch."

I glance at my sandals. I've been living in low heels or flats up here – such a relief to be comfortable. Back in Melbourne, Andreas would have expected the works: stilettos, tight dress, make-up. Trophy wife.

Daniel raises a palm. "If you'd prefer to drive, we can. That hill is a bit of a bitch to walk back up."

"Tell me about it. I tried to ride a bike up it. Remember?"

He narrows his eyes.

"The day of my interview?"

"Sorry, I … didn't take much in that day." He taps the side of his head.

We move out to the porch, setting off the security light and scuttling a couple of geckos on the walls. Within seconds, sweat prickles my nose. "Oof. Doesn't get much cooler in the evenings, does it?"

"Not this time of year."

While Daniel is busy locking up, I take the moment to remove my wrap and fold it into my handbag. Practical is one thing. Dying for a cause is another.

We stroll down the driveway and out onto the footpath. Night sprinklers from the neighbours' properties spray fine mist, refreshing and cooling our skin. A heady, sweet smell drifts from the foliage above as we wander under a tree with dangling, leaf-like yellow-green flowers.

"What is that?" I ask. "It smells gorgeous. Like ... jasmine?"

"Ylang-ylang."

"Really? How do you know that?"

Daniel shrugs. "Can't a man know these things?"

I smirk. "I wouldn't think a high-flying businessman who locks himself in his office all day would have time to smell the roses. Let alone ylang-ylang."

"Firstly, I'm not high-flying. I just inherited my father's business and happen to be good at running it. Secondly ... you got me. Cynthia's an aromatherapist. She was always pointing out trees and plants and expecting me to know what they were. Most of the time, I got them wrong, but that one's pretty distinguishable."

Cynthia? A healer? Have I got the woman entirely wrong? "Evelyn gave me a box of spiced figs with Cynthia's branding. Is that part of her business?"

Daniel frowns. "Not that I'm aware of. Huh. Maybe it's something new."

The ylang-ylang scent wafts over us again. I breathe deep. "Mmm, it's smells like ... like honey tastes."

"You know it's used as an aphrodisiac?" he says.

There's no hint of sleaziness in his tone, but I find myself increasing my pace. "Maybe we should get a move on. I'm hungry."

⬥

A million birds flutter and twitter in the massive tree growing next to the main street curb. I have put my hands over my ears to block the shrill cacophony until we've passed it.

"Nesting tree," Daniel says. "Don't want to park your car under it."

Further along, he sidesteps a rowdy group of beer-bearing blokes spilling out of a pub. From inside, yells and raucous laughter sound.

"Cane toad racing."

I shudder. "Those big fat ugly things? Don't tell me they have to kiss them before they start?"

"Ah, that would not have a good outcome."

"No princes, then?"

"Well, you might hallucinate one from the toxin."

"Thanks for the heads up."

Further ahead, on the footpath outside a pub, a familiar brindle bundle of fur lies, head resting on paws. "It's Bertie," I say, hurrying forward to give his scruff and chest a good rub. He grins, tongue lolling.

"Davy Jones. How are you, mate? Long time no see." Daniel holds his hand out to Bertie's owner who's emerged from the pub, beer in hand, still singleted, though looking fresher than our first meeting.

"Danny Boy! How the hell are ya? What are ya doing slumming down here amongst us plebs?"

Daniel's laugh is so loud, so genuine, it makes me laugh too. "Get out of here," he says. "How have you been?"

Davy runs a hand through his slick-backed wet hair, then scratches an angry welt on his shoulder. I immediately regret not wearing insect repellent. The mozzies are worse away from the breeze of the hillside or beach.

"Good now," he says. "Did me ankle a while back. Been out of work. Lookin' for a bit now though. You got somethin' for me?"

"Always," Daniel says, patting Davy's shoulder. "Go see the tour office on Monday. We're always looking for reliable crew."

"Will do, young fella."

Daniel turns to me. "This is Georgia. She's working at the house now."

Davy grins like his dog. "The ice cream lady. Bertie never forgets a face."

"Hello, Davy." I offer a hand.

He flips it over and places a swift peck on the back. "Pleasure. Any friend of Danny's is a friend of mine." He winks at Daniel.

We continue past the bank, closed clothing shops and an art gallery selling Indigenous paintings. I can't help smirking as I glance sideways at Daniel.

"Don't even think about it," he says.

I laugh. "Danny Boy? I like it. Is Davy Jones his real name?"

He gives me side-eye. Now I know where Reilly gets it from. "What do you think?"

"He seems a nice fellow. I met him on my first morning. Same pub. Brekky beer in progress." I flinch at my words, what they imply. A judgement from someone least qualified to throw stones.

Daniel stops to glance at a real estate agent's window where rows of pictures display holiday properties for sale. "Can't blame him. Lost his little boy in a boating accident years back. Wife couldn't cope, killed herself."

"Oh god. That's awful."

His jaw works as memories seem to flicker across his face. "Used to head my crew. Knew the waters here like no one else. Such a waste. I doubt he'll ever come back from it."

"But ... you offered him a job."

"I always will, and he'll never show. It's just ... I think he needs to hear it. Like ... some kind of hope to hold on to. Anyway"—he swivels back on course to dinner—"come on, *Ice Cream Lady*. What was that about?"

The restaurant is part indoor – a spacious, yet intimate bar with rows of back-lit gem-coloured bottles lining the walls, low-slung couches and soft-lit lamps – and part outdoor – an open-air dining area, its overhead creamy canvas sails dotted with shadows of fallen leaves, white-clothed tables set for two or four. The whole space has a Balinese feel to it, lots of dark-hued carved wood, torch lights and greenery. Most surprising is a narrow stream that cascades over stone steps, the entire length of the restaurant.

"We're a little early," Daniel says. "Shall we order a drink while we wait?"

"You're the boss."

"Let's forget that for tonight?" He smiles, awkward, then heads off to the bar.

I sink onto a couch overlooking the restaurant area and push away a palm frond that wants to become a hair accessory. Diana Krall's brandy-hued voice wafts from the speakers on the rafters, something about a guy who nearly drove her out of her mind but he can cry her a river now. It's bittersweet, melts me a little, makes me want to close my eyes and wallow in lost opportunities and wasted years.

As Daniel sits opposite, I straighten up and smooth my dress. He hands me a cocktail menu. "What do you feel like? Do you have a favourite?"

I don't hesitate. "Vodka martini, two olives, thanks."

He nods, puckering his mouth as if considering my choice. "Not what I would have guessed but sounds good. I'll make that two."

What would he have guessed? Cosmopolitan? Something with an umbrella?

As he motions to a waiter, his phone rings. He pulls it out of his pocket, looks at the number and frowns. "Sorry, do you mind?"

"Go ahead. I'll order the drinks."

He nods as he rises. "Somchai. What's up?" He heads to the far side of the bar where it's quieter. I watch his body language as he stands – hand on hip, head lowered, shoulders hunched, a grimace. It doesn't look good. It's at least fifteen minutes before he returns, and somehow, in that short time, his face has become gaunt.

"I'm so sorry," he says, reaching for his martini, which has arrived in his absence. He takes a good mouthful.

"Is everything okay?" I ask.

He waves my question off. "Just work. Sorry to keep you waiting."

Keen to lift the atmosphere, I launch into chat about how well Reilly is doing in school, how she's eating much better, how I'm taking her to Kuranda and the butterfly sanctuary for her birthday. Daniel nods, responding with the occasional "mmm" or "uh huh".

Another ten minutes, and I'm looking at a lone olive on a toothpick in the bottom of my glass. Oops. A warm tipsy wave courses through me, the empty stomach kind, but Daniel isn't looking so relaxed – leaning forward, elbows on his knees, head lowered.

Maybe I'm talking too much. "Is something bothering you?" I ask.

He doesn't respond.

"Daniel?" Oh god, he's having one of his episodes. I lean over and touch his knee. "Daniel? Are you okay?"

"Mmm?" He looks up, chewing the side of his thumb.

"Everything alright?"

He straightens, picks up his glass and drains it, then motions to a passing waiter. "Same again, thanks."

I think about objecting, for propriety's sake, but lick my lips. "You scared me. I thought you might be ..."

"Ah no, sorry." He pinches the bridge of his nose, as if he has a headache. "I need to go back to Thailand."

"But it's Reilly's birthday on Tuesday. She'll be devastated, especially after being at her mother's for the weekend." I purse my lips. I've been good at keeping my mouth shut about their family affairs so far. Must be the alcohol.

He rubs his chin. "Yeah, well, we all have to do things we don't like sometimes."

I fall quiet as I consider his words. Truthful, but also hurtful to a young girl who's keyed up about her birthday. "Do you mind if I ask what's so pressing?"

"Hmm?"

"What's so urgent?"

"What? It's really none of your business."

Ouch. I sit back, hold up my hands. "You're right. I just thought, I'll need to explain to Reilly why you aren't here. She's really been looking forward to—"

He catches himself, shakes his head. "Sorry, sorry. It's ... I told you about Somchai, right? My project manager? The one who was injured?"

"You did. Is he okay? I hope he's not hurt again."

"He's recovering. But it's looking like his injuries weren't accidental. He found out the site manager's been hiring cheap labour – underpaid refugees forced to live in disgusting conditions. That's not what my company is about. I need to fix this."

"That's awful. Those poor people."

"It makes me sick to my stomach. And it's putting the whole damned project at risk."

"I'm glad you're doing something about it. My ex would have bulldozed his way over there, sacked the project manager, given the site manager a raise, then visited a strip club. All in one day."

"Sounds like a nice guy. Still around?"

Tingles fly through my chest. I pick up the olive from my glass, suck it off the toothpick and chew. "Not if I can help it."

He holds my gaze, waiting, as if deciding ... "There's something else. I uh ... I don't know why I'm telling you this, but ... I'm also having some trouble with my board of directors. There's talk of a no-confidence vote because of my condition. I could lose my seat, my own company. I'm hoping if I spend some time on the scene with them, in Sydney, and if the medical trial works ... well, the long and short of it is, I hate to put pressure on you ..."

I take a moment to digest this. "I'm not against the idea, I guess I'm more worried about Margie's reaction. She didn't seem that pleased when I mentioned my possible permanency to her."

"Ah, damn. I'm creating a mess here, aren't I?"

"It's not your fault. It's a convergence of circumstances."

"Maybe I should speak with Margie myself?"

"I think she deserves that."

"Right you are. I kind of thought she might want to retire soon."

"Better not to make assumptions."

"True."

"Sooo," I say. "Has Cynthia planned anything for Reilly's birthday?"

"Sure. A Sunday afternoon tea party for her friends next weekend – that's *Cynthia's* friends and *my* weekend with Reilly. Cynthia expects me to come. I feel obligated to be there, for Reilly's sake, since I'm going away for a few days, but"—he sucks in a breath, collecting himself—"you know Cynthia. Well ... I guess you don't yet, but I'm not sure I'll be able to leave her house without committing murder."

I chuckle. "It's just one afternoon. You can be civil for a few hours, can't you?"

He shakes his head, looks toward the bar, perhaps eager for our drink order. "You don't know her. That woman could make a pope swear." He gives me a hangdog look, all big, pleading eyes. "I know you're already doing me a huge favour tonight, but I don't suppose you—"

I hold both my hands up. "Nooo. I'm not going into the lion's den with you."

"It would only be for a couple of hours. I hate the thought of being alone with a bunch of her cosmetically modified crew. They'll flay me alive. It's nauseating."

"What's nauseating, darling?" A woman hovers behind him, placing her hands on his shoulders, massaging him. "Oooh, too tense."

Daniel shrugs forward, pulling away from her, as if she's grabbed him with sharpened claws. Only her fingernails aren't clawed; they're neat, clear and shiny, kind of like the rest of her, from the short funky blond bob, to her slender hips.

The woman laughs and moves around the couch, carrying an aura of self-importance, so tangible it might be displacing air. She eases onto the couch beside me. "You must be the new nanny." Her dress is off-the-shoulder, simple, perhaps linen. Somehow un-creased, even in this heat. She smiles, almost warmly, and it's now I recognise her from Reilly's photo: Cynthia.

I give a little wave. "Hi, I'm—"

Daniel stands. "What are you doing here? And where's Reilly?"

Cynthia holds my gaze as she answers, looking me up and down. "Babysitter."

"You insist on having her on your rostered weekend, yet you hire a babysitter?"

She pouts. Actually pouts. "It's Stuart's and my anniversary. He's buying me dinner."

Daniel almost chokes. "*Anniversary?*"

Cynthia flicks something imaginary off her skirt, then looks up coyly. "Jealous? It's six months since we met."

Daniel sits again as the waiter interrupts with our drinks. He asks Cynthia if she'd like anything. She waves him off.

"Ah, excuse me," I call the waiter back.

He hesitates.

"What's this?" My glass is filled with something golden. A light layer of froth on top with a pretty piece of burnt pineapple.

Cynthia touches my arm. "Try it," she says. "It's a Pineapple Persuasion. Call it a welcome gift from me."

I'm not sure whether to be annoyed or grateful. She hasn't messed with Daniel's drink. Is that telling? I choose grace. "That's kind of you." I sip. "Mmm. Tangy but sweet. It's got an overtone of something ... spicy."

"Ginger," she says, "lime, vodka. The nutmeg on top was my idea."

"Yes, that's it." I sip again. "It's good. That reminds me. Evelyn gave me a box of your spiced figs. They're really good."

She bows her head, places her hands in a namaste position. "Of course." It only lasts a second before she turns to Daniel. "Have you taken care of that Police Check I asked for?"

I suck in a breath, look sideways at Daniel.

He's focusing on his martini, looking as if he'd like to grab the glass and down it. But when he speaks, he's calm, words evenly paced and articulated. "Have you signed the divorce papers?"

She smirks. "This is our daughter's welfare we're talking about."

Daniel's hands tighten on his knees, flesh fading to white. "Exactly."

Cynthia turns her focus back to me. "Drink up, nanny."

Like an obedient child, I pick up my drink. If I finish it quickly, will she leave? It's only a small serving. I take a large sip.

"Enjoying life in my house, nanny?"

I'm proud that I manage not to choke. "It's a beautiful house. Easy to feel at home."

"Well, yes, you've virtually taken up residence."

"I think you mean 'literally' – *literally* taken up residence."

Her eyes narrow a fraction, hardly noticeable, but satisfying. She bites back. "Loving the hair by the way. A little bland perhaps. Better get those roots attended to."

My hand flies to my scalp. "But I only just—" What a troll.

"I see he's moved you on to the business dinners. I hope you're not expecting anything more performance wise." She touches his thigh. "Darling isn't able to deliver."

Daniel doesn't react, doesn't make eye contact. God! Even if she hates him, if that's true, it's an exquisitely cruel thing to say. How I'd love to tackle this cow to the ground.

"That's enough, Cynthia," Daniel says quietly.

I can't help myself – I swallow the rest of my drink, run a finger around the rim, collecting froth remnants, then look Cynthia in the eye. "Oh, I don't know. I don't have any complaints so far." I slowly slide my finger between my lips then pull it out, sucking. "Maybe it just takes the right persuasion." *Who even am I?* I daren't look at Daniel.

Cynthia's smile stiffens. "I'm parched. Love a champagne. Would you mind, nanny? I need a moment alone with my husband." She stands to let me pass, as if dismissing me.

Husband?

Daniel clears his throat. "Georgia." His right eye twitches. "I'm really sorry. Would you mind giving us a minute?"

I grit back humiliation, can hardly speak as I pick up my purse and stand. A flash of an idea – to elbow Cynthia in the gut as I pass – tempts me. "Sure. I need to go to the ladies anyway."

Before I've taken more than a couple of steps, Cynthia calls out. "Nanny." I turn, and she beckons with a finger. Do I keep walking? Ignore her? That would be childish, wouldn't it? I return to her. She leans in and whispers. "Your tag is sticking out, sweetheart."

I'm a puzzled deer, stuck in her headlights. She spins me around, takes a second to tuck in the label on the back of my dress – if it really was sticking out – then leans in close to my ear. "We both know nothing's happening in the bedroom department." She pats my butt. "There's a good girl. Off you go."

I spin back, mouth open to ... curse her? I don't know. But she's already seating herself next to Daniel, done with me. I detour to the bar, plonk onto a stool. Rage, humiliation coursing through me. "Long Island Iced Tea. Stat."

Diana's now crooning about lips she longs to kiss and how she has never known the art of making love. Her words, her melancholy tone, seep into a bruised part of me.

"No, wait, sorry. Vodka. Double. No … mineral water. Please." And screw Cynthia's champagne. She can sit on a bottle of it for all I care.

I'm feeling a little woozy.

Daniel orders wine to accompany our meals, but I can't. Just can't. I don't know what's wrong with me. It's as if I'm looking through a vapour of rising heat. I don't understand. Alcohol never affects me like this. It's excruciating, exhausting, trying to look interested in his clients while I'm so fuzzy.

And Daniel is right: Angelo's wife, Gabby, although charming and full of camaraderie, doesn't speak much English, and I don't speak Italian, so Daniel has to constantly translate back and forth, while I attempt to interpret meaning through tones and gestures. It doesn't help that I keep glancing over Daniel's shoulder to where Cynthia sits two tables away, directly in my line of sight. She doesn't make eye contact, not once, never acknowledges me, yet it's as if I'm an addict, fascinated by something so Medusa-like I can't look away. Can a person be that nasty? *Can they?* I mentally shake my head, remind myself who I've just left behind in Melbourne. Andreas and Cynthia would make a perfect pair. Perhaps I should suggest it to get him off my tail.

As the evening wears on, the conversation turns to business and the translating becomes less frequent. Gabby and I attempt to converse, repeating and rephrasing, adding in hand gestures and facial expressions, as if that will make our meaning clearer to each other. Finally, Gabby pulls out her phone and shows me pictures of her family, pets and home. Relief. A universal understanding. She points to me. I shake my head and shrug.

"No photos."

She's taken aback. "Perché?"

I hold my hands out wide, as if I'm showing her how big a fish I caught. "Long story."

She looks sympathetic, glances at Daniel, then pats my arm. What is she thinking? That Daniel won't let me have a phone?

I hold up my water glass. "Cheers."

She reciprocates with her wine. "Salute."

We clink, drink, sigh then sink back in our chairs, resigned to waiting for the evening to be over.

A movement catches my eye. Cynthia's leaving. She stands, doesn't bother pushing in her chair – of course. Finally, finally, she looks at me. Pointedly. A little smile. Sympathy? Oooh, I so want to hold up my middle finger.

The waiter approaches, offering dessert, a cheese platter, coffee, port. I sag. Please, no. Angelo pats his stomach, shakes his head. Gabby does the same. "No grazie."

Soon, we're standing, gathering our personal effects, nodding our fulfilment of the meal. A dizziness, like the rush of air before a subway train, washes over me. I grasp the back of my chair, wait for it to pass. Thankfully, it's short lived.

Out on the sidewalk, in the heavy, not-so-fresh air, Daniel and the couple continue to chat in Italian. A word catches my ear several times – something like "chiclonay". After an eternity, Daniel shakes hands with Angelo, while Gabby and I exchange kisses on both cheeks. Angelo takes my hand and kisses the back of it. "Bella, bella."

They head off, and I almost swoon at being released to head home, to crash into bed, bury my head in my pillow. I've never felt so, so tired. So blurry.

44

Andreas

Katie called me while I was on the train home from work. My birthday had come around again.

"Tomorrow," she said. "We're getting you out of there. I've booked your plane ticket."

I thought she was joking. She wasn't.

"New Year's period. Travel will be crazy busy. There's no way he could track you, even if he uses his mates."

I listened, face flushing, heart rushing.

As the express train flew past station after station, I sat elated, surging with adrenaline. I let myself imagine a free life – without a stomach cramping from stress every time I heard a car pull up; without a demeaning stream of ridicule over my cooking, without being told I was hopeless, a piece of rubbish no one would want; without the threat of a fist in front of my face; without him.

I couldn't.

As the train drew closer to my station, I panicked, became angry. Didn't I have enough people in my life pushing me around? Didn't Katie know he would sense it? That there was no way he would let it happen?

We're only halfway up the hill. I'm sure I shouldn't be sweating this much. How long does it take to get used to this damned weather? Distraction, I need distraction. "What does 'chiclonay' mean?"

"Sorry?"

"Chiclonay. Angelo ... you guys kept saying it, outside the restaurant."

"Oh! Ciclone. Cyclone."

"Should I be worried?"

"No. We were talking about a low-pressure system, a tropical low, out on the Coral Sea. Happens regularly this time of year. It'll probably fizzle out."

I stop, lean forward, hands on my knees. The air swims, wavers. Daniel bends to pick up my purse, fallen from my shoulder.

"Hey, you okay?"

I shiver, my stomach flirting with nausea. "Is it cold or just me?"

"Uh ... just you. Is your wrap in here?"

I nod, and he pulls the wrap from my purse, drapes it over my shoulders. I pull it tight. How can I be cold and sweaty at the same time? Not good.

"This is my fault," he says. "I shouldn't have ordered so much alcohol."

I straighten, wave him off. "I'm a big girl. But I don't think that's it. Maybe it's"—I want to say it feels like being stoned, except heavier, but that's probably not something a nanny should be saying—"something I ate."

"Perhaps."

"So," I say, desperate to distract myself. "Cynthia's a piece of work."

His laugh is sharp. "She was in fine form tonight."

"I'm impressed how restrained you were."

"Pfft. Years of practice."

"It can't have always been that way."

It's bad of me, but I'm super curious as to what Cynthia meant by him not delivering in the bedroom. Did she mean he didn't attend to her needs, or he couldn't "deliver"? I can't help feeling she was fishing. Wanting to know if it was just her.

Daniel screws up his nose, rubs it. "No. It wasn't."

"Sorry. I'm prying again. You don't have to—"

He pauses and turns to me. "Look, I know Margie and I put her down. A lot. She's painful. But there's still a human being underneath. She tries. She could have just walked away and had nothing to do with Reilly."

Before I can respond, a wave of weariness seeps through my muscles and my stomach cramps. I bend, folding my arms across my middle.

Daniel grips my arm. "You okay? You don't look good."

The pain eases, and I take a breath, move on. "Tell me more."

He hesitates. "You sure?"

"Yeah, yeah. Probably wind. Keep going."

"She was excited before the birth. Had the baby shower, all the baby catalogues, the prenatal workshops. But after Reilly's birth, her enthusiasm evaporated. I couldn't understand. The second Reilly's tiny fingers curled around mine, I was totally, irrevocably in love. But Cynthia said she felt nothing, empty."

"That's so sad. We had a couple of kids at the kindergarten whose mothers didn't bond with them. The mothers were plagued with guilt, and the children were so starved of affection, they'd try to go home with anyone who show interest in them."

"Yes, we thought it was an attachment issue or the baby blues. Cynthia wasn't sleeping, hardly ate. Spent days in bed watching nothing on television. We thought she'd move through it, past it, if we gave her enough support, but when Margie came home to find her screaming at Reilly in her cot ... it shook us. Turns out she had post-natal depression. We got her professional help, but she never seemed to recover."

"That must have been awful. For everyone."

He nods. Takes a breath. Unburdened.

"And now she blames you," I say.

"Well, I could have done better."

The gravel slides beneath my feet. I yell, face plant.

"Georgia! Are you okay?"

I slowly push myself up to sitting. The effort makes me sag. I could stay here in the dirt and cry.

Daniel squats, offers his hand. For a moment, I stare at his fine, long fingers. I haven't held a kind hand in a long time. I pull my wrap tighter, bolster myself, about to refuse, but as soon as I try to stand, my back screams. "Ow! Shit." I grab his arm.

He places his other hand under my elbow, firm and comforting, not possessive, insistent. As soon as I'm upright, the pain dissipates. I let go of him.

"Okay?" he asks. "Looks like you grazed your leg." He bends and brushes me off.

"I'm fine. Just jarred my back again," I say, a swell of shame adding to my nausea. I'm reminded of my first day at high school – tripping up the steps in front of all my peers, the concerned faces staring down at me, the smirks. "I feel like such an idiot."

"Happens to the best of us," he says. "Smell that?" He points up.

It's the ylang-ylang again. Only its scent is headier, the smell syrupy enough to taste. A few insects flutter about the bracts of dangling yellow flowers.

"Divine. Are they butterflies? At night?" I ask.

"Moths. They help pollinate."

"You *were* paying attention."

He reaches up and pulls down a branch so I can get a closer look.

"They're like straggly, long-legged starfish," I say. The smell. Oh, the smell. Intoxicating. It's almost enough to make me forget how awful I feel.

"Not far now," he says as we push on.

Finally, *finally*, we reach the porch. I'm sweating worse, still shivering.

"You really don't look good. I think I should call a doctor."

I can hardly answer, I'm shivering so much. "N-n-no .... I just n-n-need to lie down."

He unlocks the door and helps me inside. "I'll make you some sweet tea. I'm sure Margie will have something stowed ... maybe ginger."

"Maybe a bucket too."

"Georgia, Georgia, wake up." Daniel is trying to pull me up from my en suite floor.

"I'm okay," I mutter, grabbing the sink for support.

"Yes, I can see that."

"Wait." He flushes the toilet – I hate to think what he's seen in there – puts the lid down and sits me on it. "Feel better?" he asks.

I nod. "Strangely enough."

He runs a face washer under the tap and wipes my face. I attempt to take the cloth from him, but he eases my hand away. "Let me."

"Fill your boots."

"Sorry?"

"Go for it. Have at it."

A giggle burbles up inside me, and for a moment, I consider grabbing the cloth in my teeth and wrestling it away from him, like a dog. *What the heck is wrong with me?*

"Okaaay. Let's get you to bed."

As he lifts me to my feet, his arm around my shoulders, I see myself in the mirror. Thank god I wore my hair up and didn't get a vomit shampoo. This makes me laugh too. Crazy. Eventually, my head clears enough to allow me to stand on my own. "I can do it."

Daniel insists on keeping a hand under my elbow. "I'm calling you a doctor."

An illogical guilt seizes me – as if I'm a kid caught swilling alcohol from their parents' drinks cabinet. "No, don't. I'll be fine. Just ... need sleep. Oh wait!" We're almost at the bathroom door when a gurgle cramps my gut. *Oh god, no. Please no.* "You have to leave me," I say.

"I'm not leaving you. You're in no state—"

I spin around yank up the toilet seat, pull down my pants just in time. "Oh god," I groan as my bowels empty themselves in a rush. "Please, please go."

He backs out the door. "I'm just outside. Let me know when you've ... finished." He pulls the door to.

Time warps. The room spins. Stench. Oh, the stench. Thank god the wash basin is within vomiting distance.

———◇———

"There's hot tea there." He points to my side table. "And a bucket there." He points to a red plastic tub. "In case." He sits me on the edge of my bed, then kneels to remove my sandals. I look down at the top of his head and have an insane urge to knead his thick hair, like a cat padding into a sheepskin. Am I stoned?

He's done, so I flop back onto the bed. "Ohhh. Sudden moves. Not good." I roll over onto my side, curled up like a kitten. "Purrr." He pulls the covers over me and tucks them under my chin.

"How's your back?"

"My back?" I giggle again. "Tell me a story." I *am* stoned.

He moves to the French doors, where moonlight is glaring in disapproval, and adjusts the plantation shutters downward.

"My retinas thank you."

He returns to me, brushes hair from my face. "You're sweaty. Are you still cold?"

I'm afraid to nod in case he suggests I drag myself out of bed for a hot shower, but an involuntary shiver gives me away.

"I'd make you a hot water bottle, but I don't think we have any ... not in this climate. Oh wait, Margie gave me a wheat bag once for a sore shoulder. I'll have a look for it. Drink your tea while it's hot, if you can. It's sweet. Might help—"

I lurch upright. He's quick to grab the plastic tub and shove it onto my lap. *Oh god. Oh god.* My stomach cramps with each retch. It goes on and on. Nothing but bile – my dinner has already gone down the toilet – but still my body spasms, until, spent, I flop back again. "I'm sorry, I'm sorry." I'm crying now, little girl sobs.

"Shhh."

***

When I come to, Daniel is wiping a cool cloth over my face. "How long?" It feels like hours, but my tea is still sitting on my side table, and the moon is still outside the window, its light cut into slivers by the shutters.

"Not long. Here, sip this. Wash your mouth out."

He hands me a glass of water, then holds up the plastic tub – rinsed and smelling of lemons. My urge is to get up, brush my teeth, but I can hardly hold the glass.

"Want some tea?" he asks as I ease back into my pillows.

"Uh uh," I mumble. "Not sure it will stay down. So tired ..."

***

I wake to the hazy glow of the television with the sound low. The whopper headache and spinning room I expected is only a dull, heavy ache. Next to me, Daniel lies on top of my sheets, his head resting in the crook of his arm, dark curls clumped with sweat. His eyes are closed, and I want to touch the lashes that almost touch his cheeks. I stare as he softly breathes, his chest rising and falling under his white t-shirt. When did he take his shirt off?

It's been a long time since I felt comfortable enough in my own skin to relax next to a man and not want to head straight for the shower and wash the stink of sex off my body. Wait ... did we? No. I'd remember that. And he's fully dressed. I lift the bed covers. I'm wearing a t-shirt. How ... do I even want to know?

His face is beautiful in sleep, soft, trusting, delicately shadowed ... reminds me of another face. Seems so long ago now, quiet voices, lying close, touching each other's face, confessions in the dark, tears even, revelations of his battered childhood. How could someone so broken in my arms, so needful of love, so tender, fulfil his own father's legacy? How could he not see that coming and want to turn it around? To just make it stop. Was it all lies? A ruse to get me to fall? Was it a long-game plan to entrap me? I'd give anything to go back to before it all began, to tell him what was to come, to warn him of himself. Everyone deserves a second chance.

God. How stupid. What a cliché. No. I would walk away if I had a do-over.

Was Daniel capable of turning like that? Were all men? I can't let myself believe it. Can't let it ruin me.

He stirs, opens his eyes, looks startled, then smiles. "Oops."

My heart. I'm lost.

"Oops." I smile back, can't hold his gaze, so turn to the television.

"Oh, sorry. Did I wake you?" He hunts around for the remote, aims it at the television.

I pull his arm back. "No, leave it on."

"You sure?"

I nod. "I know this film," I murmur. "It's Pinkie. Um ... Richard ... Richard ..."

In the grainy black and white movie, two youngsters stroll along a boardwalk. The camera pans to what looks like a phonebooth.

"Brighton Rock," I say. "Richard Attenborough. I always get him and his brother mixed up."

"How are you feeling?"

"Like bus roadkill."

"That bad?"

A small laugh. "No. Not really. The nausea has passed."

"Can I get you anything?" he asks.

"No. I'm fine. Oh, look, can you turn the volume up?" I push myself up a little, propping against my pillows. Daniel does the same.

"This is crucial, this scene. You gotta hear what Pinkie says."

Daniel presses the remote.

Pinkie, the smooth criminal, is in the booth now. The camera shows a close-up of his newlywed wife. She's just a girl, all doe-eyed and naive in her polka dot frock and prim white collar, watching her guy from outside of the booth.

"It's not a phonebooth," I whisper. "It's a recording booth. It makes records."

The camera closes in on Pinkie recording his message. He says he knows she wants to hear him say I love you, but he doesn't love her. He thinks she's a slut. He hates her and wishes she'd go back to where she came from.

"That's awful," Daniel says.

"But you gotta wait till the end. There's a twist."

We lie like this, comfortable, cosy, engrossed. And I turn to watch Daniel's face, right at the end, when the girl plays her record for the first time. Her guy is now dead – thrown himself over a cliff rather than be arrested – and this is all she has left of him. The recording starts, we hear his voice, wait for the inevitable vitriol, but the record skips and repeats over and over: "I love you ... I love you ... I love you ..."

Daniel jerks his head back, as if he's been slapped. "No! That's not right. That's worse."

I laugh, pleased I've got the reaction I was waiting for. "It's a killer, isn't it?"

"Devastating."

"It was never going to work though."

"Because they were too young?"

"No. Pinkie was asexual."

"What?"

"Asexual. Not physically attracted to her."

"Yes, I know what asexual means, but you can still be attracted to someone if you're asexual. You can still have a relationship. Care for someone."

Something in Daniel's tone unnerves me. "I suppose so—"

He seems to retract into himself, tighten. "Not suppose so. You can."

"I never said you couldn't. I just ..." Me and my big mouth. Such a klutz. What do I know of sexuality beyond my own screwed-up hetero relationship? Have I offended him? Is ... is *this* what Cynthia meant?

I search his face in the dimness. Something flickers in the shine of his eyes. He's doing that staring thing again. Unnerving. So hard not to look away. But I hold his gaze. He *wants* me to ask.

"Are you—"

"Well, good morning to you too." Margie stands in the doorway. I'm sure both Daniel and I have our mouths hanging open. "I'll put the kettle on, shall I?"

Is that disappointment in her voice? Judgement? How much has she heard? What is she thinking?

She doesn't hang about.

Daniel sighs, gets off the bed and moves to the plantation shutters, snaps them open, jolting light into my pained eyes. "You should probably stay in bed," he says.

"What are you, my dad?" It's a joke, borne of shock, but it carries petulance.

He doesn't answer. Doesn't look at me.

"Thank you. For last night," I call as he exits. *Oh geez, Georgia. Shut your stupid mouth.* I do as I'm told, sinking into my body, waiting for whatever is to come. A child banished to bed for complaining about a stomach-ache because she doesn't want to go to school.

46

Andreas

I was sure he could tell – just by the way I was walking to the car, as if I'd forgotten how to put one foot in front of the other.

As I opened the car door, music blasted from the radio. He barely waited for me to get in before taking off, banging his fist on the steering wheel in time with the bass.

"Katie wants me to stay at hers tomorrow ..."

"What?" He turned the music down.

"For my birthday ... tomorrow. Katie and I ... we'll see a movie."

"Whatever." He turned the music back up.

I sneaked a finger up to block one ear.

"Celebrate with your shitty sister," he yelled. "I've got plans."

My hope sprouted a leaf.

Throughout dinner, he continued to stay in his own world. He'd bought himself a pair of noise-cancelling earbuds. Had he bought them for my birthday, then decided to keep them? He knocked his knife on the table between bites, head nodding to his beats.

47

"Morning again." Margie stands over me with a breakfast tray.

Must have dozed off again. I blink a few times, cough to clear my clagginess, tongue a scratchy sour sponge. "You're back early." Obvious statement of the year, but what else is there to say?

"Black tea and dry toast."

"Thank you." A sharp twinge grabs my back as I struggle to push myself up against the pillows. A flicker of memory: gravel, slipping, embarrassment. "Is Evelyn okay? Has something happened?"

She places the tray on my lap. "She's fine. More pressing engagement here."

"What engagement?"

She doesn't answer but lays a napkin across my chest.

"Margie, you weren't due back for another two weeks."

"Well, someone has to collect Reilly, and you're apparently in no state."

"You ... oh damn." I slap my forehead, then the side of my face, trying to smack away the fogginess. But, what? Does she have ESP, so flew back early?

She heads toward the French doors. "Might open your patio doors, it's a little ... fuggy in here." She leans to pick a shirt off the back of my desk chair. Daniel's. It looks damp. Another memory triggers: me throwing up on him. Oh god.

Do I explain? Is she going to keep dancing around the elephant in the room?

"Margie. Daniel and I ... we didn't—'

"I know."

Knows what?

She heads into my en suite "I hear you had quite the night," she calls.

"Not really."

She returns, arms laden with vomit-stained towels and my soiled dress.

"Don't you think I know Daniel better than you?" she says. "Better than anyone? Get some toast into you."

I pick up a triangle of toast. She's cut the crusts off.

"Then let me know if you need help showering."

Seriously? Infantilising? If she thinks nothing happened between Daniel and me, then why is she so mad? Something bad must have gone down in India. "Margie. Tell me what's happened."

Her look stops me dead. "Apart from finding out our nanny is an alcoholic and inveigling her way into the household?" She shakes her head. "I should have listened to Evelyn."

My face blooms with heat. Guilty-not-guilty heat. My throat tightens.

"Well, dear, you have a day in bed to yourself. Maybe we'll see you tonight ... if you've sobered enough."

"What? Wait ..."

She doesn't.

Goddammit!

I push the breakfast tray aside and swing my legs off the bed to stand, but my back has other plans. "Fuuuck!" I ease my butt back onto the bed, take a couple of deep breaths, then try again. Nope. Not happening. What do I do now? Stay in my room like the naughty little girl she thinks I am? No way. I roll sideways, bend my knees a little and push up. Bearable. Okay, let's go. Let's go tell her what's what.

But, ugh, she's right. It stinks in here. *I stink.*

The hot shower provides some relief. Not much. I opt for my usual beach wrap for economy of movement, less pain. As I finish tying the material across my chest, the smell of bacon makes my nose twitch. I follow the trail of deliciousness.

"Got some extra for this bedraggled soul?"

Margie turns, not quite hiding her surprise. "Of course. They say a good greasy feed is the best hangover cure."

I flinch. "Not hung over, Margie. And I'm not trying to inveigle anything. Especially, if I'm not welcome ... not that it would be any of your business anyway." Good one. How to win her over.

She looks back at her pan, shrugs. "Okay."

"It's true."

"Hold it well, then, do you?"

"It was something I ate."

"Uh huh."

"Margie, it's important to me that you believe me."

She puts down her spatula and looks at me. Hard. She's never used this look on me before. It's disconcerting. Now I know why she's been the house matriarch for so long.

"What?" I say. "You can ask Daniel. He ordered the alcohol last night. I stopped after two, switched to water."

She blinks, says nothing, then moves over to the cupboard where the recycling bin is kept. She opens it, pulls out an almost empty vodka bottle. Lemon flavoured.

I'm not sure if it's anger or mortification that strikes me mute, eyes and mouth wide open like a groper fish. I suck in a breath. "You went through my things? While I was sleeping?"

"No, your washing basket. Just now. Underneath your used towels."

"That's an invasion of privacy, Margie."

She replaces the bottle and returns to the bacon, which is spitting its own disapproval. "You know where Evelyn and I met?" she asks.

I clear my throat, tight with indignation. "No."

"AA meeting."

"You're a—"

"Not me. I was there to support my husband at the time."

"But Margie, I'm not—"

"Asking for help is nothing to be ashamed of."

"I'm *not* an alcoholic."

"Tch." A that's-what-they-all-say attitude radiates from her, like heat from one of her hot pies straight from the oven.

My chagrin makes me want to stamp my foot. "I'm not! I never drink when I'm driving, when I'm minding Reilly, running errands. I take my responsibilities seriously."

"You know alcoholics don't necessarily drink every hour, every day?"

A sliver of guilt tightens in my gut. Is she going to tell Daniel?

"Well, all that aside, I'm packing some grab-and-go bags. There's a cyclone developing off the coast. You might want to do the same."

"Daniel said it was just a tropical low."

Margie picks up tongs and transfers the bacon to a plate lined with paper towel, fat slipping from the valleys of crunchy meat. "Yes, but things change overnight, don't they?"

"Margie ..." Something strange on her arm catches my eye. I move closer, reach to touch it. "Is that a bruise?"

She grabs her blouse sleeve, pulls it lower on her arm, snaps at me. "It's nothing. I bumped it. None of your concern. How do you want your eggs?"

This is not the Margie I know. And her rejection hurts. I've been stupid. Let myself become attached. I want to hit back, to hurt her too.

"Eggs?" she repeats, not bothering to make eye contact.

"Umm ... fried is fine."

"I'll bring it out to the patio. Daniel's having his in his office."

I've been dismissed, left to wrestle my shame. My back twinges as if prodding my guilt. Deserved or not.

By morning, the cyclone is officially a Category 1 and has a name: Yasi.

48

Andreas

He wanted sex.

I didn't fight it, closed my eyes, biding the minutes of heavy disgust, while I clung to a glint of dazzling hope, as if looking past his rutting and panting to a keyhole through which blazed the sun.

And on the other side, deliverance.

Afterward, in the bathroom, my reflection was a sickly ghost, mouth turned down against reasoning with the unreasonable, pupils dilated like a scared cat.

But scared cats claw and tear their way to freedom.

49

Margie stands behind me in the post office queue. I can't help but think she's come to keep an eye on me. She didn't trust me to drop Reilly at school for her first day back this morning. I'm kind of glad. I probably shouldn't be driving.

My phone rings in my pocket. "Yes? ... Really? Look, I'd love to, but"—I pause to check the length of the queue. Too long. It's not moving—"I can't right now. Perhaps in half an hour? ... Okay, I understand ... No, it's okay. Tomorrow is fine."

"Another hot date?" Margie asks.

I want to bite back. I don't deserve her jibe, but it touches some shameful place in me, some ingrained bruise. As if to provoke me, my back twinges vehemently. "Physio. Last-minute cancellation. They're asking if I can come right now."

Margie huffs at my grimace. "Look at you. Give me that." She grabs the small padded envelope I've been almost crushing in my hand and drops it into her carry bag, along with Daniel's mail. "Go. There's no point the two of us standing in line, and you're obviously in pain."

"No, Margie. Give it back. Please. I need to see it posted."

"Oh, come on. I can handle it. I'm not going to lose it between here and the counter."

"Margie! You don't understand."

She softens, eyes narrowing. "What is it?"

I lean in, my voice cracking as I whisper, "It's his ring."

A flicker of understanding in her eyes – the wisdom of a thousand battered women. "Good. Don't want bad karma hanging around you."

"It has to go by registered post. I'm sending it to my sister so she can forward it." My back twinges again as we inch forward. I suck in a breath, try not to grimace.

Margie's hand is firm on my arm. "Georgia. It's okay. You can trust me."

I hesitate, heavy with reluctance. "Well …"

"Go!" she says. "At the rate this queue is moving, you'll be back before I reach the counter. She nudges me out of the queue. "I'll take care of it. Call me when you're done. I'll come get you."

"Okay."

As I open the door to leave, Evelyn is approaching from across the street. She waves, scoots across the road. I wait to hold the door open for her wheelchair, but I don't need to – she parks the wheelchair outside and stands. On her own. Without help.

"Cat gotcha tongue?" she says, winking.

"Sorry for staring." I shake my head. "I'm just … surprised." I don't tell her I'm mostly surprised by the weight that's fallen off her in only a week. She wasn't that big to start with.

She shrugs, shoos a fly away. "Special magic from the trip. You joining us for lunch back at yours?"

"Umm … not right now, maybe if you're still there when I get back?"

"Sure. I'm staying for a swim afterward."

"Ow." My breath catches. The physio has made me bend forward, flex back, slide my hand down my right side, and it's the left-hand slide that triggers my agony. I gingerly straighten. "It hurts all over, but mainly on the right. Like something's grabbing my lower-middle back."

She asks if I'm okay to climb onto the table. I nod, lie on my stomach.

"Yes, I can feel the inflammation. Subluxation. Really sore, huh?"

"You could say that."

"How did you fall?"

"Don't ask. It's complicated."

"What happened here?" She gently touches my left rib.

"I must have pulled a muscle or something."

"No. I meant here. There's an old bruise." She presses a little harder and pain shoots around to my front."

"Argh."

"Did you break a rib previously? You may have jarred it, or refractured it when you fell. I can organise an X-ray."

"No. That's okay. It happened a few weeks ago."

I close my eyes, bury my face into the towel beneath me. I thought it was gone. Thought the residual evidence had faded – like the bruise on my neck. Thought all that remained was the invisible tension in my sinews. But it seems I have one last echo of his violence.

"Right, well, I'll loosen up your muscles, maybe do a small adjustment. Then it's just pain meds and gentle stretches."

She sets to work, squeezing cool gel onto my skin, then easing her strong fingers into my unyielding shoulders and upper back. Oh, mercy, the sweet, sweet pain. Soon, I'm almost drifting off.

She moves further down, working either side of my spine, moving gently over my sore rib. "How's the pressure?"

"Good."

She spreads more gel, presses and kneads the top of my buttocks. "You know," she says, "they say the lumbar area and sacrum is where we store all our emotions. That back pain can be a symptom of not feeling supported, of fear of loss or fear for survival."

"Mmm hmm." My throat is suddenly so tight, it's all I manage. Either her words or her nurturing touch have drawn tears from me. Soft at first, but then I have to bite down great gulps determined to erupt.

She backs off, leaves one comforting hand on my shoulder as she leans forward. "Georgia, are you okay? Did I hurt you?"

I shake my head, unable to control my wracking body. She places a box of tissues next to me, waits for me to calm. "Georgia, we're done now. I'm going to leave you for a while, give you some space. Take your time, okay?"

Eventually, I emerge, red faced, red eyed and hurting more than when I arrived.

"Do you need a hug?" she asks.

For fuck's sake.

◆

Outside, the footpath has darkened with rain, steam lifting and wafting in eddies as passers-by disturb the lace-like mist hovering over the concrete. I didn't even hear the downpour, too busy with my own to notice. The sky is still roiling, threatening. I dig my phone out of my pocket. It beeps as soon as I turn it on. A message from Margie.

Taking Evelyn home. She's not feeling well. Sorry. Broken glass on kitchen floor. Can you fix?

Of course. Hope she's okay.

Margie's still driving, I imagine. Unable to answer. I'll have to walk back to the house, pick up the Moke to get Reilly.

I stop at the chemist first, stock up on ibuprofen and paracetamol, then start the trek back to the house. A third of the way up the hill, the rain starts again. I have to pause anyway, to catch my breath from the grabby pain. I have time. Reilly won't be out of school for a few more hours. I rest on a moss-strewn log under a Morton Bay fig – the same one that drenched me on my first day – and tears spring with unfinished business. I'm wretched, eyes gritty and sore, my nose stuffy.

The tree shivers warm fat droplets on me, as if trying to comfort me with its own tears. Rivulets of rainwater gather in the red dirt crevices at my feet, platelets in open veins gathering a muddy crimson wash to coat the road, to carry away the hill itself, piece by minuscule piece, until it's exhausted from friction. Like me.

⚬

Daniel's office door is closed. Good. Wouldn't want him to see me in this condition. He'll be busy doing what he can from here to sort out the mess in Thailand. I have to give him props for not booking his flight until tomorrow so he can see Reilly on her birthday.

Margie's left a registered post receipt on the kitchen bench. Bless her for that relief. I wouldn't have blamed her if she'd forgotten.

I should call Katie, let her know the ring is on its way. First, I make myself a peanut butter sandwich and take it to my bedroom. I scrunch my face in expectation of pain as I ease back onto the pillows. It might be my imagination, but my back is already feeling a titch better. Maybe my tears were the release I needed. Or the anti-inflammatories. I doubt the physio treatment would have worked that quickly.

I dial Katie, take a bite of sandwich, not expecting her to answer.

But she does, sounding breathless. "Sis. Everything okay?"

I quickly chew and swallow my mouthful. "Heya. Sure. How's things with you?"

"Good, good. Hang on a mini." The phone muffles for a few seconds, and a door hinge creaks. "Sorry. Hang up. I'll video call you back."

I nearly cry when her face appears on my screen. Her sweet, sweet smile, her calf-like brown eyes, her ever-present long ponytail – now a tousled mess. Mascara is smudged below one eye. She's in her bathroom, sitting on the toilet; I recognise the cracked tile on the wall behind her. She won't get it fixed, says it looks like art – a dead tree in a square snowscape. How contrary to her sterile work environment. I suspect it's a tiny rebellion.

"Did I interrupt something?" I ask.

She laughs, then covers her mouth. "Not something. *Someone*. He's sleeping now. Big night."

"He?"

"Ummm ... can't remember his name. Too drunk."

"Kit!"

"What? We did safe sex."

"How do you know if you were drunk?"

"Um ... evidence."

"Ewww."

"You're such a prude. Oh wait, I remembered his name." She bites her bottom lip, scrunches her nose like Dad used to. "Jackson."

"Jackson? Isn't that ... you're sleeping with your new partner?"

She grins. "Tricky, huh? Anyhoo, wassup?"

I sigh. "Nothing. Just wanted to hear your voice."

I tell her to expect Andreas's ring in the post, how relieved I am it's gone. How my back is killing me, making me a little teary right now.

"Aww, hun, it's just tension. It'll get better with time. Hang tight." She gets up. "I need some water. My throat's as dry as the bottom of a cocky's cage."

I smile at that, a pang of reminiscence – one of Dad's expressions.

The video shudders as Katie leaves the bathroom and moves along the dim hallway – flashes of golden daisies on vintage wallpaper she's restored – white louvres on the loungeroom windows, which glare light as she flips them in passing. In her kitchen now – the collage of travel photos stuck on her fridge. "How's the man?" A tap whines and running water trickles.

I swallow, peanut butter sticky in my throat. "He's gone quiet, thank god. No more texts. Maybe once he gets the ring—"

"Not *that* man."

"Oh."

She swigs her water. "The *other* man."

I fill her in about dinner with the Italians, about meeting Cynthia, then being so ill. A blush heats my face when I reach the part about Daniel taking care of me.

"Holy crap!"

"Uh huh."

"And he held your hair back?"

"And guess what?" I lower my voice to a whisper – silly since he's down the other end of the house. "I woke up next to him." I wait, feeling wicked, but I have a small need to savour, just for a moment, a flicker of her bohemian attitude. Even if it's a false truth. And what are sisters for if not to tease?

Katie is wide-eyed and wide-mouthed. "Way to go! Was it *goood*?"

"Ha!"

"What?"

"I don't think he's interested in women. Or men. Or anyone, really."

"What makes you think that?"

I sift back over my conversation with Daniel, his sudden defensiveness after we'd watched Brighton Rock. "Something he said."

"So ... no sex? At all? You sure?"

I shrug. "No. Well ... I don't know. He's had a child, so he must have had sex. Unless ... I guess they could have gone invitro ... but there's a spectrum to asexuality, like most things in life, so I'm only guessing. But I think ... I think I could ... relate to someone like that."

Katie falls silent, drops her eyes. I can't for the life of me garner what she might be thinking. Would it be wrong to become involved with someone like him because it suited my current state of being? Would that be taking advantage

– even if he was interested? Platonic relationships can still break people.

Katie clears her throat. "Do you think it's wise to get so invested in someone right now?"

"But ... you encouraged me. You said it would be good for me."

"Sex! I was talking about a good shag. Not taking on some damaged dude. Haven't you had enough of them?"

"Kit! He's not damaged, he's—"

"Geez, I'm talking about his brain thing." She sighs, drags a handful of her ponytail into her mouth and chews on it. "I know this is really shallow of me, but I've seen enough patients deteriorate from brain conditions. What if you end up looking after a vegetable? What if he dies?"

I can't believe she's saying this. All her training, her compassion, her dedication to saving lives and this is what she says to me? "Everybody dies," I whisper.

"G, wake up. You want to go from one prison to another?"

A nugget of anger blocks my throat. Anger or ... resentment. "I'm not like you. I can't just use people like that."

She recoils as if I've slapped her.

We stare at each other a moment before I have to look away, bite my lip. "I didn't mean that."

There's an edge to her voice now. "I'm just saying you deserve to be looked after for a while. To have some joy in your life. Some normality."

My heart is a crushed, brittle recyclable container. "No such thing as normal. We're all damaged one way or another." But she's right; it was stupid thinking. I need to shape up. Do my job. It's not like I have real problems. Like Evelyn.

"Ah, sis." Katie's voice breaks. "I wish I could reach out and give you a big hug."

Crap. I'm tearing up now. "I wish you could too."

She sighs, leans into her screen. "G? Don't listen to me. I'm an idiot. I'm the damaged one. You do you."

I nod.

She sends me an air kiss. "Maybe a little affection is all you need right now."

"Maybe."

"Hey!" She bends forward out of camera shot, then straightens with something small and ginger in her hand. "Meet Smudge. Isn't he adorable?" She pushes the kitten's face up close to the phone screen, smooshes its little nose. It mewls.

"Nawww, what a darling. But what about your Kathmandu trip?"

She winks. "That's what Jackson's for."

We hang up, and I grab my pillow, squeeze it to my chest, wishing I had a mum to whinge to. *There, there. It's all going to be okay.* Do grown women ever stop needing their mother? I thought so, when I was younger, when I had to take care of our family and the bitterness of a stolen childhood had held me firm. But now I'm not so sure.

And I think I've ruined my chances with the one friend here who could have been that mother figure. Something has shifted in our household. A sullen shadow is creeping between us all.

By five o'clock, Yasi has become a Category 3.

50

Andreas

I couldn't breathe.

All day at work, everything about me ached.

He would know. Somehow, he would know.

I responded to each of his texts promptly. No chances taken.

By afternoon, I was throwing up. My manager was concerned I might have a bug that would spread to the children. She wanted to send me home.

"No. I can't. I'm fine. Just something I ate last night. It's gone now."

51

This is the coolest part of the day – not yet light enough to turn the headlights off, stars still clinging to the dark-velvet sky, a pink tinge on the horizon hinting at the sun stirring, everything sheened in condensation.

Daniel's eyes are closed, his head lolling in his hand, elbow resting on the convertible's open windowsill. An air of tiredness drags on his face. I'm not sure if he's been avoiding me this last couple of days or if he's been hunkered down with business matters before his trip. Or maybe he's had another episode, brought on by the exhaustion of looking after me. I want to ask but don't want to disturb him. A bump in the road does it for me – slipping his elbow off the sill and making him jerk his head up.

"Sorry," I say.

He breathes deeply, expanding his chest and rolling his shoulders, then rubs his face. "Shouldn't have taken that sleeping pill last night."

I slow the car, changing gears as we approach a tight bend. "Hopefully, you can sleep on the plane."

"Mmm. Maybe." He stretches his neck to one side, as if it's stiffened while he was resting, then turns to look at Reilly. "How's it going, Pumpkin?"

In the rear vision mirror, she nods sleepily. Poor thing. Having to drive with your dad to the airport because you want some time with him on your birthday is bad enough, but getting up at four in the morning sucks. He owes her. Big time. And as if he's read my mind …

"Biggest snowdome ever," he says.

Reilly manages a dopey grin. "Promise?"

"Promise."

They both settle into quietness again until Daniel addresses me. "I, uh, we haven't spoken since …"

"Since the 'night of horror'?" I offer, hoping my grimace adds some levity.

"Yes. That."

He's quiet again, so I steal a glance. He's picking at a fingernail.

"Thank you," I say. "For looking after me. You didn't have to."

"I know."

I gear both the car and my body, bracing for a hill. "I, um, wasn't sure if things were still okay. With my job, I mean. Margie seems a bit—"

"I hope it won't change your mind about staying."

I squeeze the steering wheel, shake my head. "Are you kidding? I thought you might sack me."

He laughs. "For diarrhoea?"

I guffaw, loud and sudden. "Usually, it's my mouth running off."

He chuckles. "Well, there was plenty of that too. But seriously, I'd like you to stay."

I glance again, meet his eyes, a flutter of fear rising as I wonder if there's nuance in what he's saying.

Now it's his turn to blush. He refocuses on the road. "I'm sure Reilly feels the same."

There's a murmur from the backseat.

"See? I'd take that as approval."

I wipe my eye, which has suddenly decided to water. "I guess that's settled then."

"Great."

"Great."

We drive in silence for the next twenty minutes, Daniel drifting off, head in hand again. Reilly lets out a little piggy snore, and I chuckle. I hope she's going to last the day. It'd be a shame to waste her birthday treat. I'm looking forward to the Kuranda trip myself, although the thought of the Skyrail makes me a little jittery.

Daniel suddenly speaks, startling me. "And, uh ..." He glances behind to Reilly again. I check her in the rear vision. She looks out of it, head slumped to one side, but Daniel keeps his voice low as he leans toward me. "Maybe try to avoid Cynthia while I'm away."

My own voice is an involuntary whisper. "What? Why?"

"Nothing. Just best if you stay away."

"You can't say that and leave me hanging. Has something happened?"

"No." He sighs. "I might be totally barking up the wrong tree ..."

"But what?"

"Well ... I just don't know."

God, how frustrating! "Don't know *what*?"

He chews his fingernail, suddenly fascinated with examining it. "If your illness was an accident."

"Are you kidding me?"

"Shhh." He holds his hand up. "It's a suspicion. Nothing more. We can't go making accusations."

Reeling. I'm reeling. At least he doesn't think I'm an alcoholic, like Margie, but ... Wow!

There's a horn blast behind us – I've slowed down, lost concentration. I hit the accelerator on both the car and my imagination. Reilly wakes, complains.

The last time, the *only* time, I've seen Cynthia was … "The cocktail?"

Daniel shrugs. "I don't know. Maybe. I wouldn't put it past her."

What am I meant to do with this information? Should I report her? "Has she done anything like this before?"

"I don't think so. I don't know."

"So, it's just me she has a thing about?"

"I wouldn't take it personally. She's pretty pissed about the divorce. You might just be collateral damage." Daniel wipes his forehead, brushes his hair back as if he can brush away the thought. "I'm sorry. I shouldn't have said anything. I could be completely wrong. I'll talk to her when I get back."

"Thanks. *So much.*" I'm curious now. "So you think she doesn't want a divorce? Why?"

He shrugs. "Who knows what motivates Cynthia? They say misery loves company."

At the airport, Reilly rouses herself long enough for a birthday hug but doesn't bother switching to the front seat, tiredness sucking her back into a slump.

Daniel retrieves his carry-on luggage from the boot, places it on the sidewalk, then returns to the passenger side, both hands gripping the passenger door as he leans forward. He holds my gaze, that thing he does for too long. "Take care of you both."

I search his face for clues, but he turns away.

On the drive back, I switch the radio on low. Adele's "Rolling in the Deep" is playing. As I listen to her singing about the scars of love, I glance out to the bay where the sun hovers just above the skyline, as if hesitant to start the day.

——◦◦◦——

"Reilly. Wake up, sweetheart. We're home."

She cracks her eyelids open, grumbles, but reaches for her seatbelt clip. I steady her as she stumbles from the car, then leans on me as we head to the front door. "Let's hop back in bed for a while," I say. "I'll wake you when it's time for brekky, okay?"

She nods and lets me lead her, zombie-like, to her room, remove her shoes and tuck her in. My own bed is calling. I don't fight it but set an alarm for three hours.

I swear I've only been asleep for five minutes when I'm woken by the deliciousness of pancake smell. Margie. I slip into shorts and t-shirt, then head to Reilly's room and knock. "Rise and shine, birthday girl!"

I step back as the door bursts open.

"Ready!"

How do kids do that? One minute half asleep, the next a hummingbird on steroids. "Look at you! Pigtails, hat, backpack. An intrepid traveller if ever I saw one. To the kitchen!"

"Nooo, let's just get going."

"Absolutely not. We're not due to pick Sammi until eleven. And I'm pretty sure Margie's making birthday pancakes." I pretend to spank her bottom as she stomps along the hallway, thumbs tucked into her backpack straps.

"One pancake for you," I say, "three for me."

"That's not fair!"

"Well, you'll just have to beat me to them."

She takes off, and I follow, huffing and puffing my disappointment at the possibility of missing out. I also revel in a little smugness – at how I've been able to distract Reilly from her eating woes these past weeks. Points to me, zero to Cynthia.

Margie is at the stove, one hand on hip, the other sliding a spatula under a crêpe-thin pancake. She lifts and flips it perfectly – the hand of a thousand flips. "Juice is fresh. In the fridge," she says.

Reilly dumps her backpack and opens the fridge while I lean against the doorway. "Nice scarf."

She flicks me a look, then adjusts the batik green scarf around her neck, as if she's not comfortable with it. Tell the truth, I've never seen her wear one. Perhaps it's a travel souvenir. "How's Evelyn?"

"According to her, she's fine. Nothing a good rest won't fix."

"And according to you?"

"I said she's fine." Her tone is so brusque, it makes it clear the subject is dropped.

Okaaay. Maybe her bad mood lately isn't about me after all.

"Umm, I was wondering, Margie. Do you think it's still safe to go to Kuranda with this cyclone looming?"

Reilly spins around, juice glass paused at her lips, her mouth a stricken "O".

I hold up a hand. "Just being careful." I turn back to Margie. "I was listening to the news on the car radio, and I don't like the sound of it. It's a Category 3 now."

"Just needs to be kept an eye on. We'll get plenty of warning if it's going to hit. Still way off in the Coral Sea for now."

"Okay," I say, hoping to convince myself, "Daniel seemed blasé about it. Said they have a habit of petering out before they hit land. But he said you'd know what to do."

"That's why I've come back – to pack a few more things. Suggest you do the same."

A tiny thrill flits through me. "So you are worried?"

"Not worried," Margie insists. "But prepared is best. You'll be fine. As I said, we'll get plenty of warning. Besides, they'd shut down the train and Skyrail if it weren't safe."

"Just as well," Reilly huffs. "No cyclone is going stop my birthday." She rushes over to the cutlery drawer. "I'll set the table."

"Thanks, pet. Lemon, sugar and syrup's already there."

Margie and I glance at each other. Since when has Reilly ever offered to help out? I'm about to wink, but Margie looks away.

I lean back against the counter as Reilly rattles in the cutlery drawer and Margie pours more batter into her pan. Then I look closer. There's something about Margie – a weariness to her posture, a dullness to her energy. The auburn curls that usually frame her face are a mess of frizz. I wait for Reilly to head out to the dining room before I say anything.

"Margie?"

She adjusts her scarf again, stares at her pan, face set. I think about making a joke about her "resting bitch face" – a term Reilly brought home from school and was quickly reprimanded for – but I'm sensing now isn't the time. "Margie? Are you okay?"

She looks up, distracted, but seems to focus. "I'm fine, fine. Just a little tired. How's your back?"

So typical. Always focusing on others. "It's a bit achy, twingey, but I'll be fine. I'll take some ibuprofen before we leave."

"If you get desperate, there's some Endone in Daniel's …"

She bites her lip, as if she's regretted her words. Does she think I'm a drug addict as well as an alcoholic?

"That's okay. I wouldn't take opioids when I'm driving and not with the girls in my care. Over-the-counter stuff will do."

She nods.

"But, Margie, you know I'm happy to do more around the house, to help out? Now that I'm permanent—"

She waves me off with the spatula. "By the way, Cynthia's cancelling Reilly's party this weekend. She's taking off overseas again with what's-his-face."

Seriously? Is the woman running away? After making me sick? "What a snake."

"Exactly. Never mind her daughter. Not that Reilly will care. It was never about her."

Not what I meant, but okay. "Does Reilly know?"

She shakes her head, falters, rests a hand on the bench and wipes her forehead with the back of her hand.

"Margie. Are you sure you're okay?"

"I said, I'm fine."

Her tone is edgy, irritated, and ... she's wearing her hair partially down. Margie never does that. Call it survivor's intuition, but something in me just knows. I inch closer to her, and when she's focusing on her pan, I reach up, slip her hair away from her neck, lift the scarf.

"Margie! How did you get that?"

She drops her spatula, tries to elbow me away, but I'm quicker, grabbing her arm. She snatches it back.

"Margie, what's going on? Who's doing this to you?"

"No one. It's nothing." She pats her hair over her neck again, picks up her spatula from the floor, rinses it off, then flips the last pancake before bending to remove a stack from the oven where she's keeping them warm.

I don't press her. Margie is Margie. She's not going to talk until she's ready. She straightens and gives me the plate of pancakes, which she's rested on a tea towel.

"Careful. It's hot."

I try to catch her eye, but she won't look up. So I turn toward the kitchen doorway. Reilly is standing there, her keen gaze moving between us, a tiny crinkle embedded in her flawless young forehead. "I came back to get more juice."

"Come on, birthday girl." I swivel her out of the kitchen. "Let's eat before these get cold."

At the table, Reilly fixes me with a stare, a finger twirling a curl against her face. "Is Margie okay?"

I concentrate on sprinkling sugar on my pancake, playing for time. "She's fine, sweetheart. Just a bit tired after her trip."

"But you said—"

I hold up a hand, put my spoon down. "I know. " *Take a breath.* She's way too young to learn about domestic abuse. And yet, here she is in the middle of it. And if I lie to her, what does that make me? Culpable? "Sometimes people don't act the way we would like them to. Sometimes the people we love have … issues, problems, so they don't always behave the way they should."

"You mean like Mummy and Daddy?"

"Sorry?"

"Like when Mummy screams at Daddy?"

"She does?"

Reilly purses her lips, tightens the curl around her finger. "She called him a"—she searches my face for permission. I cringe at what's coming but nod—"soft cock".

I try not to react. "Not okay."

"She said he was useless, hopeless. She hit him. I saw it."

I watch carefully now – her flushed cheeks, teeth sunk into her bottom lip, tight grip on her fork. But there are no tears. I wonder if Daniel knows any of this. If I should bring it up with him when he gets back. Is Reilly safe on her visits to Cynthia's? "I'm really, really sorry you had to see that, Reilly. It must have been awful."

"It was." She shrugs. "But I'm not a baby."

My heart pains for her stoicism. "No, you're not." I reach over and squeeze her hand. "And you're very brave to tell me. Very brave."

As she sucks in a breath, she stabs a pancake onto her plate.

"And you can tell me anything, Reilly. Anything at all. I'm here for you. And I'm here for Margie too. You don't need to worry."

She nods, resolute. I could be looking at myself as a kid – adulting before her time.

52

Andreas

Just getting on the train was difficult.

I had to force each step toward the carriage, constantly looking behind, then at the carriage doors each time it stopped at an unfamiliar station.

Katie met me at the station closest to her house. We hugged tight. Lots of tears.

"Good," she said. I'd only packed a small overnight bag.

53

Sammi is sitting on her doorstep when we arrive, elbows resting on knees, chin in hands. She jumps up and runs inside, yelling to her mother. Reilly scampers up the footpath, and I follow.

Nayla pushes the screen door open. "Happy birthday!" She gives Reilly a hug, then shields her eyes from the sun as she turns to me. "Perfect day for it."

"It is. Are you sure you won't join us?"

"No. Love to, but I've got a bunch of cupcakes to bake for a wedding tomorrow. Say, when are you coming for your next lesson? I may need an apprentice."

"Um, later this week?"

"Deal."

Sammi reappears behind Nayla. "Mummy, you're in the way."

Nayla shifts aside and Sammi shuffles through lugging a small suitcase – things for her sleepover tonight. The girls perform some sort of fist-bumping, finger-twisting, secret handshake.

Nayla laughs and rolls her eyes. "Girls, shall I bring some cupcakes over for when you get back? They're lime and coconut."

"Yes, pleeease."

They take off down the path toward the car, Sammi singing "happy birthday, happy birthday, happy birthday" on repeat between fits of giggles as Reilly bumps her off the path and onto the lawn.

—◆—

Our gold class carriage – a treat since it's Reilly's birthday – is decked out in heritage features: polished woodwork, pressed-tinned roof, brass accessories, sash windows. I had expected the repetitive clanking of heavy wheels on rails, but the train is a slow climber, brakes squealing as it pauses at scenic lookouts and points of interest. A recorded voice-over tells us it's a narrow-gauge railway – 3ft 6in – and what an amazing engineering feat it was to build by hand, and how men had to supply their own tools. How they spent weeks, months, away from their families, how physically and emotionally fraught their lives were. And here we are, tourists in a posh carriage with light refreshments and comfy padded chairs.

Reilly and Sammi chatter and point at pretty things out the window, oohing at stomach-churning drops down steep valleys. A waiter brings over a platter of cheese and dried fruit snacks, which the girls attack. I wonder if they're going to want any of Margie's packed lunch I've lugged along in a basket. The waiter returns, holds up a bottle of champagne, his eyebrows raised.

I don't even pause. "No, thanks."

Head leaning against the window, I let myself dream as the train cleaves to the mountainside, weaving through ancient rainforest – a Wet Tropics World Heritage Area. I'm learning a lot.

I try to imagine what the rainforest creatures are doing right now – cassowaries and scrubfowl, fossicking through the damp, mossy, fungus-strewn and leaf-littered forest floor. Kingfishers, pythons, tree frogs inhabiting the creeper-covered tier of trees, looking for their next meal of grubs, small marsupials, worms or insects. Thousands of insects ... I try not to imagine those.

Then I drift into a different fantasy – a happy life here, what that would look like. Permanent, accustomed to the heat and humidity, to the afternoon rains in wet season, the hectic tourist seasons, the quiet off-season when business owners face lean times and take time off for themselves. Once Reilly is older, maybe I could run my own business. I wonder if Nayla is serious about wanting an apprentice? I think I'd like baking, decorating, the constant presence of icing sugar, the taste of sweetness in the air. Margie wouldn't feel threatened then, and Daniel—

"Look!"

Reilly's pointing out the window. The train has curled into a giant, red and white caterpillar examining its own tail. The voice-over tells us this part of the track was built to allow the train to gain momentum to climb the hill.

The girls settle until Reilly calls out again. This time we're traversing a bridge over a yawning, rainforest-covered ravine, while above us, an angelic foamy waterfall laces its way over rocky outcrops. It's a heck of a long way down. Stoney Creek, a sign says. Some creek.

Another quiet period until a distant rumbling filters through. We must be approaching Barron Falls. Wet season has bloated the river into a wide brown sludgy serpent, and we're expecting the waterfall to be a magnificent monster of untamed force. As we draw closer to the station, the sound grows to a dull thunder and hiss. We're not disappointed

– the river smashes over sheer rockface, catching in stepped pools, then plummets again. The valley is unfathomably deep, the air misty from cascading, roaring water.

We stare bug-eyed until we have to put our hands over our ears as the train's brakes screech unbearably loud. We're laughing so much, I almost miss the beep of my phone.

Having fun?

For a moment, I smile, thinking it's Margie or Nayla, but .... I slap the phone face down on my lap. Why? Why now? He wouldn't have received the ring back yet. I only sent it yesterday. It's as if he has ESP and wants one last mindfuck, one last attempt to assuage his ego.

I lift the phone, flick it onto silent mode, check the setting twice, then shove it back into my pocket. I'm over this.

It vibrates. I resist, focus on the cascading water, the roar, the hazy air, a rainbow in the mist. I can't look. Won't.

Remember our first trip on a train?

My pulse seizes. I cover my mouth, snap my head up, rake the carriage, scanning each passenger. There aren't many people in here – it's quiet season. Two couples, one family of three. They're all distracted by the falls. I don't see him. Maybe he's in another carriage. Maybe he saw me through the window when the train curled around the track? No. Don't be stupid. He'd have to have binoculars. He's not here. He's just screwing with me.

Remember? You had that see-through nightie.

I shudder.

You looked so hot, babe.

Nausea. Headache. Flash back: a private room in a sleeping car, the blinds open to the outside world because he liked the danger, the risk of being caught.

You still get me hard, babe.

The train stops. Passengers disembark for photos of the falls. I want to tell Reilly and Sammi to stay on the train. To stay right next to me. But they'll think I'm a lunatic, and I'll be spoiling Reilly's birthday. They're already heading for the carriage door. I hurry after them as they get off, but hang back, searching the platform, people emerging from other carriages. The girls head straight for the lookout railing. He's not here. He's not.

After ten minutes, I relax a little. He's messing with me. It's coincidence. *How* though? How is he doing this? Is he tracking my phone? Can he do that with such an old model?

It seems an age before the train whistle blows. We all climb back in. I sigh, hugely. Take my seat.

See you at the station.

NO! NO! NO! I can't catch my breath. Hands clutch to fists. Nausea rising. Chest hurts. I'm going to throw up. What do I do? Call the police? No – he has friends. I glance at Reilly and Sammi, still mesmerised by the view. We'll have to stay with the crowd, keep close to another family. He wouldn't do anything then. Not with children around. Would he? What do I do then?

Think. Think.

Maybe there's a taxi service at Kuranda. Maybe we can make a run for it. The girls will think I've lost it.

But for now, I have twenty minutes of hell. Waiting.

I want to smash something, scream. Minutes seem to speed, yet drag unbearably. Not enough time to think. Too much time to think. Thank god Reilly and Sammi are keeping themselves occupied, chatting about what they'll do in Kuranda. I sit straight-backed, phone in lap, waiting for the next message. There isn't one.

Before the carriage doors open at Kuranda Station, I grab the girls' hands, hold them tight. "Stick together now. We don't want to get separated." They pull me forward onto the platform, too excited to notice my agitation. I'm all eyes, all tight muscles, all ready to punch, to groin strike, to rake at eyes. I must look like a mad woman, scanning every face.

We flow with the crowd, out to what looks like the township's main street – cafes, gift shops, thrift shops, a rustic pub on a corner that takes up plenty of real-estate.

"Come on," Reilly says, pulling my hand. She's pointing toward a sign for the butterfly sanctuary.

I hesitate, still scanning the thinning crowd.

"Hang on," I say. "I just need to check something." I pull out my phone, pretend to be searching for something. I've made up my mind. I'm going to confront him. Wait until the a-hole appears and bloody well stand up for myself. They say bullies are cowards within. I'm going to test that theory. There's no way I'm letting him hurt me. Not in front of the girls. Not ever.

Maybe he's not really here. Maybe he's just guessing. That's his style – he's a troll. Maybe he's still in Melbourne, and somehow knows I bought train tickets online. Maybe he doesn't know it's Kuranda. We could be anywhere.

The girls are getting antsy. I've got no reason to delay. I let them lead me on. The sanctuary is a couple of blocks ahead, but I keep glancing behind.

"What are you looking for?" Reilly asks. "Are you scared we're going to get lost? It's okay. I know the way."

I could cry at her sweet concern. "All good." So hard to smile.

Inside the rainforest habitat, we wander the dirt tracks under the meshed-in enclosure. The girls ooh and ahh at the butterflies – a myriad fluttering bright colours, shapes and sizes. I peer between wet leaves and trunks, vigilant.

"Georgia! Take our picture."

I nod, distracted, focused on someone moving behind dense foliage.

"Georgia!"

"Sorry. Yes? What?"

Reilly holds her arm out, a large non-descript brown and black butterfly sits on her elbow. It opens its wings revealing the bright blue of a Ulysses, the only one I know the name of – Dunk Island's mascot. Its wings continue to slowly open and close like luminescent satin bellows. Reilly holds out her mobile phone with her other hand. I reach for it and, careful not to upset the butterfly, snap several shots.

"Me too," Sammi says, giggling. She tries to eye the delicate emerald and black creature balancing on the rim of her peaked cap.

"Keep your head back," I say. Snap. Snap.

I give Reilly her phone back and check the battery on my own: forty per cent. The power doesn't seem to be lasting. Age, I expect. I tell the girls to continue their adventure. I'll meet them at the exit. They're safe in here; there's only one way out.

It only takes them another fifteen minutes and they head over to me. There's a queue to exit the enclosure as each person is inspected by a staff member.

"What are they doing?" Sammi asks.

Reilly lifts her chin, smug at knowing something Sammi doesn't. "They're collecting butterfly eggs from people's hats."

Sammi drops her jaw, raises her eyes to her cap.

Inspected and released, we head out to the park to picnic on Margie's lunch. On a blanket under a tree, Reilly and Sammi squeeze crackers together, oozing vegemite and butter through the holes. They each wipe a finger across the black and yellow noodles they've made, collecting the messy goo, then licking it off. I haven't done that since I was a kid. I'm tempted to do the same, but I'm supposed to be the adult here. And I'm being vigilant. Still scanning.

Something catches my eye. A few metres away, a man on a park bench. I can't see him clearly – there's a shrub, the sun's in my eyes, too many kids running around, parents calling, a ball being thrown, someone playing a guitar, a glimpse of something white and orange in the man's hands. A familiar book. My heart punches. Dizzy. The sandy hair, the stocky build. I stare harder—

Reilly screams. "Ow! Get them off! Get them off!"

She's slapping at her leg – green tree ants crawling, biting. I've read the bright green little monsters are aggressive, inject acid into their bites, hurt like hell. But worse, didn't Margie say Reilly is allergic to stings? "Stand up! Stand up!" I pull her off the blanket, grab paper napkins, swipe at her leg until I've got them all off. She's crying now, so I grab her shoulders. "Honey, are you allergic? Do you know?"

"No, no."

"You're not allergic or you don't know?"

"I don't know," she says. "I don't think so."

"Do you feel okay? Your breathing? Do you feel sick?"

"No." She sobs. I'm frightening her.

"Okay, it's okay." I pull her into a hug, glance at Sammi who's looking stricken but has had the sense to get off the blanket. "You don't have any on you?" She shakes her head.

Should I race Reilly across the road to the chemist we passed earlier? Just in case? But I can't leave Sammi here on her own. I look over my shoulder to the park bench. It's empty.

"Okay, let's pack up quickly. But be careful."

The three of us grab our belongings, shaking everything out as we repack the picnic basket.

"It hurts," Reilly says, patting at her leg, red marks swelling.

"Oh, honey. Can you walk?"

She takes a few steps, nods.

"Let's get you something for the pain."

⬥

The chemist examines Reilly's leg, asks if she's allergic. Reilly says no again, but I try calling Margie to confirm. She doesn't answer. We leave the chemist with analgesic, antihistamine and instructions to keep a close eye on Reilly for further symptoms.

"I think we'd better get a shuttle back, just to be safe," I say.

"But you promised! You said it was a 'birthday promise'."

"I know. And I feel really bad about that, but the Skyrail takes an hour and a half, and if you have an allergic reaction and we're stuck in the treetops—"

"But I'm NOT allergic. I've been bitten before."

I glance at her leg – the swelling is angry red. If there was one thing I learned in my previous life in childcare, it's that allergic reactions might not be bad the first time, but the second and third ... "Sweetheart, we just can't take that risk. Can you imagine how your dad would feel if something happened to you? While he's all the way overseas?"

Her bottom lip trembles. God. Why does seeing someone else in tears always make me want to cry too? It's as contagious as yawning. "Okay, look. You're a big girl now, so I'm going to let you decide the right thing to do."

Reilly hiccups, then squints up at me. "I get to choose?"

"Of course. Birthday girl is boss."

She nods, squeezes her hands together and scrunches her face as she considers, then looks to Sammi for support. Sammi grabs one of Reilly's hands. "It's okay. It means we get to have another trip." She looks at me slyly. "Maybe on a school day."

I open my mouth to object, but I'm flummoxed with admiration. Sammi's a little politician in the making.

Reilly sighs but nods once with conviction. "Let's take the shuttle."

"Good decision."

"And Sammi can still stay over tonight?"

I baulk, unsure of my next move, beyond getting them home. I can't have them with me at the house, not if Andreas is around. "Of course. A promise is a promise. Especially a birthday promise." Lies. I hate myself. I hug Reilly's small shoulders again, squeeze her to me. "You're being really grown up, Reilly. Your dad would be proud of you."

She manages a small smile, and I grab the girls' hands. "Let's go."

It's only a short wait until the shuttle arrives. The girls scramble on board the minibus and grab a seat together while I pay the fee, then sit behind them.

That was close.

I freeze, hands trembling. I want to turn and check if he's on the bus, but he can't be – I would have seen him getting on. I want to madly scan the street, but I don't want him to see I'm fazed. I simply sit, clutching the phone in my lap. Until it rings. I drop it in fright, have a mad urge to kick it away. But as I stare at it on the floor, the number display kicks me into action, and I scrabble to pick it up.

"Margie? I want to know if Reilly is allergic to insect bites. She got bitten by green ants, and ... No? That's a relief, I was ... What? ... God, Margie. I'm sorry. Is she okay?"

I take a breath, let Margie speak. Evelyn has collapsed. She's being rushed to a hospital in Mossman. Margie doesn't know what's going to happen next. Will I be okay with the girls?

"Of course. Yes, yes. Just go. I'm thinking of you both."

The girls turn to face me from their seats. I'm barely holding back a crazed howl, but somehow manage to smile, raise a hand, signal it's okay. Everything is fine.

Reilly leans in and whispers. "I'm here if you need to talk."

The sweetness of her innocence. Of adult words in a babe's mouth. I cover my face, bite hard on my lip, dig my fingernails into my palm. I could bawl now.

54

We're home. The girls have gone quiet, sensing my unease. They don't object when I cut them a piece of birthday cake Margie has left in the fridge and tell them to go to the lounge and watch TV, play a game or something, but stay together.

I sit out on the patio, holding my phone, deciding whether to call the police. But what do I say? Tell them I had a domestic violence order against Andreas, which I ruined by returning to him? DVOs are useless until the perpetrator does something tangible anyway. Too little too late. And I don't trust them. Not after last time.

I call Nayla instead, ask if she's able to collect the girls for the night, that I have a migraine coming on. She says she's flat out with the cakes for the wedding but can swing by later, after she's delivered them. Can I hold out? I'm on the verge of telling her it's not safe here, that she needs to come now, but a niggling voice tells me I'm overreacting. I mean, who's to say Andreas isn't still in Melbourne? That he isn't gaslighting me? Who's to say it wasn't the stress of his messages that triggered my imagining the man at Kuranda? Katie was right – I should have blocked Andreas before I arrived, but ... keep your enemies close. A fury born of deep fear boils in my gut. This time, if he is here, I'm going to deal with him.

"Sure, Nayla. Thanks. I owe you one."

I check on the girls. They're watching SpongeBob SquarePants. Normally, I'd sit with them and watch. I love that impossibly yellow, squeaky, kooky character. But after I check Reilly's bites are no worse, I head to the garage.

There's nothing weapon-like here – no baseball bat, hockey stick, crowbar – just a clean ordered space, tools hanging from a peg board, metal shelving stacked with gardening equipment, paint tins, a leaf blower, a toolbox. I toy with the idea of a long-handled screwdriver, but I'm not keen on the thought of getting that close to Andreas. And could I actually stick him with it? If I was pushed? It's all a stupid idea anyway – don't they say not to use a weapon unless you're trained, lest it gets turned against you? I'm feeding my own panic here.

Back in the lounge, I explain to the girls they can still have a sleepover, but it will be at Sammi's. Reilly doesn't seem fazed but wants to know if I'm okay. "Sure, sweetheart. I'm just a bit out of sorts."

She holds out her hand, and I curl up with them on the couch, watch the cute cartoon with its subtle messages of friendship and community, lost on me right now. My phone sits beside me, still on mute. After an hour and a half, there's been no allergic reaction from Reilly, no further texts from Andreas, and the girls have tired of cartoons. They implore me to join them in a game of Knucklebones.

⸺◆⸺

I'm getting the hang of this game now, throwing the plastic bones in the air and catching them on the back of my hand. But though my hands are bigger than theirs, the girls are quicker, more dexterous, and their lithe bodies don't have the disadvantage of cramped hips from sitting crossed legged on the tiled floor too long, even though I've pulled a cushion from the couch to sit on.

The television hums in the background, on the weather channel so I can keep an eye on the cyclone. The ticker reads "Category 3 Cyclone Yasi tracking west-southwest toward Townsville'.

"Toilet break," I say, groaning as my back grabs when I push myself up.

"Okay," they chorus, neither of them looking up. When it was my turn, it was all giggles and ribbing. Now it's razor-sharp focus and furrowed brows, fixated on making sure each other doesn't cheat.

I head to the loo, then to the kitchen to grab some salt and vinegar chips and M&Ms. I'm lost in thought, shaking the snacks into bowls, when the doorbell rings. Relief settles like warm hands on my shoulders, pressing away tension. Nayla's early.

"Mummy!" Sammi yells.

"We'll get it," Reilly calls.

The girls' bare feet patter on the tiles as they run down the hall to the front door, their giggles making me smile – they must be deliberately bumping into each other and the walls. I imagine Reilly's pigtails bouncing as she runs, and Sammi holding up her too-big, cut-off jeans as they slide down her narrow waist.

I wonder if Nayla would like to stay for wine. There's a half-drunk bottle of white in the fridge. I'm surprised Margie hasn't poured it down the drain. Guilt pauses my hand, but I shake it off. I'm not an alcoholic. Wine bottle tucked under one arm, Fanta bottle tucked under the other, I grab the snack bowls and head back to the lounge, listening for the girls' excited voices to return, telling Nayla all about the train, the butterflies, the horrid ants.

But they've gone quiet. Too quiet. It's now my brain fires the warning, sending sharp tingles to my chest. No! I increase my pace. No!

Andreas is standing in the centre of the lounge, clutching Reilly's hand. Sammi is close by, frowning, hands hidden behind her back, as if she's refused to participate in this friendly charade with a stranger. In Reilly's other hand is a Patrick Ness novel. The third in the series. The one the book café said they had just sold out of.

"Georgia?" Reilly says, voice quivering.

The Fanta bottle slips from me, thuds, bounces across the floor.

His presence is unmistakable – not a giant ogre, he's not tall, more average, but he possesses a solid, bull-like radiation of latent, unstable energy. Despite his five o'clock shadow and crumpled shirt, arrogance still radiates from every animalistic pore. A picture comes to me: Reilly opening the door, all smiles; Andreas's dark charisma taking her by surprise; him telling Reilly he's my friend, we go way back. "I bought you a present for your birthday." A predatory smile as he pushes his way in, takes her hand, leads her here.

"Hello, Georgia."

His voice rakes me, clenches my stomach. I rush to place the snack bowls and wine on the floor next to the discarded knuckle bones, then walk straight at Andreas. Holding his gaze, I take the book from Reilly, throw it on the couch, then grasp her free hand and pull her away. Andreas holds on for a fraction too long, forcing Reilly to stretch her arm before he lets go.

"Sweetheart," I say, "why don't we take Sammi to your bedroom and show her your …"

"My new laptop?"

The girl is quick. She's been nagging her dad for a computer for weeks now, but she's not being smart with me – her eyes tell me she's picked up on the adrenaline that's making me squeeze her hand too hard, that's making my voice low, strained with tight coolness.

Sammi has sensed it too, though she looks more confused than scared. I hold my other hand out to her, and she comes to me. I look back at Andreas. "I'm taking them to the bedroom. Wait here."

He sniffs, lip curling, but says nothing.

"Or why don't you wait for me out by the pool?" I incline my head toward the patio door. Anything to get him out of the house.

"I'm fine here," he says.

I bite my lip. *Don't argue.*

Sammi quietly whines. I'm holding her hand too tight. I turn and pull the girls with me. They don't resist.

I close Reilly's bedroom door behind us. Why isn't there a damn lock on the door? You know why, stupid; it's a kid's room. The girls sit on the edge of Reilly's bed, eyes wide like startled cats.

"I'm sorry," Reilly says. "I thought he was your friend. You said he was. When he sent you that text message. Remember? He called you a bit—"

"I know, I know, sweetheart." I kneel in front of her, take her hands and rub them. "It's not your fault. It's mine. I was trying to—"

Her tears come and so do Sammi's.

"Hey, hey, now. What's all this? There's nothing to be upset about. You haven't done anything wrong. I just need a few words with ... my friend, and we'll get on with our games and snacks. Okay?"

They nod, wiping their faces with their palms. Brave girls.

My hand trembles as I reach for the doorhandle. What if I call the police from here? What if we all sneak out Reilly's patio door? We could make a run for it, down the beach track. I turn around, head over to the French doors and survey the patio. Good. He's not there. But what if one of the girls tripped and fell down the stairway? I could carry one of them, not both. The neighbours? No, they're rentals; I'd be sending them to strangers.

The girls are crying again now. I'm frightening them.

Stop it. Go face him. Make him leave. "I'll be back soon," I tell them.

The walk back to the lounge is excruciating. It's as if my brain is only now allowing me to download the full recognition of danger. I thought I knew fear before, when I lived with him – the cringing against punches to my stomach, the hair-dragging across the kitchen floor to the bedroom – but this, this trembling in my bones is a new level. I'm not the only one at risk here.

I stop, lean my head against the wall. How did he find me? Is no place safe?

I try to breathe deep, calm myself, but the air catches, my chest too constricted. I push back off the wall. There's no point delaying the inevitable. He'll only come looking for me. For us.

He's near the knuckle bones, bending, reaching into the bowl of M&M's. He takes a handful, straightens, tilts his head back as he throws the lollies into his mouth, then brushes off his hand. "Mmmm. Haven't had these in a while. I've forgotten how good they are."

I space my feet. *Stand strong.* I cross my arms. *Show him you're not scared.*

"What do you want, Andreas?"

He speaks with his mouth full of chocolatey sugar shells. "Is that any way to greet a long-lost lover? No hug? No kiss?"

"Cut it. Tell me what you want."

He tilts his head. "I would have thought that was obvious."

"What? The ring? I sent it back to you."

He chews, swallows, bends and picks up the wine bottle, unscrews it and takes a couple of swigs. "Ugh. Too sweet." Now he takes the M&Ms over to the couch and sits, one arm draped across the back. "Now see, I know you're lying 'cos I didn't get any ring."

I stay where I am, feet still wide but fists clenched at my sides now – I can at least pretend to look strong. "I'm not lying. I sent it back to Katie by registered post. She'll give it to you. I have a receipt. I'll get it for you—"

He grins. "Come on. Stop playing games. You asked me here. You missed me."

"What?"

"You texted me."

"I *what*?"

For a second, confusion crosses his face. "You. Texted. Me."

"I did not. Why would I do that?"

His eyes harden, familiar anger flushing his cheeks. "You playing me?"

"I am not."

He puts the bowl aside, reaches into his back jeans pocket and pulls out his mobile. I watch, curious at my own calm now. Or is it numbness – my body preparing for assault? While he's looking at his phone, I glance around the room. Only two exits from the house – the patio and the front door, down the hall. I could sprint there ... but the girls.

"Here," he says, holding up his phone. "Your texts. You told me you wanted to see me. You gave me your address."

"I didn't. I would never—"

"You told me to pick up this bloody book! For the kid." He gestures to the novel beside him.

"What?"

"Fuck!" he yells.

I curse myself for flinching.

"Come over here and look at it."

My feet obey, though I tell them not to. I stand in front of him, reach for his phone. He snatches it away. "I said *look*. Don't touch. I'm not having you delete them."

I almost stumble back at the venom in his voice. "Okay, okay. I'll look." He holds his phone up again, and I lean forward. "Why does it say "Babe"?

"I saved it in my contacts, you idiot. Thought it was your new number. What the hell does it matter? Just the messages."

Babe: *Come get it.*

Him: *You want me to come to you?*

Babe: *Yes. I miss you.*

Him: *Babe, you make my heart sing.*

He's followed his last text with a gif of some guy dry humping a big-boobed woman. Gross. Why would he think I would appreciate that? So disgusting. How was I ever with him?

"I didn't send those."

"You're kidding, right?"

"No."

His face flushes again. A nerve jumps in his cheek, his knee bounces. "Let's see." He types a new message. Waits. Nothing happens.

"Where's your phone?" he asks.

I turn, point to the coffee table.

"The sound must be off," he says.

"I don't think—"

"Get it."

I obey again, bring my phone over. He takes it. "What's your password?"

"I'm not telling—"

He stands, looming over me, smelling of days-old sweat. "Four five two eight."

My phone lights up. He checks the message app. "There's nothing there."

"I told you."

I try to snatch the phone back, but he's too quick. "Wait." He uses my phone to text himself. He phone pings. He grunts. "Different number."

Another ping. He reads the message, then laughs. Not a happy sound. "Someone is playing us both." He holds the phone up.

Him: *Babe, I'm here.*

Babe: *Come inside. Can't wait to see you.*

I look at him blankly. "I don't know who—"

"Wait." He taps his phone, holds it to his ear, listens. "What the ..." He looks genuinely puzzled. "Who the hell is Evelyn?"

My world drops away, a frisson roiling within me, as if all my individual blood cells are panicking, trying to rush somewhere safe. There isn't anywhere.

This isn't possible. He's mistaken.

I collapse back, the couch catching me as truth folds in, suffocates me, the words rushing in at me: "You give me his name and number – in case he somehow manages to contact me. Then I can warn you."

Why? Why would Evelyn do this?

"Who is she?" Andreas insists.

I grip my hair, pull at it, desperate for pain to override the betrayal. I don't accept this. Can't.

Andreas shrugs, smiles, ugly in his satisfaction. "Whatever. I told you I'd always find you. Just didn't know it'd be so easy."

Blinding, burning fury. I rise, fists flailing. Punch. Hard. Connecting with his chest, again and again, almost throwing him off balance before he's able to grab my wrists and shake me. "Grown a pair while you've been away?" he grunts. I'm a ragdoll in his grip. Eventually, he throws me back onto the couch, and my back screams at being jarred.

"Calm down. You're gonna wake the kids." He grins at his joke, while I sit panting.

The doorbell rings.

He snaps a look toward the hallway. "Who's that?"

"My friend. She's come to pick up the kids."

He falters, seems unsure of what to do.

"If I don't let her in, she'll think something's wrong."

He flicks his head. "Get rid of her."

"I can't. Her daughter is here."

"Get rid of them all."

I push myself up, stumbling with the gripping pain. As I head to the foyer, I try to shake off his manhandling, tidy my hair, clothes, while cycling through ideas: have Nayla call the police when she leaves, drive off with her and the kids …

Nayla stands there holding a tray of six cupcakes. "You look terrible," she says. "I'm sorry I couldn't come earlier. Are you okay?"

I fumble a smile. "I'm alright." Then murmur, "Wait here. I'll get the girls."

"I'll come with you. I want a better look at you. I'm worried."

"*No.* Wait here."

Her hand snatches my shoulder as I turn to leave, eyes searching mine, immediately alert. She seems to see all of me – the fear beneath my skin; the fatigued muscles barely supporting my bones; my crazed, panicked brain. "Georgia, what's going on?"

A movement catches in my peripheral vision – Andreas's figure filling the other end of the hall, blocking most of the light. Nayla sees it too.

"Sure, I'm fine," I say, louder now. "Just this damned headache won't go."

"Are you in trouble?" she whispers.

I nod subtly, give her a big smile. "All good. Let me bring the girls out."

I make to move off, but she holds on. "Is someone here?"

My voice is tiny, shameful. "Yes."

Nayla's petite frame seems to grow in size. "Your ex?" she hisses.

I blink. How the heck does she know?

Her expression turns fierce, and she doesn't bother to keep her voice down now. "Where are the girls?"

"Back bedroom."

"Okay. Show me this arsehole."

I hold my hands up, though I sense nothing is going to stop this mother tiger. "Wait," I whisper. "Maybe we should call the police."

She huffs. "Cop shop's shut. Number diverts to Cairns this late in the day. They'll take forever to get here." She dumps her cupcakes on the hall table, grabs my hand and heads up the hall with me trailing, marvelling at her gusto, her bravery, her feline determination. Her child is in danger. She's not taking any crap.

Andreas is blocking the hallway.

"You need to leave," Nayla says.

Andreas pauses, taking her measure, then smiles. "Are you talking to me?"

"I don't see anyone else here."

He tilts his head at me, smirks. "I like your friend. Maybe she should join us."

Nayla's face is stone. "In your dreams, buddy."

Andreas laughs, turns and saunters over to the couch. He sits, crosses him arms, looks at the TV. "Holy shit. Would you look at that?"

It's a satellite picture of Cyclone Yasi, a vast white cloud mass. Enormous. Andreas leans forward for the remote, points it at the TV. The sound level rises, and he throws the remote back on the coffee table. The clatter jars me.

Nayla repeats, "You need to leave."

Andreas drapes his arm across the back of the couch again. "Well," he says, sucking saliva inside his cheek, then poking a fingernail to remove debris from his teeth, "I don't see any man of the house around. Think Georgia might need someone big and strong to look after her with this mother of a cyclone coming in. Think I might stay the night."

"Daniel will be back any minute," I say, braver now I have backup.

Spittle edges his lips. "Babe. You already told me he's away." He brandishes his phone.

"I told you that wasn't me!" I'm yelling now, gathering my own fire.

Nayla grasps my arm, pulls me back. "Shhh." She approaches him, this tiny woman full of grit. "I said *leave*."

Andreas stands, slowly, deliberately, sticks his hands in his back pockets, chest flexed. "Or what? You gonna make me, widdle girl?"

Nayla stands her ground. "You want to find out?"

"Yeah, well"—he leans over, grabs a handful of M&Ms, throws one in the air, tries to catch it in his mouth, misses —"company stinks anyway."

I almost guffaw at his chagrin, the bully bullied.

He swaggers past us, doesn't look back as he retreats down the hall. We follow, at a distance, watching his back. I want to yell something smart like "don't let the door catch you on the way out", but I'm not game. I manage to croak out, "Go home, Andreas. It's over."

He doesn't turn, just holds up his middle finger, then exits out into the amorphous, moist heat he can't punch.

The door slams and we hurry to lock it.

"Holy crap," I say, breathless, hand to my chest, shaking. "You were amazing. Thank you. I don't know what I wouldn't have—"

She places her hands on either side of my face. "Shhh. It's okay. I was just as scared as you."

"Do you think he'll leave?"

Nayla lets me go, rises on her tippy toes to look through the peep hole. "Maybe. We'll wait for a bit, then get the hell out of here."

Relief hits me now, and my legs give way, sinking me to the floor.

Nayla kneels next me. "Big breath."

I nod.

"It's the shock wearing off," she says. "Just breathe. You'll be fine." She rubs my arm.

"Mummy?"

Sammi is at the other end of the hallway, holding hands with Reilly.

"Come here, darling."

Nayla holds her arms out, and the girls run to us, breaking into tears once they're in our arms. I swallow, holding back my own. Gotta be brave for them. Show them they're safe.

"I'm sorry," Reilly says between sobs. "I didn't mean to let him in. I thought—"

"Shhh, it's not your fault. It's *not* your fault, okay? You're not to blame yourself. You didn't know."

She nods, but I can tell she's not convinced. "Daddy says I shouldn't open the door unless ..." She sobs harder, and I squeeze her harder. "I thought it was Sammi's mum."

"I know you did, sweetheart." I take her shoulders, lift her chin, wipe tears from her cheeks. "Look at me."

She raises her hazel eyes, all shiny with wet.

"Listen to me. You didn't do anything wrong. I thought the same thing. I thought it was Nayla too. No one is blaming you."

She wraps her arms around my neck. "Don't go, Georgia."

The stab of cold, cold guilt is unbearable. I haven't figured out my next move. There's been no time. Am I going to stand my ground and fight for this new life? Stand up to the bully, like Nayla? Or keeping running? But Reilly knows already: I'm going to run.

"Come on, Samara," Nayla says, rising. "Let's get your things and go home. You too, Reilly."

"No," she says. "I want to stay with Georgia."

Nayla looks at me. "You're coming too, aren't you?"

I glance at her, cowardly guilt smothering.

"You have to come," Reilly says, tightening her grip, burying her face in my neck.

Something forms in me now, some clot of resolution that still needs solidifying, but it's coalescing. I pull Reilly's arms from me, holding her hands tight. "No, Reilly. I have to stay. There are some things I need to do."

"Nooo," she cries.

"Listen to me. Remember what a big, brave girl you are. It's just for tonight. Just until I've sorted things out."

She shakes her head, whining softly. "I don't want to."

"I know, honey. But it'll be okay."

"Promise?"

I'm about to give her that, a false promise, but I can't lie to her anymore. "I will try my best. Now off you go. And you do whatever Nayla tells you, okay?"

She sniffs, nods.

"That's my girl."

The girls trail off together down the hall, arms around each other for fortitude.

Nayla's eyes are on me; I can feel her solid gaze. "Nayla"—I bolster myself with a deep breath—"I'm not running anymore."

Her eyes cut me, a fine blade. "You can't stay here alone. He'll be back. I know the type."

"You're right. He will. But I have to convince him to let go."

"You can't convince someone like that."

"I have to try. I have to. Or this will never be over."

"It'll be over if ..." Her neck muscles contract as she swallows. "At the very least, lodge a complaint with the police. Leave a message if you can't get through. At least it'll get him on the record here."

I look her in the eye, tell her what she needs to hear.

"Oh, wait," she says. "I have something in my car."

She moves to the door, checks the peephole again, then edges the door open. "His car is gone."

I'm on the verge of telling her not to go out there, but she has to get the kids home somehow. Her car is on the drive, not far. "Let me come with you," I say. "Stand guard."

She nods.

I glance down the hallway to ensure the kids haven't appeared yet, then follow her out into the dark, waiting on the garden path, twitching at every crackle of undergrowth, every creak of insect or night creature. I muffle a shriek when a flying fox rustles its way out of a tree and takes flight, its leathery wings buffeting the humid night air.

Nayla slams her car door, sprints back to me. "Here." She holds out some sort of device. "It's a stun gun."

"What? Where did you get that?"

"Don't ask."

She shows me how to shoot it. It only has one set of darts. If I miss, the unit can still stun close-up. "Let's hope it doesn't come to that," she says. "And remember what I taught you in class: throat, heel of palm, groin. Brace. Don't hesitate."

Reilly and Sammi emerge, each trailing a little suitcase on wheels. I hug them both, try to brush the worry from their faces.

Nayla squeezes my hand. "Call me. I can take the kids to someone else. I can come back—"

"Go," I whisper and close the door on their worried faces.

Before I let my mind go where it wants to – to dark thoughts – I make myself a list of things to do:

- Email Daniel – reassure him that I'm leaving, that I won't put his daughter in any further danger.

- Call Margie – update her, ask if she's okay. If Evelyn has done this to me, what's she doing to Margie?

- Pack my belongings.

I only get as far as the email before exhaustion and indecision replaces my adrenaline. I need to sit for a minute.

<hr>

It's the TV and me in the dark. One of us low-level humming on the outside, the other, inside. Evelyn … Andreas … Evelyn … Andreas. Repeat ad nauseum. Why would Evelyn do this? *How* did she do it? If she didn't want me here, she could have just told me.

Exhaustion pulls at my eyelids.

I'm waiting at the airport for Daniel, anticipating his sympathy for the turmoil Reilly and I have been through. But when he appears through a parting in the crowd, he's glowering. He grows taller as he approaches, his face tight, fury simmering. He grabs my throat, pushes me back against the car. I'm a failure, he tells me. He shouldn't have trusted me. I try to explain, but my words are caught in his grip. Thunder breaks above us, hailstones.

I wake on the floor between the couch and the coffee table, M&Ms spilled about me like a shattered rainbow of bullets. Ugh, my back. It's killing me. I drag myself up onto the couch. The television has turned itself off. Did I fall on the remote? I scrabble for it on the floor and turn it back on, needing to dispel the loneliness sucking at my bones. But as soon as I press the button, I almost yelp as a siren blares at me. A garish red, purple and green graphic – like some kid's Crayola drawing of a storm with branched lightning. The words "Cyclone Warning" flash over and over.

Yasi has become a monster. Category 5. The biggest in Australian history. There is no higher rating. It's due to cross the coast late tomorrow evening.

Nayla has messaged me. She says they're okay. Am I? I should come to her place tomorrow around three, and we'll drive to Mossman together with the kids. They have a community hall that's safe.

I message her back:

See you then.

55

Morning is rude. Creeping in through the lounge window, spying on my rawness. I try to grimace away my headache. It doesn't cooperate. A flicker of a thought about the Endone in Daniel's room. I head to my room for the respite of paracetamol instead.

My bed looks so tempting. I could collapse there for a few more hours, but the need to check my emails is more pressing. I flip open my laptop. Daniel has answered. He sounds distraught. Says he's been trying to call me, has left messages. He's glad I'm okay, but I'm not to leave his employ until he's had a chance to talk with me. But he wants Reilly and me to move to safety, both from Andreas and the cyclone. He says we need to get away from the beach area. Go further north and inland. Use his credit card. He's managed to get back to Sydney but can't get a flight to Cairns – the airport closed at ten.

Shit. How long have I slept?

I email him back:

Thank you. Don't worry. I'll make sure Reilly is safe. We're going to Mossman with Nayla. I'll let you know when we get there. All under control. Safe flight back.

I check my phone. Flat.

I head to the kitchen, put my phone on charge, make coffee, then don sunglasses as I head out to the patio with a magazine for distraction – a faint hope. I'm still wearing my shorts and t-shirt from yesterday. Crusty. The pool beckons, a soothing sanctuary. I should shower first, but ... no one's going to know. I shed my outer clothing to bra and undies and dive in.

The water's a tonic to my weariness, even though it's baby-bath warm. Eyes closed, I fling my arms, three strokes to a breath, counting each lift and push, lift and push, until I sense I'm nearing the pool's edge. And each time I open my eyes to turn, it's like waking from a lazy dream, the tiredness almost painful.

This last lap, the effort has me spent. I climb the steps and collapse on a sun lounge, close my eyes to the sun, wait for my quick breaths to slow as I listen to the intermittent pats of water dripping from my body onto the already hot tiles. It would probably sizzle if it weren't for the humidity. I consider moving under a sun umbrella, but the heat, the exercise, last night, have drained the last of my energy. I'll burn if I wait too long, but I just ... can't. The magazine suffices to shade my face. Arms too tired to hold it up.

⋯◆⋯

A vague dinging calls me from my stupor. Windchimes? Again, louder. I jerk up, magazine slipping from my face to my chest, flapping to the ground in a heap of bent pages. Fumble into my clothes, underwear still damp. Slip into my sandals, cross the patio, sun bright in my face, the doorbell, a baby's cry that refuses to go unanswered.

Two blue-clad bodies, their middles bloated by the distorted peephole view, stand on the porch. I wrestle with the lock, peer around the door.

"Yes?"

"Georgia Wright?"

"Yes. Has something happened? Is it Nayla? The kids?"

One of the officers introduces himself and his partner. Jacobson and ... the second name slips from my mind as soon as Jacobson says, "We've had a report of a theft."

The relief sags me. "No," I say, moving to close the door. "You've got the wrong house." Wait ... they know my name.

Jacobson takes off his hat, wipes his forehead with a crumpled hanky pulled from his trouser pocket. "You are Georgia Wright? Do you mind if we talk inside?"

I squint, wavering. Why can't they just tell me what they want? Ugh. This heat. I check my clothes, making sure my wet bra isn't showing through my t-shirt. Once I've opened the door fully, I cross my arms over my chest anyway. "Come in."

They refuse the offer of a seat on the lounge, stand there towering over me like a couple of sweating monoliths in short-sleeve shirts. Jacobson must be over six foot, lean except for a small petulant gut that probably refuses to budge no matter how much his wife puts him on diets.

"Ms Wright, are you"—he refers to a pocket notebook—"familiar with Andreas—"

"Yes ... no ... I mean, we were ... Has he done something?" I squint, trying to focus through a sudden nervous fuzziness.

"Ma'am? Are you okay? You look pale."

"Yes ... no. I've been out in the sun. Can you just tell me what he's done?" I search his freckled face. He has kind eyes.

"Perhaps you should sit?" He nods at the couch. "Can we get you a glass of water?"

"Thank you." I point toward the kitchen, then ease onto the edge of the couch.

Jacobson motions to his younger counterpart, who looks freshly minted, shaved back and sides, uniform still holding its firmness and colour.

When the younger officer returns, I want to gulp the water, cascade the coolness down my throat, but I'm afraid to put too much in my protesting stomach. I clutch the glass on my knees for comfort.

Jacobson opens with, "Did you remove a diamond and sapphire ring from Andreas Weber's premises?"

"*Remove*? Is he kidding? It was my engagement ring. He gave it to me."

"Ah."

Something in his tone, his sagging demeanour, tells me he's been through this too many times. I imagine him making a comment about avoiding paperwork. Or is that a police trope?

"Maybe we can sort this out amicably? Do you still have it?"

I swallow, throat thick. "No. I posted it back to my sister, in Melbourne, to return to him. I have a receipt." I move to stand, but he raises a finger. Stay.

"When was this?" he asks.

"Umm ... just this Monday gone. I guess it wouldn't have arrived yet. But, like I said, I can show you the receipt."

"No need. It's not going to prove anything."

"What do you mean?"

He grimaces. "Not to be rude, but a receipt? You could have put anything in the parcel."

I pull my shoulders back, about to unleash ... but he's right. "Did he tell you he showed up here yesterday? Forced his way in, monstered me and the children?"

"He broke in?"

"N-no, one of the children. But he's been harassing me with text messages."

"He has?"

"Yes! I'll show"—I pause, mid-stance—"Am I allowed to get my phone?" It's hard to hold back the sarcasm.

He nods, and for a minute, I'm lost, trying to remember where I last left the damned thing. Kitchen. On the charger.

When I return, I open the text app and ... "He's deleted them."

"He's deleted them?" If Jacobson's condescension was any wetter, it would be dripping. "How?"

"I ... I gave him my phone—"

The younger officer interjects now. "You *gave* him your phone?"

"Yes. I told you he was monstering me. Yesterday."

"Where?"

"Here. In the house."

"You let him in the house?" the young officer says again.

Jacobson glowers at him but says nothing.

"No! I told you ... one of the children ... Look, I had a DVO out against him."

"You had a DVO against him?" The young cop again.

I only just manage not to shout "stop repeating everything I say". Hills to die on, Georgia.

"Yes," I continue. "From when I was in Melbourne. He wasn't allowed near me."

Jacobson takes control again, and I'm surprised he's not patting my head. "Okay. Well, unfortunately, it won't be valid here. You'll have to apply to a Queensland court to get it extended."

"Seriously?"

He shrugs. At least he has the decency to look apologetic. "But if he's threatening—"

"You know what? Go search my room."

"That's not really—"

"No. I insist." I don't waste time asking if I can move now, just march over to the hallway. "Come on. At least you can tell him I don't have his damned ring anymore."

They look at each other, hardly bothering to hide their resignation, but follow.

I stand aside as they enter my room, the bulk of them seeming to take up too much space, too much air. I lean back against the doorway, attempting casualness, but I can't help crossing my arms. A flush assaults my face as Jacobson opens my wardrobe, the other my dressing table drawer, feeling about in the softness of my t-shirts and underwear.

I half expect them to shove, yank things, heft them onto the floor, like they do in TV crime shows, but they're methodical, almost polite.

A sick, guilty feeling plagues my gut as they continue. Why? It's not as if they'll find anything. And the ring was effectively mine anyway, wasn't it? Isn't that the law?

Young officer moves to my bedside drawer. I think through what I have in there: tissues, hand cream ...

"Here. What's this?" He holds up a red velvet pouch.

My mouth dries as if a desert wind has swept through it. Jacobson halts his search of my mattress – the doona and pillows askew, as if they're halfway through being stripped for the weekly wash. He scowls, leans heavy on the bed to push himself off his knees, huffing with the effort, then saunters over to join his subordinate.

"That's ... impossible!" I say. "We posted it. Days ago." *Wait*. It's as if they knew exactly what they were looking for. "Who told you it was here?"

"Do you mind we open this?" Jacobson asks, as if he needs permission.

Does he?

I nod, not believing, not accepting.

He picks at the golden drawstring, his fingers too big, too cumbersome, then uses his fingernail to get a grip and pull apart the knot. He's done it. He opens the bag, tips the contents into his palm.

I slam my hand over my mouth, almost vomiting at the gut punch: Margie? Margie has done this?

"We'll wait in the lounge. Give you a moment to ... change if you like."

"You're arresting me?"

"No, ma'am, but it's best if you make a statement. Hopefully, we can clear this up without it escalating."

56

I've never been in the back of a police car. It smells of sweat and spilled milky coffee gone sour. I glance at the doorhandle to my left. Is it locked? I think about sneaking a hand over to check, but keep them both folded in my lap. Contained. Instead, my bottom lip bears the brunt of my nerves. I've done nothing wrong. Surely, they'll believe me, see Andreas's claims are false? They'll be able to check I had a DVO – or whatever they call it in Queensland. That one of their own failed me, put me in danger. I can give them Katie's number, my old manager's phone number. They'll confirm the engagement was real, testify to Andreas's violence. That's all this needs. It won't take long.

I shift my gaze to the back of Jacobson's head. Riding shotgun, he's sunk into his seat. Probably jaded, nearing retirement. How many people have protested their innocence to him? Does he have some sort of inbuilt radar after all these years, one that senses whether people are telling the truth? God, I hope so. I need an ally in this mess.

A thousand questions swarm, but I hold back, visions of American cop shows – people yelling from the backseat, banging on protective grates and being told to shut up. Stupid thoughts. These guys are chilled. But don't they say it's the quiet ones you have to watch? I've always thought that quiet violence was more dangerous than loud. The quiet violence in Andreas's eyes when I answered back, the quiet that told me a tsunami of slaps, punches, spitting and swearing was about to unleash.

Breathe.

I've got to be patient, co-operate. They can't charge me for something I haven't done. They can't hold me. Can they?

We pass a pretty weatherboard building with a corrugated-roofed verandah, and the older policeman points. "Been to the Court House Museum?"

"No," I say. "I've been meaning to."

"First and last woman hanged in Queensland – Ellen Thomson – was sentenced there along with her lover. Hanged in Boggo Road Gaol, 1887. Good for you we don't do that anymore, hey?" He laughs.

I don't know if he's trying to intimidate me, or if he genuinely thinks that's funny.

"You Melbournians went one better," he continues. "Had the last woman hanged in Australia – Jean Lee. Pentridge, yeah? Been there?"

"Yes. It's not attractive."

That's an understatement. I did a tour there once – its imperious bluestone walls surrounding the ugly, sorrowful facility, its tomb-like shadowy cells now imprisoning nothing but vestiges of long-gone occupants' desolation. Something dark seemed to suck light and hope from every room, every thick space. The smell was musty, earthy, but I swear there was also a remnant of death, an odour of fear slinking in murky corners. I couldn't stay, had to escape halfway through the tour.

I've heard there are plans to turn the prison into an accommodation and shopping complex – a ghoul's delight of shops, businesses and apartments. Imagine looking out your bedroom window and into a prisoners' exercise yard, or onto the roofs of buildings that held such misery. Imagine what went on there. The stuff of nightmares. What sort of person would be happy to live in a place like that, with such an overtly grim history?

I shudder. Such morbid thoughts while sunshine, sea and frangipanis pass by my window. I'm not going to jail. Even if the worst did happen, first offenders don't get jail time, do they?

I wonder if I can press charges against Andreas for false accusation. Wasting police time and resources is a crime isn't it? Why is he doing this anyway? He's capable of a lot of low things, but having me hauled in by the law under false pretences? If this is his way of trying to get me back, the fool has lost it.

Why doesn't he just get on with his life and let me get on with mine? There are plenty of other women out there. He's a physically attractive man. It wouldn't be hard for him to find someone else – someone who wants the same things as he does, someone who wouldn't mind being a trophy wife, house slave and baby factory. Maybe then he wouldn't be so angry, with his words and his fists.

Impossible. It's like asking a narcissist to see reason.

The car rolls to a stop outside the police station – a neat, light-blue and cream, low-slung building, its location prime, by the sea. I must have walked past it a few times. It's funny how you never notice some things until they become meaningful to you, how they take a backseat in your awareness.

Jacobson gets out of the car, opens my door, motions me out. The younger one sits flicking the screen of his mobile but looks up briefly. "Salad sanga?"

Jacobson nods. "Yeah. No butter this time."

Young cop rolls his eyes.

Inside, two air conditioning units buzz high up on opposite walls – a duel of wills against the humidity. My perspiration prickles. The officer behind the duty desk, a compact woman in her forties, glances up from her phone call, then goes back to her conversation: "Nope ... nope ... not our responsibility. Nope ... nope ... need to sort that yourself." Her tone brooks no argument, but her caller is persistent. "Daryl ... Daryl ..." She pulls the phone away from her ear – the caller is shouting – looks at it for a second, then casually hangs up.

"Ah, Wanda, Wanda, Wanda. You shouldn't do that," Jacobson says. "One day it'll come back to bite you on the bum."

She screws up one side of her mouth. "He'll call back. Always does."

Movement in my peripheral vision catches my eye – a man getting up from a bench recessed into the left wall, almost behind me. I don't want to be rude and turn to stare, but something about him sets off my senses. He steps closer. I spin, then step back as panic pushes a tsunami of fear through my chest.

He stands, hands on hips, back to feature his groin. I can imagine his charismatic insolence when he first arrived. I wish I could have witnessed Wanda's laconic response. She'd have probably looked Andreas up and down, expressionless, then gone back to whatever she was doing.

Andreas grins, then holds his arms out wide, as if he expects me to run and hug him in a happy reunion. "Hey, babe."

I'm a millisecond from recoiling, but force myself to keep still, keep my brain from issuing a primal reaction. *Focus. You're in a police station. He can't do anything.* I bite down on my tortured bottom lip and direct my attention to Jacobson. "Why didn't you warn me he was here?"

Jacobson's face is passive, but his eyes betray his surprise. "I wasn't aware."

He heads over to the desk and hands the red velvet pouch to Wanda. They converse, but I don't take in what they're saying, because Andreas has sidled up to me.

He inclines his head toward my ear. "You know, we can make this all go away," he murmurs.

I keep my eyes focused on Wanda. Jacobson is still talking to her, but her eyes are on me now. "Is that true?" she says. "Jacobson here tells me, you have an AVO?"

"A ... DVO. Is that the same thing? I ... I did have one."

"Close enough," Wanda says, then turns to Andreas. "Sir, step away from the lady."

Andreas's smarmy expression flickers, but it's back in a second. "She's my fiancée. She's coming back with me. Right, babe?"

Jacobson takes an interest now. "You said she stole the ring."

I suck in a breath, can't believe Andreas's stupidity. Easy as that. Reality is dawning on him now. We're all staring, waiting.

He returns to his cocky, hands-on-hips pose. "I meant ex-fiancée. But she had no right to take that ring."

"You can have the damned ring," I tell him. "I don't want it."

He looks hangdog now, as if he's offended. "Babe, I don't want it. I want you. I just want us together again."

I look him in the face and speak slowly so my voice doesn't break. "Andreas, I am not going back with you. I've had enough of being your punching bag. We are over. Take your ring and leave."

Something strange passes over his face. Uncertainty? Is he finally getting it?

He reaches for my wrist, grips it. I try to pull my arm way, but he holds tight, pulls me to him. His tone is low, gritty, threatening. "I miss you, babe. You belong with me."

I flail at him. "Let go!"

Jacobson is suddenly beside me, shoving an arm across Andreas's chest, wedging him away from me. "Back off. Now!"

Andreas holds his hands up in surrender, smarmy smile back in place. "She knows I'm right. Just a matter of time."

"Ma'am. Do you wish to press charges?"

I'm about to say why bother, but, "Yes, yes, I do," comes out instead. For all the good it will do.

Andreas hawks up saliva, about to spit it at us, but changes his mind. The look he gives would have made me tremble once.

◆

A couple of hours later, Jacobson's sidekick drives me back to the house, droning about the cyclone. "Not seen one this big up here. Not in my time. Not in anyone's time." He says it might still move north or south. "Can't never tell. Sometimes they change their mind, just like a woman." He laughs. "Maybe that's why they all used to have female names."

Jerk. He needs to stop hanging around pubs with his yobbo mates.

"Guess I shouldn't be saying things like that, hey? Might offend someone?"

Idiot.

He keeps going, mansplaining how I should pay attention to warnings on the telly, on the radio. When we reach the house, he asks if I'd like him to come in with me. "Just to be safe."

I decline his chivalry, but as soon as I get inside, regret it – I've forgotten to arm the security system. Yet, some small part of me, the petulant child, doesn't care. Doesn't want to.

Screw Andreas.

Screw Evelyn.

Screw Margie.

Screw Reilly for making me care.

Screw this house with its cold white walls. Aren't houses supposed to collect the energy of their inhabitants? Don't their walls, floors, furniture, absorb all that negativity? Has this house packed it all down, its façade the cool sweetness of privilege? Will it reach a breaking point, then belch out all that trouble and misery?

I can't deal. With anything. It's never going to stop until I stop it.

Wine. The last of it.

Endone.

Margie was right. I'm a lush.

57

Somewhere in the recesses of my drugged, wine-soaked consciousness, I register the intermittent vibrations of my phone. Ugh. Go away. I almost fall asleep before it starts again. I reach a leaden arm to wrestle the phone out from under my pillow, crack a crusty eye open. It's after three o'clock. Five missed calls. Two voicemails. Not to listen to them. Don't want to hear Margie's voice.

Close my eyes.

Then open the message app. Type.

I know what you did.

So tempting to press send. To wait for a reaction. Wait for lies. But I want to see her face when I say it. See her panic, reach for excuses. Tell me it wasn't her. Tell me it wasn't Evelyn. Tell me they weren't in this together.

Why? Why hire me if they wanted me gone? I just don't get it.

The phone bounces off the bed as I drop it, lands on the floor. Stuff it. There's no one here I trust now. Not even … is Daniel in on this too? He's known Margie since forever. Well screw them all. If they want me out, I'm out.

But there's Reilly. Damn it.

The phone vibrates again. Such anger. Such fury as I roll onto my side to reach for it. Reach for a release from this hell. To tell her. Tell Margie what a bitch she is. Her and her fake-ass lover.

Arrrgh! Goddammit that hurt. I'm on the floor, the phone under me. Too much effort to roll off it. I push up onto an elbow, manage some yoga-esque manoeuvre to drag the phone out. I was right; it's Margie.

"WHAT!?"

"Georgia? Are you okay? Why haven't you called me? Has something happened?"

"So much."

"Are you okay?"

"I guess that depends on what you mean by 'okay'."

"Georgia? What's on? You sound ... are you drunk?"

"Not nearly enough."

"What's happened? Where's Reilly?"

"Don't stress yourself. She's at Sammi's. Safe 'n' sound."

Her relief seems to deflate her voice. "Are you okay? Do you need help?"

"I'm getting out. Leaving." Am I drawling? I think I am.

"Yes, you should."

See? It's true. They want me gone.

"They're saying to go to Mossman," she says. "The community hall. All the resorts are evacuating there."

"What?"

"You have to get out. It's not safe."

"I ... I just said that." I shake my head. "You got what you wanted."

"What?"

"Andreas. He's found me. Are you happy now?"

She pauses. "Andreas is there?"

"I know I don't mean anything to you, but I can't believe you would put Reilly at risk."

"Georgia, what are you talking about? I don't understand."

"THEY FOUND THE RING! Don't pretend you don't know. And Evelyn – I saw her text messages." Damn these tears.

"Georgia, you're rambling. You need to sober up. You need to get to Mossman, or at least get to somewhere away from the beach. Are you hearing me?"

"Sure." Let her stress. Let her suffer.

"The house is vulnerable on the hillside. And they say there's going to be a king tide with the cyclone. The beach area and town might flood. If you need money, use the household credit card. Take the car. Take whatever you need."

"Margie?"

"Yes?"

Can't speak, so many thoughts tying up my throat. But I can't help it; I want to know why.

"Georgia, if I could be there I would, but the road is closed. Tell me you'll be okay," she says.

"Okay," I whisper.

"Tell me."

"I *said* okay."

"Alright. Take care of yourself. I'll see you on the other side."

I hang up, drag myself outside to air my sorrows. The sea is a wrinkly green-grey carpet, the air thick with heat and drizzle. I lift my head, let the rain fall on my face, slick, melting. This calm is too oppressive.

God, I stink. I take a shower, change into fresh shorts and t-shirt. Coffee, coffee, coffee. Ugh. More coffee. Am I sober enough to drive yet? Maybe I should wait a while longer. The cyclone won't be arriving until after midnight, and Mossman is only twenty minutes away. Better play it safe. A few more hours of sleep. My weary body won't say no. After some food.

I gather eggs, bacon, bread – use up the last of the fresh food in a good fry-up. For a second, I toy with the idea of a raw-egg smoothie. Ugh. Probably a myth anyway. With my luck lately, I'd get salmonella.

The eggs are popping, bacon spitting, when a banging on the door jerks me from my thoughts. Coffee spills down my t-shirt. "Fuck! Is that Andreas again?"

I head down the hall, sprinting a little when the banging comes again. The peephole reveals a woman and man in orange overalls. SES – State Emergency Services. I pull the door open.

"You're aware there's an evacuation notice for the waterfront?"

I assure them I'll be gone long before the cyclone arrives.

"Most people along here have already gone, and we won't be able to provide rescue services once the storm hits."

I thank them and return to my overcooked breakfast. Good thing I like crunchy.

Before I settle down to nap, I work my way around each room, closing the steel security shutters. They seem strong enough to protect the windows, but up here on the hill, the house still feels prone. The shutter in Reilly's bedroom sticks a few centimetres from the bottom. Damn. Forgot that hadn't been fixed. Hope I haven't made it worse. When I press the switch to raise it again, the shutter moves up a centimetre, then jams, the motor whining. I try to manually force it down, or up, but it won't budge. *Forget it.*

My belongings sit by the front door in my carry bag and a borrowed suitcase – not stolen; I've left a note I'll return it. Wouldn't want anyone to think I'm a thief.

I lie on the couch. A couple more hours of rest. Just a couple. I flick through mind-numbing daytime television channels, muting the sound every time the glaring cyclone warning comes on with unbearable frequency, then switch to the streaming channels, settle on Con Air, but as soon as Nicolas Cage tells John Malkovich not to screw with his daughter's bunny, my eyes droop. Perhaps I was just waiting for that iconic scene ...

Beep.

It's Andreas. A photo – him and Reilly. He has her by the hair, her head pulled back exposing her throat.

Open up little piggy, or I'll huff and puff and ...

A knock at the door – a shave and a haircut rhythm – not an urgent thumping. I'm off the couch and bolting down the hall, not bothering to look through the peephole. He shoves Reilly toward me as soon as I pull the door open. She flings her arms around me, buries her face in my stomach. I kneel, tilt her head, look into her face. "Did he hurt you? Are you okay?"

She nods, terror making her mute. I stand again, push her behind me. She clings tight, a limpet on my back.

"Greetings from the Ninja's house," Andreas says. "They send their apologies for not being able to join us."

"How did you ... what have you done? If you've hurt—"

"Keep your panties on. You girls are just too easy."

Reilly's voice is muffled. "He followed us. He tied them up in the laundry."

I picture Nayla and Sammi on the hard tiles, socks or hand towels stuffed in their mouths. He must have disabled Nayla. She wouldn't give up without a fight.

"What are you doing, Andreas? This is too far."

"Babe, babe, babe. I've come to rescue you." He spies my suitcases by the door. "And just in time, it would seem."

"What?"

He raps his knuckles hard on my forehead. "Hello? Anybody home? There's a cyclone a-coming."

I slap his hand away and shove his chest. "We can handle it ourselves. Get out."

My shove surprises him, but he grabs the doorjamb and shoots his foot forward, jamming the door open as I attempt to close it. I lean in and press hard, hoping it hurts enough to make him back off.

"Go away! Leave us alone. I'm calling the police."

Reilly comes out from behind me to lend her strength. Andreas laughs, and with one push has us sprawling. My head connects with the hallway wall, and I drop to the floor, Reilly beside me. Andreas saunters in, and I stare at the sweaty, unshaven face towering above me. He looks haggard, face glowing with ruddy heat.

"You look terrible," I say, for want of something else.

"It's bloody hot! Why the hell do people come here for holidays? Offer me a cool drink, why don't you?"

"You're not getting anything from me."

"Is that so?"

I push myself off the floor, back still against the wall, signal to Reilly to get to her feet.

Andreas takes a step toward us and leans in close to my face. There's blood under his nose. Did Nayla get a punch in? I fight to keep my breathing even, clench my jaw, refuse to flinch. Nayla's words come back to me, "Brace, don't show fear."

Andreas feigns a smack to the side of my head, and damn it, I flinch.

"Ha, ha! Just kidding. You know I wouldn't hurt you, babe. I love you."

Sharp pain as I roll my fingers inwards, dig my nails into my palms, fold my thumb across tight – strike ready. A hard punch to his throat, or the heel of my palm up and under his nose would be enough to let me push him back out again. *Do it. Do it.* But what if I miss? What if he catches my arm? He'll break it.

Reilly pulls on my sleeve, wrestling me back to reality. "Sweetheart, I want you to go to your room and pack another overnight bag. Use your school satchel."

She doesn't argue. She's off, pelting down the hall.

"Going somewhere?" Andreas asks.

"Yes. But not with you."

He tilts his head. "Babe. Come on. I got two tickets out of here. We can make the flight before they close the airport if we hurry.

"You're delusional. The airport's already closed. Andreas, listen to me – you need to get out of here. Find somewhere safe for yourself. I'm *not* going back with you. I'm *not* taking another beating. That's a promise. We are done."

He widens his eyes. "Oooh, listen to the little lady talking. Anyone would think you'd grown a pair."

He presses a finger into my breastbone, tries to back me up the hallway. "*You* do as I say."

I slap his hand away and stand my ground. "You just don't get it, do you? It's over, Andreas. Give up. *Go home.*"

"Never."

Something settles over me. Not anger, not defiance, something calmer, stronger. I step toward him, take his hands in mine. They're heavier than I remember, swollen with the heat.

"Andreas, this is for your sake as much as mine. We both know there's nowhere for this to go. If you don't stop, you're going to destroy us both. Is that what you want? You say you love me. If you do, just leave. Find somewhere safe to ride out the storm. Then go home. Start again."

He swallows, says nothing for a moment, as if he's considering my words. *Please, please*, let him see, let him realise the carnage he's causing.

He flips his hands around mine, squeezes and smiles. "You know what we need? A nice refreshing beverage. Yeah, and a good long talk."

"I ... we're leaving, Andreas. We're going to pick up Nayla and Sammi, then evacuate to Mossman."

"Come on, you got time for one last drink."

"Your drinks never stop at one, Andreas. You need to stay sober so you can drive."

His face hardens. I've pushed too far.

"Okay," I say. "Just a quick one." What the heck am I doing?

He kicks the door closed behind him, then follows me to the kitchen. The knife block next to the sink catches my eye – no, he'd have me sliced up before I got in a single stab, even if I were capable of that.

"Hot or iced?"

"Are you kidding? Come on, babe. A proper drink."

I spin to face him. "If you want to talk, it's tea or coffee."

He stares. A beat passes between us. He looks away. "Sure. Whatever. Iced."

Finally, a concession.

"I'm having hot."

This might work. I take my time preparing the tea things – filling the kettle, putting it on to boil, retrieving Margie's iced tea from the fridge, pouring Andreas a tall glass. But when the kettle clicks off and I reach for it, he moves in close and places his hand over the handle. I look at him. His blood-shot eyes say everything. He removes his hand so I can pour.

"He picks up his glass and holds it up to examine its contents. Why are you having hot tea? What's wrong with this? You poisoned it?"

I sigh. "For god's sake." I take the glass from him and take a big gulp, forgetting how it gives me brain freeze. I grimace, rubbing my forehead. He laughs.

"Put some food together, babe. I'm starving."

"You're not staying that long."

Another look.

"There's not a lot. We haven't had time to shop. It'll have to be cheese and crackers."

"Whatever."

I stare at the sharp knife in my hand as I slice off a block of hard cheese, picture the blade in his gut or chest, imagine the meaty sensation of its tip jamming between his ribs, the blood spatter, the surprise on his face ... then him grabbing and pulling it out, slicing my throat.

I leave the knife on the sink, replace it with a cheese knife and turn to pass him the plate. "If you can carry this, I'll ..."

Something is missing from the bench. I scan, trying to remember what was there. It only takes a moment. "Put that back."

"Sorry?"

"Come on, Andreas. This is no way to start."

"No idea what you're talking about."

"My phone. The charger lead is still there."

He holds up a hand. "Not me, babe. Maybe the kid took it."

"Andreas—"

"Come on. Let's go sit in the lounge."

He turns and heads to the doorway. I glance back at the knife. Maybe I could hide it in my back pocket?

"Babe?"

I jerk toward him. Did he see me looking? "Um ... do you like dried figs?" I point to the white box on the bench – Evelyn's present. Oddly, just the smell of them makes me nauseous now.

"You know I do."

I pick up the figs and my tea and follow him into the lounge. We place the food and drinks on the coffee table.

"Why's it so dark in here?" he asks.

"I've closed all the shutters, for the cyclone."

"Huh."

I move to switch the lounge room light on, then stand there, unsure what to do next. He bows a little, holds out a hand – a boor of a gentleman – indicating for me to sit on the couch. I expect him to stay standing, to hold a power stance, but he sits beside me, his weight pressing down into the cushions, forcing our bodies to lean into each other.

"Oops. Too close, right?"

My obligatory smile is tight.

He shuffles over a little, the gesture giving me a stupid spark of hope.

I point to the food. "Help yourself."

He glances at the plate, then shoves an olive in his mouth while loading up a cracker with cheese. "Good," he says, spitting out the olive pip and refilling his mouth. "Can't remember the last time I ate." He moves his focus from the cheese plate to the packet of figs. "So what are these? Special or something?"

"Spiced figs. They were a gift from my employment agent."

He laughs, derisive. "Agent, hey?" He opens the box, pushes aside the tissue paper and sniffs, then pulls a face. "Some fancy shit. Too fancy for me." He replaces the box.

"So"—I pick up my tea, a small, boiled barrier between us—"What do you want to talk about?"

He shrugs. "You and me. Me and You. Us, we."

"There is no 'you and me' anymore. It was over the first time you hit me."

He reaches a hand, and I pull back as he tries to brush some hair from my face. "Please don't touch me."

He straightens, snorts, releases it through his mouth. "I know I wasn't good to you, babe. I didn't mean to hurt you, but you made me mad. You know? If you didn't talk back all the time, things would have been different. Don't you see that? It could have been so easy."

I swallow, soften my voice. "Things were never easy, Andreas. You wanted to own me. Control me. That's not a relationship. That's jail."

"Nah, you're looking at it the wrong way, babe. I'm giving you security. A home. I'm out there every day, working like a dog for you. Don't I give you the best of everything?"

He's talking as if we're still living together.

"Don't I, babe?"

"You did. You're right. You gave me everything. But I didn't ... I don't *want* everything. I don't need it. I want space, but you won't let me have that."

His shoulders sag. "I'm trying, babe. All I want is for you to be happy." He shakes his head. "Don't I make you happy?"

I replace my tea, lower my head, gather the hem of my shorts in each hand for fortitude. "Maybe you could make someone else happier. Someone who feels the same way you do. Then it wouldn't be such a battle. We're plainly not suited for each other."

His jaw stiffens, his voicing dropping to a low monotone. "I don't want anyone else. I want you."

I pat his leg. "Drink your tea. It's getting warm. Is it okay if I check on Reilly? I won't be a minute."

Permission. I wait for it.

"Yeah, go on. Leave her there though. I don't want the kid here. This is about you and me." As I push into the cushions to get up, he grabs my wrist. "We have an understanding, don't we?" He glances toward the hallway.

<hr>

A new pain fills my chest as I push open Reilly's door. The room is empty, save for her school bag on the bed, half-filled with clothes, a few snowdomes.

"Reilly?" I whisper.

Nothing.

I kneel beside her bed, lift the covers and bend to look underneath. No scared mouse hiding there.

"Reilly?" I call, louder.

A muffled bump. Her cupboard.

I open the door. She's sitting in the base, arms wrapped around her knees, face buried.

"Sweetheart? Are you okay?" I whisper.

She looks up, eyes swollen, red. "Is he gone?"

She moves to get up, but I indicate for her to stay put, put a finger over my mouth—"Shhh"—then squat next to her, smooth her hair. "It's okay. No one's going to hurt you."

"But he's going to hurt you, isn't he?" she whispers.

I swallow down the pain of her knowledge. Too young to have witnessed, to have experienced, such violence. I so want to tell her everything will be alright, but I can't lie. We both know better. "He'll probably try. But I'm going to fight him, Reilly. I'm going to fight him with everything I've got."

"Can't we call the police?"

"He has my phone. And they're probably all tied up with the cyclone coming."

"Are we going to die?"

I swallow. *Don't lie.* "We still have a few hours before it arrives. The worse won't be until after midnight."

She nods, sage in her dread.

I sit back on my haunches, look over to the French doors, the gap under the shutter. "Reilly, do you think you could fit under there?"

She leans out to see where I'm pointing. "I don't know."

"Let's give it a try, hey?"

She nods, clambers out of the cupboard, and we move to the windows. I open the French doors, and a hiss of wind blows in from the base of the shutter. The outskirts of the storm must have arrived. I kneel and give the shutter one more heft. No luck.

"Why don't we just ..." Reilly reaches for the shutter switch.

"No!" I hiss.

She jerks her hand away, panicked.

"It's stuck. He'll hear the motor."

I take her hand, try to squeeze the fear out of both of us. She looks at the gap. It doesn't seem big enough.

"If you can get through, I want you to run down the hill as fast as you can and find a neighbour who will let you in. If no one's home, run into town, to the police station. Okay?"

"But what about you?"

"Don't worry about me. I'll be okay."

She nods, gets down on her hands and knees, then lies flat on the tiles. She pushes an arm through the gap, inches her head under sideways, but her shoulders and upper back jam. "I can't," she cries.

"Shhh, it's okay. Doesn't matter."

I help her shuffle back inside just as Andreas yells from the lounge.

"Coming," I yell back.

I lead Reilly to her bed. Sit her on the edge. "Stay here, okay? I'm going to get us out of this."

"But—"

"You trust me, don't you?"

She looks unsure, beyond tears now, but nods because it's the only thing to do when you're a terrified kid and a monster is in the house and the grown up is pretending everything will be alright.

※

When I return to the lounge, Andreas has the fig box is open in his hand. He pats the couch next to him. Compulsory. "Mmm. These aren't so bad. Have one."

"No thanks."

"No, go on, they're really good."

He pushes the box at me. The smell almost makes me retch. "I can't. I think I'm allergic." I reach for my tea.

"Huh, didn't know that." He shoves two more in his mouth, his jaw working the leathery fruit.

"A lot of things about me you don't know."

He eyes me.

"Sorry. Big mouth."

He's quiet as he chews, looking around the room. "Stuff here must be worth a lot."

"I guess."

"What does this guy do for a living?"

"Building industry."

"Yeah, worth a lot. You doing him?"

"No! Of course not. Listen, can we talk about you?"

He spits a hard piece of fig into his hand and scrapes it onto the lid of the box. "Not one to talk about myself, really."

I nod. "And that's the problem."

He stiffens.

Careful. You can't reason with a narcissist.

"I mean, not the 'problem', I mean"—I put my hand on his knee, and he looks at it—"when's the last time you took a moment to think about yourself?"

He licks his bottom lip. "Never, babe. It's always you."

"I know. You think about me all the time. But you're just as important."

He shrugs, sucking fig remnants from his teeth with his tongue.

"When you're so focused on me, how have you got room for anything else in your life? Your health, your job – surely that's suffering?"

He reaches for a couple more figs and chews as if considering my words. "Go on."

Can I finally get a wedge in his brain? Put a crack in his obsession?

"It must be exhausting for you. You look so tired."

"Yeah, well, not much sleep. That's on you."

"Andreas. You need to take some responsibility here—"

"I am! I'm trying to fix this."

"Shhh."

He sags a little, presses the palm of his hand to his forehead, lowers his voice. "I am, babe. But you're right, I'm so tired." He closes his eyes, shakes his head, as if trying to loosen a headache. "Nobody understands."

"And you deserve happiness as much as anyone—"

"I do. You know I do. But you're not letting me have it."

I take his hands now, squeeze them, look him in the eye. "Andreas, you're not letting *yourself* have it."

He opens his eyes. "So this is all my fault?" His voice has hardened, risen. "It's *my* fault? Did I sneak out of our home? Did I buy a ticket and fly as fucking far away as I could?"

Calm. Calm. Stay calm.

I squeeze his hands again, bringing his attention back ... trying to hold back the demon, the putrid beast, panting to unfetter itself. "It's no one's fault, Andreas. It's just ... we're not right for each other. Our relationship is toxic. Do you think all this anger is good for you, or me?"

His chin sinks to his chest.

"You could be perfectly happy with someone else. Someone who appreciates everything you do for them. Isn't that what you want?"

"I don't want someone else." He's sulking now, wanting pity. "You said you'd marry me."

I let go of his hands, sip my tea again, carefully replace it, then look him in the eye. "Andreas. I'm sorry if I caused you pain. But being together isn't healthy for either of us. Can't you see that? I can't beg anymore. You have to move on."

"Bullshit." He reaches for yet more figs. Chews heavily. I'm grateful he's expending his energy on the rubbery fruit instead of me. Is there the tiniest chance I'm getting through?

"It's him, isn't it?"

He jabs my chest. Hard. Here come the bruises. I steel myself. *Don't show fear.* "No."

"He's got more money, a better house, car."

"Stop it. You know I don't care about those things. And there is no 'him'. He's ... gay." *Forgive me, Daniel.* "There's just no 'us'. There doesn't need to be someone else for me to not want to be with you."

Oh, hell. His face is reddening. Before I can react, he has my throat. "Don't you ever say that!"

I manage a tiny nod, my vision blurring with tears, heart wild. "I'm sorry," I rasp.

"*Never.* You hear me? There will *always* be you and me."

I stare at his nose, willing myself to pound it, to drive the heel of my hand up into the cartilage, to see him roll back in agony and fall, but what then? I'd never be able to run down to Reilly's bedroom, drag her past him, then out the front door.

Suddenly, he lets go, and I gasp, fill my lungs, twice, three times. He fists his hands, puts them to his forehead and keens. "Babe, babe. See what you do? I don't wanna do it, but you drive me nuts. Why can't you just do as you're told?" He lurches at me then, grabs me in his arms, leans his weight on me, sobs. "I don't wanna be like this. I don't. Why can't we just be happy? You're right, babe. I'm tired. So tired."

He shifts his bulk, and in a horrible instant I think he's going to pin me to the couch, rape me, here, within earshot of Reilly. But his hands slide down my arms, and he drops his head in my lap. "So tired, babe." He clings to my knees, crying.

I don't know what's happening. Is he having a breakdown? Do I dare to cling to a skerrick of hope?

I pat his back. "We don't have to fight, Andreas. I'm tired too. My bones are weary from running."

He takes a huge, shuddering breath and quietens, then bends his knees and lifts his feet onto the couch. "I don't feel well."

I sit. Breathing. Waiting. Staring down at the side of his sweaty face, the scar on his left cheek a narrow vein of white against his ruddiness. Minutes pass. Maybe fifteen. Is that a snore? I try not to move, hoping he'll fall deeply enough asleep that I can shuffle out from under him, but my back is cramping. I can't help it, I have to relax my muscles, lean back into couch. He snuffles, then resettles himself, hugging my knees. The cyclone warnings flash silently on the television. I stare at the entrance to the hallway leading to the bedrooms, hoping, by some miracle, Reilly might disobey me and appear. I'd signal for her to sneak out the front door. Once she's out, I could shove Andreas off me, bolt to the door myself. He'd be too dazed to figure what was happening.

But there are too many ifs, and the hallway remains empty, the house silent except for the low howl of the growing wind, curling around the house, as if marking it for destruction.

⸻ ◆ ⸻

I jerk awake. How on earth did I fall asleep? Nothing has changed, except the wind has strengthened, branches slashing against the house, as if they're desperate to come in and escape their own monstrous master. Is it dark out there now?

I spy a lump in Andrea's pants pocket. My phone? Easy, easy, I slide my hand along his back, gently rubbing to see if he wakes. Slowly move down over his waist, pause, hold my breath, insert my hand into his pocket, pinch the phone between two fingers, millimetre by millimetre, ease it upward, upward. Halfway now.

He suddenly pushes himself up, the back of his head nearly connecting with my face. The phone slides out of his pocket and lands in the gap behind the seat cushions, a corner still visible.

He sits up, smiles groggily. "Oh, babe. Did I fall asleep?" He wipes spittle from the side of his mouth, picks up his drink and swigs the remainder.

I don't think about it, don't hesitate – I swoop my hand to the phone, grab it, shove it down the back of my shorts, into my underwear.

"Thirsty," he says. "More?"

"Sure. I'll get it for you."

"Don't do anything I wouldn't."

I nod, pick up his glass, listen to him crunch more crackers. In the kitchen, I go straight to the fridge, get the jug of tea out and take it to the bench, grab a tea towel, pull out my phone, put it on silent. It's after nine. Shit. Dial the police station. I've half-filled the glass before the phone shows a connection. Whip it to my ear – it's diverted. *Stupid, stupid, stupid. Of course it is.* I whisper a pointless message, slip the phone between the tea towel folds.

Andreas is sitting on the edge of the couch. He looks dazed, skin waxen underneath flushed cheeks. He sucks in a couple of breaths.

"Andreas? What's wrong? Are you okay?"

He shakes his head. "Something ... where's the bathroom?"

I point. "Down there. Second door on the right."

He lurches to his feet, hand over his mouth, bolts. I'm not sure whether to follow him or grab Reilly and run. But I'll have to pass the bathroom to get to her.

I have to try.

As I silently tread past the open bathroom door, Andreas retches a great, violent heave. He's on his knees, hands on either side of the toilet bowl, spasms gripping his body. I'm reminded of my night of horror last Saturday and ... I actually feel a twinge of sympathy for him.

I step away, bare toes gripping the tiles as I slink to Reilly's room.

<hr>

She's sitting on her bed, a small carry bag beside her, hand clamped over her mouth. She's turned off the main light, so the room is dim except for the dance of pink and purple butterflies her bedside carousel lamp casts on the ceiling. Its motor whirs quietly, constantly.

She lowers her hand. "Is he sick?"

I whip a finger to my lips—"Shhh"— beckon to her. She slips off the bed, turns to pick up her bag and creeps toward me, her bag tilting her body to one side. "Reilly, what have you got in here?" I whisper.

"My snow globes. I can't go without them. What if our house blows away?"

"Honey, no." I don't have the heart to tell her she's being irrational, that we need to run, to fly. *Calm, keep her calm.* "Sweetheart, you can't—"

"WHAT THE FUCK have you done to me?"

His bellow jolts us. Reilly looks about to scream. I push her behind me as footsteps thud down the hall. Then a heavier thud – he's fallen. Cursing.

I slam the door. No lock. What now? Hide in the cupboard? The teak dresser to my right catches my eye.

"Help me." I'm not sure why I'm still whispering; the monster is loose and knows exactly where we are.

We grunt, push and pull. My back complains bitterly, but I'm thankful for the grip of my bare feet and the help of the little mat beneath the dresser that lets us slip-slide the weighty bulk in front of the door. I lean over it, listen to Andreas's muffled cursing between moans, picture him on his knees, crawling closer, thumping the walls.

Stepping back, I glance at our efforts. The mat catches my eye. Andreas will probably just push the door open and slide the damned thing out of the way. "We have to remove the mat," I say, trying not to cry out as I bend to lift a corner of the dresser. "Can you pull the mat away from the leg?"

Reilly does as I ask, and we work our way around until all four legs are sitting on their rubber stoppers. I slump to the floor, breathing heavily. Reilly sits, leans into me, and I put an arm around her, ready to brace. The child feels smaller, as if I could crush her in my armpit. "It's okay."

Andreas has gone quiet. Gathering for another onslaught? We sit silently for a while, listening to the wind. It's stronger now. It warned us, and now it's coming for us.

The lamp on Reilly's bedside table flickers. For a mad moment, I think of Margie's comment about the light circuits, and I imagine Andreas has boiled the kettle, but it must be the storm.

"What are we going to do now?" Reilly whispers.

"I don't know. Wait, I guess. Maybe he'll pass out. Or give up and go away." Words. Rubbish words. Deep in my bones, I know it. Andreas will never give up; this is his finale. It won't end until someone's dead.

Reilly trembles, lets go a single sob, then bites down on her lip. "Are we going to die?"

I pull her closer. "Hey, no. It's okay. We're okay. He's not going to hurt us. I won't let him."

Empty, empty lies.

She puts her fist in her mouth to stifle her crying. I ease it away. "Don't hold it in, sweetheart. If you need to cry, cry."

"He'll hear me." She hiccups, and I sense the tide of fear she needs to unleash.

"Doesn't matter now, honey. You cry if you need to. Heck, I might join you." I laugh, thin, edgy, a bit manic.

"But he hurt Sammi."

Her words hang, and my breath catches in wariness. What has she seen? What did the bastard do over there?

She's searching my face, eyes asking permission. I wipe a tear threatening to join the others on her pale face, kiss the top of her head, stroke her hair. I want to tell her now is not the time or place, but ... "Do you want to tell me what happened?"

She lowers her head, presses her hands together, fingers threading, then digs her thumbnail into the quick of the other. She's trembling.

"I think ..."

I give her a gentle squeeze.

"I think ... he might have—"

The bang is so loud, so forceful, it reverberates through the dresser. Reilly screams. I grab her closer, pull her face to my chest. "It's okay, it's okay, it's okay."

Another bang. "Bitch!"

Another. "I'm sick," he wails. "You gotta call a doctor." Muffled dragging against the door, softer thuds. "You poisoned me. I'm sick." He's crying, retching over and over.

I wait.

Wait.

Wait.

The wind wails outside, picking up small loose objects and smashing them against the house. Somewhere in the chaos, Andreas's moaning stops. I close my eyes. Listen. Can't move. Too scared.

I ease my grip on Reilly. She straightens, takes a couple of big breaths, sniffs a few times. "Is he dead? Can we go now?"

I so want to tell her yes. "I think we should wait a little while."

"But the storm is coming—"

"I *know*." I've spoken harsher than I mean to. "You're right. We need to go, but ... just a few minutes."

She nods. Tucks into my armpit. "Georgia?"

"Hmmm?"

"Did you?"

"What?"

"Did you poison him?"

"No. No, of course not."

But her words pause my rattling thoughts, force me to focus on a single thread: *poisoned*. What did Andreas eat? Cheese, olives, biscuits, tea and ... figs.

Figs. Evelyn again.

Time becomes surreal. I'm falling down Alice's rabbit hole.

But this new trembling, this latent energy, boiling up from some place of fury I never knew I had, is like an armour – a hardening of molten igneous rock.

❧

I grunt as I lift the last corner of the dresser, tilting it back as Reilly shuffles on her hands and knees to shove the mat back under the footing. Another grunt as I ease the dresser down, work to push both my pain and the dresser away.

We don't need to say anything; our martyred looks of "now or never" are sufficient. I ease my breath out, long and slow, then turn the door handle. With all the noise from the wind outside, I'm hoping Andreas hasn't heard us – if he's conscious. The hallway is dim, empty. I turn to Reilly and whisper, "Let's go."

She reaches for her bag of snowdomes, and I almost scold her but change my mind. "If we have to run, you have to drop it. Okay?"

She nods, solemn in her promise.

We move slowly at first, me still with bare feet, trying to avoid the slippery mess of vomit Andreas has left on the tiles. Something else, shiny, wet, coats the floor. I bend and look closer. Water. Ahead, the kitchen kettle lies on its side. He *was*. He was going to throw boiling water over us.

I hold Reilly's hand, press my other hand flat against my chest, begging my heart to quieten, to not beat so damned loud.

We make it to the kitchen doorway, and I stick my head in. Empty.

"Keep going," I whisper.

And just as we reach the end of the hallway, I slam to a halt. Andreas is lying on his back just inside the lounge room, his arm stretched across the doorway. I inch closer. His eyes are closed, bile leaking down his cheek and puddled on the floor. His face looks aged – the texture and colour of day-old white coffee scum.

We have to step over him.

I turn back to Reilly, whisper that she should go first. "I'll wait until you're across the room." She gives an imperceptible nod and holds a finger over her mouth. *Shhh*. My heart swells. Smart kid. So brave.

I coil my muscles, ready to defend her escape if Andreas stirs. She steps over his arm, avoiding the bile, then creeps along, her sneakers silent except for a faint tapping on the tiles – a metal aglet from a loose shoelace. How I hear it over the wind is beyond me.

Hypervigilance.

A nagging part of me wishes she'd move faster, so I can follow, but I don't want to hurry her, to panic her. She's halfway across the lounge when Andreas's body lets go a loud fart.

I snap my gaze to him. I must be hysterical because I want to laugh at the juxtaposition of ridiculousness and acute terror of him waking. But I've heard bodies release gas when they're dead, so ...

He shifts a little, and I jerk back.

Not dead then.

Reilly has paused. I signal for her to continue. Once she's across and standing in the entrance hallway, I take a step closer to his body, preparing to step over him. I understand now why Reilly had moved so slowly – my muscles want to seize, need coercion to move.

I lift my foot, balance unsteady, place it on the other side of him, my breath stuck in my chest. I want to squeeze my eyes shut, so I don't see the slack body I'm straddling. *Move. Keep moving*. I gather myself, lift my back foot. *Easy, easy.* I'm over!

I keep my focus on Reilly – scared to look down at Andreas, as if by doing so, I'll be inviting the monster out from under my childhood bed. If I don't look, he can't move.

But he can.

Hot fingers curl around my ankle. I scream, yank my foot from his grip, the other slipping in the bile, sprawling me face first. "Run, Reilly! Run!" I scream.

She drops her bag and takes off.

I can't help it; I look back to face the monster. He's lumbering to his feet. I scrabble to gain my own footing, take off again. I'm almost at the entrance hall, when my foot catches on Reilly's bag, and I thud to the floor. Andreas is on me in a second. He flips me over, and I scream and scream, claw at his face, my fury not enough. Never enough. One hefty backhand across my face, and I'm silenced. Then the too-familiar choke of big hands around my throat.

"What did you do to me?" he roars.

"Stop ... please," I hiss through the tightening constriction, my fingers uselessly prying his grip. A flash of Nayla's teaching – I push my arms up inside his and push out. Oh my god, it works, but only to make his elbows collapse, crashing him on top of me. He pushes himself up, angrier, slaps me again. "I gave you a chance. This is how you repay me?" He plants his knee on my chest, leans in.

I can't move, can't scream, can't ...

My vision blurs, lungs shrieking in a burning hell. This is it. I've had my last breath. This is how my life ends. No dignity. No compassion. Just unforgiving, mad, mad, hatred.

And suddenly the air is back. Sucking, great gulps of life, drawn down airways that feel coated with broken glass.

Andreas falls sideways.

What's happening?

Reilly stands, looking down at me, bag of snowdomes in her hand.

"You?" I croak.

She drops the bag, grabs my arm. "Come on, come on. We have to run."

Dizzy, I glance over at Andreas. He's hunched over, head in his hands. There's blood seeping through his fingers.

Reilly pulls at me again. "Get up!" she yells.

And I do. Somehow, I'm up, wobbly, uncoordinated, but I'm up and running again. We get to the front door, and I try to spin the lock. It doesn't budge. Deadlocked. The keys are gone from their hook.

Andreas bellows from the lounge, heavy footfalls thunder closer.

"He's got the keys," I howl.

Reilly screams, clings to my shorts. "He's coming."

We're both sobbing now. So close, so close. I look for something to throw. Nayla's cupcakes are still sitting on the hall table. I grab the tray and piff them, handfuls at a time, down the hall, smudging creamy green icing all over the floor. Maybe he'll slip over. He's only about five metres away. I throw the last one at his face. It hits him square, smashes over his eyes and cheeks. His feet hit the mess on the floor. He slides, slips, braces himself against the wall, regains his balance and wipes his face. He growls and keeps coming.

Now I remember! Yank open the hall table drawer. There it is – Nayla's stun gun. *Thank-god-thank-god-thank-god*. I snatch it up. Point. Fire.

The barbs hit his chest. He jolts to a stop, his body jerking, spittle flying, then falls to his knees, body trembling as if a giant has grabbed him by the scruff and is shaking him like a grotesque limp puppet.

The charge goes forever as I hold the gun, arms stretched out, the wires still attached. Then it stops, and he falls onto his face.

I drop the gun. Everything pauses. Even the wind seems to take a breath.

He doesn't move.

I need to search his pockets for the keys. I have to touch him.

"Stay back," I whisper to Reilly as I kneel beside the immobile monster. I reach a shaking hand toward his pants pocket.

"What are you doing?" Reilly hisses.

I freeze. Look back at her. "He has the keys."

She shakes her head. "Daddy has spares in his office."

Relief. Sweet, sweet relief.

"Can you get them?"

She nods, takes off.

I make to stand, but remember the stun gun, what Nayla said about using it for a close-up second shock. I bend, snatch up the weapon, disengage the barbs and hold it close as I back up to the front door. How many movies have I watched where the victim doesn't finish the job, doesn't stomp the groin or put a shot through their attacker's head or heart?

Reilly is back. She hands me a small bunch of keys. I give her the stun gun, tell her if he's wakes and gets close, to fire it. Don't think. Just do it.

I flick through the keys, steeling my shaking, trying one after the after until ... Hallelujah!

We're out into the storm.

58

It's adrenaline that keeps me pumping – protecting Reilly from bits of flying branches and debris, getting us both into the Moke, reversing past Andreas's car without getting us bogged in the garden. Our hair flings in our faces, rain saturating us. The gusts are strong, but not as ferocious as I expected. I'm guessing the cyclone's eye must still be some way off. I pray no trees have come down in our path.

The headlights cut across wet-slicked road as I press my bare feet on the pedals, driving as fast as I deem safe, which doesn't feel fast enough. We keep our saturated heads low, leaves and muck slapping against the windscreen, the wipers straining against the lashing rain. Rivers of muddy water rush along the gravel gutters each side of the bitumen. I snatch a glance up at the hillside beside us, its red-dirt banks, wondering if a mudslide is imminent.

Reilly stares straight ahead, dazed.

"Reilly, put your seatbelt on." She doesn't respond. "Reilly!" I yell. She turns to me, wide-eyed and fearful, as if I've slapped her. It crushes my heart. "Put your seatbelt on, sweetheart."

My gaze is back on the road, just in time to swerve around the end of a fallen branch. I can feel Reilly staring at me. She hasn't moved. What's going through her head? Does she think she had a hand in killing Andreas? Did I? Is he actually dead? Does she think *we're* going to die?

I take my hand off the wheel, pat her thigh. "Come on, sweetheart. Seatbelt."

"Oh my god," she says. "Did you smell his fart? It was so bad."

I snap a look at her. Surely she's in shock. But she's laughing now, and I do too.

We're losing it.

Her laughter dissipates, and she finally reaches down and does up her seatbelt.

We make it down to the main strip, where all the shops have tape criss-crossed over their windows. No cars, no minibuses. A tourist ghost town. We drive past the supermarket, its lights blazing in the dark, checkouts vacant. At the end of the strip, I turn right onto the only road heading out of town. We pass the beachside resorts, the cemetery, an out-of-town pizza shop, and at the Captain Cook Highway, I turn left.

"Mossman is that way," Reilly says, pointing right.

"I know, Reilly. We're going to Sammi's. Can you guide me? I don't think I remember from here." *Keep her occupied.*

She doesn't baulk at my white lie, just sits up taller and leans forward to peer through the windscreen.

A few minutes later, we pull up outside Nayla's house. I hold Reilly's hand as we pelt across the driveway. The front door is locked. I bang on it, bang again, peer through the glass pane. It's dark inside.

"They're in the laundry," Reilly reminds me.

I curse, grab her hand and take off around the back. That door is locked too. I call out. Bang again. No answer. There's a small sliding window next to the door. I raise myself on tippy toes and peer in.

"Nayla? Sammi?"

There's a dark shape on the floor. It's too hard to make out what it is, but it must be them. Surely.

"Hold on," I yell, my voice lost in the wind. "We're gonna get you out."

I flatten my hands on the glass, try pull the window frame aside. It doesn't budge. Even if it opened, I couldn't ask Reilly to climb through. I've asked too much from her already.

"Wait here," I say, pushing her into a crouch next to the back steps, out of the wind.

Three windows line the side of the house. All closed. But no cyclone-proof screens yet. Small mercies. Should I check if there's a shed out back? Check for something to jimmy one? But behind me the rockery offers a quicker solution. I heave a small boulder into my arms, swing it back, pitch it at the window. The glass shatters on impact. I stick my head through. It's a bedroom. Reaching in, I yank the curtain down over the broken glass as best I can, then climb through, waiting for the sharp sting of a shard beneath my hands or knees. I'm lucky.

I flick the light switch. Yes! There's still power.

I round the laundry door, reach for the light switch, then stand there staring. Sammi is sitting on the floor next to her mother who's slumped on her side. Both have their feet tied, hands fastened behind their backs, clothing stuffed in their mouths.

Sammi's face is red and streaked. Her eyes grow big with desperation as she sees me and tries to yell through her gag. It kicks me into action. I kneel beside her and clear her mouth.

"Mummy, Mummy," she sobs.

"Shhh, it's okay."

I lean toward Nayla, pull down her gag. "Nayla?" I pat her cheek. "Nayla, can you hear me?" She doesn't move.

Pulse. Check for a pulse, breathing.

She's alive.

I step over her legs to reach the back door, unlock, yank it open. The wind nearly blows it back in my face. Reilly is sitting exactly where I left her.

"REILLY. COME."

She rises, hurries up the steps. I slam the door. She crouches next to Sammi.

Now I can turn my attention back to Nayla. I tap her face a bit harder. "Nayla!" She stirs, moans. "Are you hurt?"

She groans as I lift her shoulders so she's sitting. Blood cakes one side of her face, all swollen, her nose at an odd angle.

"Arsehole," I mutter.

She opens her eyes now, takes a moment to focus. "Georgia." It's a whisper, but any response is welcome right now.

"Hello, Sensei."

She smiles, crooked. I take that as a good sign.

I turn to Reilly. She fussing with Sammi's leg ties, so I go to work on Nayla's. The bindings are knotted, biting into their skin. Garden twine.

"Where are your scissors?"

"Kitchen," Nayla says huskily. "Bottom drawer, next to fridge."

I'm back in a jiffy and we have them loose in moments.

"Are you okay?" I ask again. "It looks like your nose is broken." I try to tilt her chin up, but she bats me away.

"I've had worse. Let's get out of here before this cyclone really loses its shit."

She gets to her knees, and I hold her arm to support her. Before she's fully on her feet, she throws up. I jump back to avoid the bile. She takes a minute to steady herself, wipe her mouth.

"I think you may have a concussion," I offer.

"You think?" She shakes her head, then regrets it, holding a hand on each side of her face. "You're driving."

<hr>

The wind gusts the rain into horizontal sheets, plastering our hair to our skulls and slapping our limbs as we all run for the Moke and bundle in. I consider taking a minute to pull the soft top up to cover us, but the wind will probably catch it and wrench it, taking one of us out in the process.

Nayla lolls her head against her daughter, hunched on the rear bench seat. Sammi does her best to support her mum. Reilly remembers to fasten her seat belt.

The streetlights are still working, but my vision is a watery blur. I have to squint to see the road, continually wiping rain from my face. Back on the main road, we head out toward the highway. Mossman should only be fifteen minutes from here – fifteen of the longest minutes of my life.

A gust hits the side of the car, almost forcing me to skid into the gutter. The steering column feels as if it might snap under the strength of my grip as I yank the wheel back. Too far. The tail end skids. Somewhere in my psyche, I remember to not fight the skid, to straighten the wheels, accelerate, let the tyres find their grip and pull us back into the centre of the road. Thank god there's no oncoming traffic.

I stay keenly aware, on edge, waiting for the next gust, carefully holding the car steady, trying to go as fast as I can without killing us. We're on open land here, and the wind has no resistance, sugarcane fields whipped, their strappy green lengths laid flat, crops ruined. We reach the Bonnie Doon Road turnoff, and safely make the turn. A few more minutes up the road and I yell, "We're nearly there."

The road narrows, and I eye the trees lining the road ahead, begging them to hold tight as their branches are pushed and pulled violently by invisible hands. A confetti of leaves whips around us. The town must be just around the corner, surely. Just a few more …

I don't hear the snapping and cracking – the wind is too loud – but the monster of a gum tree seems to pause as it splinters from its foundations, as if wanting us to appreciate its majesty, its might, held aloft by the storm. It pivots as it falls, a beastly ballerina of nature, arms stretched wide, reaching for an invisible partner to catch it, but the wind betrays it, and it crashes – an ugly, ungraceful landing as I slam the brakes.

We careen toward the tangled blockade, wheels screaming their dismay along with our mouths. Instinctively we brace, duck our heads, the collision inevitable.

It's weird, the way the sound of the impact hits us before the thud to our bodies, grinding and grating as the inertia jerks us forward then backward, my head whacking the steering wheel somewhere in the melee, the windscreen shattering, branches smashing through, clawing their way past us. And then we're stopped, buried in a fallen forest, a leafy cocoon, my panting, my pulse, loud in my ears.

A solid limb sits wedged between Reilly and me, reaching through to the back of the Moke. "Are you okay?" Stupid question. No one's okay, but Reilly knows what I mean.

"I think so."

I turn to look back. Sammi's nose is bloody, but she looks otherwise uninjured, pinned in place by her seatbelt, shock holding her together. "You okay?" I call back.

She nods. Brave little soul. She tries to look past the branch to her mother. "Mummy?"

Neither of us can see Nayla properly, too much heavy foliage.

"Nayla?" I yell over the wind. "Nayla?"

No answer. Something sickening rises in me.

Don't think about it. Just do.

"Okay, everyone sit tight. I'm coming around to get you."

I release my seatbelt, slide out of the vehicle, grateful it has no doors, nothing to jam shut and trap us. But I have to shove, push back and stomp branches with my bare feet to get to Sammi, the wind still slapping wet leaves in my face. I lean in, unclip her seatbelt and help her climb out. We push through more foliage to the back of the car, where I tell her to sit on the road and wait. She does, arms wrapped around her knees, head tucked in. I move around to Nayla's side.

"Oh god, Nayla." The limb has pinned her, a side-branch jammed into her neck. Blood, so much blood. Her head is back against the seat, eyes wide, unblinking.

I keep moving forward, snapping, breaking branches, debris sharp under my feet, until I reach Reilly and help her climb out too. I avert her face as I send her to the rear of the car to join Sammi.

And now I drag my gaze back to Nayla, reach for her neck, feeling for what isn't there – a missing beat in the discordant raging of the storm. "No!" My body wants to sink to the ground, but I cling to the doorframe. "*Fuck you, Andreas. Fuck you storm. Fuck you God.*" And now, I think the unthinkable, move to do the undoable – bend, reach in to remove her thongs. I can't run far in this melee without something on my feet.

I move back to the girls, crouch beside them, pull their faces to my chest. A group hug of sorrow and terror. "We have to go," I tell them. We can walk. It's not far."

Sammi leans back, searching my face. "What about Mummy?"

I shake my head. "I'm sorry, sweetheart. We ... we have to leave your mummy here."

"No!"

"I'm sorry ... so sorry, Sammi. We can't take her with us."

"Nooo!" she yells. "She'll die. We can't leave her."

"Sammi—"

"No!"

I grab her shoulders, hold them tight. "Sammi, look at me. We can't take her with us. There's nothing we can do to help her. We have to help ourselves. Do you understand?"

"No! I'll stay, I'll stay."

I can't speak, can't make things easier, can't stop her pain, my own anguish. And I sob. A goddam sob that's not mine to have. She should have all the sobs, all the tears.

I grab her hand, try to drag her to her feet, but her little body tenses, her fingers digging into my palms. She screams.

Reilly's crying now too, clinging to Sammi's shoulder in solidarity.

I die inside, something burning and blistering as hate takes hold. This is on me. This is all on me. If I'd never come here, this would never have happened. The searing admission forges my veins, my arteries, to steel. I will get them to safety. I *will*.

I yank them to their feet. "*Come on*," I yell. "We can't stay here."

I pull them toward the fallen tree trunk. It's thick, at least a metre and a half in diameter, but we can climb it. I push Reilly up first, hefting her foot with my cupped hands. Up the rough bark she climbs, and over the top she goes, the wind unsteadying her. She makes it over, slides down the other side. Sammi stands beside the trunk, still crying, looking back at the car. I kneel before her, take her face in my hands, make her focus on me.

"Sweetheart, I'm sorry, but I can't … I can't make it better, and I need you to move." She doesn't budge, so I get behind her and hoist her under her armpits, almost throw her onto the branch trunk. The wind tries to throw her back at me, but I defy it, stand firm, holding her in place. "Climb, Sammi. Now!" I yell. I shove her, hating myself.

She does, still crying, clambering over the top and hopefully down into Reilly's arms. I follow her, using branches for leverage, grazing my palms, thighs and stomach, then thump down on the other side.

"Let's go."

I grab a hand from each of them, and we're running, me ahead, pulling the girls behind me. Reilly trips, and I yank her to her feet without stopping.

We're saturated, wind beaten, but we're alive, and up around the next corner are the yellow flashing lights of an SES truck doing a U-turn. I drop the girls' hands, and wave, yell into the wind as we run toward the lights. "Wait! Wait!"

A miracle. The vehicle stops. The driver is incredulous as he jumps out of his cabin. "What are you doing out here?" He holds his arm up to protect his face from the wind.

"We had an accident," I yell.

"Come on," he says to Reilly and Sammi, opening the passenger door. The wind catches it, but he grabs and holds it firm.

Reilly climbs in, but Sammi resists. I have to pick her up and push her into the cabin, then squeeze in beside her. She's still crying. "I'm sorry, sweetheart."

The driver closes our door, then runs around to his side, climbs in and slams his own. "You're damned lucky my wife's a diabetic. If she hadn't forgotten her meds, you'd be goners. That everybody?" he asks, sliding the vehicle into gear.

I look at him, words jamming my breath. I purse my lips, a sob threatening, put my arm around Sammi, pull her head to my chest, place my hand over her free ear. "My friend," I say. "She's still back there. In the car."

He pauses, looks in his rear vision mirror. "She injured?"

"No ..." I'm sick at the thought of Nayla lying there in the wild of the storm, her body lacerated by the fury; sick at the look in Sammi's eyes, as she fights me off and stares up at me with hate, accusing. I shove my knuckles against my teeth.

I have to say it. *Have to.* "She's dead."

A scream fills the cabin. Sammi's rage is worse than any cyclone's wrath.

59

We stumble down the concrete steps of a sports centre. The driver bangs on the glass doors. "Pete! Open up."

Another man in bright-orange SES gear appears and unlocks one of the doors. "Lockdown was five o'clock," he yells, struggling to pull the door back from the wind's grasp.

Pointless information. I guess he needs to feel some sort of control over this madness, his reflective gear and heavy boots not providing sufficient agency. I don't argue, just follow the point of his finger to a camping table where a police officer sits with a name register.

We all shuffle forward as one unit, the girls clinging to either side of me, their hands gripping onto my t-shirt, dragging it down.

"Get caught out?" the officer asks.

I bite back simmering sarcasm, give her our names, addresses. She records them in her ledger. Sammi shifts beside me. I look down into her tearstained, grubby face, her curls plastered to her forehead, grazes and scratches marring her perfect skin. What she's silently asking is futile, but I do as she bids.

"I have a friend still out there who—"

"Can't put lives at risk," the officer says, continuing to write. "It only gets worse from here."

"But it's ... it's her mother."

The officer stops writing and looks up. She glances at Sammi, then me, shakes her head. "I'm sorry. We can't." At least there's a semblance of sympathy in her voice. "Through there." She points.

Sammi's grip goes limp.

As the hall's heavy doors close behind us, there's a claustrophobic heat and hush, an eerie stillness, the quiet reverence of a church, against the muted moans of the cyclone. Dim. Airless. The louvre shutters all closed. The only light comes from the emergency lighting in the roof – pin holes in the firmament of the metres-high ceiling. Rows and rows of mattresses and camp beds line the floor, people's belongings, animals in crates, everything cramped around them as demarcations. Musty, sweaty air. I hate to think what it's going to be like by morning.

Over to the left is a netted-off room. I can imagine a few hours ago, kids would have been running rampage, jumping on the sprung flooring and trampolines, throwing balls around. The perfect distraction for young ones to pass the time while not driving their parents to distraction.

We head to the far end of the hall to look for space, stepping over legs, blankets, plastic bags of goods, and find a small space next to ... Davy Jones. His singleted frame is sprawled on the floor, back resting up against the wall, his eyes closed. Dear Bertie lies by his side. The dog raises his smooth hairy head, grinning and greeting us with thumps of his tail, then rests his chin on his outstretched paws.

A woman on Bertie's other side scoots over, pulling away a few bags to make room for us. We hunker on the wooden floor, Sammi between Reilly and me. People nearby either glance, trying not to be obvious, or stare, nodding silent greetings. I survey the mass of bodies, wondering if Margie and Evelyn are somewhere among the quiet throng or if they're still at the hospital.

Davy wakes and clears his claggy throat. I nod to him, and he seems to register. "Ice cream lady," he murmurs through a sleepy smile. He leans over, passes me a soft raggedy towel. "Here," he says. "Dry yourself off."

I gently towel the girls' arms, legs – careful of their abrasions – dry their hair, then my own. The woman on our other side taps my shoulder. She's holding out a plastic shopping bag. "Snacks," she says.

"That's okay."

"For the kids," she insists.

I place the bag between the girls and myself and look through it. Biscuits, chocolate, a can of baked beans, bottle of water.

"Are you hungry?" I ask them.

Reilly shakes her head. Sammi doesn't respond.

It takes me a few minutes to realise I'm shivering. I wrap the now-damp towel around the girls, pull them to me, as if closeness can repair our trauma. Sammi lets go a sob. The intensity of it resonates through my side. I squeeze her tighter, Reilly too. Sammi's crying turns to wailing, and I let go of Reilly to pull Sammi onto my lap. She's inconsolable, thrashes against me, pummels my chest.

"No, no, no, no, no. I hate you. I hate you."

Her pain is like its own storm. It whirls through my chest, my arms, uncontainable.

Bertie gets to his feet, howls a protest before Davy throws an arm around him and drags him down again. People stare, startled out of their whispering hush. The woman next to us asks if we need anything, if the girls are hurt, can she help? I shake my head.

Reilly gets to her knees, tries to put her arms around both of us. She has her own sobs. It takes forever for Sammi to exhaust herself. I keep her in my arms, whispering how sorry I am, that everything will be okay, everything will be alright.

Goddammed liar.

Someone approaches us. A woman with a bundle tucked under each arm. "Here you go, dear," she says. "I brought these along in case anyone needs them." She drops a couple of rolled-up air mattress at my feet. "I'll get the foot pump going. Won't take long." She bends, unrolls one of the mattresses – has to lay it partially across our legs because there's no room – then stands again, the round rubber pump groaning and puffing under her hefty foot.

I ease Sammi onto the floor – she slumps over, resting her head in Reilly's lap – then stand to unravel the second mattress, murmur a thank you. But as I try to blow it up with my mouth, I lose my breath, overwhelmed, tears stinging. "I'm sorry," I whisper.

"Don't be silly," she says. "Won't take a minute. We can't have you and little uns sleeping on the floor, can we?"

While she's pumping away, a voice cuts in over the PA system, telling us the men's toilets are blocked. That they need to use the disabled toilet, and not to flush anything except toilet paper. He says the worst of the cyclone will hit in the early hours, and if the roof comes away at any point, we're not to panic but to move to another area.

Move where?

Before long, we're lying on the gifted beds, their bloated forms firm yet marshmallowy after the hardness of the floor. I look at the girls curled on the other mattress, Reilly spooned against Sammi's back. Reilly has an arm outstretched, Bertie licking her fingers. I briefly wonder why she doesn't have her own pet, then turn over to stare at the ceiling, close my eyes ... and jerk them open – visions of the storm, of Nayla, of Andreas.

Outside, the storm builds, angrier, louder, yet I struggle to stay awake. Exhaustion has claimed the girls as has Bertie, who has sneaked and snuggled himself between them. The girls each have an arm across his rotund body. More comfort than I can provide.

I rest my struggling eyelids, vestiges of alcohol and Endone seeping through my waning adrenaline.

A godawful bang, dogs yelping, the girls crying out. The ceiling lights have gone out. A barrage of torch beams flick on, sweeping the ceiling. The wind is a steam locomotive, screaming and moaning a constant barrage of debris at the walls, the roof, trying to grip its claws into the building, to rip it open like a can of something pathetic, wanting to devour us mortals to feed its fury. Long strands of cobwebs billow down on us, showers of dust. Something thuds then clatter-clangs along the roof, rolling, rolling. The torches follow its progress. The internal roof supports look like they're made of steel. Solid and thick. It's not going anywhere.

The torches flick off.

Sounds of movement drift through my twilight of waking. I sit up, groggy. The louvres are open to the morning breeze, the sun a gentle glow behind them – nature daring to breathe again. I swallow, throat sore, as if swollen, and yesterday's horror rushes back.

Reilly and Sammi remain asleep, but Bertie has gone, as has Davy. Around us, people fold their blankets, deflate their mattresses, squeeze their overnight supplies into carry bags. Conversation is still low, murmurs, as if the cyclone has tempered their spirits. Half the hall has emptied. I move to ease myself up to kneeling, not wanting to wake the girls. Everywhere hurts, but my back complains the most – I'd forgotten about it.

The woman who loaned us the airbeds is nearby. She sits on a rolled-up blanket, reading, a takeaway coffee by her side. I try to call to her, but my voice is a croak. I swallow, wince at the bruised thickness of it.

She looks up. "Did you call me?"

I nod. Swallow again. "Do you have the time?" I rasp. "Sorry, I didn't get your name last night."

"Rhonda," she says. "It's nearly eight."

"Rhonda, thanks so much for your help last night. I'll wake the girls so you can have your mattresses back."

"Take your time, dear. We're not in a hurry. Roads will likely be blocked. Are you alright? You've got some nasty bruises there."

The right eye feels swollen. I touch my forehead. There's a tender lump where it connected with the steering wheel. "I'm ... fine. Thanks."

My stomach growls, reminding me I haven't eaten since I can't remember. I ask Rhonda if she'd mind keeping an eye on Reilly and Sammi while I head over to the toilets.

"Sure, dear."

The stench in the foyer near the men's is overwhelming. I push through to the women's facilities. The paper towel bins are overflowing, and the floor is littered with wet toilet paper, empty junk food packets, an unused tampon. But the toilet still works, and there's water to bend and splash my face with over the sink. Ugh, my back hurts *so* much.

A different police officer is sitting at the check-in desk. I head over to him, wanting to ask about Nayla, about how I can get the girls to a hospital to be checked over, but when I open my mouth, all that comes out is a groan as a tingling, rushing wave fills my head.

I'm falling.

60

The rub and rattle of trolleys, whispery shoes on linoleum. I don't have to open my eyes to guess where I am, though when I do, the pale green curtains are a dead giveaway.

Daniel is sitting in a nearby chair, his head lolled to one side, eyes closed. He looks haggard, clothes wrinkled, body sagged. I can only imagine the journey he's been through to get here. How did he arrive so quickly? Is the airport open again?

I wish he wasn't here. His presence means I'm going to have to explain, face the consequences of nearly killing his daughter. *Where are the girls?*

"Daniel," I hiss. "*Daniel*," louder.

He stirs, wakes suddenly. It's like watching a crumpled paper bag fill with air. "Hey." He picks up my hand. "How're you feeling?"

I nod, swallow, my throat gravel lined. "Reilly? Sammi?"

"They're both fine. They're with Margie."

"Margie," I whisper, barely able to say her name.

"She was already here with Evelyn. Remember? She took the girls home yesterday."

"Yesterday?" I try to sit up, but my body is draggy. Too heavy for my arms.

"Whoa, take it easy. You're still in Mossman, and you're probably still concussed."

"I'm what?"

He gently pushes against my shoulder, eases me back against my pillows. "You hit your head when you fainted. Don't you remember? They've sedated you. You were in quite a state, I hear. Back injury, lacerations, bruising, dehydration. You've been out for almost two days."

"Two—"

"Shhh." He touches my cheek, brushes my hair back. "Are you in pain? I can get someone."

I try to sit up again. "Evelyn ... you have to tell the police."

"What's that?"

"She poisoned me. Sent Andreas to the house."

"Georgia, you're delirious. Just rest. Come on, lie back."

Wooziness overtakes me, and I lie panting for a minute. "Nayla?"

He pauses now, focuses on my hand, squeezes it with both of his. The downward set of his mouth mars his attempt at a smile. "They've taken care of her. There's no hurry."

No hurry. No hurry for the dead. Take your time.

"Cynthia?"

"She's fine. Don't stress yourself. Everyone is safe. I'm taking care of things. You just need to rest. I ... can't imagine what you've been through, but I want to thank you for getting Reilly through this. Without you—"

I shut my eyes. *Stop speaking. Just stop.* Without me, none of this would have happened. None of it. Reilly wouldn't be traumatised, Sammi would still have her mum and ... I open my eyes again, ready to tell him to leave, but he's staring at my throat, anger in his eyes. "I could kill him."

I gather myself, readying for one more death. "Did they find him too?"

"Not yet. He wasn't at the house."

I swallow again, pain fuelling me. "I want to see the girls."

"Of course. Maybe tomorrow."

"No. I want to see them now. I need to ..." I have no choice. My body is dragging me back to the oblivion of sleep. To where I don't need to think, to make amends, to face the inevitability of what I have done.

Let me stay there.

"The police are here to see you," says the nurse. "Do you need a moment?"

"Please. Could you pass me my dressing gown?"

She helps me put it on, tidies my bed-hair, my sheets, wheels my trolley-tray away, then brings in Detective Ng – a slight woman in a fitted black suit with a collared white shirt that looks a size too big for her. I wonder if she's borrowed her partner's, spilled coffee or something on her own.

The nurse warns Detective Ng that my voice is still croaky, that my throat is still healing, and I shouldn't be pushed.

I offer the detective a seat, but she refuses. Do all cops need to stand when they're interviewing people? Is it a power thing? She cautions me, asks if I'd like a support person present.

"Am I being charged with something?"

She gives me a wry look, tugs away a lock of hair that's slipped inside her too-big collar. I get the feeling she's overdue a haircut. That she likes it shorter. "Are you guilty of something?"

I blink. "You haven't found him, have you?"

"Ma'am, let's take this step by step."

"But—"

"Ma'am, please." Her tone is enough to shut me up.

Procedure. She quizzes me on what happened. It's less harrowing than I expect, my answers coming automatically until we get to him backhanding and choking me, to the moment I really thought I was going to die and where Reilly stepped in. I stop, cough, sip water and steel my tears for Reilly, for myself.

"And then you left the house?"

"We ran for our lives."

"Uh huh. But you'd let him in the house previously?"

"Seriously? What is it with you people? You all make it sound as if I welcomed him."

"You people?" Her stare is direct, though I suspect she's not easily offended.

I stare back at her for moment. "I didn't mean ... *cops, uniforms*. You know what I meant. The other police asked the same thing."

Detective Ng smirks. "I get it," she says, "though it's no less offensive."

"*Offensive?*"

She's trying to put up a stern front, but the pulsing vein on her temple gives her away. A guilty pulse, I hope. Facts are facts are facts, until they're not. Until they're taken out of context and used against you. Surely she understands? She a cop *and* a woman. She must see this all the time.

"And I'm not blaming you at all," she says. "Just collecting facts."

We move on. She's thorough; I'll give her that. Finally, she tells me they've not found any trace of Andreas – car gone, room he'd been renting now empty. "But we've taken fingerprints from the house, and we found the taser you mentioned, so your story adds up."

Small mercies.

"It won't be hard to track him back to Melbourne, if that's where he's headed."

"Sure." And I believe they'll make a *huge* effort to find him. As much effort as it takes to forward an email and the responsibility on to someone else. Someone back in Melbourne who'll maybe do due diligence, if I'm lucky, then put it on a back burner. A very cold back burner. Friends in high places.

"And what about Nayla?" I ask.

A slight intake of breath. I've caught her off guard. She pales, wipes sweat from her upper lip. It's trickling down her neck too, dampening the strands of hair stuck there.

"Your friend ..."

She tells me Nayla's body was found some distance from the car, which had been picked up by the cyclonic winds and rolled several times. I don't ask anything more. She says they'll be doing an autopsy. That they'll need someone to identify her.

Is she asking me? I can't do that. "Daniel says her husband is on the way from Kuala Lumpur."

"Daniel ... that's Mr"—she flips through her notebook—"Moretti?"

"Yes. My boss."

"Uh huh."

Now she wants to go over the "circumstances" of Nayla's death. Why we were driving during a cyclone. How fast we were going.

"As fast as I damn well could."

Who was in the car? Did we try to avoid the accident. Who was driving?

"Who was driving? Who the hell do you think was driving? One of the kids? Nayla, from the back seat?"

I bite so hard on my bottom lip I taste blood. They need to ask these things; it's routine, standard procedure. I know this. I've watched enough cop shows.

"Ms Wright, I know this is tedious, so if you need to take a break—"

"No."

"Okay then."

"We should have stayed at Nayla's. We would have been safe."

"You didn't know that at the time. The township was under evacuation orders. You did the right thing."

"So why are you asking me such stupid questions?"

"Well, it's just—"

"Forget it. If we hadn't left, she'd still be alive."

"You don't know that. You said she likely had a concussion?"

"I ... I think so ..."

"Let's leave those answers to the coroner."

"What about Evelyn? Are you going to charge her?"

"Who?"

61

Evelyn's eyes are closed, her body shrunken, fragile, as if a press on her bedsheets would collapse her into bone and ash. This living carcass, this death's door candidate, can't be the same woman. Days ago, she seemed strong. Thin, yes, but out of her wheelchair, walking, energetic.

There's none of the paraphernalia I expected – leads, IVs, monitors – only a thin oxygen tube beneath her nose. Above her bed, firm letters on the whiteboard: DNR. Do not resuscitate.

"Evelyn," I whisper, hoping, yet not, that she'll wake. It'd be so much easier to say what I need without her conscious. But then there'd be no answers.

"Evelyn." Louder.

She stirs, eyelids flickering open. "Margie?" she croaks, smiles.

"No."

She falters, coughs a rattling breath, then turns her head from me.

"Evelyn, I'm not going away."

"I'm dying. Leave me alone."

"Don't you want your last confession?" I'm cut by my own ruthlessness, but my sympathy has long evaporated, blown away with Yasi's fury.

She groans as she turns back, closes her eyes for a moment, gathering herself. When she finally opens them, she rasps, "You think I want absolution?"

"I don't care what you want. I just came to say I know what you did."

"And you want to know why?" Her laugh is phlegmy, spittle landing on her chin. She grimaces with pain.

I hold her gaze, wait. When she doesn't speak, I wander over to the window, look through its cyclone-proof screening. The sky is still overcast, a morbid kind of grey. Fitting. I turn and lean my back against the window, cross my arms, stare.

"You fucking ruined everything," she hisses. "We were set, Margie and I. I should never have hired you."

"You call abusing the woman you love 'set'?"

Confusion ripples over her. I wait for her clarity to return. Unlike her, I have all the time in the world.

"What?" she whispers. "I don't ..."

"You. Abused. Margie."

"No ... we were happy until you arrived."

"Don't gaslight me. I had nothing to do with your sorry extortion."

She raises a hand, as if trying to thump the bed, but it falls limp. "He owed her!" she says, her attempt at yelling, guttural, feeble. "She's given her life to that family." She breaks into a paroxysm of coughing, her body jerking with each spasm.

I glance at the doorway, waiting to see if any staff come. No one. I walk back, stand over her as she tries to catch her breath. I could hold a pillow over her face. Could drain the last life from her pathetic body. Get at least that satisfaction. But I don't need to. She seems to have arranged that herself.

"You know Nayla is dead because of you, don't you? That Reilly and Sammi nearly were. That they'll likely be traumatised for the rest of their lives?"

She doesn't answer. Doesn't she bear any guilt?

I lean in closer. "What happened in India, Evelyn? Did you get ripped off?"

"None of your ... fucking ... business."

"*What happened?* What did you do to Margie? Why did you come back early?"

Her face pinches, mouth drawing into a grimace, as if she's going to cry. Not a total psychopath then. My chest twinges at her misery, and I want to thump the stupid empathy out of myself.

"Your fault," she hisses.

"What? How? What are you're talking about?"

She coughs again, painful, cloggy. More spittle. "Credit card ... paracetamol." Her voice has reduced to a wheeze.

I could shake her bones. "*What?*"

She tenses with the effort to gather her uncooperative body, then spits her words. "All that money, all that fucking money, and they killed my liver. I could have done that for five bucks at home." She laughs as she cries. "Ain't it beautiful?" She sinks back, muscles yielding, anger leaching into unconsciousness.

I stand, impotent, still needing answers.

62

Our taxi rolls through Mossman township. The ground littered with stripped foliage, trees naked, snapped limbs barely clinging. A massive Moreton Bay fig lies in the centre of the median strip, an ancient foliaged deep-green god fallen from grace. Its branches have already been chain-sawed and moved off the road. Now, SES workers are dismembering its remaining limbs. They'll need a crane to move the trunk. Will they repurpose the wood? Let it live again in another form?

Daniel tells me things are much, much worse further south. Whole townships – houses, businesses, crops, livelihoods – all devastated. It'll take months to recover. But only one person, other than Nayla, has died. "Poor bugger didn't think about the consequences of using a generator indoors."

It's wrong to laugh, but I can't help it. Must be my tiredness, shock.

Our own township seems hardly touched, just loose debris, a tin roof relocated to a neighbour's yard. Life on the main strip looks as if the cyclone was just a blip – shops and pubs all open, tourists in outdoor cafes lapping up beers, bowls of fresh prawns or loaded nachos. Though admittedly, the crowds are fewer than earlier in the week. Some must have got out while they thought the going was good.

Wish I had.

"I've spoken with Margie," Daniel says.

My throat tightens as I wait for the denial, for him to protect her.

"She's told me what Evelyn did. Do you want to press charges?"

"What do you think I should do?"

He squints out the window, a muscle in his jaw working. "It's not up to me. It's about what you think is just, right. And I guess you have to consider the toll it'll take on you." He takes a breath, turns back, looks at his hands in his lap. I get the feeling that what he's going to say next isn't what I want to hear. "I guess it also depends on whether you want to put Margie through another trauma right now. Evelyn hasn't got long."

And there it is. Margie, blameless.

"Whether I want to put *her* through trauma? Are you kidding?"

He meets my eyes now, a deep-set frown emphasising his weariness. "Georgia, we're all devastated here. Evelyn played us all. There's no good outcome, whichever way you look."

I can't help the flint in my voice. "You believe Margie is innocent?"

"I believe her when she says Evelyn was monstering her."

This deflates me. I of all people should understand the intricacies of a manipulative relationship.

"Think on it," he says. "Whatever you decide, I'll support you."

———◦◦◦———

I hesitate in the doorway, unable to step over the threshold – something fast and furious has risen in my chest. Daniel places his hand in the small of my back, a silent signal of solace.

Andreas's body is *not* going be there, sprawled in the hallway, the barbs and wires still sticking out of his chest. There's nothing left here except my fear, guilt, shame.

As I enter the lounge, Margie and Reilly are sitting together on the couch. Margie has Reilly's hand in her lap, holding on to the child as if to anchor them both in solidarity. For a stupid moment, I wonder why Reilly didn't meet me at the door. She must have heard the taxi. A mental shake of my head – she'll probably never answer the door again. Ever.

I'm not sure what to do, what to say. Sorry, sorry, sorry keeps rolling through my head. Nothing else will come.

"Georgia!" Reilly flies off the couch. I kneel to catch her. She's in my arms, crying, squeezing my neck. "I'm so glad you're back." Hiccupping sobs.

I squeeze her tighter, using her body as a stopper – a cork holding back the fermentation of my pain. This is *her* time. I must hollow myself, be the vessel she pours her hurt into. I push her back to look at her. Her wet grin makes me smile too. "I missed you, baby girl. So much." We hug tight again.

I catch Margie's eye now, and she seems to sink into herself. If I'm culpable of putting this family at risk, it's her and her lover who enticed the monster, who left an irresistible gingerbread trail right to this household, who baited his ugliness and violence. And now they may not even pay for it.

Did Margie know? She *must* have. How could she not? We will be having a conversation, she and I. But right now, Reilly and Sammi are my priority.

Daniel says Sammi hasn't left the spare room since they got home. "Monosyllables when we press her. She's hardly eating either."

She doesn't look at me when I pop my head in to check on her. Her back against the bedhead, arms crushing a cushion against her chest, she stares – a doll with huge dark expressionless eyes. If I tipped her back, her eyelids would probably click closed. It's as if her soul has leached out and blown away with the storm. How does a child get over something like this?

"Sammi? Can I come in?"

She doesn't move, doesn't acknowledge. I pad in slowly, not wanting to startle the fawn of a child with bedraggled hair. Margie says she's refusing to bathe, won't change her clothes, screams if they try to touch her. Perhaps she's trying to hold on to the last vestiges of her mother – in whatever ruinous shape that might take.

As I ease onto the edge of the bed, she turns her head, and a sense of dread sweeps over me. Hate. Deep, intense hate in her eyes. It steals my breath. *I'm her mother's murderer.*

I look down to my hands, wringing in my lap. Do I stay? Do I sit here and let her empty her hate onto me? How deep does it run? Will it drown me?

I nod, then whisper as I pat her leg. "I understand." A mistake. She jerks away as if my hand is acid, searing her. "Sammi, you need to wash. I'm going to run a bath for you, okay? You can come back here after if you want." The words "your mother would want you to" flicker in my throat. I swallow them, get up to leave.

Reilly stands in the doorway. "Why doesn't Sammi want to share my bedroom? We always share."

"Shhh."

She steps back as I pull Sammi's door to. "She needs time. She's had a terrible shock. You both have. We have to be patient."

Reilly follows me to the guest bathroom, stands leaning in the doorway again as I turn the tap on for the bath, check the water temperature.

"She won't talk to me. She tells me to leave her alone," Reilly says, the misery on her face breaking my heart.

I dry my hands, sit on the edge of the bath. "Come here."

She buries her face in my neck, her shoulders shaking. I wonder if she'll eventually run out of tears. I wish Sammi would share some. "I know, I know, honey. We all deal with sadness in our own way. We have to give her space. She lost her mum. That's ..." I have no words.

"I just want to make her smile," she mumbles.

God she's brave. Where does she get this strength from?

"You're such a sweetheart, but we can't expect her to smile just to make us feel better. She doesn't have any smiles to give at the moment."

She stands back, looks me in the face, tearfully earnest. "What if she never smiles again? What if I never see her again? Dad says her father is coming."

I touch her flushed cheek, stroke her untamed hair into place, run a thumb over the wet darkness under her eyes. "One day at a time, Riles." I straighten her t-shirt, take her hands and squeeze them. "It's all new. Give her time. As much as she needs. If you need smiles, come to me. Okay?" I smile. It's hard, false, but it's what I can muster.

"Can you ..." She bites her lip. "Can you show me how to make one of your missy things for Sammi?"

"My what?"

She points to my braided misanga bracelet, its colours faded, threads barely holding on to my wrist – a mangled survivor. My heart twists. I should let it go; it's served its purpose.

"That's a really lovely idea. We'll make one for each of us. Okay?"

Her lip trembles. "Don't leave."

"I'm not going anywhere. I promise. Now scoot, I need to use the loo." I turn her around and play-slap her bottom. "Hey, if you'd like to do something for Sammi, how about lending her some fresh clothes?"

She nods, mopes off, dragging her feet. I close the door, sit back on the bath and let my own tears come until my chest is raw, until I'm ready to face Sammi again.

To my relief, she doesn't refuse, lets me lead her to the bath, undress her and help her in. She sits limp, a small silent bag of bones and flesh, as I swish water over her, wishing I could just as easily wash away her nightmares to come. I soap her hair, lean her back and rinse. She's compliant, though I'm terrified of looking into her eyes again. Of seeing hate there, death.

Now, standing wrapped in a towel, she has some colour back in her cheeks. Heat, not health.

⚬

By evening, we all seem to move through the house in a stupor. I recognise the feeling – the energy sap after trauma, the way I felt after Andreas's attacks. The house itself seems fragile, as if closing a door too hard might shatter it, shatter us. We speak in soft tones, too afraid of breaking seals that might lance infected hurts. But we must, sooner or later, else the festering will become permanent.

Still later, when it's dark, there's a soft knock on my ajar door. Daniel pokes his head through, looking as ragged as I feel. "You okay?"

I nod, push myself higher up against the bedhead, straighten my t-shirt and short pyjama bottoms.

He edges into the room a little, hands in pockets, awkward as a teen. "What are you watching?"

"Superstore. I need some silliness." I reach for the remote.

"Leave it. I like this show."

I stare at him, unsure what to say. "How are you coping?"

"It's, uh, too quiet out there," he says. "Margie's gone home. Kids are in bed."

Fleetingly, I picture Margie wandering her empty house. How desolate she must feel, the bearing of guilt and a further death yet to come. But before I let the semblance of pity settle on me, I move over and pat the bed. "Come."

"Thought you'd never ask." He leaves his thongs on the floor, climbs up, shoves a couple of pillows behind him, then lies back, arms crossed over his chest. "Georgia, I can't imagine what you've been through."

"Shhh," I say. "I'm okay. Let's just watch. I don't want to think." But I can't help myself. "I worry for that child."

"Sammi?"

I nod.

"Me too. I just got off the phone with her father. He'll be here in a couple of days. I don't know what's taking him so long. I mean, after what the kids – and you – have been through, you'd think he would have dropped everything and come immediately."

"Odd."

"And I've organised some therapy for Reilly – the same counsellor she saw after Cynthia and I separated, so I offered for Sammi to see her too, but he said no. He's taking her straight back with him."

"So soon?"

"Says the sooner he removes her, the better."

"*Removes* her?"

He tightens his crossed arms. "Children need time to adjust, don't they? In a familiar, safe space. I mean, you've all shared the same experience. Who better to work things through with than our family?"

I think about my own reaction on entering this house again, being stuck on the threshold. "Normally, I'd say yes, but her house might also remind her of trauma."

"Point." Daniel sighs again. "You know, I'm happy to pay for counselling for you too. You've been through hell."

My instinct is to refuse. But I take a moment to consider. "Thanks. I'll think about it."

Quiet now, we settle back to watch the television.

Family. He called me *family.* I smile. Can't help it.

On the television, Amy and Jonah are getting hot and heavy in the storeroom. Timing. I wonder what's going through Daniel's mind, lying here next to me. I want to look at him, to examine his face, see for myself, but we stare straight ahead. Do asexuals get aroused by visual stimulation? Not that a comedy is that sexy, but ... I have questions.

He heaves his chest, bellows out air as if he hasn't breathed in days. "She could stay here. Being with Reilly would be good for her, wouldn't it? Maybe she'll open up, given time."

I sigh too. So much for not thinking.

"I suspect Reilly will crash at some point too."

"Hmmm."

Amy and Jonah are stripping off in the storeroom.

"I should have been here," he says.

I prod his arm. "Hey, let's not go there."

"You're right. It's not about me."

"I didn't mean ..."

Amy and Jonah are going at it.

I clear my throat. "I can try talking to Sammi again tomorrow. Though I get the feeling she despises me. The way she looks at me ... it's unsettling."

He turns from the television, shifting to face me. "I'm sure that's not true."

"Maybe anger is a good thing. If it helps her release." I chew my lip. "How was your trip? Sorry, I forgot to ask."

"Ah, you had enough on your plate. All sorted. I won't need to go back for a while."

"Reilly will be happy."

He nods.

"So will I." *Oops*. That just slipped out.

He almost smiles, then breathes deep again. So full of sighs. "The thought that I might have lost her kills me.'

"Need a hug?" I offer. There's no way he'll say yes. It just seems the right thing to say in this moment.

He looks at me, a thoughtful sadness in his furrowed brow. "You know, I can't remember the last time I had a hug from an adult."

He stretches out his arms, and we lean into each other, twist to awkwardly embrace, yet it's firm, comforting. I too have forgotten this simple pleasure. The warmth. Honest and unencumbered.

We turn back to Amy and Jonah whose awkward sexual encounter is over. We don't talk but occasionally laugh at the antics of the characters – the garrulous, cutesy, plain dumb and the unrequited. We roll on, episode after episode, until I can't keep my eyes open.

Finally, he turns to me. "I was worried we were going to lose you too."

"*I* thought I was going to lose me."

A flicker of fear springs – where is Andreas now? Alive? Dead? Will he finally leave me alone? The close-upness of Daniel's thick, dark eyelashes, of long-day sweat and heavy musk, brings me back. His lips barely touch my cheek. "Goodnight."

⸎

Morning wakes me with an intricately divine scent. Before I open my eyes, I inhale deeply, relish the honeyed smell of the sprig of bright-yellow ylang-ylang on my pillow. Something good and innocent survived the storm.

63

Sammi sits up to attention as a car door slams out the front of the house. She's focused, sharp, for the first time in days. It's unsettling.

"Wait here, okay?" I tell her.

The rest of us hurry to the porch to wait, a wall of family to greet Sammi's father.

A slim, compact man in his forties exits a limousine's back seat. He leaves the door open, leans in and speaks to the driver. The boot pops open.

As he draws closer, Sammi's dimples are evident on his sombre face. His light shirt and cream slacks are surprisingly unrumpled. He's not come straight from the airport then.

I yelp in surprise as Sammi bursts between us, hurries forward and greets her father. He holds her at arm's length, turns her to face us, pats her shoulder. "Samara, do you have something to say?"

She nods but averts her eyes as she speaks. "Thank you for looking after me."

Daniel moves forward, hand outstretched. "I'm Daniel. Won't you join us for a bite to eat? Margie's made some lunch."

He shakes Daniel's hand briefly. "Thank you, but I had a late breakfast at my hotel." He puts an arm around Sammi's shoulders.

Daniel doesn't give up. "Just a few minutes so we can make arrangements for the girls to stay in touch. They're very attached. I'm sure they're going to need—"

"Samara, where are your bags?" her father asks.

"I don't have any."

"Nothing?"

Reilly speaks up. "Yes, you do."

"No," she says, body stiff, arms held tightly by her sides. "I don't need anything from here."

Reilly stuffs her hand in her mouth, face flushed with tears.

What's happening? This man can't just drive off with Sammi like this. He needs to talk with us, to work through what's happened. Doesn't he have questions? And doesn't Sammi want her clothes, her toys?

"Hop in the car, Samara."

She does as she's told without a glance at us.

"Please, come in just for a few minutes at least," I say. "This is too harsh a goodbye for the girls. Let's all catch our breath. I mean, there's Nayla's funeral—"

"Her family are arranging her cremation. I don't see the point in delaying."

I'm not above begging, for Sammi's sake. "*Please.*"

His voice hardens as he stares me down. "It's not healthy here."

"*What?*" His words are a gut punch.

Daniel places a hand on my arm, as if he thinks I might attack the man. He speaks softly. "Sammi's been through hell. She needs to open up and talk with people who have been through this with her."

"I will provide what she needs," Sammi's father says. "She will come back to Malaysia with me. We have doctors there, you know."

"I didn't mean—"

"No. Of course you didn't."

This is too awful. I glance at Reilly, expecting her to cry out with indignation, to run at the man and flail, demand he leave her best friend alone. But she doesn't. Perhaps the pit of guilt inside me – of not wanting an angry reminder of Nayla's death – is in her too.

We numbly watch the car reverse. Sammi doesn't look up or look back.

64

It's been an awful night with little sleep. For most of us, I suspect. Margie is outside, skimming the pool for leaves and bugs. She startles when I say her name, and it gives me a tiny joy. Is it bad that I want her to pay? I could do with a punching bag right now.

"I was hoping you'd come," she says. "Time to rip off the band-aid?"

Damn her for being so astute. "Walk?"

"Beach?"

I nod.

She puts the skimmer away, wipes her hands on her skirt. "Lead the way."

We head down the road toward the beach path. It's still early, though hot enough for sweat to dampen my singlet. The sun reflecting off rain-wet leaves makes me squint. I keep my head down, watch my feet tread each sandy step, wearing the same sandals I wore on my first day here, minus the bright toe polish. Everything so familiar yet nothing the same.

The hunted innocence in me is gone. Now, I'm the hunter, Margie my game.

We hit the beach, take off our sandals and head toward the swimming net. Billions of tiny sand balls cover the smooth, damp, compacted sand, all laid out in circular patterns. The artists – sand bubbler crabs – skitter away metres ahead of us at the impact of our footfalls.

Run, run. I'm coming.

"Daniel tells me Evelyn confessed," I say.

Margie breathes in deeply through her nose. "She did."

"And that she tried to frame Cynthia."

"Yes."

"And that you had nothing to do with it."

She looks out to sea, contemplating. "I was complicit in accepting extra money from Daniel. You already know that. But I didn't realise how desperate Evelyn was to be rid of you."

"Why?"

"You were only supposed to be here a few weeks. She got it into her head that Daniel was going to retire me, that we'd lose the income, his medical payments and bonuses."

Nothing new, but guilt smirks at me. Evelyn's near-truth assumption, a niggling splinter. "You could have just told me. I wouldn't have stayed. I never wanted to get in the way."

"*I* wanted you to stay."

I wait for her to say more, but she doesn't. We keep pace with each other, birds cry, wheeling overhead. I bite down on my lip. Why is what I have to say next so hard? It feels like cutting loose a lifeline, someone I care about, someone I thought cared about me. "But you were part of it, Margie. You set me up. That's what hurts the most." There's a wretchedness in my voice, and I just don't care. She needs to know the pain she's caused.

She stops dead, turns to face me.

I brace. Why does this hurt so much? She's the one who should be hurting.

"I owe you another huge apology. You trusted me, and I let you down. And I'm so, so sorry for that. You asked me to post your ring. Told me how important it was, and I ..."

She wrings her hands.

I dig my nails into my thighs.

"But I didn't set you up. You know how Evelyn turned up at the post office as you were leaving? I'd forgotten to get a couple of things for lunch, so I asked her to wait in the queue with your parcel. I didn't want to take it with me, and I was sure I'd be back in time to handle it – you saw how long the queue was. I told Evelyn what it was and how important it was. When I got back, she said she'd already posted it. Had a receipt. But ... she must have posted something else in its place."

"And she put it in my drawer when she came over for lunch?"

"She must have. I can't see how else it got there."

I look up now, wanting to see her first split-second reaction. "Unless you did it."

She looks me full in the eyes. "I swear. It wasn't me. I wouldn't, couldn't do that to you. And I'm sure Evelyn didn't mean for things to go so awry. She thought once Andreas turned up, you'd run. Problem solved."

"She mentioned a credit card. What was that all about?"

She sighs. "You remember you borrowed the household credit card?"

"Yes. I didn't think you needed it."

"Neither did I. But Evelyn had planned to use it for backup cash once we got to India. She didn't know I'd given it to you."

"But you said you'd paid forty-thousand dollars."

"Turns out that was just the three weeks' accommodation, meals, meditation and 'healing' sessions. They wouldn't let me be present for those, but I wouldn't be surprised if chicken gizzards were involved. When they asked for more money for treatments – they had a 'menu', can you believe? – we couldn't pay without the credit card. I told Evelyn we were leaving. So they gave us the 'free' treatment – a linctus. Liquefied paracetamol, as it turned out. Massively concentrated. We didn't know what it was until the hospital tested it after her collapse. Too late by then."

I turn away, look down the beach. In the distance, a black and brown dog is running along the water's edge, a large stick wobbling in its mouth. It could be my emotions he's carrying, teetering between relief and disbelief. Can I survive in this space of distrust? Before, it was only Andreas. How naive. What a baby I was. Did I deserve this further lesson? Is this my awakening?

"I want to believe you, Margie."

We walk on.

"How is she?" I ask. "She looked pretty bad when I left."

"Not good. I can't bring her home. Doctors says it'll only be days, maybe even hours."

"Sorry" is on my tongue, but I bite it back. Evelyn doesn't deserve pity. "What will you do?"

She looks at me. "What do you mean?"

"Will you stay?"

She flushes, turns away. "Daniel's asked me to. I don't know what else I'd do. And at my age—"

"Oh, very good. Playing the sympathy card."

She sniffs, mouth tightening.

"And?" I say.

"And what?"

"Are you sorry?" Her face scrunches, but I press. "How could you not know?"

She stops again. "You have no idea."

Immediately, I tense, ready to throw back a bitter defence at whatever guilt she wants to lay on me.

"No idea what it was like. Day after day. Evelyn sitting in urine-soaked pants because she didn't have the energy to change her incontinence pad. Some days unable to swallow even soft food. The leg and arm spasms, constant headaches. The shitty looks from people who wanted to squeeze into a lift when her wheelchair was taking up too much space, needing a ramp to enter a shop when there wasn't one, narrow doorways, bruises and blisters on her hands. Some days, she couldn't wipe her own arse. And don't get me started on dealing with the fucking disability system. I'm seriously surprised she had the will to live, with death peering around every corner."

"You think I don't know fear? I lived with it every bloody day. And Nayla's dead, Margie. She's fucking dead!" Goddammit. Why do I suddenly feel like an asshole? Like I'm the abuser?

She pauses. Tilts her head back. Looks at the sky. "I'm sorry. Of course you do. Can we sit?" she chokes out.

I look at her closely, her exhausted demeanour, the haggardness in her face. The rosy-cheeked, happy Margie is gone.

Along with my trust.

We head up toward the mangroves, find a beached log to sit on. I sigh, looking out to sea, flat and silvery under the gathering grey clouds. The beach itself is still a patchwork of ocean and shoreline flotsam. "I miss sunsets," I say.

Margie wipes her face, buries her feet in the sand, looser where we are. "Me too. But you get used to it. You can get used to anything once you become desensitised."

Truth hurts.

"I never thought I'd let myself get into another abusive relationship," she says, "but it sneaks up on you. I thought it was her illness. I forgave too much." She takes my hand, pulls it over to her knee and places her other hand on top, trapping me. "You're angry. Have every right to be. I would be. I'm sorry. I'm sorry I didn't see what was happening. I'm sorry I didn't protect you. I'm sorry I didn't"—she chokes—"didn't know what a fool I was."

God, Margie. Stop. Just stop. I need to stay angry. To be able to fight. If I let go, it's all going to overtake me, swamp my resolve, my strength.

She puts an arm around me, motherly, rests her head on my shoulder.

Damned tears. "I'm sorry she hurt you too," I manage.

65

Melbourne, August 2012

Funerals. Hard at the best of times – worse when it's someone you hardly know. You stand around feeling you should do something, say something, but empathy is missing. All you can manage is relief in knowing the responsibility and sorrow aren't your burdens to bear. Yet, I knew this man, and still my empathy is zero.

It's a saggy, morose day, a dark blossoming of wet black umbrellas hovering around an open grave. A saying comes to mind and I think, no, I couldn't dance on his grave. I don't have that much hate in me, not anymore. I refuse to let his memory eat away at me like rust.

I let go a long, long, quiet breath.

Katie squeezes my arm. "Okay?"

I nod.

Eighteen months it took for them to find him, to charge, convict. And he finds a way to slip the punishment. I hope it took an excruciatingly long time. A minute for every day of suffering he's caused, will continue to cause.

His mother sneaks glances at me from across the mounds of dirt. I recognise her from the never-ending days in the

Brisbane court – a gaunt bird of a woman who seemed to shrink with every adjournment. Silent during the trial, withdrawn. Has she been saving her words up? Does she blame me? I would have that conversation with her if she wanted, educate her on the monster her son was. Set her straight on why my tears aren't for him but for that great ethereal intangible they call closure. Maybe grief for what he stole. From me, from those I love and did love.

Thuds of hand-strewn dirt. It's over. The few people present turn away, retreating to the hall where they'll fill cups and plates with wake fare, glad to have something to do with their hands and mouths, because platitudes have run their course, and who has anything nice to say about him anyway?

She's coming over, black shiny pumps sinking into soft earth. I imagine her ankle twisting, pulling her down, her neat and tidy self-worth covered in mud.

"Georgia?" Her voice carries her years, brittle, hesitant.

"Yes."

"It was brave of you to come."

Not what I was expecting. I swallow. "Had to see for myself. Make sure he was gone."

She flinches, recomposes. "I understand. He was a ... complicated man."

I don't answer. My words would be too harsh.

Katie saves me. "I'm sorry for your loss."

The woman nods, barely a lift of lips. "Thank you."

A longing hangs in the air between us. Words that need to be said but won't.

"A complicated man. Much like his father."

Far North Queensland

Way, way below there's an endless density of green canopies. An ocean too, full of creatures that can maim, kill. Not so much this time of year. Through the plane's oval window, the water glints a welcome back.

Before You Go

Did you know that leaving a review on Goodreads or Amazon is one of the quickest and easiest ways to show your support for an author? A single sentence from you (it doesn't need to be an essay) helps authors be seen by other readers.

So while you're here, why don't you pop onto one of the sites now and leave a quick review? I would be super grateful you made the effort.

Take care.

Acknowledgements

Chris Collins, my supplier of cat food, chocolate and sanity. You are my rock, my life, my heart.

My writers workshop groups for the invaluable feedback and friendship. Kathryn Moore and Sylvia Goudie who always go over and above with their time, energy and guidance. Liz Charpleix for those final, eagle-eyed catches. My AJC Publishing beta reading team – Alix, Robyn, Leanne, Cindy and Joy – for their knowledgeable and unbiased feedback. My ARC team who lent their generous support in the final flurry. And most importantly, you, my readers, who waited patiently for me to shape my words into something intelligible.

And a special mention to Queensland Writers Centre (QWC) who awarded me a mentorship for this novel. Much appreciated.

Thank you all from me and my furry editorial assistants.

About the author

Cienna Collins is an Australian author of domestic noir suspense. Her books were longlisted for the QWC Adaptable film and television program and won a Publishable mentorship. Cienna was also awarded a placement at Hardcopy – a national professional development program for writers. Her short stories have won numerous awards and have been read on Radio Queensland.

Cienna has an Associate Degree in Professional Writing & Editing and runs a successful book editing and audiobook production business, AJC Publishing. Previous to this, Cienna had an eclectic career including managing commercial mortgages, working in a legal tribunal and fronting her own function band for over twenty years.

A previous devotee of adrenaline sports, including bungee jumping, skydiving, parasailing, sky-walking, sky-jumping and volcano climbing, Cienna is now happy to be settled at home in Melbourne with her hubby and two fur-kids, writing her adventures instead of living dangerously.

Stay in Touch
Join Cienna's mailing list: https://ciennacollins.com